THE RECKONING OF CHAOS AND MAGIC
SUPERNATURAL APOCALYPTIC WAR:
BOOK 3

I0635886

---

1. http://www.coversbychristian.com/

2. https://www.myidentifiers.com/

   title_registration?isbn=978-1-968643-01-0&icon_type=Pending

3. https://www.myidentifiers.com/

   title_registration?isbn=978-1-968643-02-7&icon_type=New

4. https://www.myidentifiers.com/

   title_registration?isbn=978-1-968643-00-3&icon_type=Incomplete

Acknowledgement

I am forever grateful for the contribution Larisa Atkinson made to this book and for how she brought Mel and Ruffus to life.

It was her vision to incorporate the paranormal experience into this storyline.

Her vision and voice will continue in the next book, and throughout this series.

For that, I am forever in her debt.

Larisa, I Love You Forever and Ever.

Dedication

This book is dedicated to the Permian Basin Honor Flight, a group dedicated to ensuring that our veterans receive the homecoming they never had. They also take them on a three-day, all-expenses-paid trip to Washington, D.C., to view the memorials built in their honor. As of this writing, this group has been conducting this work for ten years, having taken just over 1,000 veterans to Washington, D.C. This is an all-volunteer organization.

These trips are profoundly healing for these veterans and, at the same time, emotionally charged.

https://www.pbhonorflight.org/

Chapter 1

Mel

How did we end up in this chaos? What was meant to be a quick trip to the feed store for supplies turned into a nightmare. Our 2000-acre home, Freedom Ranch, with its large house, shop, bunkhouse, and greenhouse, had been our sanctuary since the shit hit the fan. We knew about the gang in town, but we had no idea that their influence had spread so far. We had learned this the hard way.

Things had gone horribly awry, and our situation was dire. The gang had stormed into the store thirty minutes after we had arrived and launched a brutal attack on us. We had endured punches, stabbings, slaps, and kicks and had been thrown and dragged around. Dylan was lying motionless in a pool of blood, having been shot twice. I prayed he was still alive as the thugs dragged us out of the store and locked us into this jail cell.

Our world turned upside down after the attack, over two weeks ago. We've lost electricity, telecommunications, water supply, and more. Modern planes, trains, and automobiles were all disabled. A bomb attack claimed the lives of our president and other high-ranking officials. The government and law enforcement agencies collapsed, and gangs have emerged from the shadows, creating a world of drugs, death, sex slavery, and likely other horrors I can't even fathom.

I was lying on the floor with my team from Freedom Ranch. Gail, our veterinarian and doctor, was one of my best friends. Nick, a Marine; Madison, a deputy sheriff; and Claire, a trauma nurse, were part of our security team.

I reviewed my Krav Maga self-defense training, going over the moves in my head. This system, which incorporates techniques from aikido, judo, karate, boxing, and wrestling, is designed for real-world situations and excels in hand-to-hand combat.

3

I needed to remember how to get out of these zip-tie cuffs we were in. BG, or as I affectionately called him, Big Enos, from Smokie and the Bandit, and his goons, had zip-tied our wrists and ankles. If our hands were bound in front, the easiest way to break them would be to raise our hands above our head and bring them down hard and fast across our rib cage. But our wrists were bound around our backs. I could use some magic if I only knew how to do it.

Gail, Shelly, and I recently discovered that we had crazy magic. We weren't young chickadees anymore. We were in the prime of our lives, which was what I called midlife. I was proud to be forty-eight. Shelly was also forty-eight, and Gail, a young thirty-seven. To say we were shocked was an understatement. My heart raced, and my hands trembled. Gail's eyes had welled up with tears, but Shelly, the group's mom and cheerleader, beamed with excitement.

"We should embrace our gifts," she urged us.

I wish I understood how my magic worked, but even if I did, there were no plants around us. My magic was nature-based. We were sure Gail was a shapeshifter, and Shelly had crystal magic. Mine wasn't very helpful in this hostage situation. I'm pretty sure Gail and I felt the same—total confusion.

If I'd had a free hand, I would have slapped myself across the face, annoyed at my lapse. I knew exactly what to do. I scooched over to Gail and leaned close to the team. "I know how to get out of these zip-ties," I whispered.

"How?" Gail mouthed.

"I still have Isis, my Karambit knife, in my boot. Those fools were more interested in groping me than searching for weapons. Neanderthals! They had only one thing on their tiny minds."

"I guess it's a good thing they were perverts instead of top-notch security guys," Gail retorted quietly. "They didn't find the knife in my boot either. I totally forgot about it until you mentioned it."

We quietly laughed through our pain. I'm not going to lie, I had difficulty catching my breath. I would never admit I had forgotten about Isis, either. I'll just let them think I was brilliant, I chuckled internally.

Gail was a fan of Benchmade knives, and her current favorite was Full Immunity, which had a 2.5-inch blade with a tanto point. A cute butterfly was engraved on the blade, inspiring her name: Queen Alexandra, after the beautiful butterfly; sometimes, we just called her Queenie.

Since we were cuffed, they had left our vests on us, though they had found our other knives and extra ammo magazines. TJ's insistence on us wearing our vests, had saved our lives.

"Let's wait a few minutes to ensure they have left, then we can work on getting out of our cuffs," I murmured.

"I can flex my chest, raise my arms, and break the zip ties holding me," Nick whispered.

"That's fan-freakin'-tastic! I didn't know we could do that with our wrists cuffed around our backs. I would try as well, but I can barely function from the pain. When we get the zip ties off, keep them so we can pretend we are still tied up. Then we'll take them out," I said.

Some of us had severe injuries from the beatings we had taken. I was probably the worst, except for Dylan. I would never forgive myself if he died. I was dealing with broken ribs, a stab wound on my side, my knee was also jacked up, and I had what felt like a broken jaw.

Nick, Claire, and I probably had concussions from being hit over the head. I could tell that Gail was in pain from the punch she had taken to the ribs, and Madison and I both had hand marks on our faces, along with split lips. The inside of my mouth was raw from when my cheek had grated across my teeth when slapped, not once, but twice.

"Nick, can you stand up and see if you can get your cuffs off?" I asked him. Nick stood, flexing like Macho Man, Randy Savage, the zip ties broke, and he let out a shaky breath.

"Are you okay?" I asked, noticing him swaying back and forth with sweat running down his forehead.

"Y-yes," he shook out his wrists and rubbed them. "I got lightheaded from the exertion."

"Rest for a minute, and then you can grab our knives and cut the rest of us free."

He nodded at me as he lay back on the floor. Claire did a worm crawl to him and leaned into him. He seemed to take strength from Claire, and after a few minutes, he stood up. "What boot is your knife in?"

I rolled onto my side. "The right boot, there's a special slot along the top inside edge that the knife fits into."

I felt him messing with my boot, and then he stood up with my Karambit knife.

"That's a good hiding spot," he grinned, "I had difficulty finding it. We should have sewn some into our boots, too." He bent down and cut the zip ties securing his ankles and then the ones securing my wrists and ankles. I always keep Isis razor-sharp, so he had my restraints cut in seconds.

"It feels good to be out of those," I told Nick as I rubbed my wrists and hands to help get some circulation back into them. Looking at my wrists, I could see where the zip ties had cut into my skin, and the blood had congealed as it dried.

I moved over to Gail, retrieved her knife, and cut her restraints. Nick quickly had Claire and Madison free, all rubbing their wrists to help get the circulation back into their hands.

We met in the middle for a very quick group hug. Speaking softly to my teammates, I said "We can do this. I know we're hurting but hang in there. We'll be home soon, I promise."

I took Gail's hand and walked to the side while the others discussed a plan. "Can you do that shifty thing?"

Gail frowned. "No. I've been trying to, but nothing's happening. I'm sorry."

"Don't worry about it, sweetie. I can't do anything either. We'll get out of here the old-fashioned way." I hugged her.

We walked back to the team. "Okay, let's plan our exit," I proposed. "This will be a fight to the death, and we can't hold back. We are fighting for our freedom. We will not let them take that away. Everything is not black and white; there are shades of grey, and today, we will be fighting in the darker shades. Stay strong. We can do this. Fear None, Conquer All."

"How are we going to get out of here? There are so many of them, and they are huge," Claire questioned.

"We need to get one or two into the cell, and then we attack. We have two knives to cut major arteries, and even though Nick is beaten up, I bet he can still hold one down for us," I explained. "Our Krav Maga training will help. One of us will pretend to need help, to draw them in."

I hoped our weapons were here, if they were, we would have a better chance to escape once we were out of this cell and on the move back to Freedom Ranch.

"That's a good plan," Claire said, her voice shaking.

"I think Nick should be the bait. If he's down, they won't hesitate to come in here. They're male chauvinist pigs and will assume that we are weak and helpless. I suggest we play it that way to our audience. Little do they know what they are coming up against." I was trying to sound more confident than I was.

"What do you need me to do? If I borrow one of your knives, I can help take them down." Nick said.

"Pretend you are having a seizure, and we'll ask them to help you. Do you want my Karambit or Gail's Benchmade knife?" I asked Nick.

"Your Karambit, if you don't mind? I like the curved blade, and it's easier to hide. It also feels different than any knife I've ever held. That's a wicked knife."

"Here you go. I call her Isis, and yes, she is definitely wicked." I grinned. "Please treat her like a lady."

"Don't worry. I'll take good care of her." Turning his eyes to Claire, he gave her a wink and a saucy grin. "I know how to treat a lady."

Claire smiled shyly, walked to Nick, kissed him on the cheek, and whispered, "Be careful."

He grabbed her around the waist, pulled her close, and kissed her so hard that my toes curled.

"Okay, kids," I said as I fanned myself to cool down. "It's time to get to work."

I wrapped my arm around Gail's shoulder. "Do you want me to attack? I can take your knife, Queen Alexandra."

"No. I can do this. You can barely stand, much less take out a thug or two. It'll be okay.

When you're ready, Nick, lie down. Gail and Claire, you're on the right side of the door. Lay facing the door so your hands and feet are hidden behind your back. Madison, over here on the left with me. The door swings inward, and if there are two of them, we can use the door to pin them in. Any questions?"

"None. Pretty straightforward," Madison replied. I lay down near the jail cell door and started yelling, "Hey, help! We need help here! Our guy is having a seizure. Come on, help us, help him." I kept yelling until I heard the outer door open. One of the thugs finally came through the door. Thankfully, he was alone.

"Shut up, or I'll come in there and give you something to scream about."

Looking at him, I realized I might have miscalculated by using this approach. The guy was enormous, probably six feet six tall, 260 pounds at least, and all muscle. His bald head had a sheen, as though he oiled and polished it daily. His blue jeans were well-worn and tight on his legs, and his white t-shirt was stretched thin. Over the top, he wore a black motorcycle vest with patches. He could be a defensive lineman for any pro football team or a grizzly bear. "Our friend is having a seizure and needs help. Please help him," I said, my voice trembling as I looked up at him. The words felt thin, barely more than a whisper. I dropped my gaze to the floor, my eyes burning with panic. My shoulders hunched in tight, a subconscious attempt to make myself smaller, more pitiful—anything that might make him listen. I could feel the fear clawing at my chest, cold and paralyzing, as I stood there, hoping he'd see how desperate we were.

"Haven't you noticed we have no doctors or medical facilities since this shit happened? I'm not a doctor; I can't help you," he growled.

"Come on, man. Please. Be a decent human being and help him. Can you bring us some water and possibly find someone who can help?" I smiled timidly at him.

"Fine, we have some water up front. I'll bring you some. I want to make sure you are well-hydrated," he said, with a gleam in his eyes. "It's going to be me and you and BDSM. Then we'll add you and your little friends to our collection of whores. There are a few who are a bit worn out and need to be replaced." His wicked laugh echoed behind him as he left the cell.

We had to get out of here quickly. I looked at Gail, who had a look of horror on her face. When she noticed I was looking at her, she quickly gave me a determined nod and mouthed *dead man*.

When Bear returned, as I had named him, he unlocked the jail cell door and entered carrying a bucket.

The water sloshed around in it. "Don't do anything stupid. Oh, that might be hard with your hands and feet secured," he said, and then laughed.

"How do you expect us to drink that with our hands tied?" I asked.

"Figure it out!"

He was about five steps into the cell when Gail started to move off the floor toward him. Her knife was in a fighting position.

He froze, his mouth gaping open, and he looked around. "What the hell?"

We converged on him. Nick rolled off the floor with the speed and agility of a cheetah catching and attacking his prey. He pulled my Karambit out, and Bear started backing up, dropping the bucket of water. At the same time, I got to the cell door. I slammed it shut and moved out of the way. Nick and Gail seemed to move as one, with supernatural speed. It was like watching a macabre dance of death. Gail was going high for his head and throat like we had trained in Krav Maga, while Nick went low and severed his Achilles tendon and then both of his femoral arteries in a flash with Isis. Bear had no idea who to try and defend against. It didn't matter though, if he went high, Nick got him low, Gail had his throat in view if he went low to defend against Nick. Isis was a flash in Nick's hands as he slashed Bear. As Bear moved his hands to try and stop the blood flow, Gail sliced his neck wide open. His eyes went wide, and he crumpled to the floor of the jail cell, his blood pooling with the water on the floor around him, the life leaving his eyes.

I stood frozen and tried to process what I had just witnessed. That scene was right out of a horror film and would be burned into my brain until the day I died. I needed to toughen up. I knew how to put on a brave face. Gail and Nick were fantastic. They did what none of us wanted to and did it with determination and grace.

Covered in blood from head to toe, Gail stood there, not moving. She had a blank look on her face; I ran to her, wrapped my arms around her, and held her tight. I knew she was trying to be strong and not cry, so letting her go, I stepped back and grinned at her, "Great job, Ms. Adler, you're my hero. And Nick, you put Wolverine to shame. Thank you both." Gathering around, everyone high-fived each other.

I went to Bear's body, held my breath, and searched him for weapons and keys. I found a 9mm semiautomatic holstered to his side and the keys to the door in his vest pocket. We took a moment to catch our breath and then headed to the door to the outer area. I peeked through a window and not seeing anyone, opened the door and headed into the other room.

Our weapons and items were on a table in the center of the room. Athena was on the table. "Hello, beautiful, I've missed you," I said, holstering my gun.

We had our weapons and ammo secured when we heard voices coming into the building. "Quick, hide," I said. The room was large, at least thirty feet by forty feet, and cubicle-style desks were spread around it. I had just found cover when the door opened and three gang members walked in.

"Where the fuck is Jose? Check the cell and see if he is having fun with the girls already," a short, fat goon snarled. He was about five foot three, had a beer belly, greasy hair, blue jeans with rolled-up cuffs, a white t-shirt with cut-off sleeves, food stains down the front, and the same black biker vest Bear wore. Short and portly described him well. His new name was Porky Pig.

Waiting until they had reached the middle of the room, I surged to my feet and fired Athena, hitting Porky Pig in the chest, neck, and head, spraying his brains across his two compadres. As he fell, Gail jumped up and fired her rifle at the second tall, skinny dude. He took four rounds center mass, spilling his shredded heart and lungs across the floor.

"Nice Shootin' Tex!" I yelled at Gail, giving her a thumbs-up.

"Right back at ya."

The third gang member, in his haste to try and get away, was slipping and sliding in the gore on the floor. Nick shot him point-blank with his pistol—one shot to the head.

The room smelled of gunpowder, blood, and death as we quickly made sure none were left with a breath in their lungs. All our shots were accurate and true.

"Check them for weapons and ammo, and move quickly, we made a crap load of noise taking them out. Nick, are you good to lead us outside? Once outside, I can help you work us away from the building, and we can walk back to the ranch."

"I'm on it. Let's go," Nick said.

We followed him out of the building. Thankfully, the closest door took us out a side entrance on the north side of the building. The sun was still up. I would have preferred that the sun be down to help hide our escape, but it soon would be.

Looking back at Carson Valley Inn, people were heading towards the sheriff's office. "We're going to have to hustle. Some gang members are heading this way." Then I heard motorcycles starting up. Shit! This was going to be tough. "Heads up, people, we are about to be chased by morons on motorcycles," I panted, as we all ran to the east.

Nick stopped, "Mel, you get everyone across the road and away from here. You know the route. I'll slow these dipshits down with some cover fire."

Claire froze mid step. "We can all get away, Nick. Stay with us, and we can find a place to take a stand."

"I got this, Claire. I need you to keep moving. I've done this in Afghanistan. I'll find you," he growled.

"Please don't get hurt," Claire cried as I grabbed her arm and pulled her along with the rest of the team.

"Let's move it, ladies. We need to cross the road and swing north in the parking lot. After we cross the fence and tree line, there's a canal over there that we can follow."

We crossed the road and headed for the fence line along the canal. We had just reached the fence when I heard shots being fired. Then, an even louder shot echoed across the area. When I turned around to see what was happening, a dude flew off his bike, like a giant hand had just picked him up and thrown him. *Holy hell. Where did that shot come from?* I wondered. Nick was firing in their general direction, but his rifle didn't have enough stopping power at that distance. Gail and Madison found a hole in the fence and went through it. I was glad we didn't have to climb over it or try to cut through it.

Claire was standing there watching Nick. I tried pushing her through the fence, but she wouldn't move. I understood her plight and worry about him; I was worried, too. I looked back to where Nick was hiding in the bushes when I saw him break from his cover and head our way. He was waving for us to get through the fence and keep moving.

"Let's go, Claire. Nick will be here in a minute, and we need to keep going," I gestured to the hole in the fence.

Claire and I got through the fence and took positions on either side of the hole to protect Nick as he approached. The bikers had stopped, and their gunfire ceased as we retreated.

Nick came through the fence at a run, and we all took off. It would be a long walk through parts of the city, and I was unsure what we might encounter. I was running out of steam quickly and probably wasn't the only one about to drop.

"The shot that took out that biker was probably a 50-caliber from the sound and the impact on the biker," Nick said, as we ran along the canal, out of breath.

"I hope it's a team from the ranch. Nick, should we slow down so they can find us or keep moving?" I was so tired that I hoped he would want to slow down. Maybe it was my husband. Please let it be TJ.

"We need to keep moving as fast as possible to escape town. If it's a team from the ranch, they'll catch us," Nick said. "They'll have vehicles and can move faster than us."

"Okay, I know you're right," I said between breaths.

We were running for about fifteen minutes when I saw River View Pond. It looked so refreshing. I was hot and thirsty, and we hadn't had water since breakfast.

"Hey Nick, do you think we can start walking slower now? Just a quick reminder, we have no water for the journey back home," I stated.

"You're right. We need to conserve the water in our bodies. Luckily, it will soon be nighttime and cooler, we won't sweat as much."

We were approaching the highway when Nick stopped us. "Let's watch for any threats, and then cross. I'll stay on overwatch for you, and then I'll cross, and you do the same for me."

"Sounds good. Ready when you are," I replied.

"Go, go, go," Nick whispered.

We all took off across the highway. The casino on the other side had burned, and we used some rubble as cover. We were clear and positioned to cover him. He was about halfway across when a vehicle appeared in front of us. *Fuck! What now?* Thankfully, Nick heard the vehicle and peeled off to the left to use the building as cover.

"Stay down, everyone," I whispered to my team. I was peering over some of the burned rubble when I recognized it. "It's John's Jeep."

"Stay down until we are 100 percent certain it's someone from the ranch," Nick murmured.

When the Jeep was about fifty yards away, I could see John driving with Gavin and Shelly riding along with him. Shelly?

Gail hobbled over to me and sat down, "Is that our girl?"

"You know it. She's a force to be reckoned with when she sets her mind on something. And in this case, we were the something."

Shelly had shown up for us like the universe had sent her on purpose. I wish I'd been there to see her lay down the law—calm but firm. She was joining the team to find Mel and her friends. She was our crystal-carrying, incense-burning mama bear with fierce vibes and a heart full of justice. A wild soul with flowers in her hair and a fire in her spirit.

Gail and I stood up, and I could see the shock on their faces. We must have looked like hell from the beatings and blood. The rest of the team looked just as bad.

John stopped his Jeep, and they all jumped out. Shelly ran to Gail and me and wrapped us in a gentle, comforting, and loving hug. "You're a sight for sore eyes," Shelly said in a soothing voice.

"You both are going to be as right as rain very soon, I have that on good authority." Shelly winked.

What did she mean? Hmm ... 'right as rain', 'on good authority'? We'd have to talk about that later, for sure. That was odd.

I looked at Gail to agree, but she wasn't looking at me. In fact, she had lain down on the ground and closed her eyes.

John keyed up his radio. "Team One. We found them. They're safe."

"Where's TJ?" I desperately wanted and needed my husband. "Who else came into town to rescue us?"

"TJ and Russell were entering the Carson Valley Inn to look for you all," John replied. "They need to exfiltrate from the area and will be here soon."

Gavin and Shelly handed us water and snacks from the Jeep. "Thanks, guys." I drank the water, but I couldn't eat; my jaw hurt too much.

"Did Carlos have his 50 BMG?" Nick asked.

Gavin smiled, "Yeah. He doesn't leave home without it. Why do you ask?"

"Someone shot a guy off his bike, and it looked like he was picked up by a giant hand," Nick said, and laughed.

"That was Carlos. He found a rooftop for an overwatch position and saw you all running from the sheriff's building. Then the two bikers headed that way, so he took one out," Gavin said.

"How did you guys find us?" I asked.

John put his arm around Shelly. "We found Dylan at the feed store, and he said he heard the gang mention taking you to the sheriff's office."

"Dylan is alive?" I gasped, relief flooding through me.

"Yes. He's back at the ranch and being treated by Tracy. He lost a lot of blood, but he'll survive as long as the wounds don't get infected," John explained.

"I have been heartsick thinking we had lost him," I choked.

Interrupting our conversation, another vehicle came racing down the street, heading our way. "That's TJ!" I couldn't wait to see him, *hurry, babe*. He raced down the street and locked his brakes to stop.

I drank him in as he quickly walked to me. He was a sight for sore eyes, a gorgeous, sexy man; I was addicted to him. His jeans fit him just right. His tall, lean, muscular body sent chills down my spine.

I was moving to meet him when he grabbed me in a giant bear hug. I held on to his firm, broad shoulders for dear life.

He began asking me so many questions so fast that I couldn't understand him. I smiled, lay my head on his chest, listened to his heartbeat, and let him continue. When he finished his questions, I looked up at the adorable dimple on his chin and his sapphire blue eyes, as tears filled my eyes.

"I love you, TJ. I'm so sorry, I screwed this shopping trip up—Urgh, don't squeeze me too hard. I might have a broken rib."

"Sorry, love," he said, as he kissed every available space on my face. "This situation is not your fault. The jerks in the gang deserve full responsibility and payback," he said. Then, pulling himself back so he could look me in the eye, he told me, "You are so beautiful."

"Okay, now I know you're lying," I laughed and patted his cheek.

"Nope, I'm not lying. I was so worried. I would've been lost without you." He was checking me from top to bottom, finding my injuries.

Both teams embraced, and I sighed in relief, knowing we would all be okay and that Dylan was alive.

"I want to go home," I whimpered.

Now that TJ was here, I could let my guard down, and he would take over and let me rest.

"Yes, ma'am," TJ and John said in unison.

Chapter 2

TJ

At fifteen hundred hours, John, Russell, and I completed range training with some of our less experienced people. Mel and her team had yet to return.

"Hey John, have you or Russell heard anything on the radio from Mel and her shopping team?"

"Nothing yet. They've been gone longer than expected," John replied. "Let me check with Isabella at the watch desk and make a radio call."

I followed John inside the bunkhouse. My stress levels were building with each step as we approached the watch desk, unsure of what news awaited us.

"Isabella, have you heard anything from Mel and the team?" John inquired.

"No. Let me see if I can raise them on the radio."

"Ranch calling Mel. Ranch calling Mel. Do you copy?" Isabella announced on the radio.

After what seemed like an eternity, with no response, I said, "Let me change the channel on my radio, and you can try again. That will tell me if the radio is transmitting."

"Ranch to Mel. Ranch to Mel." Isabella tried once more to reach Mel on the radio.

"I heard your radio call, so I know you're transmitting. Let me give it a quick test from this end. TJ calling Freedom Ranch." We all heard my transmission come over the radio speaker. Everything was working with the radio. Now I'm worried about Mel and her team. I was in full-blown panic now.

"Let's get a team to go to the feed store and check," John announced. "Isabella, recall everyone and button down the ranch until we know Mel and her team's status."

"Roger that."

I was glad John was here to make those calls to secure the ranch until we had a status on Mel and her team. I couldn't think straight right now. I *needed* Mel to be safe, or I'd lose my mind. "Good call, John. Are we taking anyone else with us?" I asked.

John grabbed his radio. "Carlos, meet me in the armory and gear up."

"Ten-four."

We were on our way to the armory when I heard Isabella's call.

"All ranch personnel. Code Blue, I repeat, Code Blue."

That was our code to secure the ranch and take defensive positions in case of a security breach.

John and I arrived at the armory, and Carlos was already gearing up.

"Mel and the team have been gone longer than expected. We're going to the feed store to see what's happened," I explained to Carlos.

"Let's get the lead out, boys," Carlos said, trying to be jovial and ease some of the tension in the air.

Ruffus limped in, probably thinking he was going with us to check on Mel. "Sorry, boy. You need to stay here and heal. We'll find your mama and bring her home. I promise." He gave me those sad eyes and a few barks, I swear I saw a tear.

Less than a week ago, we were on a mission at Spider Lake to rescue hostages that the Cartel had kidnapped. During the skirmish, Ruffus had chased a Cartel member who was trying to escape and was shot as he took the criminal down. He had taken a bullet to his left hind leg. The surgery had been a success, but he was far from a full recovery. Ruffus was a hero that day.

As we headed out, people were moving into security positions. I was relieved to see that everyone took the threat seriously.

"I'm taking a route through the Ranchos, as it's faster than running along the river and the dirt trail there. Keep your eyes peeled for any danger," I stated.

"Copy that," they agreed.

I stopped just over the bridge and parked in the trees by the town.

"I'll take point. You two on me as we move in," Carlos said.

I was relieved that Carlos had taken charge. My head wasn't in the right place to make good decisions. My thoughts were solely on Mel. Something was wrong. I had never felt this lost before. I knew I loved Mel with all my heart, but this was beyond my love. This feeling was something I'd never felt before. It was like I had lost a piece of me. I *needed* to keep her safe and protect her. This was a terrible feeling.

We worked our way to the back of the feed store through the trees. Their truck wasn't there. I could see empty shell casings on the pavement. That was when the hair on the back of my neck stood up, and the nausea hit me with a force so strong that if I didn't get this under control, I was going to throw up right here.

Carlos ran to the door, "Spread out and cover me. I'll cover you two while you approach one at a time, then I'm going in the door."

We both gave him a thumbs up. He took cover near some pallets and signaled us to join him. I went first and took up a position to cover John on his approach. Being this close to the building, we could all see the many empty shell casings on the ground—blood, oh my God, blood. I had to ignore it for the moment and focus, or I would lose my shit.

Carlos gestured to the door, showing three fingers before counting down. He entered first, going to the right; I went left, and John went straight ahead.

I saw Dylan on the floor and nearly tripped over another body as we entered the back area of the feed store.

"I've got Dylan here, and another body. Let's clear the store," I said.

"TJ, check on Dylan and guard him just in case the unknown is a threat," Carlos declared. "John and I will clear the rest of the building."

I went directly to Dylan, walking past the dead guy, and shared my feelings for him with a few kicks. My clue to him being a bad guy was the vest he had on. When I reached Dylan, I knelt beside him and checked his pulse—it was there thank goodness. He opened his eyes, gave me a slight smile, and tried to sit up. I put my hands on his shoulders and eased him back.

"Relax, buddy, I got you." Dylan had so much dried blood on him, I was unsure if it was his, from the dead guy, or a combination of both. "Everything is going to be okay. Just hang in there. Where is Mel?" I was desperate to know what had happened. As I asked the question, John and Carlos returned after clearing the feed store.

"How is he?" John asked.

"He's alive," I said. "I need to get his vest off and bring me more light so I can check his wounds."

My mind was jumping all over, wondering where my wife was. *Please be okay, baby.*

"Let's get Dylan outside," Carlos instructed.

We carefully picked him up, took him outside, and laid him on the ground.

"I'm going to bring the Jeep back here and get the medical bag," John said.

"We'll take Dylan's vest off to assess his injuries and get him ready to head back to the ranch," Carlos ordered.

What? No! I didn't want to leave. I wanted to find Mel. Logically, I knew Dylan needed medical attention, but I couldn't leave Mel.

Back with the Jeep, John took the medical bag to Carlos. And gave Dylan some water, and then Carlos began to treat his wounds.

I pulled John aside and said, "I can't leave Mel, she needs me."

"I know this is tough for you, but we must get Dylan back to the ranch and treated as soon as possible."

"I'll stay and find her, then you bring the cavalry, and we'll rescue the team." I knew for a fact I wouldn't wait for the team. I would get Mel, no matter what. I would do anything to ensure her safety.

John slung his arm around my shoulders. "We can't leave you here, brother. You know that. We'll hurry and get back here as soon as possible. And we'll bring Mel and the team home safe and sound."

I said nothing, just turned and returned to the Jeep. I was so angry, if I hadn't left, I would have shown John just how angry I was.

"Ranch, TJ. We have Dylan at the feed store. He's injured, and Carlos is assessing him now. Have Tracy standing by. Mel and the rest of the team are missing. Keep the ranch on alert."

"Ranch copies."

"Sorry, guys. I couldn't protect Mel and the team," Dylan said in a rough, ragged voice as he gasped for air. "A gang was on us quickly, and I was hit in the first volley of shots. I did take one out when he went to check me for weapons." Dylan stopped for a moment, pulling oxygen into his lungs, then carried on. "I cut his Achilles tendon and then sliced his femoral artery. Most of the blood on me is probably his. One of his buddies shot at me, and I think it hit the back plate. The bullet ran across my back. It hurts worse than the shoulder wound."

His shoulder was bleeding slightly, so Carlos put some QuikClot on it and wrapped it up.

"Let's get him loaded and back to the ranch. His back is just a flesh wound," Carlos said.

John and Carlos jumped into the back seat after we got Dylan into the passenger seat and belted in.

Racing back to the ranch, I called in on the radio, "Ranch, TJ here. Inbound hot about seven minutes away."

"Copy. Tracy and a team are standing by to assist."

I came tearing onto the ranch and stopped next to the bunkhouse. Tracy had a team and a portable gurney ready for Dylan. I stood by my Jeep, ready to get back to town.

Shelly ran over in full kit. Her face was red and puffy from crying, but there was a fire in her eyes and an unmistakable look of determination on her face. A look that I had seen reflected back at me in the rear-view mirror. She quickly kissed John, looked at me, and said, "Do you know anything yet? I'm going with you, so don't even think about fighting me on this. Understand?"

"It's okay with me. We'll fill you in on what we know on the way," I said as I looked at John.

John shuffled his feet and looked very uncomfortable. "Um, sweetie," John said as he took her hands. "I think it would be best if you waited here. The Jeeps will be full when we get Mel and her team in them. Plus, we already have the search teams figured out."

Poor guy. This wasn't easy to watch. I understood his feelings, but didn't think he would win this argument.

Shelly pulled her hands back from John's grasp and placed them on her hips. She was really mad, it was almost as if little diamonds were floating around her. *Weird!* I rubbed my eyes and looked again. They were still there.

"If there is not enough room for me, remove one of the original members. I will replace them." Shelly looked at the team members apologetically and then turned back to John. "I am going, period!"

"Fine!" That was all John said. He looked at the rescue team, "Um, would someone mind switching out with Shelly?" he asked, clearly feeling uneasy.

Cole's smile was so broad it looked as if he were channeling Jack Skellington. "I can stay. It's not a problem. Shelly needs to go," he said, as he turned to walk away. He gave Shelly a wink, "You're a superstar. Rock on, sister!" and gave her a high five.

I couldn't hold back a little chuckle, and the rest joined in—all except John, who had a scowl marring his face. I felt a bit lighter with Shelly here. I was glad to have her along.

John harrumphed, "The search teams are as follows. I'll take Gavin and Shelly with me, and Carlos and Russell will go with you."

"Okay, let's go. This is taking too long. We're burning daylight!" I snapped.

"We need a plan. We have an idea of where they are, but we need to be ready for anything we might find," John spoke slowly in a calm, soothing voice as though speaking to a rabid animal. Whatever.

"Find me a good overwatch position, and I can cover you from the gang during your search," Carlos said.

"There's a place called 'The Roundup' from which you can access the roof. It's not far from the CVI front entrance and the back area of the sheriff's station; that would be a great spot, Carlos," John said. "TJ, you will approach from the northwest and park the Jeep near the ponds. You'll have a little hike, but I suspect fewer gang members will be on that side of the building. We'll go to the farm store, then when TJ is in place, we'll follow."

"Okay, come on guys, let's move. There are snacks and water in the Jeeps for Mel and the team. Let's hit the road, PLEASE! We've been here too long," I almost yelled. I was very close to becoming that rabid animal John thought I was.

Ruffus looked at me. He stood as tall as he could without his hip hurting. He was ready to go, and I'm sure he hoped we would take him. I knelt and scratched his head, "We'll bring your mama home. I promise, buddy."

He gave me a little yip and a wink and licked my face. I could almost hear him tell me everything would be okay. I'm actually kind of getting used to this stuff, or maybe I'm too worried about Mel to care about going crazy.

Finally, we left the ranch.

I pulled the Jeep up next to the ponds. "Carlos, you take point until we split," I said.

"Copy."

Carlos kept us in the shadows, tall grass, and trees as we approached our objective. After what felt like an hour, we arrived at our separation point.

Carlos headed through the brush and grass to the roof at The Roundup. Russell and I waited for him to arrive. Shortly after, we received two clicks in our headsets that told us Carlos was on the roof. We worked our way to the back of CVI, where I knew they had a door.

John and his team knew to start approaching the sheriff's building when they heard the two clicks on their radios. "Team two, moving."

I called, "At the back door." Just as I was getting ready to open the back door, I heard a loud gunshot.

Carlos called out, "Two bikers, one down and the other has stopped. I also saw five people running from the sheriff's station back door area."

"Can you still see them?" I asked with my heart in my throat.

Carlos exclaimed after what felt like an eternity, as he probably dug his binoculars from his pack. "It's Mel and the team making a break for it. I'll continue to provide overwatch. You break contact. When you guys are at the Jeep and moving, I'll follow them."

I was relieved, but I needed to see her with my own eyes before I could completely believe she was okay. We worked our way back into the tree line along the RV park and started running to the Jeep. It took us a lot less time to return to the Jeep than it did to infiltrate the CVI area. Once in the Jeep, I spoke into my headset, "Team One,

Hot Potato." That was our designated call sign for getting back to the Jeep and moving fast from the area.

"Two, moving," Carlos called as he left his overwatch position.

"Buckle up, buttercup, and hang on," I told Russell. "I'm going to push the Jeep hard."

"Not so hard that you kill us both, though. Do we know their route?" Russell asked.

"You have a point," as I slowed down from the 70 mph that I was doing to 65 mph.

"Team One, we found them. They are safe," John said, then sent us their location.

"How are they, John?" I asked, trying to keep my voice steady.

"They're good. Tired, hungry, and thirsty."

I could tell from his voice that something was up with them, though he was trying to relieve my anxiety. The drive took forever, and I rounded the last corner on two tires. As the Jeep slid around the corner, I could finally see Mel. The knot around my heart loosened when I saw no one performing major medical treatment on her or her team. I finally took a deep breath, locked up the brakes, and jumped out of the Jeep.

I ran to Mel and swept her up in a hug. "I was so worried, sweetheart. I love you. Are you okay? Do you hurt anywhere? Can I do anything for you?" A tear fell down my cheek. I heard her moan as I hugged her.

"Don't squeeze me too hard. I think I have a broken rib," she whispered through a gasp of air.

"What does the other guy look like?" I asked

"Dead."

I wanted to laugh but thought better of it. "Please call Carlos and find out where he is. I don't want to be waiting here too long," I insisted.

"I got it," Gavin said. "Team One Charlie, position."

"Just passed the pond. No back trail that I can tell," Carlos replied.

"We'll send a Jeep to you."

John fired up his Jeep, and Gavin climbed in as they took off. They returned about five minutes later with Carlos.

"I want to go home," Mel said.

"Yes, ma'am," John and I said in unison.

All eleven people squeezed into our two Jeeps, and then we headed home.

I grabbed the microphone. "Ranch, TJ. We have everyone accounted for and returning. Have Tracy standing by. We have a couple of injuries."

"Copy," Donnie announced over the radio.

When we arrived at the ranch, Tracy was ready with a team to triage our injured. I think she was unprepared for what she saw with Mel and her team. Katie ran straight to her mom, Gail, hugging her, while crying hysterically. Gail assured her she was fine, calming Katie down so she could help the injured.

Gail and Claire helped, and even though they were injured, they did what they could. Mel had the most injuries.

Gavin and Carlos started working on Nick and Claire because they had advanced medical training from their time in the Marines. Anita Tinkerton was also there to help. She was our pharmacist; she didn't attend medical school but was familiar with basic wound care.

I was sitting in the bunkhouse's main area with Joe, Ruffus, and Katie, waiting for word on Mel. I had been kicked out of the clinic.

Joe was our neighbor and a good ol' guy. He loved Mel like a daughter. I know he was as broken up as I was.

Soon, Mel's team left the clinic, looking much better than they had an hour before. I was nervous.

Ruffus kept looking at the clinic door for his Mel, put his chin on my leg, and gave me a little whimper, telling me he was worried about his mom.

"You're a smart boy. She will be back to her old, bossy self soon. Don't tell her I called her old and bossy; she would definitely hurt me." I chuckled, and Ruffus shared a big, toothy grin with me. I scratched his back, "Life's too short to worry about going crazy, so I'll try and roll with it. If Mel has to put me on meds because of all this, we'll deal with it then. Does that sound like a plan, buddy?"

"*Woof.*"

"She will be fine. She is tough and has a lot to fight for," Joe assured us.

After about an hour, they all came out: Gail, Tracy, Shelly, and Mel. Gail and Shelly had wrapped their arms around Mel's waist to help her walk more easily.

Relief washed over me like cool water. I could breathe again. I sent out a thank you to the universe as I leaped to my feet and went to meet them, with Ruffus leading the way, going directly to Mel.

"She has a concussion, and I'm sure she has at least one broken rib. We've wrapped them tight like a mummy. She has a puncture wound on her right side, which is healing quickly. There doesn't appear to be internal bleeding, but I'll keep an eye on her. She has a knee contusion, this will heal independently with proper care. She also has a minor fractured jaw. She knows she can only eat soft foods and liquids for a while." Mel made a loud grunt at that statement. We chuckled, and Shelly patted Mel's back to comfort her. Mel loved food; like the rest of us, we were all food oriented.

"Scarlett, our dental hygienist, came in and checked her and her team; everything looked good. No missing or loose teeth. She has antibiotics to take for two weeks to be on the safe side. I wanted to keep her here, but she was adamant about sleeping in her own bed tonight. The only reason I am allowing this is because I sleep down the hall from her." Gail gave Mel a small smile. "There was a significant improvement to her injuries from when we began her treatment to just before we walked out here." She looked at Mel as if they were having a private conversation that no one else was privy to. "We'll all keep an eye on her. But if she acts weird when I'm not around, come get me immediately," Gail said.

"Isn't she always acting weird," I replied.

Mel poked me in the ribs, "Watch it, mister. You could be on the couch."

"Let's go. I'll throw you in the shower and join you. We must all do our part to conserve water," I declared, giving Mel a wink as I took her hand.

"Be careful with the bandages on your puncture wound. If you need fresh bandages, let me know," Gail sighed.

"Just give us some now, and I'll change them after her shower," I said.

"Okay."

We headed to the house for a shower and bed, with Ruffus following along. When Mel was cleaned up and in her most comfortable pajamas, I fed her some cream of wheat and tucked her into bed. I lay beside her, carefully wrapping my arms around her. I wanted to comfort her, but I needed this as much as she did.

"Chef C told me that last week he'd noticed food, milk, and water bottles missing every day, and this morning, all the leftover food was gone. I did a quick inventory of our stock and supplies and found that we were missing a case of beef jerky, a large bucket of trail mix, a large storage bag of blankets, and a bag of pillows,"

I wanted to distract her from the memories and pain of what she had just lived through. But now that I think about it, that was probably not a good idea. She was a go-getter and wouldn't rest if she felt someone was being taken advantage of or if the missing items meant someone was in trouble. *Darn it, I should have kept my mouth shut.* She had that look of determination in her eyes that said she would get to the bottom of this mystery.

"Really? Well, we need to do something about that. I'll get my girls, and we'll get to the bottom of it. I also wanted to talk to you about the women that the gang has at Carson Valley Inn. They are using them as sex slaves. We need to rescue them. I'm tired now, but I will be addressing this again," she said as she yawned, closed her eyes, snuggled closer to me, and fell asleep.

"Goodnight, sweet dreams, I love you."

Chapter 3

Curtis, The Leader of the Gang

It had been a couple of weeks since the world we knew had ended. We'd lost all electricity, cars, and more. I had no idea what caused all this mayhem. However, I liked it; Gardnerville, or G'Ville as we called it, was our barrio. In the first few days of this disaster, we lost six crew members at the VFW skirmish and twelve at the Walmart dustup. Tommy, my second in command, found ten new members, and then BG and his bikers increased our number by another twenty members.

BG and his crew came from Reno and had asked to join my crew. I was no fool, I'd welcomed them with open arms.

I was sitting on the deck at the Carson Valley Inn (CVI) around 3:00 p.m. when our new biker friends dropped some people across the street at the sheriff's. I suspected they were prisoners they'd found on their travels. After they left the, BG joined me.

"What'd you guys find on your travels this afternoon?" I asked BG.

"We acquired a crew that was cleaning out the feed store. There were four fine-looking ladies and two boys. Zero killed one of their boys after he sliced Grunt's femoral artery. We dumped them in the jail since you said it was empty, and we could use it if we had prisoners," BG explained.

"Great, we'll bring the ladies over later tonight for the fellas to play with." I grinned. "I'm sure the boys will like the new chicks."

"I left Jose over there to guard them. They had some excellent tools with them. We'll bring those back from the jail when we drop off the playthings," BG drawled.

"Sounds good," I replied.

"Where's your girl at?"

"She's chillin' at the house that we just obtained. It's nicer than the one we had here in the city." I wouldn't reveal to anyone that the house had power and running water. If I did, they would all want to come over, use the shower, and take our food.

"What do you guys have planned for the evening?" I asked.

"If you don't mind, we'll grab the new ladies and break them in," BG said with a chuckle.

"That seems fair. Why not send someone over now to bring them back? I'd like to see them before you roughnecks try them out."

"I'll be right back."

BG returned with some guys. "Curtis, this is Hector, Mario, and Ian. Curtis is the leader of the crew here. Run over and grab the girls we snatched up at the feed store. Bring them here. Take care of the guy they had with them. We don't want to have to feed him, you catch my drift?"

"You got it, BG," Ian replied as they turned to leave.

"Hector tends to beat on women he plays with. Whatever girl he plays with tonight, she will be down for the count for at least a few days. He enjoys beating them for hours," BG said, a smirk tugging at the corner of his mouth like it was just another joke.

"That's cool, man. That's why we have a few extra girls here," I snickered.

I watched BG's crew walk into the sheriff's department building when we heard muffled gunfire.

"What the hell was that?" BG yelled. "Joey and Leon, get on your bikes and head to the sheriff's building to see what's happening. Shit, never mind, chase down our prisoners and bring them back. Now. Move it!" BG screamed.

I called for my crew to gather up and get ready to help as Joey and Leon took off on their bikes. They had gone about 100 yards when I heard a loud boom, and Leon was picked off his bike and thrown to the ground. His bike continued for another fifty feet before it fell over. Everyone stopped when they saw the giant hole in Leon's back. We all knew he was dead.

BG started roaring. "Move it assholes! Get the prisoners before they get away." Everyone was looking around for where the shot had come from and was afraid to move and be the next victim. They knew that if the gunner targeted them, their day would end, just like Leon's.

BG stood rigid, fists clenched at his sides, chest heaving with silent rage. His jaw grinding so hard, I thought his teeth might crack.

I looked at BG as the veins in his neck and forehead throbbed. "We have plenty of girls for fun tonight," I said, trying to calm him.

"Fuck that. Someone just took out one of my best boys. I want someone's ass for this. You don't have a handle on your territory. It's time to take control of this town and show everyone who is in charge," BG bellowed.

I gulped a mouthful of air, wondering if BG and his crew would try and run us out of town. "What's your plan?" I asked, keeping my voice firm, eyes locked on his. I couldn't let him see the fear—not when they needed a leader.

"We're going to go break some heads until someone tells us who those people are," he hissed.

Then, I noticed most of the crew were standing around the entrance, looking for answers and directions.

Tears welled in the eyes of one of the amazonian women, catching the light as she tried to blink them away. Up close, she appeared to be even bigger than BG. I was unsure who I would bet on to win a wrestling match between the two.

BG turned to the amazonian. "Sorry, Matilda. I know you and Leon had a thing. We'll get revenge for Leon. I plan on taking out those bimbos and their crew. We will find them soon."

"I will flay the shooter's skin from his living body," Matilda choked out, her voice trembling with rage and grief. Her teeth clenched so tightly it looked like she might shatter them, and her eyes shimmered with tears she refused to let fall.

BG raised his voice for everyone to hear. "Search the area. I want the shooter, now! Did anyone see where the shot came from? They had to have been here to rescue the prisoners. Speaking of the prisoners, someone get over to the jail to check on the crew. Now! Get the lead out." Everyone scrambled like cockroaches when the lights came on to do his bidding.

I looked at BG. "We can bury Leon down near the river. It will make a nice final resting place." I could tell that dealing with burying a friend was not one of his strong points.

Matilda spoke up. "That would be fine, and he would've liked that. Thank you."

I could tell that she was fighting back the tears. The other amazonian appeared and hugged Matilda.

"It'll be alright. We'll find that sniper and make him pay."

"Thanks, Deirdre. I know we will."

Deirdre could have been a twin to Matilda. She was 6'5" tall, all muscle, and her black hair was crew-cut. Her arms were as big as my thighs. Either one of them could pop my head off my body, like squeezing a pimple.

BG's crew and mine were walking into the jail. Five minutes later, they were headed our way with their heads down. Well, it didn't look like they had good news.

When they stopped before us, the one who had clearly drawn the short straw spoke to BG.

"Jose, Hector, Mario, and Ian are dead. Jose was in the cell with his neck and legs cut wide open. The prisoners took their tools back."

BG started yelling and cursing. "What the fuck, and who the fuck, are we dealing with here? Who are those people? Four bitches and one dude took out Jose. How does that happen? I want their heads on sticks, now!"

People scrambled and headed out in all directions, looking for the women and the team who took out Jose. I was sure the sniper was long gone, though I wouldn't tell BG that. He was pissed enough.

Gunfire came from one of the neighborhoods. What the hell was happening today? After an hour, one of BG's crews returned.

"Everyone we have talked to knows nothin' about the crew that escaped or the gunman that took out Leon."

"Keep searching, Angel. Someone knows something about those people. I want answers," BG yelled through gritted teeth, fists clenched as he waved them around, punctuating his anger.

I wanted to know why there had been gunshots, so before Angel could leave, I asked him "Hey, Angel. Were you guys being shot at? I heard gunfire."

"No. We shot some random people to inspire others to talk. It didn't work. We took out fifteen people in the hood." Angel said as he turned and headed back across the street.

"What's the plan if no one talks?" I asked.

"I guess we'll have cleared all the houses by then. Everyone on the crew can pick their own house," BG growled.

"It's getting late. I'm headed to the house to hang out with Fiona. My boys know where I live and can get hold of me if they find anything," I said, as I headed to my red Ranchero and home to Fiona.

Chapter 4

Mel

The morning sun shone brightly through the window as I rolled over. I looked at the clock, and tried to jump out of bed, but my body didn't want to cooperate, and my head fell back on my pillow. It was almost 8:30 a.m. I don't remember the last time I slept in this late. I put my hand on TJ's side of the bed and found my other snuggle buddy, Ruffus. He was lying with his head on TJ's pillow, looking at me with a cute little grin. "Good morning, my cutie patootie. How are you feeling? You're looking good."

Ruffus barked and whined until I scooted over. Then he rolled over so I could snuggle against his back. I relaxed, listening to his breathing and feeling his little heartbeat as I slipped in and out of dreamland for a while.

It was so good to be home. Yesterday was terrifying. We were lucky we escaped when we did; had we been taken to the gang's leader, things might have ended much differently. A shiver ran down my spine at the realization.

Everything became foggy when we returned to the ranch last night. I bet Gail slipped me something to put me to sleep—that stinker. I needed to check on my team and make sure everyone was okay. I don't remember seeing them once Gail got hold of me.

I slept well last night, considering what we all went through. I only woke up a few times from nightmares, but TJ never let me go; he held me all night.

There was a quiet knock on my door, and then a head of wild, bone-white hair peeked around it, and then another one popped in below it. "Vibe check?"

"Feeling good, Katie, come in, my beauties."

Gail and Katie ran in, and carefully lay down on the bed, turning me into a Mel sandwich, with Ruffus on one side and Gail and Katie on the other.

Katie was an adorable mini-Gail. She was fourteen but thought she was twenty-one. They both had the most amazing natural bone-white hair I'd ever seen. Gail had a pixie cut, and Katie's hair was long; so long that it almost touched her bum. They both had bright green eyes with flecks of gold. She called me her auntie. Katie was my little peanut. I loved that kid.

Gail kissed my cheek, "How are you feeling?"

"I'm like a chipmunk locked out of a coffee shop, a little nuts and no energy."

Katie giggled. Gail patted my head, "Heaven forbid my little chipmunk can't get to her coffee. I'll go get you some."

"Let's have our coffee on the porch," I said as I sat up and tried to move my big lump of fur. Ruffus wouldn't budge. "Come on, sweetie, let's go outside." That worked. He was up and out the bedroom door in a flash.

"How are you doing, Gail? You look great, as usual. I'm diggin' on the haystack of chaos on your head."

She grinned, smoothing her hair. "Thank you. I worked hard on this look and am happy you like it. I'm feeling pretty sore this morning, hoping for average after lunch."

"How was the team doing last night?" I asked

"There are a few bumps and bruises, but they'll recover. Dylan took the most damage with the gunshot wounds, but he's a tough guy. Tracy fixed him up, and he's taking it easy for a while, but he'll be back in action with no adverse side effects."

I was so relieved to hear that. When Dylan was shot, I thought we had lost him. I really screwed the pooch yesterday. That was a hard lesson to learn.

Katie played fetch with Ruffus, while Gail and I sat on the porch with our coffee. I listened to the water rushing over the small rock waterfall into a little pond by the porch, the birds singing, and the breeze rustling in the trees, and my anxiety melted away.

Shelly and Raven walked onto the porch with coffee in hand and a plate full of homemade croissants that Chef C had sent over.

I snagged a warm, flaky croissant from the plate, "Mmm, good morning, ladies. Raven, I'm happy to see you. I've been looking forward to getting to know you better. I wanted to remind you to ask if you need anything. I can't understand what you're going through, I've never lost someone close to me, but I'll do everything I can to help you."

A few days ago, when TJ and his team had gone to the Rubicon to rescue some hostages that had been kidnapped by the cartel, Raven's husband, Sean, had been killed right in front of her. TJ had offered her a place at the ranch, and she'd accepted. I met her the night they returned and felt an instant connection. She was special. She was a beauty. TJ told me she was thirty-four years old. She was the same height as Gail at five foot two, in great shape, with an athletic build, and had the deepest, darkest, longest black hair I'd ever seen; it had a blue sheen, and she had long, thick lashes that complimented her beautiful gray eyes. I didn't even know gray was an eye color, but wow! She was gorgeous.

"I wanted to talk to all of you today, so this works out perfectly," I said.

Shelly sat on the porch swing, her legs swinging back and forth. "What'd I do now?"

"I have a few other things I want to discuss with everyone, but since you asked, I'm curious what you meant yesterday when you said, 'you're going to be as right as rain very soon; I have that on good authority.'"

Shelly and Raven looked at each other and nodded.

"Let me start from the beginning. Raven and I have been hanging out and getting to know each other. I've shown her around and have been helping her get acclimated to her new home. She knew the three of us were different, so she immediately asked what kind of magic we had. I wouldn't start our friendship with a lie, so I admitted the amazing things that had been happening. I told her about my groovy crystal magic and how you, Mel, have a magic touch with nature," Shelly looked at Gail and smiled. "We talked about what might be going on with you, Gail. She has some ideas that we'll share later. She is special, too."

Raven picked up from where Shelly left off. "Firstly, let me thank you for letting me join your community and live in your home. I can't tell you what it meant to me to find a safe place to live and make new friends when, not long ago, I lost everything and was alone. Before this mess began, I was a teacher; Sean and I had a good life. We enjoyed camping, fishing, and hiking, and he was teaching me woodworking. I enjoyed sewing in my spare time, but all of that's over, and this—" she waved her hands around, "—is my new reality. I'm not complaining; I love it here. I miss my old life with Sean." She took Shelly's hand and smiled. "This girl has been a lifeline. I know the goddess has blessed me with her. I always could talk to spirits. I've studied the occult for many years and continued my education, until I lost everything at Spider Lake." She took a shaky breath and looked at each of us; we smiled, and she continued. "When Shelly came to me frantic that you two were missing, I requested help from the spirit realm. A spirit friend came to me and told me what was happening with the shopping team. I passed the message on to Shelly, and here we are. I'll share my knowledge with you, and help you make this transition as easy as I can."

I was speechless. I glanced at Gail. Her mouth was hanging open, and she was staring at Raven. "Um, sugar, close your mouth," I whispered to Gail.

She snapped it shut and smiled at Raven. "You're like the ghost whisperer," Gail whispered in awe. "Can you contact Elvis and invite him over?" Raven laughed.

I looked at Gail "We'll talk about that later." Gail stuck her bottom lip out, and began to pout.

"Fine," she said, giving me the side eye.

Gail exhaled loudly, "Raven, Welcome to the family. Thank you for sharing that with us. We've been struggling, well, mostly me. I'm scared and confused. I would love to talk to you more. I know that what I thought were dreams are actually reality, and when I'm in the woods running around on all fours, it's really happening."

"I'm with Gail when I say, welcome to our family, and now our team of four, Raven. We are happy to have you here with us. We've got each other, and we're going to figure this out. I know there's a reason we are all here, but I don't know why. I feel it. So much has happened these past two weeks; we'll figure it out together. I've started a list—"

Gail burst out in an uproar of laughter, "Raven, now's as good a time as any to share a quirk of Mel's. She loves lists. You'll find them all over the house, in the greenhouse, and even in the bunkhouse dining room. Not a day goes by that she isn't working on one."

"Rude!" I frowned but winked at Gail.

"I think that's a great quality," Raven smiled at me.

"Thank you, Raven," I looked at Gail indignantly.

"Yes, I agree it's important to keep track of things that need to be done, but our marvelous Mrs. Mel takes it to the extreme. She has lists for anything you can imagine. Example number one: I found a list on the coffee table last week for how she wanted to organize her pantry. It listed by-products and positions: shelf one, dried beans, and dry pasta. You get the idea." Now, everyone was laughing their booties off.

I was trying unsuccessfully to hold back a laugh when I saw several of my potted plants had grown a little and were swaying. I could hear their happy laughter. Phil, my philodendron, wrapped one of his long vines around my arm, working his way to my shoulders. I smiled and sent out extra love to my babies. "How are you doing today, Phil?"

"If I were any better, I'd be triplets!" he responded. I was the only one who could hear my plants, but it was evident to my friends that something was happening.

Raven got up from the swing and sat next to Ava, my Lavendula, also known as a Lavender plant, and cooed, "You're quite the beauty, and your fragrance is lovely!" as she fluffed her leaves. "This is amazing; I've never seen anything like it. What are they saying?"

"They were laughing with us, and Phil," I pointed to him as he continued to curl around my shoulders, "he told me, 'if he were any better, he'd be triplets!' Ava, that's the beautiful lavender plant's name. She likes you and would like you to visit her more often, oh, and she's requested some banana peels." I smiled.

"I'll make a point to visit her every day. And I'll see what I can do about some banana peels," Raven said, as she pulled the hose over to give the plants some water.

"Thank you, Ms. Adler, for sharing one of my favorite habits with the class. She's correct. I'm a list-making fool. I love my lists. I want to readdress an earlier topic I attempted before I was rudely interrupted." I winked at Gail.

"You are very welcome, Mrs. B," she giggled.

"When we were in the jail cell, Bear told us that they had women they used as sex slaves; that is unacceptable and needs to be stopped. I've already spoken with TJ, but I'll talk to him and John about putting a mission together to rescue the women. What are your thoughts on this?"

Gail instantly stood and looked determined as a bulldog with a bone. That told me she was ready to kick some booty.

"I'm in. We need to save those women and take out the slimeballs while we're at it."

Raven and Shelly agreed.

"I have a few more things I'd like to discuss with you. To begin with, I would like to start patrolling Rancheros this week. We can build teams after we see how the first patrol works." I looked at Gail, "We are a bit messed up right now, but I honestly feel so much better than I did when I fell asleep last night; I don't understand how I could be feeling this good already. I can take deep breaths, and I know I could eat something more solid than cream of wheat. I just wolfed down a croissant. It's unbelievable. Gail? What's going on? How are you feeling?"

"I wasn't as hurt as you were, but I'm back to one hundred percent. I'm unsure how or why we're healing so quickly, there's no reason. But if I had to guess, I would say it has to do with the magic."

"Are you three game to join me on patrol?" I asked, crossing my fingers.

"Count me in," Gail said. "But why are we starting the patrols in Rancheros?"

"I would like to secure a buffer between us and Gardnerville. The gangs there are dangerous, as we found out firsthand yesterday. From what I have been able to ascertain, Rancheros hasn't been hit as hard by the gangs, and I want to get in there first and establish a strong protection presence. That way the gangs won't have a chance to get a stronghold over the town."

Raven and Shelly nodded in agreement.

"I'm all for that, but I obviously didn't bring any of my weapons. Do you have any I can borrow?" Raven asked.

"Girlfriend, we have any, and everything, your little heart desires."

Her eyes lit up with excitement, "Do you have a katana?"

That surprised me. I didn't expect her to ask for a katana. "I do, I have a few. And of course, I will give you one. Is that your weapon of choice?"

"Yeah, I loved my katana. Of course, I had many other weapons, but the katana was my baby. I called her *Snake Venom*. I would work out with her every night."

"We will get you outfitted with everything necessary for patrolling," I said.

She had a beautiful smile—the first genuine smile I had seen since I'd met her. I'm glad I could be part of that moment.

"There are a couple of mysteries we need to solve. We must dig deep, pull out our best Nancy Drew skills and attitude, and get to work."

Shelly took a huge bite of her croissant and spoke with her mouth full, "I would prefer to be Trixie Belden."

"Cool, channel her—"

Gail spoke over me, "Um, excuse me, bossy lady—"

"Whoa. I think you meant to say, 'boss lady.'"

"Nope. I said what I meant. Bossy lady, I would also like to choose my alter ego if you're Nancy Drew, and Shelly is Trixie Belden. I want to channel Sherlocka Holmes," Gail enthused.

"I didn't mean that we need to have alter egos; it was just an example of—never mind. And by the way, you pronounced his name wrong. It's Sherlock, and—" Geez! She did it again. I shook my head. I was beginning to get a headache.

Now Gail stood with her hands on her hips, "No again, times a million. I want to be Sherlocka Homes! Get it, not the dude, but the dudette version. Understand rubber band."

This had been a long day, and it wasn't even noon. "Okie dokie smokie, Sherlocka it is. Since we've opened this box of worms. Raven, who would you like your alter ego to be during our investigations?"

She had been quiet the whole time, grinning. I think she enjoyed the show.

"Hmm, well, I guess I'll channel Jessica Fletcher."

That got a round of applause and cheers.

"Booyah! Great choice. I love *Murder, She Wrote*," Shelly yelled, and she danced around the porch.

"Great, Trixie, Sherlocka, and Jessica, can I please begin?"

"By all means, I am not sure what is taking you so long to get to the point, but I wish you would," Gail responded in her best Ann impersonation. We giggled.

"Pardon, I would like to add some information to this conversation." Raven wanted to get into the fun. I was glad she felt comfortable with us. Sometimes we could be a bit overwhelming.

"Yes, Raven, what would you like to share with the class?"

She stood in front of us like the teacher that she was, "Did you know the stage before frostbite is known as frostnip?"

She waited patiently for a reply, clasping her hands in front of her, but we all sat there in stunned silence. I wasn't sure where to go with that. Raven smiled, "I love fun facts. I have some doozies I'll be sharing with you. Some are very educational."

I gave Raven a thumbs up, "I look forward to learning from your infinite knowledge."

Mystery number one. "TJ told me that last week, Chef C began to notice that food, milk, and water bottles were missing. The same thing happened every morning; all the leftover food was gone yesterday. TJ did a quick inventory of our stock and supplies and found that we were missing a case of beef jerky, a large bucket of trail mix, a large storage bag of blankets, and a bag of pillows. I'll get my whiteboard out from storage and set it up when we begin our investigation. It'll be our mystery board to keep track of our clues. Also, while we are investigating the case of the missing food, let's keep our eyes and ears open for a person who has been breaking into my greenhouse and destroying some of my plants."

Shelly stood and stretched her hand out in front of her, and we all joined her, putting our hands on top of each other. "One for all and all fo—"

The moment all our hands touched, time slowed to the point that I saw a hummingbird next to us, and I could see each flap of her wings. The birds floated mid-air, and a squirrel looked as if it was frozen as he climbed up a tree trunk. Ruffus sat with Katie on the stairs, looking at us. They weren't moving. Suddenly, my wrist was burning; I tried to pull it away, but I couldn't. A golden rope bound our hands.

"W-w-what's going on? It won't let me go. It's burning!" Gail shrieked.

It was over as quickly as it began, and we all yanked our hands away.

I stared dumbfounded at my right wrist as I tried to shake the pain away. "Um ... do you have a mark on your inner wrist?"

"Yes," they whispered in amazement.

Katie ran to us, took her mom's wrist, and was grinning like a mule eating briars.

We all had the same tattoos—and they were beautiful. The tattoo was the Tree of Life, with a Celtic quaternary knot at the base where the roots would be. Four lines wound up and around, to form the trunk, and then four large branches formed around the top. Each branch was different and simply stunning. Iridescent sparkles of every color of the rainbow surrounded one branch. Another had gold and silver wisps that wound around the branch. The next one was so cute; tiny animals were sitting on top of the branch, others hanging, and birds flying. Lovely symbols of air, water, fire, and earth surrounded the last branch.

Raven, ever the teacher, raised her hand, "Is your tattoo moving? Mine is moving like it's alive. This is magic, no doubt."

Holy cow, the tattoo *was* moving. I sat back in my chair, not feeling well, and tried to catch my breath. "This is Un-Freakin'-Believable!" I said between breaths.

We looked at each other and nodded, speechless.

"Whatever is going on, I am pretty sure this," Raven held up her wrist, "means we are meant to work together. I don't know what the task is, but I guarantee that whatever it is, it's important. We are connected, bound together."

Chapter 5

I woke to the smell of coffee and Ruffus's head on my pillow. That damn dog would work his way between Mel and me and then take one of our pillows during the night. We both were having nightmares about what we had been through the past couple of weeks, so it was good to have him there. He relaxed us. He had his bed on the floor, though he liked ours better.

I crawled out of bed, and Ruffus picked up his head to look at me. "You want to go downstairs, buddy?" He chuffed at me, laid his head down on Mel, and closed his eyes. "I guess that means no. Take care of Mel for me." I headed downstairs to get my morning cup of java.

John and Shelly were sitting on the front porch drinking coffee. "Morning, you two. How are you doing today?"

"Living the dream, though it might be a nightmare," John replied.

I laughed.

"Let's head to the bunkhouse for breakfast. I'll go upstairs, wake Mel, and meet you there," I said.

"Sounds good."

I'd spoken to James and Cassie the day after Mel and her team were taken from the feed store. I told them I wanted her to rest for a few days, and then we would put a team together to take them to his parents' home near Topaz Lake.

Mel and her team were progressing well, and I figured we could make the quick twenty-mile drive south. We would take two Jeeps and a trailer to take them some extra food if their parents had none or were low.

When we arrived at the bunkhouse, I went to talk to James. "Hey there. Are you and Cassie ready to go see your parents?"

48

"Yeah, but honestly, I'm going to miss Chef C's food," he chuckled.

"I bet. It's very good. We'll leave here around ten hundred hours. I'll gather the team and prepare two Jeeps for the trip."

"Thank you, TJ. We appreciate your help," James replied.

When I sat with Mel, John, and Shelly to eat our breakfast, John asked, "What are you thinking about, brother?"

"I'm trying to figure out how much security we'll need to take James and Cassie to his parents' home. What's your opinion on the security team?"

"Two, in addition to you and me, should suffice," John replied.

"After breakfast, let's gather the team and plan for the trip," I said.

"Copy that," John said as he got up from the table to find the additional security for the trip.

John returned a while later with Bonnie and Carlos. "I found these two first, and they agreed to make the trip with us."

John detoured to where James and Cassie were sitting. "We're going to plan the trip to your parents' home. We need to discuss this, and then we'll pack the Jeeps and gear up."

I gave James and Cassie a weapon each. I wish we had held some weapons training with them. Hindsight is twenty-twenty.

Mel was in the shop as we packed. It was amazing how quickly she was healing. She and Cassie were sitting by the Jeep, and I could see Mel whispering words of encouragement to her. Mel also gave Cassie a quick overview of the gun she was carrying.

Thanks to Mel's whispered words, Cassie was much calmer when we were ready to hit the road.

We finished packing the Jeeps with extra food and weapons and were ready at zero nine forty-five hours.

Ruffus was sitting with Mel, and I debated taking him until he leaned into her and laid his head on her lap. It looked like he wanted to stay and care for her. "Are you staying here? You're a mama's boy," I teased him.

He gave me a few quick barks as if to say, 'Yes, I am, and proud of it!'

I hugged Mel, kissed her, and rubbed the top of Ruffus's head before leaving.

We had our usual loadout of a suppressed AR-15, 9mm pistols, and plenty of ammo. I also grabbed my Daniel Defense AR-10, chambered in 308. If I needed to reach out and touch someone, I could. Carlos had his 50-caliber BMG with some real reach.

We completed our radio checks and headed for Highway 395 and Topaz Lake.

I led the group, hoping for a quick, easy trip. It was not to be. As I rounded the corner at the village of Carter Springs, I saw a roadblock with no way around it. I quickly keyed my radio. "Roadblock just around the bend. Four people behind the three vehicles blocking the road," I snapped. We had agreed to keep some distance between the Jeeps for situations just like this.

"Stay cool, and let's see what they want," I said.

Carlos sat in the passenger seat and pulled out his pistol; I did the same thing. I knew John and Bonnie would be getting into position. If this went south, we would deal with it.

It was a standoff that I was beginning to think would take hours to end as the people on the other side of the vehicles looked at us like aliens.

I heard John in my ear. "We are in position. I have the two on the left. Bonnie has the two on the right. Ready when you are."

I looked at Carlos, who clicked his microphone once. "I am going to step out and see what they do," I whispered to Carlos and Cassie.

As I opened the door to stand behind it, I kept my pistol in my hand, though out of sight of the adversary across the way. We were only about thirty yards from the vehicles, so I could take a shot with my pistol if I had to.

"What do you want?" I yelled at the four people at the roadblock. "Can we pass through?"

"We don't want to hurt you. We want your food," one responded.

He was at least six feet six tall and probably 180 pounds soaking wet. The skin hanging off his arms and around his belly suggested that he was struggling to find enough food to eat and had lost weight due to the world situation.

I heard John in my ear. "I got Flabby's head in my sights. Can you see anyone, Bonnie?"

"I can just see the top of the two on the right through the side windows," Bonnie replied.

"If this goes south, Bonnie, just throw rounds their way, and I will come out firing to assist," Carlos murmured.

"We are not giving up any food," I told Flabby.

"Well, then we might be at an impasse," he declared.

"If you let us pass, we could bring some back, though there are no promises. If not, this will not end well for you," I asserted.

He laughed, "There are four of us here with guns trained on you three, and I think little miss in your back seat is too scared to pull a trigger."

"I only see you out front here, and you will be the first to go down. My Recon Marine friend will take out the two on your left before they can even blink, and after I have put three rounds into you, your other friend on your right will get three rounds. All of this done in less than five seconds," I calmly declared.

"Do you even need Bonnie and me?" John asked.

"No."

"What did you say, smart ass," Flabby asked.

"My Marine friend asked if I wanted his help, or could I handle all four of you on my own," I said, as I laughed.

"Haha. You're not very funny, and I think we can take you and your Marine friend. Then we will have your little girl back there as a new play toy," Flabby proclaimed.

That was my trigger point. "Execute, execute," I said into the radio. Flabby's head exploded from John's 5.56 round, and his second shot hit him dead center in the chest.

Bonnie was shooting into the car, and the two on her side were keeping their heads down as Carlos bailed out of the Jeep with his pistol in hand. He jumped over the rear deck lid of the bright red Camaro with such grace that *Starsky and Hutch* would have been proud. He started firing at the two before his feet touched the ground.

In typical Marine Corps fashion, the first guy took two rounds to the chest and one to the head. The second guy was trying to bring his old bolt action rifle around to fire at Carlos, and it might have worked if he was not so close to the car. His rifle barrel caught in the wheel well, and Carlos fired again, three times, two to the chest and one to the head. Both guys were dead in less than five seconds. Carlos was spinning around to fire at the remaining threat just as I cleared the back of the pickup that was backed up to the Camaro and fired four rounds into the chest of the fourth and final threat.

"Clear," I called over the radio.

"Clear," Carlos called.

"We'll be there in a minute," John said into the radio. "Driving up now."

I walked back to check on Cassie. She sat with her arms wrapped tightly around herself, shoulders shaking, chest rising and falling between uneven breaths. Her eyes glossy with tears she couldn't hold back, and her jaw trembled from the effort of trying.

"We had to do this," I said gently, trying to steady my voice. "I hope you understand. They would have taken you—and they would've tried to kill us."

Cassie jerked her head up and looked at me. "They would really do that?" she asked, her voice barely above a whisper.

"Yes," I said, not wanting to sugarcoat anything. "They would have abused you before they traded you for more food." Cassie was as white as a ghost, as I explained this to her.

"Well, maybe I should learn how to use a gun," she stammered.

As she was trying to pull herself into a seated position, John pulled up, and James jumped from the Jeep to run over to her. "Are you okay, sweetheart?"

She nodded slightly. "Yes, I was scared ... when bullets were flying everywhere," she said, then she turned to look at Bonnie. "Were you scared?"

"Yes and no. I've been training with these guys from day one. I was also a competitive shooter prior, so I know how to handle a weapon. This was a little scary, though I trusted my training and my team," Bonnie replied.

"Wow, you are brave, Bonnie. I was so scared."

"I hate to break this up, ladies, but we need to keep moving. Let's grab their weapons and anything useful and move the bodies, then we can push one of the cars out of the way," I said.

"Let's make it quick. I think we've garnered some attention from the little community here," Carlos advised.

We pushed the red Camaro out of the way and were soon moving again. We hadn't been moving for long when John announced, "We'll be turning left onto Topaz Park Road. That will take us to James's parents' home."

Carlos responded with a single click. We passed Holbrook Junction without incident and, about three-quarters of a mile later, made the left onto Topaz Park Road.

Cassie gasped shortly after we made our turn. "Their home burned down," she stammered.

Wisps of smoke rose from what had once been a gorgeous lakeside home. The two buildings next to it were also burned.

"Extra alert, everyone. Something went down here," I exclaimed over the radio.

John stopped his Jeep next to mine. We all met in front of the burnt husk of the home.

"Let's set a quick perimeter. We can see if the embers are cool enough to walk through the home," I growled. I hoped they had escaped before it was set on fire. "John and Bonnie, can you set the perimeter while Carlos and I check the home?"

"Copy," I heard in my earpiece.

"James and Cassie, do you want to stay here? I'm not sure what we will find, and it appears to be a mess in there," I said.

"We need to help," James stammered.

"Okay. Be careful. We have limited medical abilities here," I replied.

We moved into the remains of the home; many areas were too hot to enter and inspect. "With all the debris in here, I'm not sure we would even find a body," I muttered to Carlos. "Let's get out of here," I announced to everyone.

When we were outside, I asked James, "Do your parents have any friends they might have gone to when the home caught fire?"

"One thing I'm not seeing is empty shell casings. It doesn't appear that there was a gunfight here. Did your parents have any weapons, James?" John asked.

"Dad had a couple of ARs, even though my mom did not like guns. I think he also had a couple of pistols, though I'm not sure what kind," James responded. "They have a couple of friends in town. We can check their homes."

"Load up. We are burning daylight. John, lead the way with James giving directions," I said.

I followed John into the little town, where we drove to a two-story home on Beatty Street. It was painted robin's egg blue with white trim, though it appeared to need a little work. "Keep some separation, not much for cover here," John said over the radio.

"We will stay back and find some cover," I said, "Carlos might be able to find an overwatch position."

They replied with a single click. I backed up around the corner onto Kit Carson Drive and parked.

As Carlos exited the Jeep, he asked, "Can I use the Jeep hood as a platform?"

"No problem," I said as I exited the Jeep.

"Cassie, it's best to wait for us in the Jeep. Are you good with that?" I asked.

"Yeah, I feel safe in here," she replied.

I grabbed my AR-15 and moved down the street to find a position to cover John, Bonnie, and James.

I found a short retaining wall and set up behind it so I could watch the other team. I shared our position with the others.

"Copy. James and I are headed for the door, and Bonnie is covering us from the Jeep," John replied.

John and James headed for the door and knocked. As I looked at the home, a curtain moved. Someone was there. "The home is occupied; someone looked out the window," I informed the team.

About twenty seconds after they knocked, the front door cracked open, and then it was flung open by a man in his fifties. He was around five feet ten, with a beer belly, a bald spot on top of his head, and primarily gray hair around the lower edges. If it was colored red, he could have been Bozo the Clown.

"Their parents are here. Everyone, muster up," John announced.

"Carlos, would you bring the Jeep here?" I asked.

"Ten-four."

I stood up and started across the street when the man pointed in my direction. I could see John talking to him, and then he relaxed. Bonnie was moving John's Jeep closer, and as I arrived at the front door, Carlos pulled up with my Jeep and Cassie.

Cassie was out of the Jeep in a flash, ran up the porch, and hugged the gentleman at the door. I could see a couple of women hanging back. The first one appeared around the same age as the man who answered the door, and the other appeared to be around seventy.

When we all arrived, they invited us inside. We assembled in the kitchen, and James introduced us to his parents and the other couple. His parents were Barney and Betty. Betty was around five feet two and was pleasantly plump with brown hair peppered with gray. Her eyes were deep blue, and she wore tan tactical shorts, a light blue shirt, and slippers with what appeared to be a green hopparoo, a kangaroo, and a dinosaur combination on them. Barney's outfit matched Betty's, minus the slippers. I bet they both shopped at the local 5.11 store.

The other couple were Kurt and Leandra. Kurt was five feet six, skinny, with white hair. He probably weighed around 150 pounds. He wore cut-off blue jeans, a yellow T-shirt, and Birkenstock sandals with black socks. Leandra also wore jean cut-offs and a blue T-shirt.

"What happened to your home and the other buildings?" I asked Barney.

"We were cooking ramen for lunch on our camp stove when something happened to the fuel tank. I think it leaked, which caught fire and then spread to our home. The wind pushed the embers and flames to the other two structures. We got out with our go bags, a couple of weapons, and the clothes on our backs," Barney recounted.

"I'm sorry to hear that. I'm glad you were able to get out with your lives," I replied. The fire probably saved their lives. Camp stoves can put off deadly carbon monoxide.

"What are we going to do now?" James asked. "We came here to live with you."

"You can stay here," Barney insisted. "We should really ask Kurt and Leandra first."

"They can stay here, but we don't have enough food to feed six people for more than a month," Kurt stated.

"We can take some of you back to our ranch. However, we'll have to figure out the sleeping arrangements. The bunkhouse is almost full," I explained.

"Our truck runs, and we have a thirty-foot travel trailer parked in the storage area by the road," Kurt said softly. "Although it depends on how far we travel, we don't have much gas."

"We've extra gas with us if you need any. You are all welcome to join us at the ranch." I said to them.

"I think we will remain here," Kurt said. Probably a bit too fast, as Leandra glanced at him.

"Okay, Barney, let's get your truck and trailer and get moving," I said. "Kurt, if you and Leandra change your mind, we are about twenty miles up the road. If you have a handheld radio, I can give you the frequencies we monitor."

"We have a GMRS handheld. Will that work?" he asked.

"Yes. That will work. Its range is limited. You might have to walk to the top of the hill for it to reach us at the ranch," I replied.

They said their goodbyes, and then Barney headed around the back of the house with a set of keys for his truck. He pulled up out front with his truck and waved us to follow him. We moved out to the frontage road and found an enclosed area with around twenty RVs. He connected and pulled out towards Highway 395. We gathered up and briefed the trip back. John would lead, Barney, Betty, James, and Cassie in the middle, and I would follow. "Keep a little distance between us, so if something happens, you have room to stop or maneuver," I told them. "We only have about twenty miles to go, so if we have no hiccups, we should be at the ranch in thirty minutes or less."

"Sounds good," Barney said.

As we were moving along Highway 395 going north, I said to Carlos, "I hope we have no issues on the way home."

"Agreed," he said.

When we cleared the top of the pass, I keyed up my radio, "TJ calling Freedom Ranch, how copy?"

"Freedom Ranch, loud and clear. Standby for authentication. 'Navy Chief.'"

"Navy Pride," I responded.

"Authenticated. How is your trip and status?" Charlie asked.

"Headed home. Plus, four. All healthy," I responded. The ranch knew we planned to leave James and Cassie in Topaz Lake, so the plus four told them we had them and two extra people with us.

We made good time and soon pulled into the ranch property. We stopped at the bunkhouse, where Chef C met James and Cassie.

"Welcome back, though if you are back, that probably means there was trouble down there," Chef C said to James.

"My parents' house had burned down; they were staying with friends, so we brought them back here. You get your wish, another cook at your service," James said with a bow, chuckling.

"Not how I wanted it to happen, though I'm glad to have you here."

Barney yelled at me over the sound of his truck. "Where do you want me to park our trailer?"

"Follow me, I'll show you where to park. After lunch, we can figure out power, water, and sewer for you."

"You have power and water?" he asked.

"We have enough solar power for the ranch, which also powers our well," I said, as I grinned. What a day! I'm glad to be home. "We will give you a tour after lunch."

Chapter 6

Ruffus

Ruffus here, protecting my kingdom as I heal from the gunshot wound I received while on the Rubicon trail. I was shot while I pursued the enemy. The team was on a rescue mission to save some people who had been kidnapped. Gail, our doctor, fixed me up, and I was healing quickly. That was what she told me at my last appointment.

I was the lieutenant commander of a special top-secret mission that demanded a great deal of my time. I can't share the details. Needless to say, this was a life-or-death situation, and I was the right dog for the job. I did have some subordinates who helped me, so it did take some of the burden off. I attended to the mission details several times a day. I've just returned from attending to my duties, and now it's break time.

I could only play for a while until I needed sustenance and rest. It was good to run and jump again with my little hoomans. I played with them, watched over them, and kept them safe. I appreciated it when they scratched the top of my head and brought me treats. I'll catch up with them later.

Speaking of treats, it was time to visit the Treat Wizard. He was magical with food and always gave me something delicious to eat. I think he had a never-ending supply of bacon! We had a connection that I just couldn't put my paw on.

I ran into the room with all the food, and there he was. "Hello, Mr. Treat Wizard," I said as I sat beside him. "It's that time again."

Sometimes, I played the pity card with the Treat Wizard, which trumped almost anything. He usually gave me precisely what I wanted. I needed lots of food to heal quickly, real food, not the hamster turds my pets tried to feed me.

"Well, hello there, Ruffus. How are you doing this pleasant day?"

"I'm better than I was, but not nearly as good as I'm going to be when I get some bacon in my tummy. Thank you for asking," I replied.

"So, whatcha got for me today? Bacon?"

"Here you go, buddy, some splendid bacon."

"Oh my gosh, so good. Thank you, Mr. Wizard." I gave his hand a lick and was on my way. I sat under a tree and contemplated life. It was a pretty good one. I was still not over what TJ did to me the other day. It was the day after we had all the yummy pork; my Mel went missing. TJ was extremely upset, and I was too. Although I was still sore then, I wanted to go with him and rescue my mama. He wouldn't let me. I couldn't believe it. But then, not too long later, he came back with Dylan, who had been shot. He was going to leave again, so I tried a second time to grab a seat in the Jeep. Again, he turned me down flat. That wasn't right, and I would make him pay for his treachery. I would start with his underwear drawer and see how he'd like them apples.

It was my job to protect my pets. I should have just followed them. Oh, well, what's done is done. But, next time, I won't be so nice. I was in charge, and he knew it. This was my domain. *Harrumph.*

I was almost in dreamland when I heard wings flapping right by my head, the wind from the wings blowing in my ear. I opened one eye and was about to tell the bird to beat it when, lo and behold, a beautiful tiny creature hovered in front of me.

She was six inches tall, with shiny, iridescent rainbow colors covering her body. She sparkled with diamonds. The two horns atop her head looked like solid gold swirls. The claws on her paws were as shiny gold as her horns. Long, thick, multi-colored eyelashes surrounded those big, beautiful eyes, which were a kaleidoscope of colors. The colors shimmered all the way to the tips of her wings.

I sat up. "Hello, little one, where did you come from?" I asked as I tilted my head to one side, and then the other. "What are you doing here?"

She landed gracefully on the ground before me, so I lay my head level with hers between my paws.

"It is a pleasure to make your acquaintance, Sir. My name is Princess Adalinda, a Dragonette, and the youngest daughter of Queen Aubriana of Shangri-La."

"Welcome, Princess Adalinda. My name is Ruffus, king of this domain," I said as I bowed my head.

"Thank you. I have always wanted to explore other places and was granted this request by my mother. I would like to stay if Your Highness will allow me the pleasure. I think two or three of your moon cycles will allow me sufficient time to explore and gain knowledge of your kingdom.

I was excited and so happy to have a new friend. I couldn't stop my tail from wagging a million miles an hour even if I had wanted to.

"I will grant you permission to stay, I said, trying to contain my enthusiasm. "Would you like me to give you a tour of my kingdom?"

"Oh, yes, Sir Ruffus, that would be lovely."

"Wonderful. I will take you to my home and introduce you to my pets. I'm sure we have adequate accommodations for you, Princess."

I held open the flapping thing on the door, that let me in and out of the house, for Princess Adalinda.

"Thank you, kind sir. You have a lovely Kingdom. I'm pleased to be here."

"I can't wait for you to meet Mama Mel. She's the best. She lets me cuddle with her, and I bet she would let you cuddle with her, too," I explained as I ran into the living room.

"Mama, look who's here, a princess that came to visit my kingdom."

Mama turned, her face scrunched up, and her mouth opened like she was yawning or preparing to take a big bite of bacon.

Where's the bacon? I want some. I'm so hungry, I wondered.

Princess Adalinda sat down on my back, so I walked to Mama Mel and nudged her hand with my nose. "I would like to introduce my new friend, Princess Adalinda. Princess Adalinda, this is my Mama Mel.

Chapter 7

Mel

My house was clean. I was happy, and it was a beautiful day in the neighborhood.

I put the cassette tape of *The Sound of Silence* by Disturbed into my battery-operated boombox and sang loud and proud in my best glass-breaking voice. Twirling around the room like I was a prima ballerina, Phil, my Philodendron, and Willow, my Bonsai Green Weeping Willow Tree, were happily singing and doing their version of dancing with me.

I heard Ruffus come into the living room, barking happily. I smiled and turned to give my baby boy some sugar, but the sight before me stunned me into silence. My voice didn't work. Ruffus continued to bark and smile, showing me his pearly whites. He bounced over to me, touched my hand with his nose.

I knelt and kissed Ruffus's sweet face, never taking my eyes off the most incredible creature I had ever seen sitting on Ruffus's back. Well, that and I didn't want it to bite my face off.

"Hi, little man. It looks like you have had an adventure today and made a new friend." I sat down face to face with the radiant little beauty.

"Um ... hello, I'm Melanie, but you can call me Mel." I held my hand toward her, then realized she was the same size as my hand, so instead, I held out my pinky for her to shake. Oh, brother, I didn't know what I was thinking. She wouldn't know what I was doing. At that moment, she shook my pinky with her cute little paw and sparkling gold nails.

"It is truly an honor to meet you, Ms. Melanie. Ruffus has shared many wonderful things about you. I am Princess Adalinda from the Dragonette Clan in Shangri La." She put her little paw over her heart and bowed her head.

What the fork! She just talked to me, but her lips didn't move. *Ruffus talked to her? Where's TJ? Deep breath, in—out—in—out. Good, there you go, girl. You got this. Open your mouth and say something.*

I bowed my head. I didn't know the proper etiquette when meeting royalty.

"Your Majesty, thank you for coming to our home. I am honored you feel we were worthy of your benevolent presence." *Was that too much? No, I'm sure it was great.* I could rock this royalty stuff. I felt pretty good about myself when delicate sounds of laughter came from the two, interspersed with snorts, roars of laughter, and *hhuh, hhah* sounds filled the room. I think Ruffus and Princess Adalinda were laughing at me.

"Excuse me, what is so funny?" I asked, indignantly. Ruffus, are you laughing at me?"

Ruffus looked me directly in the eyes, smiled, and nodded his head.

Okay. Moving on.

"I must apologize, Ms. Melanie; that was inexcusable. Please forgive me," Princess Adalinda said in the sweetest little voice. You may call me Adalinda. Her Majesty is my mother, the queen. I am honored to be in your presence. I appreciate you allowing me to live with you in this beautiful castle. Thank you."

What? Why is she honored to meet me? And whoa, live here?

"Miss Adalinda. Where did you come from, and how long do you plan to stay? We do have plenty of room for you."

"I came from Shangri-La, and Sir Ruffus has granted my request to stay for three moon cycles.

I gave Ruffus a sideways glance. *Sir Ruffus, hah!* "The more, the merrier. Welcome to the family, Adalinda. I have a question for you. Did you say Ruffus talked about me? I think I misheard."

"Oh, yes, he did. He loves you and your mate very much; you are his Mama."

Tears filled my eyes as I carefully pulled Ruffus to me, trying not to disturb the princess sitting on his back. I gave him hugs and kisses, saying, "I love you, too."

Sweet baby Jesus! TJ! What was I going to do? He didn't know what had been going on, the beautiful magic that had been happening to me and my girls. I had been waiting to explain everything because I didn't know what was happening either. I'd just be honest. I didn't understand anything, so I really couldn't explain it. *Honesty is the best policy. Right?*

I made a plate of snacks for Adalinda and cut them into tiny pieces. Then, I set up an area on the coffee table for her, placing a measuring cup upside down for a chair and the plate and cup atop a small square block I'd found in the garage. Ruffus also got a small plate; fair is fair. I found a thimble in my sewing kit and filled it with peach tea for her. I sat and talked to her while she enjoyed her food. I needed a distraction; my nerves had hit a ten on the Rictor scale.

"Ms. Melanie, the food is most delicious; what do you call it," Adalinda asked.

Pointing out the food, I said, "Deviled eggs, pecan-stuffed mushrooms, meatloaf, and vanilla walnut monkey bread for dessert."

She had just taken a bite of the monkey bread and immediately spit it out, "I do not eat monkeys! They are my friends," she scolded me.

I held up my hands in surrender," No, Princess, it's not an actual monkey; we don't eat them either. It is made of biscuits, sugar, cinnamon, butter, and a few other things, but absolutely no monkey."

"Thank the Dragon goddess."

Ruffus ran to the door; I knew what that meant. TJ was home.

"I'll introduce you to my husband, but I need to break it to him slowly so as not to scare him, okay?"

"Of course, Ms. Melanie."

TJ stepped inside—and instantly slowed, sensing something was off. His eyes swept the room, stopping short when he caught a glimpse of movement near the hallway.

Before he could process it, I launched myself into his arms like a tactical cuddle missile, legs wrapped around his waist and lips on his ear.

Ruffus was walking around his legs, sniffing him for new scents, and trying to help me distract him.

"Hi, babe, I missed you so much," I murmured between kisses, pressing my cheek against his and subtly trying to block his line of sight. My arms clung tightly around his neck, part love, part human blindfold.

He staggered a step but didn't drop me. "Mel ..." he said slowly, his hands steadying me at my waist. He pulled back just enough to see my face and study me, his piercing blue eyes locking onto mine.

"Melanie. Love of my life. What ... exactly are you hiding behind that hallway door?" His voice was amused, but he was suspicious, and way too perceptive.

I grinned. The game was up.

"Well," I said, slipping down from his arms and brushing imaginary dust from his shirt. "Promise you'll keep an open mind? Because ... she's technically family now."

Adalinda flew out and landed on Ruffus's back, staring at us, grinning like a Cheshire cat.

I'm going to be honest; she was adorable, but when she smiled like that, showing all her tiny pointed, razor-sharp teeth, it kinda freaked me out.

"How did it go today with James and Cassie? You were gone for quite a while? Is everyone okay?"

"I'll fill you in later. But right now, I would like to hear what you don't want to tell me about our new family member, as you called her."

I huffed, *Fine. You asked for it.*

I looked over TJ's shoulder at Adalinda and held out my hand. "Would you like to meet my husband?" I asked her.

She nodded, still smiling like a creepy cat. She flew to my hand and landed, and I brought her closer to TJ.

"TJ, may I present Princess Adalinda of the Dragonette clan in Shangri La, to you."

Adalinda bowed, "Sir TJ, it is an honor to meet you."

TJ didn't move at first. His gaze flicked from me to the small dragonette perched daintily on my hand. She looked like something out of a fairytale—until she opened that sharp-toothed grin again. I watched TJ's posture tighten, just slightly. Not enough to call it fear, but he was reading the room like a man trained to walk into chaos and make sense of it.

"She talks," he finally said, his tone unreadable.

"She does," I replied softly. "And she bows, apparently. Very polite for someone with teeth like a mini chainsaw."

Adalinda huffed and crossed her tiny arms. "I do not *eat* humans. That's just rude."

TJ raised an eyebrow. "Is that ... a joke?"

"She's learning," I offered. "She hasn't threatened anyone, hasn't burned down the house, and Ruffus likes her."

At the mention of his name, Ruffus barked once and nudged TJ's leg, then circled Adalinda protectively, like he was her bodyguard.

TJ crouched slowly to get on their level. "Ruffus doesn't like just anyone. You know that."

Adalinda hopped from my hand to TJ's knee without warning, balancing with supernatural grace. His hand twitched, but he didn't pull away.

"You can trust me," she said, looking him dead in the eyes with eerie sincerity. "I gave her my wing. That means protection. Loyalty. Family."

TJ looked up at me. "She gave you, her wing?"

I nodded. "That is like giving your word."

He studied Adalinda again, then reached out one finger—offering it like a handshake. "Well, Princess, if Ruffus trusts you, and Mel's still in one piece, I guess I can try."

Adalinda bumped his finger with her forehead in reply.

"I still want a full debrief," he said, standing up and brushing off his knee. "And if she burns my gear or eats my protein bars, I'm reevaluating."

"Noted," I said, slipping my arm around his waist. "But ... admit it. You're kind of into the tiny dragon thing."

"I admit nothing," he said, though the corner of his mouth twitched. "But this is officially the weirdest day I've had in a while."

Adalinda let out a tiny giggle. "You must not get out much."

TJ's face paled, and I thought he was going to pass out. I grabbed his arm, led him to the couch, and carefully sat him down.

"Uh honey, I think Gail needs to give me a checkup. I've been having weird episodes recently, and just now, I thought I heard the princess talk to me."

I took his hand and held on tight, hoping to comfort him.

"It's going to be okay. Let me start from the beginning, and I will tell you what has been happening."

So, I told TJ about the plant magic and all the other crazy things that had been happening. When I finished, TJ wasn't moving; it was hard to tell if he was breathing. Oh no! I hope I didn't break him.

"So, you can hear my thoughts? I wondered how you seemed to know what I was thinking. I would prefer it if you stayed out of my head," TJ said and frowned.

"I'm sorry. I didn't do it intentionally. You think very loudly. I'll try to figure out how to block out your broadcasts, and maybe you can learn how to turn the volume down on your thoughts." I said.

"Ten-four."

"Are you okay?" I asked.

"Yes? No? I don't know. Did Ruffus really talk to Princess Adalinda?"

"Uh-huh."

"Ruffus, come here, buddy," TJ whispered.

TJ and Ruffus just looked at each other, and Ruffus smiled happily at him.

TJ shook his head, "Okay, this is going to take some getting used to, but I believe you. I wish you hadn't lied to me. We promised to always be honest with each other.

"I didn't lie—well, not exactly. I was confused and still trying to figure it out."

He looked at me, raised one sexy eyebrow, and waited.

"Fine—sorry. Happy?" I huffed.

"Yes, thank you," he said, as he kissed me. He turned to our new friend and took a deep breath.

"Um ... hello Princess, it's wonderful to meet you as well."

She smiled, nodded her head, and went back to Ruffus. Ruffus had started to run around, and Adalinda took the opportunity to dive-bomb him, over and over. They were going to sleep well tonight.

"Mel, I have had some weird stuff happen to me, too. I thought I was losing my mind, and maybe I still could be."

I sat quietly while he explained how he'd heard and understood what Ruffus was thinking and how it seemed like Ruffus understood what he said.

"You're not losing your mind, TJ. We have a special dog-son. There are times I feel I understand him also, and I know he understands me. So, if you're losing your mind, then so am I."

We sat there for a long time in silence. I was trying to organize everything in my head; I wasn't sure what was happening with TJ and me. What a hot mess!

"Ahem. Would it be possible to show me to my living quarters? I'm in need of rest," Adalinda said as she enunciated each word, with deliberate grace. She was definitely a princess.

"Oh, my stars! I didn't even think about that. TJ?"

"Tonight, if you would like, you can sleep in Ruffus's doggie bed. I can build you something permanent later," TJ offered.

"Ruffus invited me to sleep in his big bed, and I accepted. Thank you. I will retire now. Please lead the way."

What did she mean by 'big bed'?

Holy hell, my body hurts. Even though I didn't want to move, my bladder was calling. Every direction I tried to move was blocked by either TJ, Ruffus, or Adalinda. They had all kept me awake most the night, trying to cuddle with me. I'd finally fallen into a deep sleep a few hours ago.

Good morning. How'd you sleep?" he asked.

I chuckled internally. *We needed to do something about the sleeping arrangements.*

"Good morning. I slept okay, but I need coffee. I also think it would be a good idea if you built a special little house for Princess Adalinda. Maybe we can set it up in the library."

"I would prefer to have a home set up here, with you," Adalinda said.

"Well, okay. It looks like you're going to be busy building two little princess castles," I snickered as TJ groaned.

When we finally reached the kitchen, the house was empty. Darn, I'd wanted to introduce the girls to Adalinda.

Sitting on the porch with our coffee, TJ and I watched Ruffus chasing butterflies with Adalinda sitting on his back and hanging onto his collar. It was one of the most adorable sights I'd ever seen. Her beautiful rainbow-colored scales glittered in the sunlight. Adalinda was laughing so hard she was snorting little puffs of sparkly smoke.

"Well, TJ, are you ready to reveal the newest member of our family to the rest of the community?"

"Nope!" TJ said as he crossed his arms. Mmm ... I loved watching his bicep muscles stretch his sleeves to the point that it looked as if they would rip apart. I knew what he was trying to do. He had learned that distraction technique from me. It wasn't going to work, but it was so tempting.

TJ laughed. "Almost had you, didn't I?"

"Yes, you did, mister. Let's go to breakfast and get it over with. But I am uncomfortable talking about what has been happening to me."

He pulled me to my feet and kissed me, "You win, let's go."

We followed Ruffus and Adalinda into the bunkhouse dining room, with Adalinda riding atop Ruffus's back. Ruffus barked loudly, smiling, and walked directly to Chef C.

All eyes turned to Ruffus and our little princess, and silence filled the room.

"Ruffus, come," TJ said.

Katie ran to Ruffus and Adalinda and sat next to them on the floor. She was cooing over Adalinda, who had flown onto her shoulder. TJ and I stood together, and I began. "Good morning. We want to introduce you to our newest family member." I held my hand out, and Adalinda flew over and landed with the grace of the princess she was. "May I introduce Princess Adalinda of the Dragonette clan in Shangri La." She bowed her head and smiled. Thank goodness it wasn't her Cheshire cat smile.

Gail, Shelly, and Raven approached us and curtsied. "Welcome, Princess Adalinda; it's a pleasure to meet you," Shelly said.

"I am honored to make your acquaintance, Ms. Gail, Ms. Shelly, and Ms. Raven. I am looking forward to many grand adventures with you all," Adalinda replied.

The tension in the room was so thick it felt hard to breathe.

"She is beautiful. I am so glad she chose to join our family," Gail said loud enough for everyone to hear. My girls were terrific. That was all it took to break the ice and release the tension. Questions began coming at us from every direction.

TJ held up his hand. "We don't understand what is happening either. Ruffus brought the Princess home yesterday. And yes, she can speak telepathically. She isn't a threat; she is a part of our family, and I expect her to be treated as such."

Good job, TJ.

Ann stood in a huff, her arms crossed, nose in the air, and her usual scowl. She wore the same grey and black high-buttoned-up dress shirt as always, and a long skirt with prints of black, grey, and white flowers. Her dark hair was pulled back in a tight bun.

Shoot, not now, Ann. If she says something rude about Adalinda, I will end her.

"Ann," TJ said, not raising his voice—he didn't need to. Now is not the time for conflict. Please sit down if you don't have something constructive to say," TJ informed her.

"Excuse me! This is not a totalitarian dictatorship. I have a right to speak just as much as them," she pointed her finger at Gail, Shelly, and Raven. "And you will not control what I say."

"Fine, Ann, what would you like to add?" I asked, as I watched her husband, Chef C, try to get her to sit down. Her daughter, Bonnie, had her head down. I could tell that she was embarrassed by her mother's actions.

"I do not agree to that," she said, shaking off Chef C, as she pointed at Adalinda. "That *thing* should not be allowed to stay! Why do we not have a say in this decision? It could be a vicious murderer, and I will not stand for it—"

That was it! I am done taking crap from her. "Then sit down and shut your pie hole! She is not a *thing* or an *it*! We do not judge a person, or in this case, a dragonette, on their appearance or race. There are good and bad people everywhere. Stop making general assumptions!"

Ann came over and stood in front of me, intentionally invading my personal space. I was not going to back down and she was not going to intimidate me. "Adalinda, please go back to Ruffus," I said a bit abruptly. TJ, Gail, Shelly, and Raven stood beside me as Chef C stood beside Ann, pulling on her arm.

"You little twit! Do not speak to me that way. I will destroy you!" Ann screamed in my face.

"Back off, slutwaffle!" I said. I raised my fist to knock the crap out of her, but her husband finally pulled her away from me.

TJ and my girls moved to stand between us. I was fuming. The plants around the room were screaming angrily, and my head was about to explode. Everything around me was tinted red, and I was dizzy. I must have begun to fall because TJ grabbed me, and the next thing I knew, I was lying down, looking up at him.

"W-w-what happened?" *My head is killing me. I remember being so angry at Ann that I wanted to smash her, but not much else.* "How long have I been out?"

"There was a disagreement with Ann, and after you put her in her place, you passed out, you've been out for about two minutes," TJ said as he smoothed my hair down.

Ruffus was sitting by TJ, and Adalinda was sitting on my stomach. Her sweet little face was scrunched up with worry. "It's all right, Princess," I said, grinning at her. "I'm okay now. Ann made me so mad that I felt out of control. I wanted to hurt her. TJ, I'm not like that. What's happening to me?" I asked.

"I feel like a broken record, but I don't know. Let's roll with the punches—not literally, Mike Tyson," TJ said.

He cracked up. He thought he was hilarious. I'd give him this one. It was pretty good.

We both laughed as Adalinda and Ruffus joined in.

"Just call me Mikey Jr."

"As long as you don't start biting ears off," TJ said and then laughed while covering his ears.

"Help me up, please," I asked. "I need some peace." I needed to go to my greenhouse. I wanted to check on my babies. Someone had been breaking into my 'Mad Scientist Laboratory,' as TJ called it. They were destroying cross-bred plants a few at a time. Whoever it was, they were playing with me. Why not destroy all of them and get it over with? I'd find out who was doing this and put a stop to it one way or another. I thought the only people who knew about this room were TJ, Gail, and Shelly, but obviously, I was wrong. There was no doorknob, so someone also knew how to get in. The only way in was to push a specific knot on the wall.

Crossing my fingers, I walked in. My heart dropped. The place was a mess. My plants were ripped out of their pots, leaves torn off the stalks, and broken, pots thrown across the room, and the potting soil dumped on the floor.

I cleaned up the mess and fed, watered, and talked to them. I spent the next few hours relaxing in the greenhouse. By the time I headed home, I felt much better. I said good night to them as I headed out the door, and double-checked that it was latched.

Chapter 8

Mel

The house looked magical. Everything was set up for our girls' slumber party. The living room was full of blankets and pillows. Adalinda helped me string twinkle lights across the ceiling from corner to corner. I positioned an extra-long table covered with every kind of munchie I could think of and delicious drinks to the side of the room.

TJ and John were on their way to Carson City, so we had the house to ourselves.

This morning, I woke up with the sun and began cooking, cleaning, and playing with Ruffus and Adalinda. Katie was in and out all day, checking on Adalinda and playing with them. She already loved our little princess as much as she loved Ruffus.

The whiteboard stood in a place of honor, in the middle of the room. I was ready to begin our investigations. Written on the left of the board was 'The Case of the Missing Food (and blankets and pillows)', and on the right, 'The Case of the Plant Murderer.'

Even though Gail, Shelly, and Raven live with us, tonight is about taking care of Gail, having fun, of course, and doing a little investigative business. I wanted to help Gail get control of what was happening to her. I didn't want her to be afraid anymore. I also wanted to properly welcome the newest member of our group, Raven.

Initially, Gail thought she dreamed she was running in the woods on all fours, but then she would wake up either outside or in her bed naked, covered in dirt and leaves. Hopefully, tonight, we'll figure out what's going on and help her.

Katie knew what was happening with her mama, Gail, and me, and she was fascinated. She asked a lot of questions that we didn't have answers to. She wanted a part of the magic so badly that she was constantly trying to change into an animal or make a plant move. She was getting so depressed that she had even tried twitching her cute little nose. I hoped she would come into her magic. I'd shared everything I knew with her. I had taken her with me when I went to check on my plants, I'd introduced her, and we'd talked with them. She loved it.

Katie was going to have a slumber party of her own tonight with Melissa Prime. Her room was all set up like ours, with twinkle lights, blankets, pillows, games, and enough food, snacks, and drinks that they won't need to come out for a week. I'm sure Adalinda and Ruffus will go back and forth visiting both parties.

I was having such a great time chatting with Katie and Princess Adalinda as Ruffus snuggled beside me, that I didn't hear Gail, Shelly, and Raven come in.

Gail started babbling as soon as her foot crossed the threshold, "There she is, Princess Adalinda. I'm so excited to get to know you. It's awesome that you can talk. You're so pretty, colorful, and sparkly. Are you full size, or will you get bigger? Not that I think you should get bigger, you are perfect—"

Adalinda's sweet, melodious laughter filled the room interrupting Gail's enthusiastic flow of words. "Thank you. You are quite lovely as well. I am as big as I will get. Standing six inches tall. I speak telepathically, which means I speak with my mind."

"That is outta sight, Princess," Shelly replied as she curtsied. "Mel, your pad looks far out. I'm ready to party. Whatcha got for munchies, girl? I'm starving?"

I pointed to the table, "Help yourselves, ladies, fruits, veggies, bread, dips, sandwiches, lots of sweets, and our slumber party signature cocktail is, drum roll please, Peach Cobbler Martini."

I felt like I was living in a fantasy; everything was wonderful—plant magic, dragonettes, crystal magic, and shapeshifting. I wondered what would happen next. At this point,

I was numb to changes; it was becoming the norm. The girls took Princess Adalinda's arrival surprisingly well. I bet they were in the same boat as me. Life had never been this exciting. It just felt right.

With a mouthful of food, Gail showed us exactly what she was enjoying. Gross.

"Mel, this Jalapeño Popper is so good. You're becoming a great cook. Have you been working with Chef C? Maybe it's the magic; keep working on it and let us be your taste tester."

"Thank you, but could you please close your mouth when you chew?" I teased.

Gail snickered. "Copy that. I have a question for you, Mel. Should women, in the *prime* of their lives, really be having a slumber party? And by prime, I mean forty-eight, forty-eight, thirty-seven, and thirty-four."

With indignation and a slight grin, I stood with my hand over my heart and replied, "Well, yes, of course, Ms. Adler, we should be having the time of our midlife. Kids aren't the only ones who can party at night; thus, we're having a slumber party!" Hah.

Smiling, I bowed as I received a round of applause.

"Have any of you figured out anything about our tattoo?" I asked, looking at my beautiful tattoo. I was still in awe and I'm sure I wasn't the only one.

"It must represent the four of us," Gail said, looking down at her tattoo. "I'm not worried about it. It's just so cool. I've never had a tattoo. I'm glad I'm sharing my first one with all of you."

Katie's eyes moved eagerly to each of us, before landing on her mother. "I want a tattoo. Can I get one like yours, please? I'm sure we can find someone to ink it."

"No, you cannot get a tattoo. We didn't ask for ours; it just magically appeared. If you happen to get a magical one like we did, that will be fine. But otherwise, that's a no, ma'am, on the tattoo front," Gail replied to an unhappy Katie.

I hugged Katie and whispered in her ear, "We'll figure something out. It's time for your party to begin. Melissa should be here any minute."

Raven stood in the middle of our circle, "The average nose produces about a cup full of nasal mucus daily!"

"Er ... Raven, that was a great fun fact. I'm sure I speak for all of us when I say, thank you for grossing us out," I said, with as much sarcasm as possible.

"You are most welcome. There's plenty more where that came from."

"Eeww, I'll wait for Melissa on the porch." Katie waved as she closed the door behind her.

Catching Raven up on the gossip around the ranch, laughing at a silly little story about Ruffus, when a man appeared beside her. I knew he was a ghost, but he almost looked corporeal. He looked almost solid, but there was a glow around him that was unnatural, and no matter where the light hit him, he didn't cast a shadow. I almost peed my pants from the shock of seeing him, but I was also trying to be cool. Raven smiled at the man. She didn't realize we could see him, so she said nothing.

Being the groovy mama she was, Shelly always just went with the flow and spoke her mind. She stood and walked to Raven and spoke to the man standing next to her. "Hey man, you're from the spirit realm; this is rad. I'm Shelly." Then, pointing over her shoulder, she introduced us.

Raven looked shocked, "You all can see Sean?"

"Holy Mother of Pearl! He's your husband."

TJ and his team had gone on a rescue mission at Spider Lake a while back. Raven had been a hostage, and her husband had been able to escape and contact the ranch. Sean was killed by the cartel right in front of Raven. It had devastated her. She had no one left. TJ had offered to bring her to the ranch, and here we were.

He was handsome, with dark shoulder-length hair and light blue eyes. He had obviously been in good shape when he was alive. TJ had told me that Sean looked like a modern-day Jesus, and that description described him to a T.

Shelly sat next to Raven. "For sure, sister, we can see him. This is amazing. I've never seen a spirit before, but I've read about them. Has he been with you the whole time?"

Raven was speechless. Sean's translucent hand hovered just above her skin, shimmering faintly in the dim light as it rested over her shoulder like a whisper from the past. He nodded. "I've been with her since I left my physical body. I've been watching what's been happening with all of you, and I'm not completely sure, but I think there is something otherworldly about your bond. I suppose that's why you can see me. But I'm no expert. I'm new to all this."

Adalinda and Ruffus were right there to join in the fun. This was definitely turning out to be a grand adventure.

"Should we name our detective agency?"

"For sure," Gail said, "I already have a suggestion. Sherlocka's Sleuths? It's a great name, right?"

"Er, why don't we all make suggestions? I'll write them on our mystery board, and then we'll vote."

"Fine," Gail stuck out her bottom lip, pouting.

Sheesh, that was close.

"Sock it to me, Sleuths," Shelly proudly announced.

"Good one, next."

"Gail and Associates! That would be a great name. I would vote for it," Gail snickered.

I ignored her. "Anyone have a *good* name?"

"Karma's a Bit—"

"Thank you, Ms. Adler. Let's move on. Next idea, please," I grinned at Gail and whispered, "Good one."

Raven jumped up and shouted, "Specter Surveillance!"

That was very creative. "Thank you, Raven." I added it to the whiteboard.

Shelly smiled," Serendipity Investigations."

"Excellent name."

Princess Adalinda flew to me and stood on my shoulder," Ruffus insists the detective agency's name should be 'Ruffus's Angels.'"

"Very nice, Ruffus. Thank you," I said, holding back a giggle.

Adalinda smiled, "I also would like to present a name, Charmed Four Investigation."

"Unique, I like it, Thank you."

"Magical Investigations."

"Mm-hmm, I like it; wonderful choice, *finally*, Gail," I winked at her.

Sean floated to the mystery board, "What about Shadow Sleuths?"

"Nice one, thanks, Sean."

"How about Sleuth Squad," I said, as I added it to our list.

"Ok, write down your choice, and I'll collect them," I said. Two minutes later, I'd gathered the paper from each person and was standing next to the whiteboard again. I announced the name of our detective agency.

"And the name of our agency will be, Charmed Four Investigation!"

"Let's start adding facts about the cases. Who, what, when/how, where, and why?" I said as I wrote the prompts down on our board.

Gail jumped up like a jack in the box, "Should we add Stakeouts, too?"

We all agreed that stakeouts were going to be necessary. I wrote notes down as the others shared their thoughts.

We know:

What: Stealing food and supplies

Where: Kitchen and supplies areas.

When/How: Sneak into the kitchen at night when Chef C leaves, and before he arrives at 4:30 a.m.

Why: To help someone outside the ranch or to barter with.

Who: No idea.

"Let's check the recordings from the cameras by the gate and see if anyone is giving the supplies away or carrying them out. I wish we had some by the bunkhouse," I said, adding, "we should probably add more around the ranch."

Shelly stood up, "Since we have no idea who to question first, we should keep our eyes and ears open and slyly ask random people sneaky questions. And plan a stakeout in the kitchen ASAP."

We all nodded in agreement.

"Great, now that we have a plan of attack for the missing food case, let's move on to the plant murderer case

Before we began the case of the plant murderer, Shelly explained to Raven about my private room, where I work to crossbreed plants and trees.

"Our board is now officially our murder board," I said.

What: killing my plants.

Where: Greenhouse secret room

When/How: At night, after everyone has gone to bed. And they know about security teams' routes.

Why: Does someone want to mess with Mel? By killing a few plants at a time. Why are they doing it at all? – They don't like Mel?

How: did they find out? Did they overhear us talking, or did someone see Mel go in?

Who: Ann is at the top of the list; she hates Mel.

"We'll start with Ann and see what she says," I said

"Now, let's get to the partying!" Raven sang as she got up and turned on my boom box. She began to sing *"Stand by Me"* by Ben E King while Princess Adalinda gracefully flew around her head. It was so sweet, I had a lump in my throat. We joined her during the second chorus, hugging and singing to each other. We sang our way to the front yard and fell on the grass, reveling in our friendship and peace.

My stomach dropped. "Oh, crud, ladies—we've got a problem. Don't move. Don't make a sound."

Fear has a way of short-circuiting common sense.

I should've known that someone would inevitably do the opposite when I said that.

Gail jumped up, her eyes wild, got into her fighting stance, and yelled at the top of her lungs, "Where?"

I've never in my life seen anything like it. Standing at least twenty feet tall, black, though not just black, but like it was sucking the light out of the space it inhabited. Floating out of the body were twisted arm-like branches with spikes. Oh, sweet sugar in my coffee! The creature had *four* eyes that were as big as dinner plates and glowing blood red. Evil, malicious intent rolled off it like the smoke from a flaming barbeque. The disgusting smell of sulfur was all I could smell. I could no longer smell my sweet flowers.

A strong wind hit us all and threw Gail to the floor. Raven jumped up and began chanting something in another language I didn't understand. Her long black hair was floating around her head, not controlled by the wind. It was something otherworldly. Her eyes were glowing bright white, and a skull shadow covered her face.

The wind swirled around us as I crawled and tried to reach Raven. Before I could reach her, one of the black, spindle-like arms grabbed me as some of the spikes punctured my waist and threw me against a tree. I lay on my back, attempting to catch my breath while chaos ensued around me. I rolled over to push myself off the ground on my hands and knees while trying to regain my breath. Being thrown against the tree took the breath out of me, and I was sucking air that my lungs failed to utilize. Raven was standing in the middle of a whirlwind, chanting. Shelly was lying against the porch, and Gail was headed toward me.

"What are we going to do?" Gail screamed above the howling wind.

Ruffus bounded to our side, while Adalinda clung to his collar, her tiny claws digging in to keep from being torn away. She hovered low, close to me, wings tightly folded against her back, but the wind still tugged at her like it wanted to toss her from the earth. Strain etched her face, every muscle working to keep her grounded. Ruffus's ears were pinned flat, his stance wide and braced against the gusts.

"That is a demon; I do not know the type."

"A what?" Um, demons don't exist, right?" I knew in my gut she was right, but I'd never imagined I would be face to face with something so evil. If we don't stop it, it will hurt my friends. That can't happen. "How do we kill it?"

"Raven is weakening the demon, but you must destroy its physical body. Call your magic and throw everything you have at it."

At least we were outside; that would help me.

"Thank you, Adalinda. Please take Ruffus and go to the house where it's safer. Come on, Gail, let's get to Raven and Shelly."

Raven was still chanting and holding tough, but she needed help.

I spoke telepathically with my plants. *Come on, babies, I need help. Get that jerk.*

A huge vine burst from the ground and began wrapping around the demon, but it wasn't working. He was easily pulling them off. Crap!

"Gail, we all need to use whatever magic we can against him."

Shelly called to every rock and stone in my yard and pummeled the creature. I called on my plants again, begging; this time, giant vines rose with thorns the size of my arm and began to wrap around the demon. Raven was chanting. Adalinda was shooting fire at him, and, OMG, Ruffus was attacking it. "Ruffus! Get out of here!"

Where was Gail? "Gail!" I looked around but couldn't find her. A vast black, dog-like animal suddenly appeared and started to tear the demon apart. It was at least fifteen feet tall, with three heads, a set of horns atop of each, and fire flaming from each head. The tail had spikes running along the top and ending in an arrowhead. The freakin' eyes were glowing eyes. I sucked in a breath as I realized it was Gail.

I grabbed Raven and Shelly's hands, and we stood against the raging wind. It felt like static electricity was running through my body when we connected. I didn't know what to do, so I repeated what Raven was saying, and then Shelly joined in chanting, *"Non-recipient relinquish,"* over and over, while Black Dog Gail continued to rip it apart.

The demon looked like it was starting to crack apart, and then lava started to flow to the ground. The rotten egg smell intensified, and smoke clouded my view. Black Dog Gail sat back and watched with her six red eyes, in glee as the demon exploded into ash.

Ruffus, Adalinda, and Black Dog Gail ran to us.

"Um ... Gail, sweetie, is that you?" I asked.

All three heads looked at me, grinning like crazed animals, showing all her sharp, pointed teeth as her tongues hung out of all three of their mouths, dripping with what I'd guess was black demon blood.

We sat on the porch, waiting for Gail to change back, but nothing happened.

"I can't change back!" Gail yelled at us, her voice sounding strange as it came out of one of the dogs' mouths.

Shelly looked stunned. That, even after everything we had just been through, she still couldn't quite believe a giant three-headed dog was talking to her, and that that giant three-headed dog was her friend. I couldn't believe that would surprise her. I knew we had a deep connection. Four days ago, after we escaped from the gang in Gardnerville, I had started to hear Gail's thoughts. I explained to Raven and Shelly what I thought was happening.

I stood in front of Gail on my tippy toes, trying to reach her middle head. Holy Canoli! One of her heads was bigger than all of me. I patted her enormous paw instead. "Relax, girlfriend, breathe in—out—in—out." I continued to talk to her, soothing her fears. Finally, she began to change back. Her paws went first, turning back into her human feet, the change working its way up her body. The skin of the dog went from black, to gray to her final tanned skin. She sat there naked as the day she was born, smiling like the cat that ate the canary. Shelly came running out of the house with a robe for Gail.

"That was awesome. I was amazing!"

Adalinda flew to Gail and landed on her shoulder. "Yes, Ms. Gail, you were most definitely spectacular. Why did you choose to turn into Cerberus?"

"I've been reading *Skin Games* by Jim Butcher. When you told us we were fighting a demon, the first thing that popped into my head was a wicked, cool dog from the book—then boom, I'm a three-headed dog."

"All of you were incredible, Shelly, the flying rocks! You go girl, that was amazing!" I said.

"Thanks. I don't know how I did it; I just wanted to punch the dude, and rocks started flying at him."

I watched Raven, she was relaxing in the rocking chair like it was just another tranquil evening on the ranch. "Raven, what did you do? And how did you know to do it? You were wicked cool."

"You already know I've grown up being able to communicate with the spirit world. Sometimes, mischievous spirits, called poltergeists, terrorize people. I try to help innocent people whenever possible, so I learned to banish them. I knew this was worse than a poltergeist, but I tried anyway. I was winging it, but it seemed to help."

I was so tired that I could barely keep my eyes open. I checked the wounds around my waist, and saw they were already healing. "All this magic and healing that my body is doing, tires me out," I said.

"I hope this was a one-time attack. We need to be prepared in case it happens again, which means training harder than ever before. We'll also add more weapons training. I am so out of shape." I needed to tell TJ about this incident and find out if we could participate in the training sessions with the security teams.

We made it into the house and fell onto the blankets on the floor. We didn't care that we were filthy, covered in dirt, blood, and demon ash. When my head hit the pillow, everything went black.

Chapter 9

TJ

John, the security team, and I were sitting outside by the fire pit, taking a break after our training and lunch, when Melissa Primm, Billy's daughter, came running out of the bunkhouse, yelling for me.

I stood to meet her, "Slow down, Melissa. What're you yelling about?"

"Someone from the Carson City Army National Guard is calling on the radio for you or John. They don't have a security code. What do you want me to do?"

"Let's go see who it is," I said to her as we walked back to the bunkhouse. Brian, Chef C's son, sat at the radio.

I took the microphone, "Freedom Ranch here. Who's calling?"

"This is Gunner from the Army National Guard facility near Carson City. I'm trying to reach TJ or John at Freedom Ranch. We were there for training last year."

"I'm TJ. I remember when you attended the training. John is also here. Share something that will convince me of who you say you are."

"For an old Navy guy, you showed us young Army bucks a thing or two about shooting and rubbed our noses in it," Gunner laughed.

I looked at John. "Did you hear the gunfire in the background while he was talking?"

"I did. I remember these guys and gals. Great group."

"We remember you. What can we help you with?" I inquired.

"We're under attack by a gang from Carson City. They have killed many of our fellow soldiers. We could use some help to flank them and a place to bug out to."

"Let me talk to my team. Monitor this frequency, and we'll get back to you at the top of the hour."

"Copy."

89

I turned and looked at John. "We need to help them. Mel would be angry if we didn't.

"Brian. Put out a call for Tracy, Gavin, Dylan, Madison, Billy, and Nick to muster here. We need to plan a rescue mission," John instructed.

Brian did as he was told, and our team soon arrived in the bunkhouse, looking expectantly at me and John, waiting for us to tell them what was happening.

"Okay, team. We have a situation in Carson City with a group of Army National Guardsmen. John and I have worked with these guys and gals before here on the ranch. They are in trouble with a gang attacking their base. It sounds like they are holding them off so far, but they have taken heavy losses. They would like us to come up and flank the gang and allow them a way out. We'll talk to them in about ten minutes and can ask them questions. After the call, we'll head to the armory to check our gear. Then, we will pack the Jeeps. We'll travel at night with our NVGs." I was glad we had two snipers, we could break up into teams of two for the attack. "Do you have any questions?

Hearing none, I grabbed the microphone at the top of hour, fifteen hundred. "Freedom Ranch is calling Carson City Army National Guard, do you copy?"

"Carson City ANG, we copy Lima Charlie," Gunner repeated.

"We have the team standing by. Can you give us a sit-rep," I asked.

"There are ten of us left. We have probably thirty or more gang members shooting at us. We're hunkered down at the armory with some of our armored vehicles outside for additional protection. Do you know where our base is?"

"John and I have been there before. We'll take some of the trails in the hills south of there to approach. Where are most of the gang members congregated?"

"South and east of us. They're using a few hills as cover to shoot into our compound. They have us pinned down in the armory now. When can you get here?"

"We'll leave soon. We have NVGs and will attack after the sun has gone down. We have two snipers. Thoughts on where to put them?" I asked.

"Carson City has a public works area, and the back side has enough elevation that you should be able to see the perps on the two hills looking down into our facility. They have people spread around the front gate just off the highway. If you can give us enough of a break, we can get into one of the Stryker's here and use the M2 gun to help," Gunner elaborated.

I was sure I could hear his grin through the radio when he commented on the Stryker vehicle and its use of the 50-caliber. It would wreck someone's day when that gun started firing.

"We have mobile radios and will let you know when we'll attack. Be ready to move," I said.

"Copy. We have enough people to drive the vehicles we have parked outside. We have two heavy transport tactical trucks and trailers loaded with ammo, weapons, and other gear."

"Ten-four. We'll be there soon." I ended the radio call.

"Team, get some rest. We'll head out around nineteen hundred. It should still be daylight when we arrive. We might have to hike in a little bit, as the dust from the dirt roads will give us away in the daylight," I explained.

We met at eighteen thirty in the armory, grabbed our gear, performed buddy checks, and loaded into the Jeeps.

Mel approached, "Be careful."

"Always," I said, as I kissed her.

We drove roughly thirty-three miles and would have to hike the last two miles. We made good time along the BLM roads, slowing down the last five miles to keep the dust down. We crossed the bridge over Carson River, found a location to stash the Jeeps, and started hiking along the river line.

I sent John and Billy to the abandoned buildings to find a position to eliminate the threats at the base's front gate.

I knew there was an abandoned tank about a quarter of a mile hike in, so I sent Tracy and Gavin up the hillside to find a position near it. They could also give us a sit-rep of what they saw on the two high spots where the gang was taking shots from into the Army facility.

We had been hiking further along the river when Gavin reported in. "Six threats with long guns are 550 yards from my position, and eight threats are located 1050 yards from me."

We soon found the dried creek from the public works yard, and Dylan and I started working our way up the draw.

Nick and Madison went to a higher elevation to get eyes on the threats on the hills.

I reported, "Twelve threats near the bottom." I didn't see armor or vests like ours, so that was a plus.

John called in, "Team two in position. Ten threats."

I switched channels to contact our friends at the base. "Carson City ANG, Freedom team calling. Copy?"

"Carson City ANG here, Lima Charlie," they replied.

"We're in position. Will wait till twenty-three hundred to start the fireworks," I reported. "Let's get the party started, and after about two or three minutes, you join in. We should be able to clear them out quickly."

"Carson City copies."

"I'll have our team on your frequency and will give you a five-minute heads-up," I declared.

"Copy,"

I switched back to our frequency and informed the team of the plan. After a quick comms check, we settled in for a couple of hours to wait and observe.

Around twenty-three hundred, I called the teams. "Teams, check-in and status."

"Team Two. In place and ready."

"Team Three. In place and ready."

"Team Four. In place and ready."

"Carson City ANG, ready."

"Team One, in place and ready," I informed the teams. "Ready to execute in five minutes. It appears that the gang are mostly sleeping. Team Three and Four, you will kick things off on my call. That will kick this beehive, and we'll start swatting. Any questions?"

"None," the teams replied.

"Dylan, when we kick this off, you take the threats on the right side and work in, and I'll start on the left and work in. You good?" I inquired.

"Sounds like a plan."

After waiting for what seemed like an eternity, I called out. "Standby teams. Ten seconds on my mark. 'Mark.'" We all counted the ten seconds down in our heads. "Execute," I announced.

"Sending," I heard from Gavin and Nick. We suddenly heard a shot, and the group in front of Dylan and me jumped up and started running around. The sleeping ones scrambled to get out of their tents, trying to figure out what was going on.

I started shooting at the group from the left, double tapping each one. The first threat I engaged took two 5.56 rounds center mass and splattered his heart onto his buddy behind him. While he was falling, my second set of shots took the second threat high on his chest and exited his back with a bloody, gory mist across their fire. My third target took two rounds directly to his face, removing the back of his head. Thankfully, their campfire was not a blazing bonfire, or it would have made our NVGs ineffective. My first three targets went down quickly . We had planned to hit them fast and hard, and it was working.

I heard Dylan working the trigger on his AR as fast as his finger would move. The threats on the right were falling as his hits ended their life and sprayed their gore across the ground.

We had six targets left as best as I could tell, and they were starting to get organized as they realized where the threat was. Their shots were starting to zero in on us, and we had to take cover. "Moving," I called as I headed further to another boulder on the left.

Dylan called, "Moving," around the same time, and I knew he was headed further to the right, to another cover that we had spotted earlier.

There was very little moon out, and that played to our advantage with our NVGs and optics. Once at my new location, I spotted two threats firing at my previous position. My first two rounds took the guy on the left in the neck and just about separated his head from his body as the bullets exited through his spinal cord. I quickly shifted my aim to the second threat, shot two more rounds a little lower, and he hit the ground with his lower throat missing.

Dylan was again working on targets from the right after he relocated. His rounds were deadly accurate, and he dropped his targets with efficiency.

I couldn't see the last two threats, and called, "moving" to relocate again. I dove behind a boulder as one of the last two remaining threats saw me and fired in my direction. I was hit with sand and rocks as I fell into a ravine. Their focus on me, opened them up for Dylan to spot them and quickly finish them off with headshots that dropped them like hot potatoes.

We both called "Clear" at the same time and moved in to check them and gather up their weapons.

Gavin and Nick were still firing their BMG 50-caliber rifles, though I wasn't sure how many threats they had eliminated. I'm sure the gang was in chaos from Gavin and Nick's accuracy with their rifles. The distance that they were shooting from, gave the gang no chance of returning fire.

"All secure," I announced.

Nick alerted us, "Team One heads up, two threats headed down the hill."

"Team One copies." I looked up the hill, and spotted the threats headed down at almost a full run. "Dylan, about halfway down."

"Copy," he acknowledged.

I sighted in on the left threat and pulled the trigger three times. My first shot went low between his legs, and then the second impacted his belly, and the third shot hit center mass and ended his life when my round connected with his heart, sending blood and gore out his back. He tumbled the rest of the way down the hill, leaving a bloody trail along his path.

Dylan's shots connected with his threat in the knee, and as he was falling, the second shot hit center mass, and the third and final shot entered the top of his head as he was starting his tumble down the hill. He was dead before his body connected with the ground.

"Team One, area secure again," I said.

"Team Three, all threats down," Gavin called.

"Team Two, area all secure," John declared.

That left Team Four with their objective to finish clearing. At about that time, I heard Nick call, "Team Four, all secure.".

"Carson City, ANG, you are clear to come out. Area secure," I declared.

"Carson City ANG, copies. Did you guys leave anything for us?" they asked.

"Negative ghost rider," I declared, while laughing.

"Is there a back gate, or will we have to walk to the main gate?" I queried.

"No, the back gate is not near that side of the facility," Gunner replied.

"Team One will grab the Jeeps and meet you all at the front gate," I sighed. I knew we would have the longer walk, though it would be best to get the Jeeps back under our control and inside the fence.

Dylan and I took off across the field towards our Jeeps. We would have about a two-mile hike, though Team Four would have about the same to get to the main gate.

Since we didn't have to worry about stealth, we made excellent time getting to the Jeeps and had them rolling towards the main gate in no time. When we arrived at the main gate, the Army guys had a Stryker sitting there, looking very menacing as we approached. This particular Stryker, an eight-wheeled vehicle, also had a 50-caliber machine gun on the top that also had a gunner standing in the turret. I saw Gunner near the back of the Stryker, and he waved us through the gate and then closed it behind us. He pointed towards the other vehicles sitting near their administration building. I figured that was where he wanted us to park.

We parked the Jeeps, and he jogged up to meet us.

"It's good to see you guys. John and the other team members are inside, getting some water. We'll head to the armory in a few minutes and pack up what we can. We have a lot to take, and the trailers are parked near the armory already."

We headed inside to meet the rest of the Army team, and after handshakes and introductions, we discussed the plan for getting them back to the ranch.

"Hey Gunner, where's your radio? I want to call the ranch and let them know we have defeated the gang and are good to go," I said.

"Our comms room is in the back room. I'll show you."

"Nice setup here. Wish we had one like this," I commented as we walked into their radio room.

"We can take the radios and gear if you want it. I have a comm's guy who can break this all down for transport back to the ranch," Gunner confirmed.

"That would be great," I said, grabbing the microphone and checking the frequency for calling the ranch. "Away team for Freedom Ranch, do you copy?"

"Freedom Ranch. We copy Lima Charlie," Mel replied.

"ANG is secure. There were no injuries. We will pack things up and then head home," I stated.

"Ranch copies. Estimated ETA?" Mel asked.

"We have a lot to pack. Estimate five hours before return to home base," I informed Mel.

"Copy, five hours."

I could hear the stress in Mel's voice. She always worried that something would happen to us or them while we were away.

"We'll be careful on the trip home, plus we have extra firepower tagging along," I said.

"Copy. You know me, though. See you soon," Mel ended the radio call.

I looked at Gunner. "Let's see what you have and what we can pack from the armory. I want to be on the road while it's still dark."

"No problem, we have a lot of toys to get packed. We have two tactical trucks and large trailers to pack. I think we can get all the weapons and ammo packed and then some other things as well," Gunner stated.

"We are about out of room in our bunkhouse, so if you have one of the large crew tents and cots, that would be great until we can figure out the sleeping situation," I explained.

"We have some of the new modular systems that we can set up, and they have everything we need in them," Gunner said.

We headed back to the teams, who were sitting around telling stories. "Okay, people. We have a lot to get packed up, and I want to be out of here in four hours so we can travel while it's still dark. Handloading the trucks will take some time, so let's get the lead out, people," I announced.

Walt spoke up, "Most of the weapons and ammo are in crates, and we can use the pallet jacks to move the crates into the trailers. The trailers are already backed up to the loading dock, so easy peasy."

We all headed to the armory and started loading the trailers and extra ammo in the Strykers and Mine Resistant Ambush Protected vehicles, or MRAPs as they are known. The Stryker is an armored fighting vehicle designed for rapid deployment and adaptability across various combat scenarios. The MRAP is designed to safeguard military personnel from lethal threats of improvised explosive devices and ambushes with a V-shaped hull that deflects blasts away from the crew.

"Gunner, I think I see more than enough stuff to fill the two trailers. Have a couple of your people pull the Strykers and MRAPs up to the loading dock, and we will fill them with ammo. I know you can have different weapons mounted up top, so what does each one have?" I inquired.

"The two Strykers have the M2 .50-caliber machine guns, and the MRAPs have the M240B 7.62 mm machine guns. Two Humvees have 50-caliber mounted, and the other two have 40 mm grenade launchers installed," Gunner explained.

Everything was quickly loaded, and the armory finally sat empty. It was amazing that it all fit, though each vehicle was packed like a can of sardines with ammo. The ANG team would drive the Stryker and MRAPs with two people each. The heavy haul trucks would have one person each, and that accounted for all the ANG team. We would have some of our people driving the Humvees home.

"Hey, Gunner, did we get the radio system from the administration building?" I asked.

"Yes, Liam, our comm's expert, pulled everything. It's in the Stryker with him," Gunner said.

While moving my right hand in a circular motion above my head. "Let's move it, people. Keep your eyes peeled and alert for anything."

We headed for the gate, where Gunner jumped out of his MRAP to let us all out of the base.

"TJ calling Freedom Ranch. Inbound with an ETA of zero six hundred. All personnel accounted for."

"Copy, and just in time for breakfast. I hear Chef C working his magic already," Mel added.

Now that I thought about it, I hadn't eaten anything since we had left the ranch. No wonder I felt so tired and out of it.

When we were five minutes out. "Freedom Ranch, we are almost home, hungry, dirty and tired."

"Copy."

We pulled up next to the bunkhouse, and it looked like everyone was awake to greet us. Ruffus ran out to see me, put his paws on the driver's door windowsill, and gave me a little whine. I reached out and scratched his head. Mel was right behind him.

"Ruffus, get out of the way. I want hugs and kisses from my man. Well, maybe after he has a shower. He stinks," Mel gasped, holding her nose.

Ruffus gave her a little yip in acknowledgment that she was right.

Everyone was checking out the new military equipment that we brought with us and introducing themselves to our new family members.

I looked around for Matthew or Russell and finally saw them both near one of the Strykers. "Hey guys, can you see if we can get these trailers into the shop? We can unload them later. One of them has a large tent in it, and the ANG folks might need help setting it up. If they want to sleep right away, they can grab some sleeping bags and crash in the shop on the workout mats. Those are pretty comfortable. I know firsthand and have been face down on them many times from sparring with Mel."

Mel pinched my side. "You might end up there again if you're not careful, buddy."

"No problem. If the ANG folks want to catch some sleep first, we can let them crash, and then we'll move the trailers into the shop. That way, we don't make too much noise," Matthew replied.

I headed into the bunkhouse with the team, and Ruffus went straight to Chef C for his morning treats. I wonder what our chef had for us this morning.

"Chef C, what delectable delights do you have for us this morning?" I inquired.

"French toast, eggs, and bacon," he replied.

Sitting down, I demolished the food put in front of me. When I had finished breakfast, I headed to the house for a shower and a well-deserved nap.

Chapter 10

Mel

What a night. It wasn't exactly what I had planned for our fun girls' night. Amazingly, though, our injuries were completely healed by this morning. I could get used to this.

After our showers, I sat on the porch sipping hot tea with Gail and Raven. There was no coffee this morning. We needed to relax, which meant no caffeine, although Gail had added a shot of After Shock to spice up the tea with yummy cinnamon.

Gail and Raven were adding information to a new book that Raven had insisted we must have. She called it our Grimoire. We were documenting everything that had happened, new magic and rituals.

Made of thick tobacco-colored leather with an impressive brass lock, it was fourteen by twenty inches. It was thick and heavy, and the cover was amazing. There were raised letters that said Book of Shadows. The sparkling jewel-colored stones in each corner and atop the lock were spectacular. In the middle was an intricate tree of life. It looked like it was made of gold, but I was sure it was just painted metal. I hoped it was just painted because if it were real, this book would cost more than our ranch. It was a showstopper.

Raven told us Joe had given it to her. He'd found the book at a garage sale a few years back and thought it was cool, so he'd bought it. They had been talking one day about how important it was to document everything we were learning and doing and had offered it up to her.

Shelly and I worked in the yard to get it back to normal. Shelly was getting the hang of her magic by moving the pile of rocks where the demon had exploded into ash, back to their original places. She was having fun moving them through the air, one at a time.

I took great joy in healing my plants, and the grass that was nearly destroyed during the demon skirmish. They perked right up as I talked to them, while I checked on their leaves and flowers. The burnt, dead grass came back to life even better than before.

I was sending out love and talking to my plants. I'd brought Phil, my Philodendron, and Willow, my Bonsai Weeping Willow Tree, outside to enjoy the day with us. Phil was talking my ear off as usual, but I loved it.

Between writing her interpretation of last night's events, Gail changed her hand into different animal paws and claws: a lion, a tiny mouse, a bird, and gak ... a slimy, webbed, reptilian foot.

Raven had a couple of ghostly visitors she was talking to. An older lady wearing a sun dress. Her hair was pulled back into a ponytail. She had a kind face and smiled when she caught me looking. Standing beside her was an older gentleman wearing bib overalls and a blue pocket t-shirt. He had wispy white hair that wasn't long enough to need a comb. He was smiling, looking at the woman adoringly, and holding her hand.

"Shelly, do you want some help moving the rocks? Wilma volunteered Fred to help you," Raven giggled.

Shelly, making the rocks dance through the air, smiled and laughed, "Fred can help if he wants to, but I'm almost done."

"Ahem"

We turned around to see Joe standing there watching us practice our magic. Everyone abruptly stopped what they were doing, the stones that Shelly had been moving, falling to the ground with a thump.

Joe was like a father to me. He was always there when I needed him. I loved him.

"Heya Pops," I said, as I went and gave him a hug. "How are ya doing?"

He patted my back, "I can't complain, but sometimes I do. It looks to me like you ladies are having a great day."

I turned and looked at Gail, Shelly, and Raven. I couldn't lie to him. I heard the unanimous approval through our telepathic link.

"Come on, Joe; you want a cup of coffee and a cinnamon roll?"

We all sat on the porch and told Joe about our magic. He listened while munching on his cinnamon roll and didn't interrupt.

Joe patted my arm, a smile on his weather-beaten face. "You're doing just fine, Melly. As are the rest of you. Just keep practicing, and it will work out."

"Wait one cotton-pickin' minute!" I blurted. "Is that all you have to say? I said magic! Did you hear me? Magic!"

"I heard you, young lady. There's no need to yell, I'm not deaf. I met the lovely little princess Adalinda the other day, remember? She is adorable and magical."

After hearing the compliment, Adalinda flew and landed on Joe's shoulder, blushing. "Thank you, sir. I think you are quite lovely and magical also."

That was weird of her to say 'magical.' Maybe it was a dragonette compliment.

Joe took my right wrist and said, "Now let me see those tattoos. Do you have any idea what they mean? They're very detailed."

"We've been working on that. The theme of four is obvious and must represent us. That's all we have. Please tell me if you know what it means," I begged.

"I know that the Tree of Life represents connection, strength, family, growth, rebirth, and tranquility. But there are many different beliefs. Your tree is unique to the four of you. It represents each of you and who you are together. Well, that's what I think."

"So, if the theory is that this is about us. The branch with the tiny animals would represent Gail because she can shapeshift. Shelly would be the branch with the colorful sparkles because she is our crystal queen. Raven speaks with spirits; the wisps of gold and silver represent her. But what is the last one? That's supposed to be me? I guess that's nature. Right?" I asked.

"I think you are on the right track; there isn't anything to worry about now. Just keep doing what you are doing, and everything will be fine. If you need me, all you have to do is ask," Joe said.

Raven stood up, grinning. I chuckled to myself, I loved her fun facts. I hoped it wasn't going to be gross.

"Excuse me, friends, it's that time again, did you know it is impossible to hum and hold your nose."

Of course, we all had to try, and darn it if she wasn't right.

"Well, ladies and Ruffus, it's time for breakfast. I'm starving, that cinnamon roll didn't last too long. Would you care to join me?"

"We would love to," I said, wrapping my arm around Joe. Gail, Shelly, and Raven joined us. We walked arm in arm, high kicking like the Rockettes. Well, all of us except for Joe, that is.

We sat at a table in the back corner to discuss our strategy to catch the thief. I needed to express my gratitude to Chef C. This breakfast was one of the best meals I'd ever had.

This delicious meal included a Tomato, Basil, and Caramelized Onion Quiche and Patatas Bravas, which were crispy fried potatoes tossed in a spicy salsa brava and served with garlic aioli. He also served meat for the carnivores but always remembered the herbivores, like me. I was not a fan of meat, and there was always something extraordinary for me to eat.

Gail stuffed a huge bite in her mouth. "How does Chef C cook like this? I didn't know we had all the ingredients for this stuff. He's a miracle worker."

He was a miracle worker. It was almost like he was magical.

"Since we're all here, let's start with the food thief case. Gail, you, and Shelly, or should I say Sherlocka and Trixie Belden, should talk to Chef C and see if you can find out more information about the theft. Raven or Jessica Fletcher, and I, Nancy Drew, will talk to Ann. She's a busybody, so if there is information out there, she'll have it."

Gail stood up to leave, "You can call me The Great Sherlocka anytime, but I don't think that's a good idea, Mel. Ann despises you, she won't talk to you."

"I can be professional. She enjoys gossiping and being the center of attention, she'll talk. If for no other reason than to prove she knows more than I do. Meet us back in the greenhouse, and we'll compare notes. Good luck."

Going our separate ways, I took a deep breath and smiled when we reached Ann, "Good morning, how are you doing?"

Crossing her arms over her chest with a condescending sneer, "I'm fine. What do you want? I'm busy."

"Ann, this is Raven—Raven, Ann." Raven put her hand out to shake Ann's hand, but Ann shook her head.

"Again, I ask. What do you want?"

"We were just wondering if you heard anything about the missing food and supplies. Do you have any idea who could be doing it? I know you know everything that goes on at the ranch. We would appreciate anything you could tell us. "

Talking to Ann like this made me feel dirty. I hated having to kiss her rear end, she however, was loving it. Her posture straightened, and the sneer grew into a mocking smile.

"Of course, I can be of assistance. You're right, I do know everything that happens at the ranch. That is what a great leader does." Ann's self-righteous tone lowered a little as she imparted the next bit of knowledge, as if she thought she might be overheard. "If I were you, I would watch Scarlett Toume. She leaves the ranch quite often, I am sure she is doing something nefarious."

Raven smiled at Ann, "What do you think Scarlett is doing when she leaves?"

Ann harrumphed and rolled her eyes, "It is obvious she is selling the food and supplies to gain personal profit! She doesn't need the food and supplies; we provide everything. It is so obvious, any idiot would be able to see that. Really, Melanie, you should be able to deal with this situation easily. This is one of many reasons I know I am the person who needs to lead our community. You and TJ should step down quietly, I would hate for something terrible to happen to you or your husband."

Was that a threat? Ann was evil. Trying to smile, even though it probably looked like a grimace, I said, "Thank you so much, Ann, you have been a great help."

We turned and headed out of the bunkhouse. As soon as we were out of earshot of Ann, I said "Let's go to the porch and chat about our discussion with Ann."

When we were on the porch, Raven grabbed a chair and sat down. "You weren't kidding when you said Ann was a demon spawn. She's horrible. It felt like she was sucking the life out of me. I'm drained, and we weren't talking to her that long."

"She's a piece of work, that's for sure. I've learned to block her and keep her out of my personal space. I used to feel drained and even depressed sometimes after talking to her. It was as if she were siphoning off my energy like she was a theoretical energy vampire. Now, I picture building a brick wall, piece by piece, around me. She doesn't drain me anymore. I should have told you. I'm sorry. Are you up to talking to Scarlett? I can talk to her if you want to wait here for me."

"I'm fine. But I don't think you were wrong about her taking your energy. I've heard about people, through my studies in the occult, who claim to be psychic or energy Vampires. They feed off the life force of other living creatures, leaving the other people exhausted. I always assumed it was fictional, but after meeting Ann,

I think whether she knows it or not, that's exactly what she is. I'm feeling a bit better, let's go talk to Scarlett."

We walked over to the garden where Scarlett was working.) Scarlett looked up with a smile, pausing tending the tomato plants.

"Scarlett, hi. This is Raven, we're looking into the missing food and supplies. Have you heard about it?"

"Yeah, that's crazy. I don't know why anyone would do that."

"Hi Scarlett, it's nice to meet you," Raven said. "We've heard that you leave the ranch often. I hate to ask, but what do you do? It's dangerous to leave with the gang's going around killing people."

Scarlett shot us a look, her brow tightening into a deep frown. Something in her eyes said she didn't like what she saw—or what she was about to hear. "Um ... what? Do you think I'm stealing the food? Well, it's not me. I would never do that. I walk to Ruhenstroth, which is only a mile away. I've been working at the fish hatchery to surprise everyone with fish on Fridays."

Putting my hand on her shoulder, "I'm sorry, Scarlett. We didn't think you had truly stolen the food and supplies, it's just that we need to follow every lead we get. Is there anyone who can corroborate your story? Have you seen anything suspicious lately?"

"It's all right. I understand. Chef C knows what I'm doing. He has gone with me a few times. We wanted it to be a surprise, so I didn't tell anyone else. I do hope you find the thief. I don't know if I would call it suspicious, but I have noticed Quinn Pherson always seems to have new clothes and other things. Maybe I'm just jealous; he's a nice guy. I really don't think he would do that."

"Thank you, Scarlett. What you and Chef C are doing at the fish hatchery is great. You're going to make a lot of people happy," I stated.

We headed for the kitchen to check out Scarlett's story. I leaned against the counter, "Chef, I have a quick question for you."

"More questions? Gail and Shelly just left after asking a lot of questions," Chef C sighed.

"Sorry, I know you're busy. I want to verify that you and Scarlett are planning fish fry Fridays, and that she has been working at the fish hatchery," I asked, ashamed I was even questioning him.

"Yes, we'd planned to surprise everyone, so please don't spread it around."

I hugged him, "I'm sorry, we were just checking Scarlett's story. We won't say anything about the fish fry."

He patted my back and let me go, "You are forgiven, now get out there and find the scoundrel stealing my food."

We left Chef C for his magical meal prep and headed to the greenhouse. "Let's meet the girls and check on the plants."

When we entered the secret room, I saw that more of my beauties had been destroyed. Gail and Shelly were cleaning up the mess. "Who the hell is destroying my plants?" I screamed. "I might have to sleep in here to find the culprit," I said.

I sat on the floor to pick up the destroyed plants. *I'm so sorry.* "We have got to stop whoever is doing this. We can head back to the house and add any new information to the board."

Getting back to the house, I went over to the board. "We cleared Scarlett, her story checks out with Chef C. We need to question Quinn Pherson next." I added his name to the board. "Did you guys find out anything new from Chef C?"

"He said he put a few locks on his cabinet, and when he came in this morning, the locks were broken off. So, someone knows what they are doing," Shelly filled us in.

I added it to the board. Gail stood by the mystery board, "We should try to get fingerprints at the greenhouse and then compare them with samples we get from our suspects."

"How do we get the fingerprints off the items?" Raven inquired.

"All we need is baby powder—turmeric powder would work well too—a soft paintbrush or makeup brush, and tape. Add the powder to the area, lightly blow on it, then put a piece of tape over the fingerprint and carefully lift it. Then we can transfer it to another paper with notes about where it was found or add the suspect's name," Gail explained.

"Great, let's do that. I know we all have things to do as part of our jobs on the ranch. So, we'll split after we collect the prints from the greenhouse and get to work. Also, after meals, let's collect glasses to start our fingerprint comparison. we need Ann's. That woman hates me. I wouldn't put it past her to kill the plants."

Chapter 11

Mel

As I ate my breakfast, I kept my eye on Ann, I wanted to make sure I got her cup. I needed her fingerprints, not that I had anything to compare them with, but if I ever found her prints in the greenhouse, I'd nail her to the wall.

The fingerprint data we collected from the greenhouse was a bust. We'd only found Shelly's and mine.

Carlos, John, TJ, Gail, Shelly, Raven, and I were planning our trip to the schools and library to collect schoolbooks and any books we could find on the supernatural, whether fiction or nonfiction. Katie sat quietly listening. She was still worried about her mom, Gail, leaving the ranch.

"TJ, are you joining us for the trip to town and the libraries?" I asked.

TJ looked at me with his sexy eyes, though I knew, that he knew that he had things to do around the ranch.

"I have a few things to work on in the shop and armory, so I won't go with you today. Be careful, and call if you have any issues," TJ said.

We left the ranch around 9:00 am. Shelly and Raven were in John's Jeep. I was driving TJ's Jeep with Gail sitting shotgun, and Carlos in the backseat. Gail had twisted in her seat so she could whisper with Carlos. He knew about Gail's shapeshifting and was very supportive. I'd seen them practicing behind the house, I was thankful he was so supportive.

"Please be careful, Gail. I've seen the worst of society in this town. Don't take unnecessary risks," Carlos pleaded.

We were headed towards our first stop at the high school. We hadn't encountered any trouble during the trip, thank goodness. I didn't want another mess like the feed store debacle. As we entered the parking lot, Carlos said, "I saw a group past the intersection sitting at a roadblock. Please park behind the school so we're not spotted. I can keep an eye on them from the roof. John will help with security also."

"Good call, Carlos," I noted.

I parked on the furthest corner of the school, away from the roadblock. The door was unlocked. These electronic locks probably defaulted open when the power failed.

We quickly found the library and located the books we needed for the required school subjects and fun reading. Everyone had carts, and we piled them high.

"We're about done here. We'll get these last carts out to the trailer and loaded, and then we can head for the county library," I said, using my radio.

We quickly drove away from the high school, heading for the county library.

We all gathered at the door, and I hoped it would be unlocked, too. "Phooey! The door's locked."

"I have a Halligan tool to unlock it. It's what I like to call my master key," Carlos said. He quickly opened the door, and we entered the library's dark, musty interior. Without power or central air, the building had become stuffy.

I looked at John and Carlos, "Please wait outside and watch for trouble." They nodded and shut the door behind us.

As we were getting our book carts, I felt a cool breeze; I looked around, but no windows were opened. Just as I was about to ask if anyone else had felt it, Shelly gave a little yip. I looked, and what, to my wondering eyes, should appear, but my favorite librarian.

She looked almost the same as the last time I was here checking out books. She was five foot four, with chin-length brown hair and blond highlights. Little reading glasses sat on the end of her nose, and her brown eyes twinkled with mischief. She wore a long, flowing floral skirt and a white chiffon shirt.

She came up to me, "Well, look who it is, one of my little bookworms. How are you, Mel?"

"Um, I'm doing okay, Ms. Shaw. How are you? I, um, didn't know, um, about ..." I waved my hands around her.

"I understand, it came as a shock to me as well, but I've been a busy bee as always, keeping my library nice and organized."

"What happened to you?" I asked. "Since the attack a few weeks ago, things have been a mess. I had wanted to get to town and check on my friends, I'm sorry I wasn't here sooner," I whispered, as tears filled my eyes.

Trying to pat me on the shoulder, she explained, "Now, now, don't you go crying, or so will I. This isn't any fault of yours, we were all trying to survive—some of us did, and some of us didn't. I'm okay, chickadee. The reason I'm in this situation is because of that hoodlum, Curtis, the gang leader. He's a thieving criminal and murderer. He must be stopped along with the rest of his idjits."

"I'm so sorry, Ms. Shaw. We will do everything we can to stop him and his gangs," I vowed. My girls had gathered around me, so I did the polite thing and introduced Ms. Shaw.

"Please call me Stella, it's a pleasure to meet you, Shelly, and Raven. Hello Gail, it's been a long time since we last saw each other. We don't need to be formal anymore. Everything has changed."

Raven came and stood next to her, "Would you like to move on to an even better library where your family will be waiting for you?"

"Yes, I think I would like that very much. But let me help you find what you need just one more time," Stella replied.

We had made four trips to the trailer with our carts full of books when my radio alerted me to activity outside.

"Heads up team. We have threats headed our way. There are four people in an older model Ford Thunderbird," Carlos whispered.

A few seconds later, we were at the main door, rifles in hand and our war faces on. "We'll be back, Stella, and we'll make sure you move on to a bigger and better library," I said as I focused back on the task at hand.

"Gail, Raven, and Shelly, you three find cover in the trees along the road. I'll go to the dumpster for cover," I said as I looked at my friends, who all nodded like they knew it was about to get real, very soon. "Ten-four."

"Carlos has the call for when we start shooting," I said.

I spoke to them through our link. *Let's keep our telepathic link open. If we see an opening to use our magic, do it, don't hesitate to take the jackholes down. Remember, we are stronger together. We've got this. Let's do this for Stella."*

We moved to the cover positions.

"In position at dumpster," I called out on the radio. My other teammates called in their positions.

"We have another vehicle stopping behind the first one," I whispered through the radio. I had to shift my position, or they would be able to see me.

It was a bright red Ford Ranchero with two people in it. I had always wanted a coupe utility like that. She was a beauty, fire engine red, and in pristine condition. I had a poster of it on my bedroom wall growing up. The driver was a skinny guy, probably five feet ten tall and around 175 pounds. The female was around five feet seven tall with curves in all the right places. That was not my thing, but I was a bit jealous. She was gorgeous; her long black hair had perfect curls.

"The new arrivals are yelling at the first group," Carlos commented. "I bet someone saw us leaving and are trying to find us."

"The four guys in the gray car have rifles, and they are looking down our street here," Shelly quietly informed us.

"Does everyone have eyes on a target?" Carlos asked.

"Yes," we replied.

"Okay, my Charmed warriors, we got this. Use your weapons or magic or both. Let these creeps have it," I sent through our link.

"If they make a move down the street, I'll start shooting," Carlos declared.

I could only see the two at the Ranchero. If we started shooting, I would have to be fast to eliminate both threats.

"Standby to execute," Carlos proclaimed. "Execute!"

I opened fire on the skinny guy first with as many shots as possible with my AR-15. One of my shots hit him in the shoulder, and one hit him in the stomach. I sent an ivy vine to wind around the woman's legs while I shifted my aim to the chick's head, but as she looked down, the vines shredded off her easily. She looked directly at where I was hidden, grinned, and waved at me. Then she grabbed the guy I shot and dragged him to the cargo bed of the Ranchero. She was fast, I mean lightning fast. Before I knew it, she was behind the wheel and took off smoking the tires. There was something about her. I couldn't put my finger on it. She was different. How had the vines fallen off? She'd looked straight at me. This was worrisome.

Carlos and John called two threats down. "Cover me. I'll check these guys to ensure they won't bother us again," John growled.

I moved up a little bit and could see John checking the bodies.

Screams of terror were coming from the right of me. Raven was having fun with one of the threats; her skull shadow had slipped in place over her face, and she had a couple of ghosts attacking him. Stella was one of them. She was laughing and looked like she was having a great time. She squeezed his neck until he went silent and fell to the ground. "How do ya like them apples, buddy? Paybacks a, um, well, you know what it is." Stella screamed with delight.

How were the ghosts able to touch him, much less hurt him? What a sight. *"You go, girl!"* I sent to Raven.

I watched in awe as Gail snuck behind one who had positioned himself where no one could get a clear shot at him. She shifted her hand only, probably so she didn't shred her clothes, and stuck her extra-large bear-clawed paw through his back and pulled out his heart, squeezed it, and threw it atop his fallen body." Shouts of excitement came through our link.

"All clear and way to go, Gail," Carlos called.

I moved from my cover position to chat with John. "We got the books we needed from here. We have one more thing to do; then we can hit the last two schools."

"Ten-four."

Shelly, Gail, Raven, and I walked back to the library to help Ms. Shaw crossover, but I had to ask. My curiosity overran my brain most of the time. "Quick question: How were your ghosts able to touch and hurt that dude?"

Raven was smiling so wide it looked like her face would split. "I shared my magic with them. It's a little draining but so worth it."

We stood there in awe, "That's incredible, girl, you rock!"

We all stood around Stella, holding hands. I didn't know what we were doing, I was following Raven's lead.

"I'm a little weak," Raven explained. "I'd appreciate it if you could share some of your energy with me. We don't have candles or crystals. Let's make our intentions known and send her peace and comfort."

As I closed my eyes and remembered all the happy times I had spent at the library with Stella, I wished her the best, and gave her love and peace. I felt warmth surrounding me, and as I opened my eyes, I saw that Stella was enveloped by a bright light that radiated love.

Stella looked at each of us with a beautiful smile and said, "Thank you. I will be back if you ever need me. Goodbye for now." She rose and shimmered into the light and was gone.

There were no words to describe what I had just witnessed, and I knew I would never forget it. We all hugged and cried a little, then got our heads back in the game.

When we walked outside, Carlos was standing by the door. He took Gail's hand and looked at us, saying, "Nice job, ladies."

I was checking out the fabulous Ford Thunderbird. "Let's take this beauty back with us. Finish checking these guys for more weapons and useful items. Then put them in the trunk of the car," I said. "We'll load those last carts of books and then hit the road."

We rolled down County Road, taking a little detour to remain in the older neighborhoods. We crossed the highway and parked near the middle school's entrance.

I was greeted with an unlocked door at the school's front door.

"Same routine," I announced on the radio. We entered the darkened school and turned on the lights on our rifles to find the library.

Once in the library, there was light from the skylights so we were ablet to turn off the lights on our rifles.

We soon had four carts full of books. We found many schoolbooks, which would make Raven and Joanne, our two school teachers, happy: the children, probably not so much. We made a total of two trips with overflowing carts. "John, Carlos. We have everything we need from this school," I called over the radio.

"Copy."

They soon joined us at the vehicles, and we were off to our last stop at G'ville Elementary School.

The last school was just around the corner, and it took us about two minutes to get there. We all knew the routine and were in and out in thirty minutes.

We soon headed home with our books and a Ford Thunderbird.

"Ranch, book scavenging team. Headed home, see you soon," I called on the radio.

"Ten-four, Ranch copies."

After we dropped off the trailer, I saw Quinn. "Can you guys take the supernatural books to the house? I'm going to chat with Quinn about the food thief. I'll meet you at the house in a few minutes," I told my girls. I was sure Quinn didn't steal the food and supplies. He was a deputy on our security team, but I had to follow all the leads, no matter how ridiculous.

"Quinn," I called as I tried to catch up to him. "Hi, how have you been?"

"Good, thanks. What's up?"

Ugh, I hate this part. "It's nothing really. I'm just checking in with you. We haven't talked in a while. I noticed you were wearing a sharp new outfit the other day. It was nice. Have you been going into town to get some new clothes and other things?" *Mel, you are such a liar.*

"Um ...yeah, I didn't know it would be a problem. I'm always armed, and I go straight to my old house and grab what I can."

Thank goodness. "Oh no, it's not a problem at all. However, you might ask someone to accompany you next time. I can tell you from experience there is a gang in town that won't hesitate to kill you. I want you to be careful."

"Okay, ma'am."

"Would you have any idea who would be taking the food from the kitchen?"

"I don't know who could be doing this. I don't want to point fingers at anyone. I think everyone on the ranch is trustworthy, but obviously, not everyone is. I'll keep an eye out for anything suspicious."

"Thanks, Quinn."

An hour later, we were working on magic with Carlos, Sean, and Princess Adalinda in the backyard, while Ruffus napped under a tree.

"I brought some glasses back with me, and I'll get the fingerprints off them tonight and record them," I shared with the group.

"Great. I wish we had found some prints in the greenhouse, but we'll keep checking," Shelly replied. "Is Quinn our thief?"

"No, I've cleared him. Now, we have no suspects. It's time to plan a stakeout in the kitchen."

"Sweet!" Gail cheered.

"Okay, ladies and gentlemen, a quick fun fact break. A man's testicles produce ten million new sperm cells each day—enough that he could repopulate the entire planet in six months!"

"Wow ... I don't know what to say to that. Um ... thank you?" I whispered.

Princess Adalinda landed on Raven's shoulder, "That is truly amazing, Ms. Raven. Your knowledge is indeed miraculous. I would love for you to return home with me one day so you could share your knowledge with my people," she said, while grinning that creepy Cheshire cat smile.

Raven bowed her head, "I would be honored, Princess Adalinda."

Shelly stood, "I want to place more protection crystals around the ranch property. I don't want another demon or any threat to be able to enter our land. We'll bury crystals in all four corners of the property. I have black tourmaline, onyx, obsidian, smoky quartz, and Shungite. They will guard the ranch and dispel negativity. Selenite is a potent crystal that can charge itself and other crystals. We will add those as well. I'm cleansing them at the moment, and will have them charged and ready in a few days. Sound good?"

"That's a great idea. We should do that as soon as possible. Joe gave me some books about green witches and rituals I've been studying. I can help with the ritual. I don't know why he would have those types of books, but I won't complain. He also left some for you all, as well," I said.

Gail and Carlos were behind some trees, where she was practicing her shapeshifting. She had her robe, but when she shifted back to her human self, she had no clothes on; if it were just the girls, she wouldn't care, but even though Sean was a ghost, he was still a man.

Sean and Raven were working on calling ghosts and having them do what she requested.

Shelly and I practiced manipulating our elements. She worked with stones, crystals, and rocks. She could manipulate even the tiny pieces of rock in the sand and dirt into different shapes. It was amazing.

Adalinda was helping me work with nature; today, we were focused on plants. I could make them move on command and could communicate with them. I've been working on how to heal. I got a lot of practice the day after the demon attack; our front yard was a disaster. I had also tried to save my plants that had been destroyed in the greenhouse. But I haven't been able to heal all of them. I hated it when I heard them suffering.

Adalinda was sitting beside me. "I want you to help this little fern." I nodded and sat next to a sick and yellowing fern.

"Feel for that spark deep inside you and fan the flame. See it growing into a raging fire," Adalinda instructed me.

I felt the magic deep down. It was like a tickling sensation in my stomach. I pulled it, trying to bring it to the surface. When the tingles began to surround my body, I knew it was working, so I pushed the magic into the little fern. Oops, I pushed a little too hard and the little fern grew at least four feet tall. Now she was singing, 'Oh, happy day.' She thanked me and kept chattering, I listened for a while.

"Er ... well done, Ms. Melanie, although I believe you put just a tad too much healing magic into her. But do not worry; you have accomplished your task. I am very proud of you. I can feel the well of magic inside you. When you harness it, you will continue to do even greater things."

I blushed; it felt good to receive the praise. "Thank you."

It was time to change things up. "We have time to get some training before dinner. Do you all want to join me? We can head to the shop for some hand-to-hand and then hit the range."

They all jumped up, "Let's do it!"

Chapter 12

Curtis, The Leader of the Gang

I woke up with Fiona's naked body next to me. She was an exquisite creature. She loved sex more than any woman I had ever known. It was as if she were possessed, she couldn't get enough. I rolled over and looked at her, her chest rising as she slept, her long, black curls spread across the pillow, and the sun glistening around her like a halo.

I snuggled in close to her and could smell the sweet scent of the lilac perfume she had put on last night after our shower. It belonged to Wilma, the previous owner of our new home.

Fiona must have felt me moving around on the bed. She woke up and rolled over to look at me.

"What are you looking at, my sweet man."

"Your sexy body."

"You want me again?" Fiona asked and gave me a sly smile.

I started to roll on top of her, but she pushed me down and jumped on me.

"I'm in charge again."

We collapsed after our, how many rounds of sex? I'm not even sure how many times we had sex last night and this morning. That woman was crazy for sex.

After resting for a few minutes, I leaped out of bed, "Race you to the shower."

"No fair. You're closer to the bathroom."

"I'll let you win," I promised her.

We soon finished our shower and were dressed. After that workout, I was hungry. "Let's go to CVI and have breakfast. Lisa's a great cook. After we eat, we can get a crew to search houses again."

"I'd love that," Fiona said with delight.

We were soon headed to CVI in our red Ranchero. When we pulled up, some of our crew were out front. They looked a little rough. It must have been a good party last night.

Fiona and I climbed out of the Ranchero and headed to the dining room. I looked in the conference room, and it was a mess. Bottles were everywhere, women were tied up and looked like they had been ridden hard. Tony was guarding the door.

"Good party last night?"

"Yeah, boss. Most of the guys are still crashed. I think these girls are done after last night," Tony chuckled.

"I hope our crew didn't kill any of them?"

"No, boss. When I checked them all this morning, they were all alive, though well used," he said, grinning.

Fiona and I entered the dining area, and I went to the kitchen. Lisa was working the grill like a pro, cooking potatoes and corned beef hash sizzling. It smelled good, and my stomach growled at the sight of the food on the grill.

"How long before breakfast's ready," I asked.

"You can take your plates now. I'll start putting this into serving bowls."

"Thanks." I grabbed plates for Fiona and myself and filled them up. Fiona had our coffee and sat at a table in the corner where we could observe the room. The handful of people awake at this hour looked worn out, shadows under their eyes and movements slow—still recovering from last night's chaos. Or maybe they were just lost in thought, remembering the five we didn't bring back.

Yesterday, we lost four of our crew at the sheriff's office when the prisoners escaped, and one of them was killed with a high-powered rifle. BG was pissed, and rightly so. All the deaths were from the crew he brought from Reno.

A few other guys and the two amazonian women walked in. "You want to help us clear a few more houses this morning after you eat?" I asked.

"Sure. Can we bust a few heads?"

Matilda looked rough. She must have cried herself to sleep last night, dealing with her boyfriend Leon's death. "We'll head to the upper-class part of town, we can search and destroy if needed."

"Okay," they all agreed.

After our breakfast, we stood at the front doors of CVI. I put my arm around Fiona's shoulders and looked at Matilda. "We'll take our car. Do you have access to one of the trucks?"

"We do," Matilda mumbled, while shielding her bloodshot eyes with her hand. She didn't smell of booze, though I could tell that she had slept in her clothes.

"You ok? You look tired?" I asked.

"I'm fine. I didn't sleep well last night. Was thinking about Leon, and our plans for the future. I'm not sure what I am going to do without him? I'm three months pregnant with his baby," she said, and then started sobbing.

"Do you want to stay here?" I asked.

"No. I need to get my mind off Leon, so it will be good to get away from here for a little while," she said.

"Let's go. Just past the sheriff's office, we'll head north. I'm sure they have some fine things that we can transition ownership of to us," I said.

Fiona giggled as I finished my statement. She was happy this morning. She wore her 5.11 camouflage pants and shirt while carrying her Smith & Wesson M&P Shield 9mm.

"Follow us," I said, over my shoulder as we headed for our red Ranchero. "Dibs," I called.

"Fine, you can drive."

We were getting ready to leave when one of the guys from our north roadblock pulled up. Decker ran to me, "Ledger saw a couple of vehicles leaving the high school and heading down County Road. We're on our way to check them out. I'm not sure how many people were in the vehicles."

"Matilda and Deidra, you can stay here. Fiona and I are on our way to head off these fools running around our town."

Fiona and I took off without waiting for an answer. We quickly found our team at the intersection of County Road and Library Lane. We didn't waste time. As soon as the car stopped, we jumped out and hurried over to join them.

"Where'd they go?"

"Not sure. Ledger saw them cross the road at the roundabout, and they were gone by the time we got down here. We went to the curve up there, though we didn't see them." Decker mumbled.

"You sure you buffoons saw a vehicle? How much have you been drinking or sampling the drugs?"

"None, we're clean," Ledger responded.

"You four walk down the street, and Fiona and I'll walk through the parking lot here looking for these fools. Be ready to move if we see something," I shouted.

"Yes, Boss," Decker replied.

Fiona and I hadn't even made it off the street when the sounds of gunfire erupted around us. I was looking around when I saw a muzzle flash in front of me and felt pain in my shoulder and then my stomach.

I felt Fiona grabbing me. As I looked down, I saw vines winding their way around Fiona's legs. Then they were sliced apart and fell off without so much as a touch from her. That was freaking weird. *Holy shit, am I losing my mind?* She placed me in the cargo bed of the Ranchero and then burnt rubber as we left the firefight. Damn, this shit hurt.

I must have passed out because, the next thing I knew, I was lying down on the couch in our living room.

"Fiona, help me, please," I gasped through the pain, "don't let me die. We have so much to do in this town to make it ours,"

"I'll do what I can for you. Let me find a first aid kit."

I couldn't move my arm, and my stomach was on fire.

I had just closed my eyes when I felt Fiona sit next to me. I opened my eyes to see her holding her pistol with a look of finality, no sadness or remorse. Why didn't I see that before?

What the hell was wrong with her eyes? They burned—red-hot, like molten lava—and the air around her shimmered faintly, as if reality itself couldn't quite hold her. A cold knot tightened in my stomach. She was beautiful, yes—breathtaking, almost unreal—but something deep inside me screamed that this wasn't right.

"So, I'm guessing Fred and Wilma weren't your first kills."

Fiona changed in an instant. No longer was she the beauty I slept next to every day; now, she was a misshapen nightmare. Her eyes were now as black as night and had grown at least two sizes larger. Gone were her long eyelashes, replaced with what looked like a few twigs. Fiona's cute little upturned nose was gone, replaced by two holes in the middle of her face. Her long, soft curls of black hair became straight, thin pieces of grey and black straw. Her venomous smile was a nightmare that was so frightening, I was ready to die to be out of her presence. Her teeth lengthened and became deadly pointed spikes as her face elongated, and half of her face formed a malicious scowl as drool dripped down the corners of her mouth. She stuck her tongue out to lick some of the drool, and it was split into two pieces like a serpent's tongue, licking both sides of her mouth at the same time. I was probably hallucinating due to the loss of blood.

When she spoke, it was as though fingernails were scratching down a chalkboard. "No, Fred and Wilma's deaths were just two of millions who have met their end by my hand."

"What are you—"

"I am ending your pain. See you in hell, baby."

Chapter 13

Fiona, The New Leader of the Gang

Curtis and I had fun this morning. One thing I could say for him was that he had stamina, which pleased me. He was always ready and willing to take care of my needs.

After breakfast, one of Curtis's numskulls told us there were intruders in town. We changed our plans and left to find the idiots who thought they could enter my town and get away with it.

When we arrived, I felt something very familiar, but I couldn't put my finger on it. There were supernaturals here, and they were powerful, yet a few of them were still discovering the magic that boiled at the surface. This should be interesting.

Curtis was yelling at the underlings, but I was focusing on my enemies.

Gunfire exploded around us, and I saw Curtis get shot. Not great, I didn't feel like finding a new plaything. As I grabbed Curtis to throw him into the car, little vines began to wind up around my legs; this was hilarious, child's play. With a single thought—*Disperge*—the vines fell away.

Now I knew exactly where the little witch was. I smiled and waved at her, then put Curtis in the cargo bed and headed home.

When we arrived home, Curtis was out cold. Instead of carrying him again, I levitated him to the couch. He didn't look good. The color had left his face, he had blood everywhere. A shot to the shoulder previously would not have been fatal, though I was not sure about the gunshot to his abdomen. I was thankful that I could levitate him inside, then I wouldn't get his blood on me. I could tell he wasn't going to make it, I could already feel his soul beginning to make the journey to the underworld. I guess I'll have to find a new toy after all. Humans were so fragile.

Curtis begged me to help him. *Ugh. I'm sorry, sweetie. It's too late for you. This town would be mine soon, and then I'd expand my territory and gain all the power that was due to me. I would never let a man take what was mine.*

"I'll do what I can for you. Let me find a first aid kit." I said to Curtis in my most sympathetic voice. The kind of voice that made people feel cared for—right before I shoved a knife into their heart. Playing nice wasn't my style. It gave me the heebie-jeebies and made my skin crawl like I'd hugged a wet snake.

I went to my bedroom, pretending to look for a first aid kit, it was time to say goodbye, baby.

I sat next to Curtis and had my gun pointed at his head, when he opened his eyes. I was irritated. Couldn't he just shut his damn mouth for once.

"So, I'm guessing Fred and Wilma weren't your first kills," he said.

He was finally getting the true picture. It had taken him long enough. However, I was a very good actress. Playing the innocent little woman was too easy, and he'd eaten it up.

I might as well show him who he had been pleasuring and ogling every day. When I was finally my true self, I smiled at him, enjoying the fear rolling off him. It tasted so good.

"No, Fred and Wilma's deaths were just two of millions who have met their end by my hand." I laughed.

"What are you—"

I interrupted him, "I'm ending your pain. See you in hell, baby." Summoning my demonic powers into my right hand, smoke curling around it, I felt the power gain strength. I pointed a finger at his head, and sent a lightning bolt into his brain, searing his brain in an instant. I took great pleasure in silencing him forever.

I celebrated the beginning of my reign by taking a long hot bubble bath while I drank a perfectly chilled bottle of Louis

Roederer 2002 Cristal Orfevres Gold Medallion Champagne—a lovely bottle for the bargain price of $12,500.00.

I put on my Armani Privé, a sculptured, sequined, floor-length dress that hugged my curves perfectly and showed off my gorgeous double Ds.

It was showtime. Tony was at the door as usual. I stopped to talk to Tony.

"Tony, I need to talk to BG, Bobby, and Ruben. Can you send someone to find them and ask them to meet me in the private office, please."

"Sure thing, ma'am. Where's Curtis? Everything okay?" he said as his eyes undressed me.

"Everything is fine. Please do as I asked," I purred and then walked inside, swaying my hips as I felt his eyes on my ass.

BG had joined the gang recently. He came from Reno. Bobby was the gang's enforcer, and Ruben was our drugmaker. I felt a strong magic coming off all three of these men. I wanted them in my ranks, but if they disagreed, I would end them.

I poured myself a snifter of brandy and sat behind the desk. About fifteen minutes later, the door opened, and all three men entered the office. I stood, walked around to the front of the desk, and leaned against it.

"Thank you for coming so quickly; please take a seat."

They sat in silence. Confusion clouded their faces.

"There have been some changes to the leadership. Curtis is no longer here to continue his duties. I am the new leader of the gang." I watched their reactions very closely; if any were against me, they would die. There were no changes from Ruben or Bobby, but BG had a wicked grin on his face.

"BG, is there a reason you are smiling?"

"Yes, ma'am, just happy; his time was up; he had no control and was weak."

"Okay, So I assume you have no problem taking orders from me."

"No problem at all," BG said, still grinning.

"Bobby, Ruben, do either of you have any issues with this new development?"

They both responded, "No, ma'am."

"Great, I called you all in here to make you each an offer. BG, you are a natural-born leader, and I would be honored if you would be my second."

BG nodded with a slight smile, "It would be my pleasure to serve under you."

"Bobby, it would please me if you would continue to be my enforcer."

Bobby stood, "I will continue my duties, ma'am," he said with a respectful bow and then returned to his seat.

"Ruben, I want to expand your role in the organization; of course, you are a master drugmaker and will continue that, but I would like to move into potions as well," I explained.

"I know you all are of the supernatural variety, as I'm sure you are aware I am as well. You don't need to disclose anything at this point," I said as I walked to my chair behind the desk. "It's time to share our surprise with the rest of the gang. Please have everyone join us in front of CVI. I would like the three of you to stand with me."

Fifteen minutes later, Ruben came in, "They are ready, ma'am."

"Thank you, Ruben." I fluffed my hair, pushed up my girls, and sauntered out the door, followed by BG, Bobby, and Ruben.

Giving my boys a wink, I turned to face the G'ville gang and ran my hands over my body, emphasizing all my curves.

"Hello, everyone. Thank you for joining me for this impromptu meeting. Firstly, I need to let everyone know that Curtis was shot today while attempting to rid our neighborhood of invaders, trying to take what is ours. Sadly, he did not survive." Shouts of disbelief surrounded us, and angry yells demanding justice came.

I'd had enough. I held my hands out in front of me, igniting them with bright red fire, and gave my new underlings a show of my power.

Gasps and then silence fell across the crowd.

"I understand how you feel, and I promise I will find these murderers and put an end to them, but for now, let's move on to some good news. I will be taking over as your new leader," I said as I began to juggle the fireballs. "BG will be my second."

As soon as I finished talking, Tommy stormed up to the front of the crowd.

"No!" he shouted. "I'm the second; BG just got here; he can't take my place—"

Ugh, I figured this would happen. Tommy was a little slug who thought he would be in charge. It was time to set an example. I put both hands over my head and gracefully threw both fireballs at Tommy. When the fireballs hit, he instantly exploded, sending white ash everywhere!

Everyone moved back. Dusting my hands off, I asked, "Does anyone else have a problem with me or these men beside me? Speak now or forever hold your peace." There was nothing but silence from the crowd. "Very well, moving on." I pointed to Bobby and Ruben. "Bobby will continue to be the enforcer, and Ruben will be our drug maker. We will take control of this town and the surrounding communities. I want to expand our territories. I have great plans for us, starting with ridding our world of those who murdered Curtis," I declared to the gathered crowd. I turned on my heel to enter CVI and called for my leadership team. "Let's go to the office. We have some things to discuss, and I have a task for someone," I said.

"Yes, Ma'am," they all blurted out.

In the office, I took my seat at the desk, pulled out the twenty-five-year-old scotch, and poured us all a glass. "I need someone to go and get Curtis's body and the couch from the house and dispose of them someplace out of the way," I told them. "Next, we need to figure out where the group that shot Curtis lives. I want their heads on stakes by the end of the week. Any questions?"

"None," they all said in unison.

"Good. Let's work on cleaning up this town."

Looking at BG, I could see his eyes undressing me. I might have to take him to the house tonight. No, I would make him wait.

Chapter 14

Mel

Tonight was the night we would begin patrolling Rancheros. We wanted to create a buffer between ourselves and the Gardnerville gangs. This would also ensure that the gangs didn't gain a stronghold over the small community. We were making a statement that we would protect those who couldn't protect themselves.

I went to my weapons room, which I called my meditation room. It was a secret room in the main bedroom hidden behind a bookcase. I was there to find some swords and katanas for Raven to choose from. She had come to live at the ranch with only the clothes on her back. She'd requested a katana, but the swords called to me. It was hard to explain, but I knew I needed to take them to her.

I laid the weapons on the table, and to my surprise, she chose a sword. I handed Raven her new sword.

"She's a beauty. She is an Oakeshott Sword. Here's the scabbard, which is made of gold, as well as the grip and guard. I have never had a chance to train with her, so you are her first partner. Joe gave her to me a few years ago and told me to hold on to her; he said someday someone might need one. That is so weird; how did he know that? Anyway, her name is Joyeuse."

"Thank you. She's the most beautiful sword I've ever seen. She feels good in my hand, like she was made for me."

Shelly and Gail looked at the other swords and katanas I had brought out. They both had a sword in their hands. Their faces shone with happiness and awe. It was strange that Joe had also given me those two swords with the same instructions. I was beginning to think this fate thing was real.

"What do you think of those beauties?" I asked.

Shelly was in her own world of fighting but answered anyway, "I love it; she feels like an extension of my arm. Where did you find her? I want one."

"I agree with Shelly." Gail chimed in. "I must find one of these. She's perfect. Look at the sheath and hilt; the dark-light color. The vertical-striped pattern is mesmerizing. The engraved rings and flowers on the hilt are beautiful. Whoever made this sword was a master."

I was going to make their day, "Well, ladies, they are yours. Joe gave me the same instructions for those two swords. Shelly, your sword is named Clarent. Gail, your sword is Durendal. Since you're all taking swords, I'll go get my favorite."

I came back with my beauty. "Meet Excalibur. I know what you all are thinking. No, we don't have the authentic Four Swords of Power. Those were just mythical. Joe named them and wanted me to keep the names."

"If we are going by the namesakes of our swords, let me see if I remember some of the folklore." Raven paced as though she were teaching a class. I bet her kids loved her. I had learned so much from her. "Excalibur is known as the sword of ice—a symbol and embodiment of power. Offensive and defensive powers are inherent to a leader. The scabbard keeps the wearer alive and prevents a wound from bleeding. It's the strongest weapon in the world. It can cut through steel and wood. The Lady of the Lake offered the sword to Merlin.

"Clarent is the sword of fire and the twin to Excalibur. King Arthur owned her as a divine ceremonial sword. She kills by burning her prey in various ways. It was also said that Mordred stole Clarent and used it to kill King Arthur.

"Durendal is the sword of air and was owned by Roland. She was carved out of stone, well-polished, and is three feet long. She was forged through alchemy and magic. She is immensely powerful, impossible to destroy and symbolizes valor and heroism. And Gail, the first Shadowhunter weapon maker, Wayland, and Smith were responsible for creating your sword and Excalibur.

"Joyeuse is the Sword of Earth and was wielded by Charlemagne. It means Joyful. It was used to coronate the kings of France in the thirteenth century. It is now housed in the Louvre. When unsheathed, it was said that it would shine as bright as the sun. It can also change into thirty different colors."

Raven took a deep breath and finished her lesson. "That's about all I can remember, but I do know if these were the true Swords of Power, we would be virtually unstopped," she giggled.

"Adalinda, do you and Ruffus want to go on patrol with us tonight?"

She saluted me, "At your service, Ms. Melanie."

Gail lost all color in her face and looked like she was in shock. "Um ... Ruffus would also like to patrol with us tonight," she whispered, trying desperately to catch her breath. "I can understand, Ruffus," she continued as she fell on the couch. Ruffus attacked her face, giving her kisses and barking happily. "Umm, Ruffus, what made you start talking?" Gail asked quietly. Then Gail nodded and said "Magic?" while Ruffus was barking and whining.

I sat beside her, took her hand, and spoke slowly and softly, "That's so awesome, chica. You're so lucky, and I'm jelly. What'd he say?"

"He said he has always talked, and he asked me, 'What made me start listening?'"

She took a deep breath and smiled, still clearly uncomfortable but dealing well with this new development.

"I bet you're hungry. Let's go to dinner and relax before we leave to patrol tonight."

"Yeah, that's fine," Gail replied.

Gail looked at Ruffus, "Sheesh, okay. Ruffus would like us to hurry. He's hungry and wants to see Chef C now."

Dinner was terrific, as always. Tonight's menu included Homemade Macaroni and Cheese with extra cheese and a buttery bread crumb topping, as well as chicken al pastor with almost charred pineapple and toasty spicy chicken, tender and juicy, served with white onion, fresh cilantro, and homemade corn tortillas, with beans and rice. I'm sure some would look at the menu and wonder why we had mac and cheese with tacos, but I knew Chef C made it for me. Dessert was homemade angel food cake with strawberries and whipped cream, thanks to Cassie and James Donald, our new pastry chefs. They had recently come to live at the ranch. They'd owned a bakery before the world went to heck. They are brilliant sweets creators. I was thrilled when they joined our crew. If I could eat sweets for every meal, I would do it.

Adalinda had a beef empanada made especially for her. Chef C added extra beef with a few veggies and potatoes. She loved meat, and he knew it. She was already hooked on Chef C's cooking.

Carlos and Gail sat across from me. He had his arm around her shoulders and spoke softly, comforting her.

Shelly forked a large piece of pineapple and held it up, "The chicken is amazing, and I love the pineapple, but we don't have pineapples on the ranch. What's going on, Mel?"

"This isn't the first time I've noticed ingredients we don't have on the ranch. This is another mystery we need to figure out. I'm not complaining, just curious."

When we had all finished dinner, we stood up from the table.

"Carlos, meet us at the shop in an hour, and we'll head out to Rancheros."

"Will do."

We dressed in full kit, meaning full uniforms with weapons, everything we would need for the patrol. We strapped on our swords, added our guns, knives, and extra ammo, and ensured we all had our radios for communications. I put Ruffus's vest on him as well. Once he had it on, he knew it was time to go to work.

"Adalinda, are you ready to protect the citizens of Rancheros?" I called.

She flew out of her castle and hovered at attention. "Yes, Ms. Melanie." She wore the most charming outfit, dressed to blend in like she was going on a secret mission. She wore a black tutu with a place for her tail and a black tank top, through which her wings fitted perfectly. Atop her head, she wore a black fedora hat that went right over her golden horns.

"You look perfect, Princess. After you," I said, as I opened the door for her.

We met Carlos at the shop. Gail and Raven rode with him in the Thunderbird.

Shelley, Ruffus, and Princess Adalinda rode with me in TJ's Jeep.

We arrived at Rancheros as the sun was setting, parked the Jeep and walked down the street. The cool breeze was wonderful considering we were in full gear from top to bottom. The armored vest always made me sweat.

Ruffus was running ahead, clearing a path. Everything was quiet. When we walked by a cute little bungalow-style home, a woman was in her front yard waiting for her puppy to do his business. The puppy, a Boston Terrier, came running toward me, barking happily. His mama freaked out, calling him, yelling for him to come back, and running full speed to get him. I held my hands up to reassure her that I was not a threat to her fur baby. She grabbed him and held him close to her chest, "Finn, you know better than to run away from me," she told him as she kissed his cute little black nose. Then she got a terrified look on her face when she spotted Adalinda. "Wh ... wh ... what is that flying thing?" She started to back up while trying to hold Finn, who wanted to get down and play with Ruffus.

"I'm sorry," I said, still holding up my hands. Ruffus and Adalinda made a beeline straight for little Finn. "That is Princess Adalinda, from Shangra-La. She is harmless. Yes, she is a little dragon."

"Oh, okay," she said as she put Finn down so he could play with his new friends. "I didn't mean to yell like a crazy person, it's just that I have never seen a dragon before. You know it's not safe around here, especially at night. You all should be locked inside. I'm babysitting this little cutie for my sister, and I would be in so much trouble if Finnegan got hurt."

"I understand. As you can see, we have some babies of our own. We're here to help; gangs have been terrorizing nearby towns, and we want to put a stop to it. We'll be patrolling and sending other teams to help as well. Hopefully, we'll get it under control soon," I said.

"Thank you so much. We need all the help we can get." She reached out her hand. "My name is Larisa Atkinson; you are welcome to stop by if you need anything during your patrols. I'll let the town know what you're doing. I'm sure they will want to help in any way possible, too."

Larisa smiled as I introduced my team. She then picked up Finn, waved, wished us luck, and ran to the house to lock herself and Finn in for the night. Once she was in the house, we all turned and carried on with our mission.

Once the sun set, everyone was locked in their homes; no one wanted to risk running into a gang. That was precisely one of the many things I wanted to stop. I didn't want people afraid to leave their homes. We needed to feel safe in our communities and live peacefully with our neighbors.

Rancheros was a beautiful town with a population of just over 12,000. The backdrop of the mountains was spectacular. TJ loved going to their golf course. He'd made me promise to make sure the golf course was secure. He was planning a day on the course with his buddies.

We were patrolling the golf course on Lakeview Drive when I spotted familiar faces. "That's Mike and Mary Mulligan from Gardnerville. I'd recognize Mike's Vietnam Veterans baseball cap anywhere; he never leaves home without it. They're preppers, we used to swap survival tips with them. Solid people," I told my team, smiling as I walked toward them. "Hey Mike, Mary, how are you guys doing? It's been a while. I've been meaning to check in with—" I stopped mid-step. My breath caught.

"They're dead ... Mike has a hole in his forehead."

Before anyone could respond, the air grew icy, goosebumps raised the hair on my arms. A whispering wind curled around us, tugging at our clothes, and the grass at Mike and Mary's feet began to blacken. With a shriek like tearing metal, they levitated a few inches off the ground, their eyes glowing with unnatural light.

"Hungry," dead Mike rasped, his voice distorted—like something else was speaking through him—as he lunged at my throat.

Carlos moved faster, intercepting the creature with a brutal twist of his hands, snapping its neck and tossing the body to the ground in one fluid motion. A thin mist leaked from Mike's mouth like escaping steam. Carlos stood like a wall of stone, his six-foot-five frame shielding me completely. Not a drop, of whatever passed for blood, touched me.

The team sprinted up. Raven unsheathed her sword in a blur and cleanly decapitated Mary as she floated toward us, fingers clawing the air.

"What the hell were those things?" Gail shouted, her voice shaking. "That wasn't Mike and Mary. That was ... something else!"

Carlos reached out and steadied her. "Those weren't human anymore. They were ... possessed. Spirits. Wraiths. I don't know."

I knelt beside Mary's lifeless body, drew my sword, and began stabbing—each strike fueled by adrenaline and fear. "Are they really dead? What do I need to do? I don't like ghosts—or whatever these are. Not one bit."

Raven gently took the sword from my trembling hands. "It's okay, Mel. They're gone now. The kind of entity that uses the dead like puppets needs a vessel. Cut off the head or sever the connection, and the spirit can't linger. That's basic folklore—but apparently, it's true now. So yes, stab away if you need to."

"Thank you for that truly disturbing fun fact," I said, managing a weak smile. "Feel free to keep sharing for the rest of your life."

Ruffus pressed close to my side, and Adalinda landed on my shoulder. The warmth of their presence filled me with a sense of calm. Whatever this was, I wasn't alone.

"I hope that was the last of them," I said quietly, scanning the golf course. "But we need to talk—figure out where they came from. If these spirits can just rise from the ground or crawl out of buildings, we're in trouble. This isn't The Walking Dead—this is worse. Unless Daryl Dixon shows up with his crossbow, I'm not signing up for this

Gail giggled and high-fived me, "I think Daryl would be a great asset to our team."

Carlos grabbed Gail around the waist and picked her up as she wrapped her legs around him. "You don't need Daryl. You've got me, babe!" He kissed her with so much heat that we all turned around, even Sean, Raven's ghost husband.

Gail was a lil' firecracker, but she knew how to handle her big guy; when she spoke, he listened.

While we gave them some privacy, Shelly and I decided to serenade the lovebirds.

Raven and Sean danced and laughed like we didn't just decapitate two strange paranormal creatures. At the same time,

Adalinda was flying in circles around our heads, and Ruffus was howling right along with us.

As Shelly and I turned to bow at our cheering fans, the air shifted. A chill swept across the lawn. I looked up and froze.

We were surrounded.

They emerged from the earth like mist made flesh or slipped through the rotting wood of the old park building—translucent, humanoid shapes flickering like broken film. Their eyes burned faintly. Shadows clung to them unnaturally.

"Spirits! Don't let them touch you!" I screamed, yanking Athena from her holster and drawing Excalibur in my other hand. There were too many to count. These weren't the slow creepers from *The Walking Dead*—they moved with eerie grace, drifting forward like they didn't belong to the laws of gravity or time.

"Adalinda, Ruffus—you need to get out of here. We can't risk them touching you. Who knows what they'll do."

"Do not worry, Ms. Melanie," Adalinda replied calmly from overhead. "We will be fine, I promise. You do what you were meant to do—vanquish these mother fluffers."

Mother fluffers. New favorite expression. Noted.

I shoved down the rising dread. I couldn't worry about them right now. I had to trust her. I had to *fight*.

The spirits shimmered as they drew closer. Some were still draped in the echoes of the lives they once lived—business suits, biker vests, jeans, shredded dresses. Their bodies flickered and twisted unnaturally, as if something far older and darker now inhabited them. Some were missing parts—hands, faces, chests torn open—but they didn't bleed. Instead, black mist trailed from their wounds. The air smelled like scorched iron and grave dirt. A few of them had once been our neighbors.

As if choreographed, Gail, Shelly, Raven, and I closed ranks—back-to-back in a tight circle, ready for war. Carlos was already deep in the fray, his sword whirling with glowing runes, slicing through incorporeal forms. Every hit turned the spirits into ash and falling whispers.

"We've gotta help Carlos!" I shouted.

We widened our circle. Spirit after spirit charged us, and we cut them down—each strike laced with holy fire, or maybe just sheer rage.

"I need to reload! Cover me!" I yelled as I ducked, jamming a mag into my sidearm.

We fought with everything we had. I ran toward the nearest entity. "You're the disease, and I'm the cure!" I shouted, slicing through its form with a satisfying flash. The spirit exploded into a swirling cloud of ash and disappeared into the wind.

"Rock on, Cobra!" Gail yelled, giving me a bloody thumbs-up.

I grinned—until Shelly shoved me aside.

A corrupted spirit in a tattered leather vest lunged at her, crawling with worms that slipped between dimensions. She met it with Eden, her Glock. "Smile, I'm about to blow your mind!" she said—and blasted a glowing hole straight through its head. The thing let out a scream like cracking glass and vanished.

Two more charged at me. I decapitated one with Excalibur, but when I raised Athena to blast the other—

Click. Jammed.

"Oh balls!" I hissed, shoving Athena back in her holster. The spirit leapt at me. I barely had time to raise a hand and close my eyes.

I braced for pain.

But there was none.

A soft *crackle* rippled over my skin, like warm rain. I opened my eyes slowly.

The spirit was gone.

Beneath me: a smoldering pile of ash.

"What the—?"

I looked at my arms. Dust clung to my skin. I sneezed—*gross*—some of it went up my nose, maybe in my mouth. "I've got dead spirit in me!"

Carlos grabbed my arm and yanked me upright. "Mel, we've got more incoming. Move. Also—that lightning trick? Wicked cool. Keep doing that."

"Lightning?" I blinked.

Then I felt it—something Adalinda once told me about—the spark. It flared in my chest. I saw it in my mind, fanning into flame. Heat raced through my body. My veins felt like rivers of fire.

Okay, Melanie. Focus.

Lightning. Think lightning.

Destroy the spirits. Save your people.

I ran straight toward them, screaming my battle cry: "DIE, MOTHER HUMPERS!"

I threw my arms up, felt the power building. The sky responded.

I yanked my arms down like I was dragging lightning from the clouds—and I was.

A bolt ripped from above and slammed into the spirits. They detonated in a flash of light and vanished into ash.

Then everything tilted. I collapsed to the ground, utterly drained. My vision dimmed, and darkness swept in.

The next thing I saw were Ruffus's warm, wet eyes as his nose touched mine.

"What happened? I'm so tired ..."

Gail grabbed my cheeks, her voice firm. "No going back to sleep, sunshine. Let's go home."

As they helped me up, I remembered. "The spirits. Are they ...?"

Shelly pulled my arm around her shoulder. "Gone. You got 'em all."

Later, I dragged myself into the shower, desperately trying to rid my body of the lingering feel of spirit ash. I tossed my battle-torn clothes straight into the trash. In the mirror, I froze.

Golden streaks shimmered through my hair.

Maybe it was the ash. Maybe it was the lightning.

I scrubbed my skin until it tingled, washed my hair five times, brushed my teeth like a woman possessed, and gargled salt water. If salt worked on demons, maybe it worked on paranormal residue too.

Still scared to look again, I pulled on my silky Scooby-Doo pajama short set and fuzzy purple socks. Then I finally braved the mirror.

Holy cannoli. The golden streaks were still there. The grey was almost ... gone?

My dark brown hair—normally aged mahogany with silver peeking through—gleamed with gold. My skin looked smoother. My lavender eyes had deepened into a richer, almost amethyst hue.

This wasn't normal.

But it was me now.

And something told me... this was only the beginning.

We were sitting on the porch, trying to relax with a cup of Peace and Serenity tea. This was a blend I had created after the run-in we'd had with the demon three days ago. It was exactly what we needed tonight. The tea contained Lemon Balm, Lavender, Catnip, Valerian Root, Chamomile, and Peppermint to relieve stress and anxiety, ease stomach pain, and help with sleep. Ruffus was sleeping on my feet, and Adalinda was snoozing on my lap. They gave me peace and comfort, but after tonight, I needed more. We were all feeling raw after the battle with the paranormals, but I wanted information.

"What happened tonight? I remember running toward the paranormals, and I wanted to blow those Slutwaffles to kingdom come. I drew my magic to the surface, and I watched them explode. What happened after that?"

Gail got up and knelt beside me, "You did so well, chica. You took out all the incoming supernaturals with your lightning. I bet there were at least fifty, probably more. Whatever you did, it was an awe-inspiring sight. We are so proud of you. I guess we know why your hands were sparkling when you and Ann were having a disagreement a week ago. You have a new power. We'll figure it out. Anyway, when you decided to take a nap on the lawn, we finished up the stragglers." Gail hugged me and lifted a strand of my now gold-streaked hair, "And this sister is an added bonus. Not only are you a green witch, but you're more. That's exciting!" She kissed my cheek and went back to sit beside Carlos on the porch swing.

"Carlos, can you please share everything you know about these supernaturals. How did you know that's what they were? They looked exactly how I imagined a spirit wraith would, but I didn't really think that's what they were. I thought spirit wraiths were fictional, like in my books. I don't understand what's going on. Magic, demons, ghosts, and a dragonette. I love our ghosts and dragonette." I reassured Adalinda, Sean, Fred, and Wilma. "I'm so happy you all are here. Is there anything else that may be coming our way that you know about?"

"Let me start by saying Gail is correct. You have a new power that is related to the elements. That could be a long conversation, and it looks like the four of you are about to fall asleep where you sit. When you expel as much magic as you did tonight, your body pays the price. It takes an exorbitant amount of energy to do what you did, which is the reason you passed out. You need to sleep. Ruffus and Adalinda are already zonked out. Can we talk about it tomorrow? I promise I'll tell you about the paranormals."

I really wanted to know now, but he was right; I was exhausted, "Fine, we'll talk tomorrow for sure."

"Good night, sweet dreams."

Chapter 15

Mel

This morning's sunrise was simply stunning—a masterpiece of nature. Today was a new beginning, and I would embrace it. I sat with my tea and a book about protection rituals under our tree in the backyard. The tree, a mysterious entity that had appeared about two weeks ago, was a sight to behold. Its species remained unknown; its leaves were adorned with indescribable colors. It seemed to whisper secrets of the universe through its rustling leaves, standing tall and proud, a sentinel of majesty, at least 100 feet tall and four and a half feet around the trunk, beckoning me into a world beyond my wildest dreams.

With my Master of Science in Plant Breeding and Genetics and a Minor in Horticulture, I was no stranger to the world of flora. Yet, this tree, with its enigmatic beauty, was unlike anything I had ever encountered in my years of research and study. The mystery of its origin intrigued me, and I couldn't help but wonder where it had come from.

Gail, Shelly, and I had seen it for the first time together while taking a walk.

Shelly had been excited as always; she was our free-spirited mama. She said it was 'magical' as she'd laughed, danced, and pulled us to the tree.

I couldn't have stopped myself if I had tried. I put my hand on the trunk of the tree, and my world had changed in an instant. I was no longer in my backyard with Gail and Shelly. I don't remember much, just bits and pieces that had come back to me. I remember that wherever I was, it was beautiful and peaceful. Surrounding me was the same kind of tree I had just touched. I'd felt a kind of peace and contentment that I'd never known. I never wanted to leave. Which was odd in itself; I would never want to leave TJ, my partner, or my gal pals, who had been with me through thick and thin.

Then I'd heard a mysterious and soothing voice. It'd said something about *time*. The next thing I knew, I was looking up at my friends.

Since that day, I've returned to the tree several times. I hadn't had any other experiences like that, but I felt peace and tranquility, which I gladly accepted in these times of battles and death.

I leaned back against the trunk of the tree and had begun to read when I heard a voice. I knew in an instant who it was. I stood up and turned to face the tree.

"Greetings, Madame Melanie. I'm Alana White, but you may call me Alana. I'm honored to have made your acquaintance. I'm similar to what is known as the White Oak tree on this plane of existence. I symbolize power, justice, honesty, endurance, longevity, and strength. However, I'm not of this world."

I was getting used to this stuff, so I went with the flow. "Hello, Alana. I'm honored to meet you. You are beautiful and inspiring. It's delightful to have you here. Do you know what's going on around us? Magic, demons, everything is a hot mess and I'm wondering why."

"When you were born, a clock began to tick, and things began to fall into place to bring us to this moment in time. Fate plays a role in everything we do. I don't know why or what is happening. I just know I was sent here to help you."

Well, that was cryptic. "No worries, whatever is to come, we'll all face it together. Um, do you happen to know anything about lightning magic?"

"I'm sorry, I don't."

It was worth a shot. I sat back down, leaned back against Alana's trunk, and studied the raised circle surrounded by magnificent, colorful flowers and bioluminescent mushrooms near the tree. A few of the mushrooms looked familiar. I had come out here several times in the evening with some books about mushrooms, and some of them looked a lot like the Green Pepe, which is odd because they are native to Indonesia, Japan, Sri Lanka, Australia, and Brazil, not Gardnerville, Nevada. It glowed pale green. Another one was called the Lilac Bonnett. They were native to Great Britain and Ireland, so they shouldn't be able to grow here. They were exquisite with bell-shaped caps that glowed soft purple. Every day, more and more flowers and mushrooms would appear around the circle, another magical miracle to add to our grimoire.

Now, I couldn't concentrate on reading, so I began practicing my magic. I wanted to create some sparks, smoke, fire, or anything from my hands. Nothing happened. I was so focused on trying to bring the spark inside me to the surface that I didn't hear my partners in crime-solving walk up and stand in front of me.

"Good morning, Toots!" Gail shouted.

Grasping my chest, trying to get my heart to slow down, I said, "Whoa!" Girlfriend, take it down a notch. You scared the bejesus out of me." Princess Adalinda, our dragonette, flew to me and landed on my shoulder. In an instant, my heart slowed, "Thank you, little one."

Shelly sat next to me. Her outfit was groovy: a tie-dyed tank top with matching socks and cut-off jean shorts. Her light blue eyes sparkled, and her long, deep, auburn red hair was pulled up in a high ponytail. "We've been trying to get your attention for a few minutes; you look like you're constipated. Are you okay?"

"Sheesh, I was working on my magic. I can't even get a spark today, and no, I'm not constipated but thank you for asking," I said with as much sarcasm as I could muster.

"Maybe you don't want it bad enough," Raven said, holding up her hand to stop me from interrupting. "I'm not saying you don't want it but think about it. The first time it happened you were angry and probably wanted to punch Ann in the face. And last night, you were probably afraid for your and our lives."

"Okay, that was very insightful. You're probably on to something."

I introduced the girls to Alana White, and let them chat, while I kept trying to find my spark. When I finally took a break, Gail, Shelly, and Raven were standing around the circle of flowers and mushrooms, discussing the possibilities of what it could be.

"Any ideas, or is it just a scenic anomaly?" I asked as I went and stood beside them. "The flowers smell delicious. It reminds me of a fresh batch of sugar cookies."

Shelly took a big whiff, "Really? To me, they smell like patchouli and sandalwood, just as calming as my incense."

Gail sat next to a beautiful chartreuse flower. "Hmm, that's not what I get. They smell like *Good Girl Gone Bad* by Kilian perfume. A lovely fruity floral fragrance."

"That's odd. I smell the ocean breeze, salt, fruits, and sunscreen, and I can almost feel the sand between my toes. I wonder why none of us smell the same thing?" Raven said.

"I would say it's something very magical," Joe said as he walked up behind us, with Carlos, TJ, and Ruffus following close behind. "You missed breakfast; how could you? That's against the law 'round these parts, partner. Plus, Chef C was distraught." He winked and hugged me.

"We'll make sure to have lunch or dinner in the bunkhouse, and I'll apologize," I said, grinning. "How are you doing, pops?" I said, as I returned his hug.

"Better now that I'm talking to you."

"You're a smooth talker."

Joe grinned and handed out bags with large, fluffy blueberry muffins for each of us, even putting one on the blanket for Adalinda.

"Hi, sweetie," I said, walking to TJ and kissing him.

"Joe, are you here to help Carlos explain what's going on and give us some information about the paranormals we fought last night?" I honestly didn't think he knew any more than we did. I was teasing, but when he replied that yes, he was here to help us understand, I was a bit dubious.

We all sat around Alana. Ruffus sat on my lap and kissed me. "I missed you too, love bug. Now, please sit next to me; I can't breathe." I giggled at the look on his face; it was as if he was shocked I would say such a thing.

"Before we begin this informative meeting, I'd like to share something," Raven beamed. "The world's termites outweigh the world's human population by ten to one. If we put all the termites together, they would weigh 445 million tons."

I slapped my hand over my face, another nightmare to add to my growing list. "Thanks, Raven. That was very informative. And I did say in haste last night that you were welcome to share fun facts forever. I think it might have been due to the stress and anxiety of the paranormal situation, but I never go back on my word, so I look forward to more educational fun facts."

"Great, I have thousands of them." She smiled and gave me a thumbs-up. That stinker knew exactly what she was doing, or she didn't catch my sarcasm. Raven was already part of the family. She was my annoying little sister, I chuckled to myself.

"I don't want to overwhelm you, ladies, so I'll share just a few tidbits," Joe began. "This beautiful circle is called a Fairy Ring. This circle was created by fairies dancing and celebrating." He held up his hand to stop my questions. "The fairies use the mushrooms as stools to rest between dancing. There are many myths and legends, but what you need to know is that this Fairy Ring is also a portal to their world."

"Another world? How do you know this?" I asked, not believing a word he said. I was sure he was pulling my leg.

"I have been alive for a very long time and have traveled the world. I've learned a great deal in my travels."

"That didn't answer my question, Joe. I don't consider sixty-seven a *very* long time. What aren't you telling us? Are you magical, like we are?"

"Yes and no. I'm a magical being, but I'm not like you. I'm something different, but that doesn't matter right now."

"Hold on, I thought you were teasing me. You freakin knew what was going on. Why haven't you talked to me before now? I've been a wreck. We've fought a demon and strange paranormal beings! I don't know what's going on, and I'm scared! You left me alone!" By the time I finished my tirade, I was screaming and crying, so of course, now my magic was working. My hands were on fire, and it felt good. I wanted to burn his bum.

Joe took my hands, but my fire didn't burn him. Why?

"Come on, Melly, just listen; I've been here the whole time. You just haven't seen me. I would never let anything hurt you. And you were never alone. You'll always have me, but you also have your sisters, TJ, Ruffus, Adalinda, and now Alana."

"You know Alana?" Jerking my hands from his, "I *have* been hurt, Joe." I shook my hands to try to put out the fire, but it wasn't working.

Joe took my hands again and looked me in the eyes with the love of a father, that I saw often from him. "It's going to be okay, sweetheart, I promise. Now, take a deep breath. Yes, I know Alana. I'm sorry I didn't speak to you earlier about everything."

Slowly, my fire dissipated until it was completely out. "Thanks," I whispered. I knew Joe loved me, and he would never hurt me on purpose, but knowing it in my heart and my head were two different things.

He patted my hand and continued, "By now, I'm sure you know you heal quicker than a human—"

"Are you inferring that we are not human?" Shelly asked, panic filling her voice.

"You are all special, more than just human. You will learn more in time."

I let it go for now. My brain was hurting. Whether this was true or not, we would figure it out.

Carlos took over the information overload, "Okay, let's move on to some spirit wraith fun facts." He grinned at Raven, our fun fact queen. "Spirit Wraiths can be created by being called or bewitched. Separate the head from the body, and you kill the spirit wraith. Always aim for the neck, which you all did quite well last night. Spirit wraiths are slow and only want food in the form of new bodies. The living is their food. They are undead humans and spirits, but not like vampires." He held up his hand, "Before you ask, yes, vampires are real, but we'll discuss them another time. Obviously, someone sent them to attack, but we can't find a trace of who could be doing this."

Gail turned to face Carlos, "How do you know about this? I thought you were just being an understanding boyfriend when I told you what was going on with me."

Carlos looked at Joe, "I have to tell her." Joe nodded but said nothing.

Poor Gail was pale, almost as white as Sean, our friendly ghost.

Carlos sat facing her and took her hands. "Mi Amor, I care deeply for you. I have been honest about everything, but there is just one thing that I have omitted. I have been on Earth for many years. I was sent to protect *The Chosen*." Gail started to speak, but Carlos kissed her softly, "Please let me finish, Mi Corazón."

Carlos was struggling; he was breathing heavily, and I could see the sweat on his forehead. This must be huge.

"My true name is Raguel. I'm the Archangel of Justice and Harmony. I didn't lie; it just didn't come up. I should have told you. Please forgive me."

Silence. You could have heard a pin drop, no birds chirped, the leaves in the trees stopped rustling with the breeze, absolutely nothing moved. I've never heard such a deafening silence. This was too much.

Gail looked like she was going to throw up, her eyes welling with tears. She slowly pulled her hands away from Carlos, and in a whisper, I almost couldn't hear, "No, this is too much, Carlos. Why are you lying to me? I've heard some crazy stuff, but this is going too far." She got up to leave. He tried to grab her hand and begged, "Por favor, te amo. Eres mi todo."

Shelly asked quietly, "What did he say?"

"Please, I love you. You are my everything," Joe replied.

I jumped up and ran to Gail, "Come on, munchkin, sit with me. Don't leave; we'll figure this out."

Begrudgingly, she let me take her back and sat with me, but she wouldn't look at Carlos.

"Please continue." I was proud that I kept my voice from shaking. I felt numb. I didn't believe all this; it can't be true. TJ grabbed my hand. He must have felt my distress.

Joe took over, "Your tattoo is a magical gift that created a quaternary union between the four of you. You are now connected beyond anything in this mortal realm."

"Melanie, Gail, Shelly, and Raven, you are the Chosen Four. You are destined to do great things. We are here to help and guide you. We'll begin a training program that will encompass physical strength and agility, magical skills, weaponry, and supernatural education." He paused, but we said nothing. It was getting hard for me to breathe; I couldn't seem to catch my breath.

"I'm sure you have noticed that you already have acquired a dragonette; she will be by your side as well. And Alana is a wise being, and she will assist you in any way she can. There is a war coming, and Mel, you will lead the fight for justice. The four of you will be at the center of it all, but you won't be alone. Many are already here, and many more will come to fight by your side. Whoever sent the paranormal beings will continue to send more creatures to try and stop you," Joe explained.

At this point, I was in full-blown panic. I jumped up. I couldn't breathe, I couldn't speak or ask for help. In the blink of an eye, Joe was by my side, and Adalinda was sitting on my shoulder.

In a soothing and mesmerizing voice, Joe said to me, "You're okay, sweetheart. Slow your breathing. Look at me."

As soon as my eyes met his, I began to relax, and I could finally catch my breath. He helped me sit back down, and Gail put her arm around me.

"What if I don't want to be one of the 'Chosen Four.' I can't do it, Joe. For Pete's sake! I'm forty-eight years old. And have you noticed I'm not in great shape anymore? You know how much I love my sweets. I love you, Joe, but I can't do it."

"You can do it, and you must do this, Mel. You, Gail, Shelly, and Raven were chosen for a reason. If you four don't stand up and accept your destiny, I fear our world will end."

"Wow, no pressure then." Each word held a buttload of sarcasm. I shut my mouth and leaned against Gail. Ruffus put his head on my lap, and Adalinda sat quietly on my shoulder, playing with my hair.

"How is this possible? Did our magic come from our parents? I don't even know who my parents are. Is there a way you can help me find them or at least find out what kind of magic they have?" Raven asked.

"I don't know of a way to find your parents, Raven. I'm sorry. But most assuredly, your magic came from them," Joe replied.

"What about my baby girl, Joe? Does Katie have any magic? I don't want her involved in any of this. She's only fourteen. She knows what's going on. She thinks it's amazing, and she also believes she should have magic. Please tell me she won't be a part of this mess and will never have magic," she said, seemingly desperate for the answers she wanted to hear.

"Joe looked at Gail with pity. "Katie will most certainly share the gift of magic. We'll work with her when she begins to manifest her powers. I don't know what her magic will consist of, but I can feel it already. She is very strong, and the older she gets, the stronger she will become."

Gail put her head into her hands and sighed, "I wish that weren't the case."

I spoke to my besties through our link, *"Let's get out of here, have lunch, and then work out."* I received votes of approval. "Thank you. We'll continue this another time. We need to absorb this information. Peace out." We got up, I flashed a peace sign, and we left them sitting by Alana.

Later that evening, Gail, Shelly, Raven, and I were back at the Fairy Ring, sitting on a blanket by Alana with a pitcher of peach cobbler martinis, wearing our pajamas and fuzzy socks.

We brought Ruffus's big doggie bed so he and Adalinda could snuggle up and snooze.

We raised our glasses, and I looked at each sister sitting with me, "A toast to my sisters from now to eternity. You are gifts to my spirit and part of my soul. May the goddess fill your hearts with happiness, your minds with knowledge, and your bodies with much pleasure! I love you all. Cheers!"

We toasted, laughed, cried, and hugged until we had no more tears to shed.

Chapter 16

Mel

It had been a week of adjustment. I was still not sure if I could be what Joe wanted, but my unwavering loyalty to him was a testament to my dedication. I was willing to do anything for him, so I was trying. He had been working with us girls, training us rigorously with weapons, hardcore hand-to-hand combat, and long lessons about this new, enigmatic supernatural world we had been thrown into. This world, unlike anything we had ever known, was filled with creatures of myth and magic, where the laws of physics were often bent or broken. I was confident that I knew what I was doing when it came to hand-to-hand combat skills because I had trained in Krav Maga for years. But that was baby steps compared to the training we were getting from Joe and Carlos. Sometimes, I thought they were trying to kill us.

Our magical training was also in full swing. While I was still grappling with my elemental magic, my green magic was starting to shine. The struggle to understand this new supernatural world was real and I was deeply immersed in it, trying to make sense of the unexplainable. Every day was a battle, but I was determined to conquer this new realm of knowledge.

Our investigations continued, and despite our best efforts, the culprits remained elusive. The mystery was a constant source of frustration, but Joe's unwavering drive to keep us occupied was a tribute to his dedication. I was grateful that the greenhouse had remained untouched this past week, but my resolve to uncover the truth about the plant's destruction was unyielding. I was determined to find the culprits, and that determination was not going to falter.

As the sun rose on another beautiful day on the ranch, I was half sitting and half lying on my porch swing, wrapped in a blanket, reading our Grimoire. TJ was engrossed in some paperwork, sitting in the rocking chair. Adalinda and Ruffus were snoozing under a tree, curled up together.

It was my turn to add more information about our lives and the magic we'd learned. There would be quite a few pages. We'd learned so much in the past week. My head ached with the weight of new knowledge, a tangible reminder of the vast, uncharted territories of power that we're beginning to navigate. Doubts and fears mingled with excitement in my heart. I'm not yet fully convinced by everything Joe and Carlos shared with us last week, but I'll add it to our book.

The gang were gathered around our usual table at the back of the room for the breakfast of champions. Sean, Raven's ghost husband liked hanging out with us. He always had his two cents to contribute to the conversation, and although TJ and John couldn't see or hear him, I could tell them what he'd said. Fred and Wilma, our new ghost friends, were flitting around the room, having a grand time. Most of those in the community couldn't see them but it didn't matter to them, they were just thrilled to be here. Ruffus and Adalinda were hanging out with Chef C.

Breakfast was another success, thanks to Chef C, Cassie, and James. They were a great team. Today's menu was a feast for the senses. An oatmeal-glazed breakfast cake, rich with the flavors of cinnamon, and a nutty glaze, was a sweet start to the day. Beyran Corbasi, a Turkish soup, was a hearty dish made with rice, shredded lamb meat, garlic pepper paste, and lamb broth, served with a wedge of lemon and Turkish bread. To top it off, I'd made a delicious nut and seed granola with yogurt. It was a perfect balance of crunch and creaminess.

Raven slurped down the last of her breakfast. "This soup was delicious. I've never had soup for breakfast, but I loved it, and the warm bread melted in my mouth. That breakfast was a delight. My taste buds were having a party in my mouth. Where did the lamb come from? I haven't seen any around the ranch."

"We don't have lambs. We've noticed extra ingredients in our meals on more than one occasion. I don't want to complain, but I am curious where he is getting some of his supplies. Chef C is a good man, and I trust him, though I will ask him about the additional ingredients that he uses that I know we don't have here at the ranch," I replied to Raven.

"Chef C would never do anything illegal," Katie said in a huff.

"You're right; I'm just curious."

"I would like to go on the coffee mission today," Katie announced to everyone at the table. When no one said anything and looked everywhere except at her, she turned to Gail, "Mom, can I go with you today?"

"No, I don't think that's a good idea. Why don't you and Melissa work in the greenhouse while we're gone? I'm sure your Auntie Mel would love the help."

I began to speak up when Katie burst out in a world-class whine.

"I don't want to work in the greenhouse. Why can't I go with you?" Katie said, with an attitude that could only come from a teenager. "I'm old enough, and I can help. Bonnie and Isabella get to go on missions, and they're only a few years older than me. It's not fair."

"Bonnie and Isabella are almost eighteen, highly skilled with weapons, and have been training with the security team since they arrived at the ranch. If it's okay with TJ, you can begin more extensive weapons training and join the training sessions with the security team, but you will not go on a mission until you are at the skill level of the others."

"Pleeeease."

"I said no! There are too many unknown factors out there, and I will not take a chance with your life."

"That's not fair—"

Gail cut Katie off, "That is enough. If you don't drop it now, you will go directly home. Do not pass go, do not collect $100.00. Understand?"

Katie jumped up. "Fine," she said, and stormed out of the dining room.

"She's so melodramatic, just like her Auntie Mel," Gail giggled.

"Katie is a smart kid; she also gets that from me." I mused. "While I have everyone here, I want to plan a mission to CVI and rescue the women being held captive and used as sex slaves. It's unacceptable and I won't stand for it any longer. We will discuss the details later. Gail, Shelly, and Raven are in, who else wants to join us?" I asked.

Hands went up around the table. "We can pull some others in if needed, thanks for volunteering. Well, on that note, who's going with us this morning on our coffee mission, as Katie calls it?" As soon as I asked, Ruffus and Adalinda came rushing over to our table.

"We're going," Adalinda informed me.

"Copy that."

TJ swung his arm around my shoulder, "I'm in, babe, and Bonnie and Isabella requested that they be on the away team if that's okay with you."

"Sounds good." My besties gave me a nod of approval.

"You know I'll be going," Carlos stated as if it was already a fact.

Carlos hadn't been too far away from Gail since he dropped the bomb that he was Raguel, the Archangel of Justice, and sent to be our protector. She was slowly warming back up to him, but she was not happy with him at the moment. I'm sure she'll forgive him—well, maybe.

"Okay, we've got our team. It seems like a rather large group to shop for coffee, but as I always say, the more the merrier. Before we leave, I want to have a quick chat with Ann. Can one of you let Bonnie and Isabella know they're on the team? TJ, will you and Carlos hook up the trailer to the MRAP for me?"

"We leave in one hour."

"Good morning, Ann," I said as I approached her in the dining area

She looked at me with her usual self-righteous expression. "What is it now, Melanie?"

"I was wondering if you have heard of anyone breaking into the greenhouse and destroying our plants?"

"Why would I know that."

"You told me that you know everything that goes on around the ranch, so you're the first person I came to."

"Well, that's true. Let me think. Hmm, I believe it would be Joanne Primm."

"Why is that?"

"She is jealous of anyone smarter than her. She's a teacher and feels she should be the smartest. From what I understand, you are working on things that are well above her pay grade."

It was interesting that she mentioned that she knows what is happening in my lab. I'll file that for later.

"Great, thank you, Ann. I will speak with her. Have a nice day."

Back at the house, I added Joanne's name to the mystery board but didn't remove Ann's name. She wasn't getting off that easily.

There were a few coffee cups in the sink, but instead of washing them by hand, I concentrated on my magic, saying *Lava Sicco Scrinium.* I pointed at the cups and then the cabinet, pushing my magic and intention just like Joe had taught me. It was working, but when I got to the part where the cups were supposed to go to the cabinet, only one made it; the other two hit the floor; I guess my magic had pooped itself out. Darn it.

TJ walked into the kitchen dressed in full kit ready to go. Va-Va-Voom! He was quite a sight when he was dressed to kill.

Maybe we could postpone the coffee run. Before I could get my request out, TJ said, "Go gear up, and I'll clean up the mess."

"Thanks, handsome."

I assembled the weapons I would take today. I was sure it would be fine, but I wanted to prepare for the worst scenario. I laid out a few pistols and rifles, my sword, *Excalibur*, knife, and *Isis,* and I grabbed *Deimos*, my Benchmade dagger. At just over seven inches in length, she was easy to conceal, the perfect size for everyday carry, and good for close-proximity combat. I kept adding weapons and ammo until TJ walked over, laughing at me.

"I think you have enough weapons, love. Are you going to be able to walk with all that? Looks heavy."

It seemed that every time I left the ranch, something terrible happened. I've learned my lesson. I would always be overprepared for anything. I would never admit he was right, but it was heavy. I took off a pistol and put it on the bench. "There, are you happy now?" I said, pretending to be exasperated.

He bent down and nibbled on my ear, "Very happy."

We left the ranch and were on our way to the coffee warehouse. We had a lot of coffee back at the ranch, but one could never have enough. I was getting into the zone, preparing for the worst but hoping for the best, when sweet little Raven decided it was time to share her words of wisdom.

"I've got a humdinger of a fun fact for you. There is a coffee with a special ingredient—This brand uses cat poop coffee beans. It is one of the most high-priced coffees in the world. The coffee is made from beans that an animal has digested. It's then advertised as an elite coffee. We could feed some coffee beans to Ruffus, and when he poops them out, you can find them and voilà—gourmet coffee."

"Ack, thank you for that mental picture, Raven, and no way am I feeding Ruffus coffee beans." Now, I would probably think about that every time I drank my coffee.

I jumped out of the MRAP when we pulled up in front of the coffee roasting warehouse. "No cars in the parking lot; it looks clear but never assume, you know what happens when we do that."

"Yep, makes an ass out of u and me," TJ announced with pride as though he'd won a prize.

"Very good, TJ," I said, giggling, as I kissed his cheek. "And that, sir, was your prize."

"Okay, team, we're here, let's get to work and get this done as quickly as possible."

Two hours later, we had the trailer loaded to the door with every kind of coffee bean and flavor we could find. "Good job, team, pack your asses into the MRAP and get home."

I felt the hair on the back of my neck rise up, and I looked around. I couldn't see anyone, but I knew someone was watching me. It felt malicious and predatorial, and I was the prey.

The evil intent hit me with such force that I was rooted in place. Goosebumps covered my body, and my throat was suddenly dry. It felt like she, and it was female, I realized, was trying to get into my head. I felt her prodding and poking. In that instant, I built my protection barrier around me and tried to keep her out. It was as if she was trying to figure out what I was, and she was freaking strong. What the heck was she? She was most certainly not human. I slowly turned and saw the beautiful but scary woman I had seen when we were at the library a little over a week ago.

I keyed up my radio. "Trouble. Six threats. Lock and load."

There were some men behind her, but I focused solely on her. She hadn't taken her eyes off me since I'd turned towards her. I knew my team would worry about the others.

I could hear gunfire and fighting going on around me, but I focused on the main threat. A fireball headed straight for my head. I dove out of the way, but not quickly enough and it caught me on my right thigh. Sweet Baby Cheeses! I was on fire! Water! I freakin' needed water. I was about to stop, drop, and roll when, out of nowhere, I was doused in ice-cold water—what the heck! I looked up to see if someone had poured water on me, but there was no one around. The fire was out, thank the goddess. I felt pain radiating from my stomach and down my leg, but I didn't have time to worry about it. If I didn't get my head in the game, I was dead. She now had two fireballs in her hands. I could really use some help here. I knew I could do this—lightning, where are you? I grabbed my gun and my dagger and sent several shots toward her head. Then, with a flick of my wrist, the dagger flew straight for her gut. It looked perfect, they were going to hit my target, but a few inches in front of Psycho, they stopped. The bullets hit the ground, and my dagger flew back to me and landed in my hand. Huh? Did she send the dagger back to me? No, surely, she wouldn't do that. I put the dagger back in the sheath, while still trying to call on my magic as the two fireballs headed my way. I fell to the ground and covered my head just as they flew over me, hit a tree behind me, and turned it into dust.

This chick was laughing like a hyena; she was psychotic.

"It's time for you to die, and don't worry little freak, I'll send your friends to their deaths right behind you," Psycho informed me in a hair-raising shrill voice.

"That's not going to happen. I don't know who you think you are. I won't let you touch any one of my friends; you aren't worthy enough to breathe the same air as them. You may have a pretty wrapper, but I see you for who you really are; you're wicked, selfish, and ugly as sin." I was on a roll. I had to keep it going. I could feel the heat beginning to flow through my veins.

"Why are you doing this?" I bellowed.

A deafening scream followed by more fireballs than I could count were released from her hands. I called on everything I had, trying to concentrate through her nightmare scream. I could feel blood dripping out of my ears, but I pushed through it, not knowing what was going to happen. Finally, a huge wall of fire erupted in front of me—it was magnificent; it absorbed the fireballs on impact. When the wall dissipated, I felt the fire and electricity flowing out of me. It was an adrenaline rush. I wanted more! Everything was an enigmatic shimmery red.

"*Fulgur Temptatio!*" I screamed. I don't know where that came from, but I followed my instincts. "*Fulgur Temptatio!*" I raised my arms to the heavens, feeling the fire magic dancing around me. As I looked skyward, I saw that my arms were on fire. I looked at my body, a startling glow of red, blue, and orange flames had engulfed me. It was mesmerizing—I breathed in the fire, reveling in the feeling of power, of funneling more magic. I screamed "*Fulgur Temptatio!*" one more time and then I brought my hands down and pointed them at Psycho.

The sky grew dark, and huge, ominous black clouds rolled in. In that instant, hundreds of lightning strikes were aimed at Psycho. She took hits left and right. Every way she turned, she was struck. If I hadn't believed she was supernatural before, I did now. I don't know how many strikes she took before she disappeared. I hoped she was dead, but I'm not that lucky.

My hands were still pointed at the empty spot where Psycho once stood. I could feel my hair floating around my head as if a breeze were carrying it. I was still burning; the fire was alive as it danced and swayed around my body. She wanted to stay. She was comforting and warm. She was a part of me, and I of her. I was so immersed in my happiness that I didn't feel someone take my hands until he turned me and spoke.

"Mel, look at me. You need to put the fire out now. You did good, but it's time to stop. Do you understand me?"

I'm so confused, who is that? I closed my eyes and let the warmth continue to grow. Someone shook me.

Then I heard a voice I recognized, but who's was it? The voice continued to talk. I couldn't understand what was being said, but the voice was all-encompassing. I opened my eyes, and through the red haze, I saw someone—TJ. What was I doing? I needed to get control.

"TJ," I rasped. My throat felt like sandpaper. The fire was gone. I was standing there naked and confused.

TJ grabbed me, wrapped a jacket around me, and held me tight.

I looked around to check on my team. "Is everyone okay?" I heard 'yeah' all around. Three bodies were on the ground, and the rest of Psycho's team was gone. "Looks like you guys did well. Water, please." It wasn't easy to speak. My throat hurt so bad.

Gail gave me a water bottle and took me from TJ. We walked to the MRAP. "Come on, sweetie, let's get home." My girls surrounded me, wrapping their arms around my waist and shoulders.

I wanted to check my hair, but my arms were pinned in the jacket. Man, I hoped I still had my hair and eyebrows. I have a lumpy head and would look horrible if I was bald.

Chapter 17

Mel

I stood in front of the mirror. TJ helped me check myself for burns or other injuries. I was more worried about my hair and eyebrows. Thank goodness I still had them. There wasn't a burn anywhere on my body. It appeared that the fire had also burned away old scars. That was crazy cool. I was weak and tired, so TJ helped me shower and get dressed.

The team and Joe were sitting on the porch when TJ and I walked out. Chef C had set up a table and brought lunch for us.

Joe sat at the head of the table wearing one of his famous T-shirts. I have never seen him wear the same one twice. He must have a whole room full of them. Today's shirt got right to the point. No explanation was needed, I knew exactly what it meant. *Some People Need a Fist Bump—To the Face With a Footstool!* It had a picture of a silhouette swinging a footstool.

I sat next to Joe, "Hi. Great shirt, I love it. Are you having one of those days, too?"

"Nope, I wore this in honor of the ass-whooping you all put on the enemy today."

We ate in silence. I was grappling with the fight with Psycho and her goons.

When we finished lunch, I sat on a blanket on the grass. I needed to be close to nature and absorb her strength. Ruffus and Adalinda curled up next to me and fell fast asleep. Gail sat behind me, French braided my hair and shared her side of the fight.

"Did you know your hair has more gold highlights, and seems to have grown a little longer? It's so healthy. I'm going to be honest with you. I thought when your fire went out, you would be bald and completely hairless, which in some ways would have been great not to have to worry about shaving, but have you seen people without eyebrows? That's just creepy."

I snorted out a laugh that I felt in my gut. She always knew how to make me feel better. "I was relieved to see my eyebrows were there too."

Gail patted Adalinda and Ruffus while they slept, "Princess Adalinda was awesome during the fight. She was shooting her fire at the jerks. It's a potent fire. They had a hard time putting it out, and that gave us more time to cause damage. Ruffus was just as vicious; he was attacking, pulling chunks out of their legs. It was a sight to behold."

Shelly piped up. "You were stunning when you were on fire. It freaked me out at first, but when I knew you were okay, I enjoyed the show. Your hair looked like bright flames of blue, gold, and red floating in an ocean around your head. It was totally groovy!"

"Tell me what happened with you all; I heard the battle raging behind me. Do you think Psycho is dead?" I said as my eyes closed, enjoying Gail messing with my hair.

"I don't think she's dead. She probably ran off to lick her wounds," Carlos replied.

"Carlos, how were you able to hold my hands while I was on fire? Is that an Archangel thing?" I asked.

He chuckled, "Yes, it is an Archangel thing, as you so eloquently put it."

Gail smiled at Carlos. "BG, the big dude that kidnapped us at the feed store, was there; he and Carlos were tearing each other apart. They were the same height, but Carlos outweighed him in muscle."

She was definitely getting over her anger toward him for lying to her about being Raguel, the Archangel of Justice and Harmony.

"I only saw bits and pieces, but what I could see was freakin' amazing. Carlos was deadly and beautiful. They were well-matched, although if Carlos had had a bit longer, I know he would have taken BG out." Gail said.

Carlos slowly scooted over to sit by her. "Thank you, Mi Corazón." He took her hand and gently kissed her knuckles. He was doing a good job of wooing her back.

"Carlos, what does being the Archangel of Justice and Harmony entail?"

"I'm what you would consider a sheriff. I fight injustice and work to help others live in harmony. I keep the fallen angels and demons on a leash and ensure they don't cause problems. I serve judgment, terminate evil spirits, and cast fallen angels into Hell when needed. I also release other angels to punish the unrepented when the time comes, and provide guidance to those who need it. There is much more; maybe we will talk more later, but for now, we need to figure out what we are up against—"

"I want to know everything, Carlos. You and I will talk later," Gail interrupted in a no-nonsense voice, then turned back to me. "There was another man, not as big as BG, but still huge. He was bat shit crazy. Shelly, Raven, and I took him on. We were wearing him down when the lightning started, and they took off. We were awesome! You should have seen us. Raven had some of her friendly ghosts attacking, choking him and trying to pull his arms off, while Shelly was pummeling him with rocks and dirt to his face, and I attacked in the form of a Brazilian wandering spider. I was seven inches long but shrunk to five inches to make it easier to crawl under his pant leg. I bit him several times. It was glorious to see him filled with pain."

"Yes, Mi Amour, you were a sight to behold," Carlos cooed. "The Brazilian wandering spider is deadly, and if he had been human, he would have died a horrible death within a few hours from lung failure, fever, vomiting, and paralysis."

Getting back to business, Carlos continued, "I know who BG truly is. I was about to tell you when I was so rudely interrupted," he winked at Gail and continued, "I can't believe I didn't sense him sooner. This is very bad. His name is Azazel. He's a fallen angel who corrupts humans with his evil. He's loyal to Lucifer and has many powers. He can change his appearance, manipulate minds, and control energy; he also can cast magic spells. Those are just a few. He's dangerous and must be stopped. I don't know what he's doing here, but it's not good; he has a plan, and his plans always end in total destruction. The three that were killed were humans. TJ shot one, and Bonnie and Isabella shot the other two. I'm not sure what the other creature was. I couldn't get a good read on him; he was cloaking what he was. And as far as the creature that you fought with Mel, she's the leader and is something incredibly dangerous and evil. She was cloaking her magic as well, so I only caught brief pulses."

"Well, crap, I wasn't expecting that," I murmured.

"Excuse me, what's going on?" Bonnie asked.

Oh no, I'd forgotten Bonnie and Isabella were here. I'm sure they knew some of the crazy stuff going on after meeting our new friend, Princess Adalinda, but I don't think they knew about all this stuff. Thankfully, TJ spoke up and saved me from having to explain.

"I apologize, ladies. Everything has been crazy and confusing lately. I forgot to keep you in the loop. That was wrong, especially with you going on the coffee run." TJ filled them in while I lay back on the blanket and closed my eyes. I needed to get my head around what was going on.

Joe had been so quiet throughout the conversation that when he finally spoke, I jolted awake and sat up.

"Things are moving along more quickly than I anticipated, and it's time to be proactive. Your protectors will move close to you. What I am about to tell you will be another shock, but I can't wait any longer. Mel, your home is sentient. She will make the necessary adjustments to ensure your safety."

I held up my hand to stop him, "What do you mean 'sentient,' 'she,' and 'necessary adjustments'?"

Joe heaved a heavy sigh as though he were dreading this, "She is aware, conscious. She can perceive and has feelings and emotions. She can see, hear, touch, taste and smell." He held his hand up to stop me as I opened my mouth to argue, "No, she doesn't do these things the same as you or me, but she does it; you don't have to question everything, my inquisitive Melly," he said as he gave me a wink. I grinned and nodded for him to continue. "She can respond and will help when needed. She has the ability to expand your home to allow others to move in, among many other fascinating abilities. Come with me, and I'll show you what she has done for you."

We went into the house, and Joe took us to a whole new hallway. Off the hallway was another bedroom and a full bath.

TJ put his arm around my waist in case I passed out. "Why, I mean, how, um, when?" I couldn't put a full sentence together. So, Joe came to my rescue.

"Your home added this bedroom and bathroom for Carlos. He'll be moving in to give you more protection."

I looked at TJ, and he just shrugged his shoulders as if to say what can we do? He was taking all this better than I was. I'm glad he was here.

I took a deep breath, "Welcome to the family, Carlos," then I glanced at Gail to see her reaction.

She frowned, crossed her arms over her chest, and looked at Carlos, who looked as happy as a lark. This would be interesting.

I clapped my hands with a huge smile on my face, "This is great! Bring it on. Isn't it great, Gail?" I smirked, and she gave me a look of indignation that told me she wasn't pleased with the turn of events.

I wasn't thrilled about having a sentient home, but I didn't want to make her angry; she could make our lives miserable. So, I patted the wall next to me. "Ahem, thank you so much, Ms. House, this is lovely." There, that wasn't so bad, I could do this.

The house rumbled and shook a little. I grabbed TJ, and he just laughed at me.

Joe laughed right along with TJ. "Don't worry, Melly. She's pleased you liked it—that's her way of showing you."

Chapter 18

Fiona, The leader of the Gang

I landed in a heap on my bedroom floor and gasped for air. I had never been this damaged before. What was she? Who was she? I had to get rid of her, or she would ruin my plans. As I lay there trying to heal myself, I released my glamour and felt relief when I was back to my true self. It didn't take much magic to create and hold the glamour, though the lightning strikes broke my arm, singed my hair, burned my human and non-human skin in multiple places. I was running on empty. I had worn this glamour for so long that it was second nature to keep it up. A glamour spell changed my true appearance into the appearance of a human creature men seemed to enjoy looking at. I didn't always look like this; when I was created, I was far beyond any beauty ever known. As time passed, the choices I'd made created who I am today. I was pleased with what I had become. I had evolved beyond anything that could have ever been imagined.

I heard the front door open. Ugh, not now. I needed more time to heal. I put every last ounce of my magic into one push, threw them out, and locked down my house. Then the world vanished into black.

I don't know how long I lay there, but as I opened my eyes, I felt much better. I needed to get cleaned up and make an appearance. I needed to ensure no one had tried to take my power and position.

I walked into CVI, my headquarters. It was pandemonium. I screamed, putting some magic behind it. "Shut up! What's going on?"

Everyone stopped, and silence filled the room. BG and Bobby walked to me. "No one has been able to contact you for a few days, and these imbeciles were panicking. I was about to blow them up just to get some peace."

"Well, I'm here now, and we have a lot to do. I want to know who we are dealing with, and I want them dead. Bobby, go get Ruben and meet us in the office," I instructed.

Five minutes later I was sitting behind the desk, waiting for them to arrive.

Bobby and Ruben walked in and sat down, waiting for instructions. They were good little minions. This was going to work out well.

"Thank you for joining me so quickly. We need a plan and need to end this threat. Do any of you know who we are dealing with?"

BG spoke first, "I know who one of them is, although I don't know where he is now; he must be shielding his true nature. His name is Raguel, the Archangel of Justice and Harmony."

No! What is he doing here? That wasn't right. Something more was going on than I realized. "If Raguel is here, more is at play here than I initially thought. We must eliminate him first and do it quickly.

"Ruben, you are a phenomenal drug maker; I also know you have a talent for potions, and I want you to create some deadly ones. We need to use everything in our arsenal to defeat these miscreants."

"Yes, ma'am."

Chapter 19

TJ

I was sitting on the porch, trying out some of the new coffee we had brought back yesterday. This stuff was good, strong, and black; it was just how I liked it. John came out onto the porch with a cup of coffee and sat on the rocking chair next to me.

"Be careful. That new coffee is strong. You might want to find the sugar and cream for yours," I said, laughing.

"Yeah, whatever. I can handle this coffee, and we Army guys usually never had sugar and cream for our coffee, though I am sweet enough and don't need to add any sugar, sugar!" he commented as he took a sip and smacked his lips. "What kind is this?" he inquired.

"I think this is their Caffe Verona blend. Very tasty on this cool morning," I responded.

"It is excellent," John drawled.

About that time, I heard footsteps in the house, and Ruffus exited with Adalinda riding his back like a cowgirl. "What up, buddy? Ready for another fun day on the ranch?" I murmured, while scratching him between the ears.

Adalinda reached out to touch my hand, and when she did, I received a shock, my hand tingling. "Morning, Mr. TJ. I hope you slept well and are well rested. I suspect it is going to be a busy day," she declared.

How would she know that? It was starting out as a good day, though.

Mel soon joined us on the porch with her own cup of coffee. "Morning, sexy. I see you found your way into our new coffee?" she said.

"Why yes, yes, I did. You going to spank me for getting into this coffee?" I asked as I gave her my best little kid smile.

"Easy there, mister or I will send you to your room," Mel said, as she giggled.

"Don't tease me with a good time," I admonished. "Is there anything planned for the day?"

"No, I think we will continue to work on our magic training with Joe to hone our skills. We have a threat in town, and we need to be at the top of our game to defeat her in the future," Mel said.

"Let me have your cups, and I'll take them inside. Then we can head over to see what Chef C has for breakfast," I said.

"He *is* magical in the kitchen," John declared.

Mel and Shelly looked at John like he knew something that the rest of us didn't.

A mouth-watering aroma of bacon sizzling on the grill, French toast, and fresh blueberries as a topping greeted us as we entered the bunkhouse. Ruffus and Adalinda ran us over as they made a beeline for Chef C and his treats. I was sure that Ruffus winked at us as he went past us as fast as he could, skidding to a stop in front of Chef C. Watching Adalinda hanging on for dear life was funny.

I looked at Ruffus and Adalinda, "Leave some for the rest of us, will you."

"There is plenty, TJ," Chef C responded as he handed more bacon to those two.

"Hey, TJ," Melissa shouted from the radio. "Ely is calling for you. It sounds like your dad on the radio," she stammered.

I rushed to the radio, it was unusual for my dad to be calling this early. "TJ calling Ely, you copy?"

"We copy loud and clear. Authentication. Who visited you in Millington, Tennessee?" he questioned.

"You, grandma, and little sis while I was in training. Where did you work when I was born?" I queried.

"Worked for Uncle Fred in Redlands, California."

"Authentication complete. What can we do for you this early?" I asked.

"We have thugs attacking the ranch here. We're in a lull now. I know we put a hurt on them, though we have lost a few of our friends here while defending the ranch," he said, his voice dipping when he mentioned the loss of his friends.

Dad lives at his ranch near Ely, Nevada, which has 1,200 acres. His house is built into the hill for natural cooling and heat. He is also a prepper and has storage areas built into the hillside. He has a shop and other buildings on the property to keep equipment, or people out of the weather if needed.

"Do you need us to come help? It will take at least a day to get there though. Not sure what the roads will be like, and cities like Fallon and Austin could be a mess," I probed.

"We could use some help, as we are down to eight people here to defend this place from those thugs. My security cameras are still working, and it appears that there are around twenty thugs left. We do have a few surprises left for them if they get close enough," he said.

"We will get a team together and head that way. Do you want to stay there after we defeat the attackers, or do you want to come here? If you want to come here, do your old trucks still run to haul the big trailers back with everything you want to bring here?" I asked.

"I think we will go there if you'll have us. The old trucks still run, so we can load everything up. We also have a couple of RVs that we can bring if they are not all shot up."

"That sounds good. We will get a team ready and head that way. I will give you a heads-up when we leave Freedom Ranch," I told him.

While I was having the conversation with my dad, the team gathered around to listen. When I turned around, they all had their hands up to volunteer to go on the rescue mission. "We need to leave some people here to guard the ranch, though Mel and her magical team can probably handle just about anything," I said. "Here is what I would like to take for vehicles: one Stryker, MRAP, Heavy lift truck, and two Humvees. For personnel, John, Nick, Gavin, Madison, Bonnie, Gunner, Tracy, Claire, Dylan, Skyler and Liam. For those who have not used the weapons on the Stryker or MRAP, you will move around and get some training during the trip there. Any questions or concerns?" I asked the group. "Dylan, you up for this trip. It was not that long ago that you were shot? We can take Quinn if you're not," I said.

"I am good to go. Our medical team worked their magic on me," he declared.

Isabella raised her hand. "Can I come? I'm part of the security team, and I would like to be trained to drive these vehicles and use the weapons."

I looked at the team and received thumbs-up signals. "You're in like Flynn," I agreed. The younger crowd looked at me like I was crazy. "It means that you are accepted."

"Cool," Isabella gasped. She then ran over to hug me, and then she hugged Bonnie and screamed, "Wonder twin power activated," they said.

We laughed at their antics.

"Okay, team, let's head to the shop and get the vehicles ready to head out. It's just over 200 miles to my dad's ranch, so plan on around five hours with no issues along the way," I recounted to the team.

In the shop, Gunner asked, "Are we taking one of the trailers with us? If we do, we will have to unload it first."

"No, my dad has a couple of big semi-trailers and the trucks. I want an extra truck just in case we have issues with one of his old as dirt trucks," I declared. "Everything on his ranch is old, like him." I laughed.

"We do have a bunch of ammo in the Stryker and MRAP, though probably more than we need. You want 50-calibers or the M240B's installed?" Gunner asked.

"There is no use in changing anything out. We probably don't need all the ammo in each one, though. We can remove some to lighten the load and make room in case we need it. We need to pack some food for the trip. Plan for five days' worth of food," I informed the team.

We started grabbing buckets of Mountain Home food to put in the two big vehicles, along with water and ammo for our rifles and pistols. I pointed out the camp stoves, water jugs, cots, and tents. We had just laid our kits out near the vehicles when Katie came running in, and we all stopped. "Chef C has lunch ready. The last one there has to do dishes," she shouted as she ran back out of the shop.

"Darn that kid. She is so fast," I exclaimed as I took off for the bunkhouse after her so I wouldn't have kitchen patrol duty.

Chef C had huge hamburgers for us for lunch, along with the typical fixings. Mel had made one of her special teas, Peach Pleasure, to accompany lunch. It was a blend of Oolong tea, peach, cinnamon, and a few other delicious flavors.

We were soon all back in the shop, grabbing our gear and completing our buddy checks. Gavin and Nick were watching our new arrivals from the National Guard and gave me a thumbs-up that they had passed the initial test.

Mel came over and hugged me before I loaded up. "You and your team have this. I know you'll all return safely to the ranch," she whispered into my ear before placing a big kiss on my lips.

"You keep kissing me like that, and it might delay our departure," I said as I pulled her in close.

She giggled as she extricated herself from me. "When you get home, sailor."

"Listen up, team. Here are the assignments for each vehicle. Gunner, Tracy, Gavin, and Isabella, in the Stryker. Liam, Nick, and Claire are in the MRAP. Dylan and Madison in the heavy haul truck. John and Skyler are in one of the Humvees, and Bonnie and I are in the last Humvee. I will lead the route, and we will follow the old Pony Express Trail. That will get us around Fallon. The trail near Sand Mountain then follows Highway Fifty. We will take a detour around Austin and Eureka and then rejoin on Highway Fifty until the exit for my dad's ranch. When we make that final turn off the highway, I will call him on the radio to get a reading on the situation at his place. If it's not dark, we will wait for darkness, so our NVGs give us the advantage of working in the dark. Questions?"

"Sounds like a plan," Gavin said.

"Burning daylight," John insisted.

I twirled my hand above my head, and we all loaded up and headed out. We completed communication checks as we rolled out of the ranch and headed east.

As I was driving the Humvee, I went through all the controls with Bonnie. "You will get to drive this and the other vehicles, so pay attention and be ready to jump behind the wheel anytime."

"No problem. I am looking forward to driving this and the other vehicles and shooting the guns if we get the opportunity," she squealed with delight.

"We will stop every so often so we can get everyone trained on the different positions and weapons on the two vehicles with the mounted weapons," I explained.

We were working our way north from the ranch to find the Pony Express Trail and make the turn to the east. After about forty-five minutes of driving, I announced a stop to change drivers and positions in the gun mounts. This allowed us a chance to stretch our legs and water a tree or two.

We soon found Highway Fifty and were making excellent time along the paved road, stopping only to stretch our legs. Due to its length and the lack of interest along its route, Highway Fifty is known as the loneliest road in America.

"Heads up, team, we are making a left turn for the detour around Austin. We will be able to look down into the town as we work our way around the town. Keep your heads on a swivel, though," I asserted.

We had made the climb into the forest when I spotted some children walking along the road. "Heads up, I see some kids walking along the road. It could be a setup. Keep the MRAP back a little bit, and have the Stryker pull up next to me. Make sure the 50-Cal is ready if anyone comes out of the bushes," I growled.

Who would use kids as bait to try and assault us? In the state the country was in, it was hard to guess who would take the low road.

The children seemed leery of us as we pulled up next to them. "You kids all right? Where are you from, and where are your parents?" I inquired.

What appeared to be the oldest one said, "We're from Austin, our parents are being held captive in town. We're hungry. We've been up here for a few days running from the police in town who are locking people up if they don't hand over their food and work for them," he said to me. He looked jittery, and his eyes were darting to each of us.

I could see the tension in his body, ready to bolt if we made a wrong move towards him or the others. The other kids were hanging back, and shifting from foot to foot, ready to run if they sensed something wrong.

"You're not going to hurt us, are you? You look like Army guys. My dad was in the Army before I was born and said you guys always help people."

I smiled at the child. "Your dad is smart, and he is correct that most Army troops are not going to hurt innocent people. We are not on active duty in the Army anymore, though all of us have served our country. What is your name? My name is TJ."

"My name is Clay. The other kids here are my brothers and sisters or cousins. Do you have some food? We haven't eaten today."

"Let me get the rest of my team up here. We have some food for you. We will have some questions about the thugs in town. Are you okay with us asking you questions about the town so we can see if we can help rescue your parents?" I asked.

"Yes, we can answer your questions," Clay nodded.

"Team, tighten up. Get out some food for these kids, though keep an eye out for trouble," I advised.

The last two vehicles pulled up, and the team bailed out, set a perimeter around us and went to work using the stove to heat water to feed the kids. Their eyes were big as saucers when they saw the food being quickly prepared for them. In no time, they were busy devouring the food from the Mountain Home pouches.

They asked for a second helping. "We had to scrounge for berries and other edible food on the mountain, though there is not much up here," Clay said, looking up at me.

I nodded to the others, and the children were given a second helping from the Mountain Home pouches. We started asking questions about the town and the officials holding their parents' captive. The kids knew their town well and gave us a good map of where people were being held and where the town leaders were hanging out.

"Will you help us get our parents out of jail? Please," the children begged.

I looked at the team, and they all nodded yes. "We will help get your parents released. We'll need to wait until it's dark, as we work better that way and have some special tools to help us see in the dark," I told the kids.

"Now that we have a plan, let's get some rest before it gets dark in five hours. We'll need someone on watch. I will take the first hour, and you all figure out who is taking what."

"Copy," they all said in unison.

Chapter 20

Mel

The sun had just risen over the horizon, and I was in one of my new favorite places on the ranch, sitting next to Alana, our magical White Oak tree in our backyard. She shared her peace with me. Sometimes, we chatted, and sometimes she was quiet so I could reflect on the hot mess that my life was. She had become a friend.

Our house was sentient. That was unbelievable. If I hadn't seen what she had done, adding rooms, I wouldn't have believed it.

I leaned back against Alana's trunk, "What do you know about sentient beings, such as a home?"

"It's a magical miracle for an object, or in this case, a home, to become a sentient being. It's extremely rare and only happens when the object becomes aware. As the object begins to grow, the goddess will encourage the growth with magic or cause it to revert back to an inert thing."

"Why would the goddess stop the miracle?" I asked, confused.

"If the being has ill intent or malice in its core, it must be stopped before it causes harm."

"You're sentient. Did that happen to you?"

"No, not like that. I'm alive like all trees, but in my world, my kind is born with this knowledge and ability to communicate."

I spent another hour with Alana, then headed to breakfast. When I arrived, the gang were seated at our table. I hugged Joe and greeted my gals and Carlos. TJ and John were on a rescue mission to help TJ's dad in Ely, Nevada.

Ruffus and Adalinda were sitting exactly where I knew I would find them, outside the kitchen and enjoying their breakfast. Chef C was so good to our babies. As I made my way to get my breakfast, the delicious aromas wafting out of the kitchen made my mouth water. I stuck my head in the kitchen, saying, "Hiya, guys. Something smells delectable, as always. What's on the menu?"

Cassie walked to me with a sample of one of her creations, "This, my lovely, is a cinnamon-apple Babka, buttery pastry wrapped around apples, with brown sugar, cinnamon, and ginger, topped with a powdered sugar glaze."

"Heaven, I'm in heaven!"

Chef C brought me a plate of Chilaquiles, which he had filled with vegetables instead of chicken, and a side of hashbrown. I had to wipe the corners of my mouth, "How do you all create such wonderous meals?" Cassie brought me an overloaded plate of her Babka, and I thanked everyone again and went to my table.

Before I destroyed the beautiful presentation, I took in the aromas of fresh tortillas, spicy red chili sauce, cilantro, onions, garlic, and vegetables from our garden, all surrounded by melted cheese.

After breakfast, I updated the team at the table again on the situation at CVI and the women we were going to rescue. When TJ got back with his dad, we would implement our plan and save those poor women. This needed to be taken care of; it weighed heavily on my mind. My heart hurt for these women.

Of course, everyone was on board and ready to kick some evil booty.

"Tonight is the night; we will put our detective caps on, Gail as Sherlocka Holmes, Shelly as Trixie Belden, Raven as Jessica Fletcher, and me as Nancy Drew. Our first mission is a stakeout to discover who is stealing the food. We'll meet when it gets dark and hide in the kitchen."

We were all excited. Gail clapped her hands, "This is so much fun!"

"Ahem," Joe obviously had something to say. He looked at me. "Sweetheart, the man's name is Sherlock; there is no a at the end."

Poor guy thought I was illiterate and was looking at me as though he felt bad for my lack of knowledge.

I grinned at my father figure. He was so kind, not wanting to hurt my feelings. "I know, pops. You'll have to talk to Gail about that. She insisted she was the female version of Sherlock, thus Sherlocka."

Relief flooded his face, and he chuckled, "Okay, I get it. Rock on, Ms. Sherlocka Holmes." Joe patted Gail's hand.

"On that note, I need to talk to Joanne Primm before she leaves. I'll talk to you later," I said, and I headed over to Joanne.

"Hi Joanne, how are you doing? Is the school ready to open?"

She smiled, "Yes, we will be ready to start teaching in a few days. I was so pleased to see all the wonderful books you and your team brought back for us."

"I'm so glad. I have a quick question for you. I'm not sure if you've heard, but someone has been breaking into the greenhouse and destroying some of our plants." I watched her closely for any change in her expression or body language. The only change was a look of horror.

"No, I'm sorry to hear that. I don't know who would want to destroy our food sources, but we need to find out and stop them before any more damage is done. What plants are they targeting?"

I didn't sense she was lying. I thought I was a pretty good judge of character, and I believed her. I wasn't sure how much to tell her, but if I expected the truth from others, that was what they deserved from me in return. "I've been working on genetically producing mixed species of fruits, vegetables, and trees. Would you have any idea who could be doing this and why?"

She looked down and grasped her hands in front of her, "Wow, that is amazing. I would love to see them and help you any way I can. I don't have the same skill set as you, but I'm willing to do whatever you need." She smiled hopefully at me. "I don't want to speak ill of anyone at the ranch, but the only situation I can think of that has any correlation to this problem happened years ago. Jolene Clean was young, and she belonged to a group that was angered that people were creating life. They believed that no human should try to play God. They protested organizations that were cloning sheep and other animals. Some of the protests became violent, and that's when Jolene left the group. She isn't an aggressive person, and that was too much for her."

"Thank you, Joanne; I'll look into it. You are more than welcome at the greenhouse any time. I would love to show you my babies."

Back at the house, I updated our mystery board. I added Jolene Clean to our list of suspects on the plant murder side and noted that Joanne was cleared. Gail, Shelly, and Raven came in. They studied the board, and I filled them in on the interview with Joanne and my reasoning behind clearing her as a suspect. Thankfully, they agreed with my assessment.

After dinner, the Charmed Four Detective agency met at the house to get ready for our first stake-out.

When we came out of our rooms, I burst out with a belly laugh. We looked like rejects from a mystery movie. We were dressed in black from head to toe, including putting our hair in a black cap. Gail had black stripes on her face and was carrying what I suspected, was what she had used, which she was going to put on our faces.

Gail had us sit in a circle on the floor with her in the middle. One by one, she marked up our faces with a black body makeup stick.

"This will help conceal us even more in the dark," Gail explained.

I rubbed my cheek, and not much came off, "But will it come off?" I probably should have asked that before she covered my face.

She laughed like it was a crazy question, "Of course, it'll come off," she paused, "I hope."

Shelly pulled a basket around in front of her. "I have prepared our stake-out necessities: flashlights, candy, cookies, nuts, dried fruit, bottles of water, blankets, and some books."

She was the mama of our group, and she always took care of us. "Thanks, Shelly. It's perfect. I didn't even think about that. You're as smart as a fox. Okay, ladies, are you ready to dig deep and become your detective alter egos?"

Raven stood upright, placed her hands behind her back, rocked slightly on her feet, and smiled at us, emulating a teacher's demeanor.

"Before we head into the unknown, I would like to share some much-needed information; I have numerous facts that I can share throughout our investigations that will help us. We are detectives; we must speak the lingo. A *B&E* means breaking and entering, which is what we are dealing with tonight. At the same time, trying to catch the thief. A *BOLO* means 'Be on the lookout.' Also, if I say *BPA*, that means bloodstain pattern analysis, which is the way blood is found at a crime scene. I want you to be prepared." Her silly sarcasm wasn't lost on me; I loved this girl; she made me laugh all the time.

Returning her sarcasm as best I could, I stood and said with a serious tone conveying the gravity of the moment, "That was very informative; you are a fountain of knowledge. I want to state for the record that I hope you do not say BPA; I feel that would be a very bad situation to be in." I was trying to carry it off like Raven did, a great actor, but I wasn't. I laughed and my amigas joined in.

I would like to say we were stealthy, but nope. We sounded like bulls in a China shop. Finally, in our positions, hidden in the shadows, we waited.

"Remember, we'll watch and follow them when they leave. It's showtime," I whispered.

"This is kind of boring," I said, and I stuffed another piece of cookie into my mouth.

"We do what we must to catch a criminal," Gail said, grinning. She held her flashlight, waving it around the room, trying to spell her name. "Remember when we were camping a few years ago, and we borrowed someone's flashlight to go to the porta-potty at night?"

"OMG, that was hilarious and sad for the poor man we borrowed it from." I looked at Raven. "We took turns holding the flashlight for each other, and when we were done, I'm not sure who, but I suspect it was me who dropped the flashlight right into the port-a-potty. Obviously, there was no way we were going to try and get it, so we had to explain what he had done to the poor man's flashlight. I should have started by saying that we'd had a few drinks beforehand; I'm sure that contributed to my clumsy attempt to shine the light for Gail. Looking back, I don't know why it was so funny, but we couldn't stop laughing. I feel bad for the guy. I wish I had given him a new one. Oh well, live and learn."

Raven and Shelly were cracking up.

"Oh, and I should mention if Mel ever makes you a croissant sandwich with cheese, you should always check it and make sure she didn't leave the piece of paper that divides the cheese slices. She tries to be helpful, but sometimes it's a failure." Gail roared with laughter, remembering the strange texture in her sandwich.

"Let me start by saying that I was making that sandwich for you, my dear Gail, out of the kindness of my heart while you were driving. I was squished in the back seat amongst a mess of camping supplies. So, I think I did a good job with what I was working with, plus you got some extra fiber." I defended myself while trying, unsuccessfully, not to laugh.

Once we got our giggles out, I wanted to address something that had been on my mind. "Raven, I'm sorry you didn't know your parents, that's rough. We all understand. Gail, Shelly, and I grew up in the L.A. Orphanage in California. We were dropped off as newborns and never knew our parents either. Shelly and I were found on the same night, so we grew up together. Gail was found by the door eleven years later. By that point, Shelly and I were much older and didn't know her. When Shelly and I were eighteen, we had to leave the orphanage. We tried to stay together, but sadly, living on the streets was hard, and we got separated. Not long after, we were all contacted by universities that stated we had been accepted into their programs, our education had been paid for, and so had our supplies and housing. Of course, we didn't apply, but we took it as a sign to continue our education. None of us knew this until we finally reconnected. We were sent to different schools." I smiled at my besties.

"By a crazy coincidence, we found each other again when our husbands became friends while camping on the Rubicon seven years ago. When TJ and I moved here four years ago, I instantly bonded with the lovely Gail Adler, our local veterinarian, when I took Ruffus for his first appointment. From that time forward, we were inseparable. Shelly spent a lot of time here, and Gail and I went to her house in Jackson, California. We became sisters. None of us know who our parents are. I even tried at one time to find mine, but there was absolutely nothing to find, not a paper trail, nothing. I figure I was born off the grid and dropped off the same night." That was a lot to unload on Raven. Maybe it wasn't a good idea. Raven sat so still; if her eyes weren't open, I would swear she was asleep. Her ghostly hubby, Sean, sat next to her, holding her hand; he looked at her and us in bewilderment. That was new; he was actually holding her hand; how was he doing that? Another question for later.

"Are you okay, cupcake? You don't look so good." I asked Raven.

Shelly got up and then came back with a bottle of water and gave it to her.

"Um, no, I don't think I'm okay," Raven whispered, while looking at Sean.

I scooted over to sit beside her and took her other hand, she was trembling. "What's wrong? I didn't mean to upset you. I just wanted you to understand that we all understood what you had gone through and that we're here for you.

Sean began to speak, but Raven cut him off. "It's okay, sweetie, I can tell them." She paused as if to compose herself, "I was raised in the L.A. Orphanage also. They said I was dropped off at the door when I was a newborn. That would have been fourteen years after Mel and Shelly had been left there. I left when I was eighteen. I attended a university and obtained my teaching credential because of help from an anonymous benefactor."

Now, we were all rooted to our spots. It couldn't be a coincidence that all four of us lived similar lives and met again years later to fight a supernatural war.

I explained my theory and it was met with murmurs of agreement.

"It would seem that someone has been controlling our lives. But who could do that?" Shelly asked.

The door slowly squeezed open, and I froze. Let's continue this discussion later. The perp is here." I whispered.

The door closed, and I heard footsteps, but no one was there. Cabinets opened, and food floated out, the same as with the refrigerator. Then the food disappeared also. This is crazy. Are they ghosts? Why would ghosts need food? When they finished and walked out, we quietly followed. There was a quick flash, and I saw Ruffus with Adalinda sitting on his back, and three hooded figures carrying the food. Then they were gone again. We tried to follow them but eventually lost them.

Back on the porch with an extra-large pitcher of peach cobbler martinis, we were trying to figure out why Ruffus and Adalinda had been stealing the food.

I slurped a large drink of my martini, "Obviously, Adalinda won't tell us what's going on. She has had numerous opportunities. She knew we were investigating the stolen food. This began before she joined our family, so Ruffus and the other three invited her to join their mission. What do you think about the disappearing act they put on tonight?"

"I believe it was a cloaking or concealment spell. Someone in the group had strong magic. I'm guessing it was Princess Adalinda. To be able to cloak three people, a dog, and a Dragonette, would take a great deal of power." Raven, our witchy wonder, usually had good leads for us. She had spent years studying the occult and was well-versed in the magical world.

"That makes sense, thanks Raven. Let's act normally when they come home and not give anything away. Then, tomorrow night, we'll follow them when they leave the house. But between now and then, we need to work on a spell that will help us track them. I was reading about a locator or tracking spell in one of the books Joe gave me. Let's study it, follow the culprits, and solve the mystery of the missing food." I said as I held up my cocktail glass. "To the Charmed Four investigators, to always getting our perps."

Chapter 21

TJ

"Okay, team. Rise and shine. Let's send some bad people to meet their maker and help these children be reunited with their parents," I growled.

I didn't like people who thought they could be the supreme commander in the little town and run it like a dictator. We all felt the same way in these situations.

Gunner, Skyler, and Isabella were in the Stryker and were Team Stryker. Liam, Tracy, and Dylan were in the MRAP and Team MRAP. Bonnie and I were Team One. John and Madison were Team Two. Gavin was Team Three, and Nick and Claire were Team Four.

The plan called for Gavin to find an overwatch position on the east side of town. He was taking one of the Humvees to help him get closer. It was going to take us about two hours to get everyone in position. The Stryker and MRAP would be positioned on either side of town, and once we started the fireworks, they would come into town to help take out the threats that came out of the woodwork.

Bonnie and I would work our way across the main street and enter the sheriff's station, where the kid's parents were being held.

The mayor and sheriff had appointed themselves the supreme commanders of Austin. Clay had been observant and could tell us where they lived. They had other minions working for them, though we hoped once we eliminated the sheriff and mayor, they would drop their weapons.

The plan called for John and Madison to take down the sheriff, and Nick and Claire to grab the mayor.

Gavin was soon in an overwatch position. "Three in position. The main street is clear, and there are no heat signatures anywhere," he announced.

"One in position," I called.

John announced, "Two in position."

"Three ready," Nick called.

The two vehicles called in, ready from their positions on either side of town. Thankfully, the town had not installed barricades on the roads into town.

At twenty-three hundred, I called, "Execute."

There was no back door at the sheriff's station, so we had to run around to the front door. I went first, going left once I was through the door. Bonnie entered behind me and went right. There was a guard asleep inside. Our entry woke him up, and I yelled at him not to reach for his weapon, which I could see in a holster on his hip. "Watch the door to the cell area while I deal with this dip wad," I called to the others.

Even with having him dead to rights with my rifle pointed at him, he still went for his pistol. My two shots hit him, center mass and sent a mass of blood and gore across the room behind him. As he was falling, I could see the life leaving his eyes and smell the death in the room along with the spent gunpowder.

I yelled at Bonnie watching the door to the prisoner area. "Do you see anything?"

"Clear," she yelled back.

I checked the dead guy for keys to the door and cells and headed for the door.

When I opened the door to the cells, I knew it was bad. The smell of decaying flesh overcame my senses, and when my tactical light shone on the bodies, I could see how bad it was. My stomach contents wanted to reveal themselves. I stopped and looked at Bonnie as the smell assaulted her nose and the color drained from her face. "This is going to be bad. If you don't want to enter, I understand. This will be something that you can never unsee," I said.

"I either see it now or I see it later," she said, squaring her shoulders back, looking like she was preparing to go into a fight. As she entered further, the stench hit her harder, like spoiled meat left out in the sun. She gagged and doubled over with bile rising in her throat that she was working to keep down.

I put a hand on her shoulder to steady her and let her know I was here.

The smell of death emanated from the cell area. It was so bad I was trying not to retch. There were a total of five cells. The first two had at least eight dead bodies that appeared to have been shot while they were in the cell, they looked to have been there for a while. The last three cells had four people each, though at least they were alive.

'How could these animals do this?' I asked quietly.

I looked at Bonnie. "You, okay?"

"I think so," she mumbled.

I saw a tear run down her cheek, and along with trying to hold down her stomach contents, she just looked anguished. I would need to talk to her later about this.

The people in the last three cells looked terrified and probably had no idea what we were going to do since someone had shot the people in the first two cells.

"We're here to help you and reunite you with your kids," I explained. "Where are the parents of Clay?" I asked.

A balding man wearing a stained white t-shirt and blue bib overalls, that had not seen a wash in a couple of weeks, raised his hand. The blond woman standing next to him, wearing a pink t-shirt that said "Pink" and camouflage pants, also raised her hand.

As I was unlocking the cell doors, I told them, "We found Clay and the other kids on the hills to the north of town. They explained what was going on and asked us to help. We have a team here who is rounding up the sheriff and mayor and their cohorts."

"Oh, thank the lord," the woman gasped. "I was so worried about our kids and their cousins. The sheriff said he had them working the fields to feed the town. We were so worried," she said.

I heard John on the radio. "Team Two. The sheriff is dead. He tried reaching for a gun when we entered, and it didn't end well for him. He had some women in bed with him," he announced.

Nick and Claire chimed in. "Four. Mayor in custody."

Gavin called out. "I have four people in the street with AR's about 200 meters from the sheriff's office."

"Bonnie, here are the keys. Get the doors open, and then we will see if the people in the street are a threat."

We soon had everyone out front, closing the door to the cells to try and decrease the stench coming from that area.

"Stryker and MRAPs. Move into town and see if the people in the street are a threat. If they shoot at you, you are cleared hot."

"Copy," they both replied.

I knew if the people in the street fired at either vehicle, the weapons mounted on them would eliminate the threat in a couple of seconds.

I looked at the people we had removed from the cells. "Stay here. We are headed out to check on this group in the street. The sheriff is dead, and the mayor is in custody. Let's move, Bonnie, I nodded at the buildings in front of us, "we can stay alongside the buildings. MRAP & Stryker. Be careful; Team One is along the south side of the street, so be careful of friendly fire."

I could hear both vehicles moving towards the people in the street. Gunner in the Stryker used the loud hailer. "You in the street. Drop your weapons. If you fire on us, we will return fire. You are surrounded."

Bonnie and I were moving that way, and as we passed the saloon, I saw the people in the street drop their weapons.

"Gunner, I will move in and check them for more weapons. Cover me."

"Copy," he replied.

"Let's go, Bonnie."

I moved closer to them and said, "If you have any other weapons, drop them on the ground. If I find anything else on you, I will shoot you. Are we clear," I shouted at them.

I could see the shock on their faces when Bonnie and I stepped up to face them. I saw a couple dropping knives and pistols on the ground.

Bonnie and I moved in and checked them for weapons. Finding none, we moved them to the side of the street.

A fat guy, who must have felt like he was in charge, spoke up. "Who are you guys? What are you doing here?" he asked.

"I will be the one asking questions here. Who do you guys work for?" I asked.

Fatso looked at me and scowled. "I am not answering your questions," he snapped.

I walked up to him. "I don't want to hurt you, but I will get answers. So don't push me," I growled.

"What are you going to do? Sick your little girl on me," he laughed.

I laughed at him. "She would have you asking for your mommy so fast; you would wish it was me working you over, you fat pig." I looked at Bonnie. "You want this light work?"

"Na. I don't want to listen to him crying for his mommy," she retorted.

He started to laugh when Bonnie stepped up and kicked him in the knee. As he was falling over, she swung the butt of her rifle and hit him on the side of his head. He was on the ground before he even realized, screaming for her to stop.

I looked at Bonnie. "He is not crying for his mommy yet," I admonished.

His friends all took a step back at the beating he received from Bonnie.

"I have more tricks up my sleeve," she proclaimed. "Answer his questions, or I will start again."

"No," he screamed. "I will answer your questions."

"Who do you work for?" I inquired.

"The sheriff," he said between sobs.

"Who shot the people in the jail," I shouted.

He looked at me and sobbed. "The sheriff made us do it, he said he would lock up our families and take our kids if we didn't," he stammered.

I wanted to shoot him right there, but I needed to be better than that. John, Madison, Nick, and Claire arrived at our location. Nick and Claire had the mayor with them, who was pulling against them as they pulled him towards the group. He was yelling and screaming for them to let him go.

When he saw our military vehicles, he shut up. "Who are you people? This is my county and jurisdiction. Any military in this area work for me, as appointed by the governor," he declared confidently. "Let me find the sheriff, so he can arrest you."

"Where did you get the orders from? We don't work for you or the governor," I said.

"This is my county. I set the rules here."

Oh, this was going to be good. I could see some of the town residents starting to gather around us. The gunfire had probably woken them up. I keyed my radio. "Keep your eyes peeled for weapons. The four in the street worked for the sheriff. This fudge stick thinks he is the supreme commander here."

"Who were you talking to? I am the area commander per our incident command plan," he declared.

I ignored him and walked up to some of the townspeople. "What has he and his fellow thugs been doing around here since the lights went out?" I queried.

A gentleman stepped up with a Desert Shield hat on. "He and his cronies were running around taking our weapons, food, and our kids. They had the kids working the fields, cleaning their houses, and who knows what else. They even took some of the younger wives and single women for their pleasure, is what I heard."

"John, cuff the four over there. I am going to take the mayor for a little walk to the train station," I snarled. "Let's go, Mr. Mayor. We are going for a little walk."

"I am not going anywhere with you," he snarled.

I twisted his arm up behind his back, causing him to stand on his toes to prevent me from breaking it. "Move it," I shouted.

We walked over to the back of the Stryker. "Where are the rest of the kids? Where have you and your friends been storing the food that you took from the townspeople? Last question, where are their weapons?" I asked as I pushed him against the back of the Stryker.

"I don't have to answer your questions. I don't report to you," he sneered.

I punched him in his large stomach, and as he bent over, I grabbed the back of his head and pulled it back up by a handful of his greasy hair.

"Ooww," he screamed. "You can't treat me that way. There are rules, you know."

"I am only going to ask you one more time. Where are the kids, food, and weapons? Answer my questions, or I will beat you within an inch of your life, then I'll turn you over to the townspeople who will take the last remaining inch," I explained, as I slapped the side of his head.

If looks could kill, he had it. I pulled out my knife and grabbed his right hand. I pinned his hand against the Stryker, slammed my knife blade against his thumb, and sliced it clean off. His scream resonated off the valley walls as he held his bleeding thumb to try and stop the flow of blood.

"You want to answer my questions now? You still have another thumb and eight fingers left," I said, as I pressed the knife against his remaining thumb.

Between sobs, he managed to say, "The kids are in the big building just down the street. Most of the food is in there. Their weapons are in the courthouse."

"Now, was that hard?" I challenged him. "Are there any guards with the kids? If you lie, I will remove the rest of your fingers just for lying to me," I growled.

"Yes, two guards. Take me there, and I can get them to come out," he pleaded, a death grip on his severed thumb with his other hand. He was holding his thumb tight to stop the blood flow with his left hand, and the knuckles were white.

We walked back around the Stryker, where I briefed John and the team on the kids' location.

I took the mayor, John, Nick, and Bonnie with me. "Make sure these four don't go anywhere and see what the townspeople need. Keep them out of the sheriff's office, though," I told them.

We got to the front of the building, where the mayor indicated the children were being held. "Mayor, if those kids get hurt, I will personally cut your limbs from your body very slowly so you die an extremely painful death. Are we crystal clear?" I whispered in his ear.

He gulped and nodded. "Yes," he croaked.

I could see sweat running down the side of his head, fear was radiating off him

He walked up the steps and knocked on the door. "Hey, Jim Bob. Open up. It's Mayor Cleatus. I need you and Petey to come on out," he called.

"Hey, Mayor Cleatus. What was the screaming I heard earlier," someone inside asked.

I was standing behind the mayor; John and Nick flanked the door, and Bonnie was to my left. When the door was cracked open and whom I suspected was Jim Bob started to step into the doorway, Nick and John drove him inside with their rifles in his face. I heard them yelling, then John called, "Clear. All kids are safe."

They walked out with Jim Bob and Petey in flex cuffs.

Jim Bob and Petey looked at the mayor. "What is going on, Cleatus? Who are these Army guys?" Petey asked.

"I don't know. They now own the town. They killed the sheriff," he blubbered.

"We don't own the town. We are giving it back to the townspeople to manage," I said.

I was sure I saw a smirk appear on the mayor's face when I mentioned giving the town back to the residents. "You won't be here to try and rule this town much longer," I whispered in his ear.

He whipped his head around so fast to look at me that I was afraid he might break his neck. "Why not? I live here just like they do," he stammered.

"We aren't leaving a dictator here or your cronies here either," I retorted.

"Hey John, do you have any more cuffs for this dirtbag?"

"Yes, we have more. You want the standard ones or the ones with razor blades pre-installed?" he joked.

"Razor blades. I want this dirtbag in pain if he tries getting out of them."

We returned to the area with the residents and our team. "Team, gather up. We have a few things to figure out before we can leave here," I announced.

We gathered up away from the residents so they couldn't hear us, though we could still observe everyone. "We need to get the kids from the hills and bring them back down here. Someone take the MRAP since it has the most room while we figure out a plan for the dirtbags here," I instructed.

Liam and Nick headed off with the MRAP to grab the kids while I gathered up the residents. "Who can run this town as a leader, or leaders, and not become a dictator?" I queried.

A gentleman with the Desert Shield hat stepped up. "My name is Doug Needles, and I ran against Cleatus in the last election for mayor. I am not saying that he bought votes, though it seemed fishy that he had so many votes, and I had so few. When I talked to people, not many commented that they had voted for this dipstick."

"There is not much we can do now other than remove him and his cronies. Would you be willing to set up a city council to run the town and help all the residents survive?" I asked him.

"Yes. We can gather everyone up at daylight and run an election. We have enough fields and hunting areas to survive. The town has a natural spring that feeds a tank, so we have fresh water. We will survive," Doug replied.

I heard the MRAP returning, and as soon as it stopped, the doors opened, and the kids jumped out and ran to their parents for hugs and kisses. I could see the relief on the parents' faces that their children were ok. I think they all had tears of joy at their reunion. There was one little boy looking around. I grabbed Clay and his parents and asked, "Who is he, where are his parents?"

Clay spoke up, "That's Joey. I am not sure where his parents are."

Clay's mom gasped. "His parents are in one of the first cells that you passed when you entered the jail area," she said, tears running down her face. She walked up to Joey. "It will be all right, son. You can come live with us. The sheriff did something with your parents."

"I want to live with my mom and dad," he gasped. "What did the sheriff do?"

Between sobs, she said, "I am sorry, Joey. They are dead. You need to know the truth."

He broke down crying, and Clay's mother hugged him. Some of the other mothers gathered around to console him.

I grabbed Doug. "Will Joey be all right with Clay and his parents?"

"Yes, Sir. They are good people. We will all help like we always do. We only had about 160 people here before the lights went out," he proclaimed.

Gavin and Nick approached me. "Can we have a minute of your time? We have a plan for the dirtbag leadership here."

"Sure. What's your plan?"

"See if Doug wants all of these dirtbags out of his hair or just some of them. Those he wants gone, we can take them over the hill, and, well, you don't need to know the rest."

I looked at them. "Not sure I really like the unknown, though I appreciate you guys willing to take the dirtbag leaders over the hill and take them to the '*Barber to get clipped*,' as Mel calls it."

We all laughed.

I walked back over to Doug. "I have a question for you. We can take care of the mayor, but what about the rest of his cronies here? Can you and the citizens handle them, or are some of them really loyal to the mayor?"

"Two of the four over there, including the one still on the ground, are his kin. They will be a pain even with him gone. The rest will become upstanding citizens again," Doug emphasized.

The one on the ground was the one Bonnie had put down. That girl had a mean streak in her. I pity the man she marries.

I pointed them out to Nick and Gavin, and they grabbed Liam, loaded the three former dictators into the MRAP, and took off.

They were gone about thirty minutes when they returned and announced, "Problem solved. Barber has clipped them."

I announced to the team. "Let's head to the top of the pass and get a little rest before we head out. Doug, we will head out and get out of your town. We will be back through in the future. Don't let us down."

"We won't. We have this now," he emphasized.

"I trust you Doug, don't let us down. Team, load up, and let's roll." We headed to the top of the pass and a pull-out that went behind some rocks, and set up camp for the rest of the night.

Before turning in, we grabbed some Mountain House food and then slept.

Chapter 22

Camped above Austin, we all started to wake up as the sun came up. It was a tough night, and I still had to talk to Bonnie. Four hours of sleep was nearly not enough, and it was going to be another long day. We didn't know what we would encounter in Ely at my dad's ranch.

I wish Ruffus was with me to help motivate me this morning and get out of this sleeping bag. We could have also towed the trailers with the tents behind the Humvees, and I would have slept better than on the hard ground.

I climbed out of my sleeping bag and found the nearest tree. When I came back into camp, the team were milling around, and Isabella was grabbing a bucket with the breakfast food in it. I grabbed the water to start filling pans and heating them for our breakfast.

While that was happening, I saw Bonnie and headed over to her. It looked like she might have had a rough night. "Hey Bonnie, can I have a word with you?"

"Sure, TJ. What's up?"

"I wanted to talk to you about what you saw in the jail. I want you to know that you can talk to any of us. That was a grizzly scene there. Nick, Gavin, Carlos, or John probably have the most experience with scenes like that from their time in the sandbox."

"Thanks. It was a little tough to get that scene and smell out of my head last night," she muttered, her shoulders hunched like she was still trying to forget.

I saw Gavin and Nick standing over near the water and waved them over.

"Hey, guys. We saw some really horrendous things in the jail last night. I was checking on Bonnie. She struggled to sleep last night. I am sure you guys have seen some really bad crap while you were deployed. If you have any ideas on how to help Bonnie through this, I would appreciate it," I asked.

Nick pulled Bonnie into a hug and whispered something into her ear that I could not hear. I could see tears running down her cheeks and saw her sob into his shoulder. Gavin stepped up to talk to her, and again, I was unable to hear it. I figured they had it under control and stepped away.

I was heating water for breakfast when they all walked back. Bonnie came over and hugged me. "I will get through it, and I am sure that will not be the last time I see something like that in my life," she whispered to me.

"We're here for you. Don't let it eat you up, okay? Talk to us and let us know how you feel," I whispered.

I looked over at Gavin and Nick, and they nodded, trying to smile, and not doing a great job of it.

We finished breakfast and .we had a quick brief about the rest of the trip to my dad's ranch. I discussed our detour around Eureka and the mine on the western side that we would pass by.

We loaded up, and I let Bonnie drive the Humvee to help keep her mind off last night. Once we were at the right turn that would take us around Eureka, and off Highway Fifty, I started giving directions. It wasn't long before we were at the mine on the summit of the hill. The gate was open, and we headed on through. I called for a stop near the mine office buildings. Once the dust settled, we all climbed out of the vehicles to stretch.

As we climbed from the vehicles, an old miner came out of the office. He was probably around 80 years old, wearing a Korean War Veteran hat, dirty old coveralls, and a grey T-shirt that might have been white when he first bought it. He spit a wad of brown tobacco juice on the dirt. "I usually run most folks out of here, though you folks look mighty official with those military vehicles. What can I do for y'all," he asked, looking at our group one by one.

I approached him with my rifle at the low, ready. "Most of us are former or retired military, though we are not official these days. We were passing through and just stopped to stretch our legs, sir. We will be no bother and will be moving along in a few," I acknowledged.

I reached out my hand to shake his. "My name is TJ, and this is part of our ranch security team headed to Ely to help my father, who has a pest problem from a local gang. Not knowing the status of the situation in Eureka, we thought it best to skirt around the town and avoid any conflicts."

"I am Todd, Todd Ockert, and the caretaker of this old mine. Y'all can stay for a while if you want, although I don't think I could really make you leave even if I wanted to. You have some serious equipment there," he smirked.

"If you really wanted us to leave, we would. Is there anything we can help you with, like food, water, weapons, or ammo?" I queried.

"I am good on the first three. I don't have much ammo for my old M1 Garand, though," he said, holding his weathered hands palm up as if to show them empty..

"As a matter of fact, I do," I replied. I walked over to the Humvee and opened the back. Sitting next to my AR-10, I had over 1,000 rounds. I pulled out two ammo cans that held just over 200 rounds each and handed them to the old vet.

He looked like Santa Claus had just dropped off the best gift of all. "Why, thank you, sir. I am very grateful for these and will use them wisely," he declared.

"If we come back this way and have an ammo can or two left over, I will be sure to leave them for you." I lifted my chin and looked past him towards the town. "How are things down there?"

"The town is in good shape. They have a good mayor and city council that are helping everyone survive. They help those who have nothing and make everyone work in the community garden and farm. They brought all the farm animals in close to the town and have security to protect everything," he said, a grim smile on his face.

"On our return from Ely, we might try to pass through the town, though this will be our primary route. If you don't mind us returning this way?" I asked, watching him for his reaction.

"I don't mind you coming this way. Feel free to stop, and we can chat. I don't get many visitors up here, especially now," Todd quipped, with a wry look.

"Thanks for the information, and the ability to pass through again. We'll head off your mountain now, we need to get to my dad's ranch. Stay frosty."

"Have a good trip, and I hope to see you all on your return trip. Again, thanks for the ammo." he said, holding his hand out to shake mine.

I shook his hand, gave him a nod and a salute and then shouted, "Load up, team. We're burning daylight here." As we left the mine, Todd waved at us. I sure hoped we saw him on the return trip and had time to chat about his military experience. All Vets have a story or two that they love to talk about from their time in the service.

Back on Highway Fifty after bypassing Eureka, we headed east toward Ely. We turned off the highway after traveling around fifty miles for the final route to my dad's. I parked in the middle of the road, as I didn't expect any other vehicles on the road today or in the future and climbed out of my Humvee. I waved everyone up to me, so they could hear the conversation with my dad.

"Ely Ranch, Freedom Ranch actual. How do you copy?" I asked. I was about to call again when I heard the reply come through.

"Freedom Ranch actual, we copy, loud and clear."

"We just turned off the main road. Need a sitrep for our plan," I said.

"We're in the bunker. We have eight people here. Our cameras show around twenty-five people on the hills around us and along our security walls. It has been hard to count them all, though. Starting at 12 o'clock, we can see what appears to be a group of four by our security wall. At 12:30 and around 700 yards out is what I think is their base camp. At 2 o'clock, I see two people on the hill acting like snipers. At 3:30 in the ravine, there are four threats. At 6:30, I see another four people in this ravine. The last group at 9 o'clock on the west sidehill, our cameras pick up three threats in a sniper den. Be careful though, I thought I saw some of them moving around in ghillie suits."

As the report came through over the radio, the team had been looking at our topographic maps of the area. I looked at Gavin and Nick. "You guys see anything that looks like you would have a great overwatch position?" I questioned.

"Yes," they both replied, each with a nod of their head.

"I will take this hill to the west of your dad's. I'll take Claire with me so she can eliminate the threat just down from us," Nick said.

Gavin pointed to the hill to the southeast of the ranch. "I will take this hill. It gives me a good view of the ranch, other than their base camp."

"I think I can see their base camp from my position," Nick pointed out.

"Probably won't be an issue, as I want the Stryker and MRAP to come in and level them with their machine guns," I said. "Bonnie and I are Team One and will take the furthest east position. I might need some help with the group on the hilltop, Gavin."

"I can do," he replied.

"Team Two is John and Madison on the hillside on the northwest position. Team Three is Dylan and Skyler, and they will approach from the ravine on the south. Nick and Claire, you have the big hill on the southwest side. Gunner and Isabella will be in the MRAP, and Liam and Tracy you'll be in the Stryker. Everyone has experience with driving the vehicle and the mounted weapons, so you all figure it out," I told them. "We have a couple of hours of daylight left, so let's get some rest, and then we will infiltrate in the darkness. Let's plan on heading in around twenty-two hundred, and if we can kick the hornet's nest at twenty-three thirty, we should catch them flatfooted.

"Sounds like a plan, Stan," a couple of them said, while the rest gave me head nods and thumbs up.

"Figure out a watch rotation of probably an hour each, I don't care which one I have,"

We all grabbed an MRE to eat and pulled out our bedrolls to catch a little sleep. Liam woke me up for my watch rotation. "You have the last watch," he croaked through his sleepiness.

"Thanks, man. I hope you get a little more sleep. I'll start coffee and water for our breakfast pouches before I start waking everyone." He gave me a thumbs-up as he climbed into his sleeping bag. I made a quick trip to a tree and then walked around our area looking for threats. I sure wish Ruffus was here. His ears would hear any threat long before mine.

After the perimeter check, I grabbed the water jug and the stove to start heating water for coffee and breakfast. At about twenty-one forty-five, I started waking everyone up, handing them coffee and breakfast. Despite the fact they were tired, they gave me smiles and head nods when they received their coffee and premade breakfast pouch.

"You all know the routine. Let's get things stowed in the vehicles, perform our buddy checks, and get our war faces on," I announced.

I grabbed my radio to call my dad. "Freedom Ranch actual calling Ely Ranch. You copy?"

"We copy," my dad replied.

"We are headed into our planned positions. Monitor this frequency for the start of the fireworks," I said.

"Ely copies and standing by."

"Let's move it, ladies. Stryker and MRAP teams, head out to your staging point, and when we kick this hornet's nest, you know your targets. Come in hot and eliminate their camp," I said. "When you are at your planned location, call it out."

"Copy," they all said in unison.

I looked at Bonnie and nodded in the direction we needed to go. We had the furthest to go. Team Three and Gavin were following us as we'd be traveling past their kickoff locations.

We had been walking through the trees and brush when Nick called out. "Sniper Team One, in position."

Shortly after that, John called over the radio. "Team Two in position. Ten threats at the camp," he reported.

"Sniper Team One, sitrep," I requested.

"Ravine has four threats. Two appear to be sleeping. Three threats at nine o'clock and all appear awake," Nick announced.

We dropped Team Three at their location and kept moving. We soon dropped Gavin on his hilltop.

"Sniper Two is in position. There are four threats at three o'clock. Two o'clock still has two threats. They appear to be a sniper team," Nick reported.

Bonnie and I arrived at our pre-designated point. "Team One, in position. Vehicle teams, you in position?" I queried.

"Ten-four," they all responded.

"All teams, standby. Ready on my call," I announced. "Ely ranch, you ready?"

"Ely Ranch is standing by on your call," they replied.

"Vehicles, start inbound. We will kick off the rest of the fireworks when you fire your first shot." I received two clicks in response.

I could see Bonnie shifting her weight from one foot to the other. Her finger nervously touching the safety on her rifle, and her breathing came in sharp and shallow, almost like she was holding her breath. I reached over and touched her shoulder. "Remember your training, and you will do fine."

She looked at me and nodded.

As we moved closer to our threats, our NVGs allowed us to see them when we were still about 100 yards out. It felt like the vehicles were taking forever, though I knew they had some distance to cover when they called out. "Contact and engaging."

Bonnie and I jumped up and started running to close some distance to our threats. At about thirty yards, we started firing our AR-15s.

My first couple of shots took the guy on the left, in the center of his back, and ended his life as the gore exited the front of his body. I moved my sights to the second threat, and as I was firing three rounds into his back, I saw a guy in a ghillie suit roll over and pull a pistol.

He was fast—faster than I expected. His pistol came up, and two shots cracked off before I even had him in my sights. The first one punched into me low, just under the vest. White hot agony bloomed in my gut like I'd been lit on fire from the inside out. The second one hit square in the vest, slamming into me like a sledgehammer. I staggered, breath ripped from my lungs, trying to move, trying to bring the rifle up and return fire. But time had slowed, and the pain didn't wait.

Thank God I had a vest on. I was able to get my rifle pointed at him and finally pulled the trigger before he could fire any more shots. I mag-dumped my AR into him and then took a quick look at Bonnie's threats. They were all down and dead.

I could hear the machine guns from the Stryker and MRAP firing at a high rate of speed, and I knew the threats in the camp did not stand a chance against those weapons.

My abdomen was on fire from the bullet wound, and I keyed my radio. "TJ here, I'm hit," I shouted.

Bonnie looked at me with shock in her eyes and stepped over to me. "What do you need?" she screamed.

"Check the threats and ensure they are dead while I grab my IFAK." Thankfully, there was a rock nearby that I could sit on while I examined my wound.

I could still hear gunfire from around the area and hoped that no one else was injured.

Bonnie appeared at my side and saw me pulling up my blood-soaked shirt She grabbed my first aid kit and pulled out the bleed-stop items. "Turn off your NVGs. I need to use a flashlight to check your wound," she muttered.

I closed my eyes to try and preserve some of my night vision, though I wanted to check my wound also.

"Looks like the bullet passed right through your side, and the hole is only about three inches apart," she whispered.

"Did it remove my love handle?" I gasped as she poked my wound and put QuikClot powder on it.

She shot me a shocked look. "How can you joke at a time like this, TJ," she hissed. "Hand me those bleed-stop bandages and the Israeli bandages, and I'll wrap this up. You will have to pull up the rest of your shirt so I can wrap this."

As Bonnie was taking care of my wound, I could hear Gavin and Nick picking off targets with their sniper rifles.

Bonnie looked at me. "Do you have a second Israeli bandage? You're too fat for just one," she laughed.

Now it was my turn to look at her and ask, "Really, you're calling me fat?"

She just laughed at me and grabbed my hand, pressing it to the bandage on my stomach. "Hold the end of this bandage while I wrap it around you. Then you should be good until we can get you to Tracy or Claire."

A different rifle from one of ours rang out, followed by Skyler calling out, "Dylan is hit. A sniper hit him. Find that sniper," she screamed. We heard an intake of breath come over the radio. "Fuck, he's gone. His head is about gone," we all heard her say over the radio.

"Fuck." I hung my head in a silent prayer. I looked at Bonnie, as she had stopped tending to my wound. She had her head down in a silent prayer for our friend. We had almost lost Dylan a while back when he went into town with Mel and a team. You never know when it's your time.

They were team three and working to take out threats on the south side of the objective.

"Where did the shot come from? I need a direction," Nick screamed over the radio.

I grunted in pain as Bonnie wrapped the Israeli bandage around me. "Put that light out. We look like a beacon out here with it on. We will finish this in the dark," I whispered.

"All done. You can pull your shirt down," she advised.

As I pulled my shirt down and packed my IFAK, I said, "Thanks, and good work. Let's move over towards team three," I said, gasping from the pain in my abdomen as I moved. I reached into one of the pockets on my vest and pulled out two Motrin in a single use package. Ripping the packaging open, I dry swallowed the pills, hoping they would kick in soon and help relieve some of the pain. "Ely, are your cameras still working? Give us a sitrep on threats."

"Threats at the camp are out of the game. The sniper den on the eastern hill still appears to be playing. Threats at three o'clock are not moving. It looks like two are still moving at the six-thirty position. Threats at the nine and front gate are not moving," they explained.

"Snipers, you got a shot at that sniper den on the hill?" I asked. "We still have two threats over near Team Three. Can one of you eliminate them?"

Gavin said, "I got what I could. It appears that their sniper and spotter are hiding behind a rock."

"Nothing I can see either," Nick replied.

"I got sights on the two live ones, though they won't be for long," Gavin declared.

I heard two quick shots from Gavin and his 50-Cal BMG.

"Threats down," Gavin called.

"Change of plans, Bonnie. We are climbing the back side of that hill." I keyed my radio. "We are moving to come up the hill behind them. Everyone, keep your heads down, except our snipers. Send a round their way occasionally so *they* keep their heads down," I announced.

"Copy," I heard from everyone.

Bonnie and I backtracked a bit so we could work our way up the hill from behind. Every step sent a fresh bolt of pain lancing through my side where the round had torn into me. We got to the base of the hill, it loomed above us like a silent threat. I leaned against a tree, catching my breath. I wish the Motrin would kick in. I leaned toward Bonnie and whispered. "Go slow. This hill is steep—and I'm not moving as fast as I was. We don't want to give ourselves away."

I could see her head nod as we started working our way up the hill. It was slow going, and about thirty minutes later, we were at the top. I clicked my radio once to let Nick and Gavin know we were at the top. They both sent a round in that direction, and as soon as I heard their round ricochet off into the night, I jumped up to clear the top of the hill, fighting through the pain in my belly. Bonnie was at my side with her rifle up.

Through my NVGs, I could see the sniper and his spotter crouched in between a couple of big rocks. They had a great view of the battlefield below them, though that was going to end soon as I started pulling my trigger, sending 5.56 mm death into their bodies.

Bonnie was firing at the same time, and we each fired five shots into the sniper and spotter, ending their lives.

"Cover me. I am going to check them," I whispered to Bonnie.

I walked up and fired a shot into both of their heads, ensuring their killing spree was done, and splattering their brains onto the hilltop.

I keyed my radio. "Sniper den eliminated," I announced. "Ely, any other heat signatures other than us?"

"Negative. Looks secure," they announced.

As I turned and looked at Bonnie, I could see the first rays of the sun coming up. "Let's work our way to my dad's ranch. We can catch some sleep before we pack this place up."

"Sounds good, though I'm not sure I can sleep after all this excitement," she proclaimed.

"When we come down from this adrenaline rush, we will crash hard," I said. "All teams. Work your way to the front of the ranch. Keep your head on a swivel, though. On second thought, sniper teams. You good to stay put for a little while on overwatch?"

"Copy," they all replied.

"We will get you some relief soon," I announced.

Chapter 23

Mel

There was a quiet knock on my bedroom door. I tried to stretch out, but I couldn't move. Adalinda was sleeping across my throat, with her head lying over my mouth and nose. Ruffus was snoring while he was lying on top of me from my thighs down to my toes. "Jesus, Mary, and Joseph! Are you two trying to kill me?" I mumbled from underneath them.

"Come in and save me, please. My babies are trying to off me."

Gail and Katie ran in and jumped on the bed, bouncing us and freeing me from my captors.

"Good morning, Auntie Mel."

"Morning, sunshine," I said as I wrapped my arms around her, hugging her tight.

She picked up the sleepy dragonette and carried her like a baby, as Ruffus followed them out the door. When the door closed, and I was sure they were gone, I whispered, "Are you ready to catch five little thieves tonight?"

Gail laid down, and covered herself up with my blanket, "Yup. Have you figured out how the tracking spell works so we can follow Ruffus tonight?"

I grabbed the book of spells Joe had given me and showed her what I was working on. "I'm confident we can do this one. It seems easier than the rest and doesn't require scrying."

We got our coffee and went and sat on the porch. Ruffus and Adalinda were chasing each other on the grass in front of the house. Adalinda was giggling while Ruffus gave doggy chuffs that sounded remarkably like he was laughing.

After breakfast, we went our separate ways to get our work done. As I made my way to the greenhouse, I saw Jolene Clean, the next suspect I needed to interview regarding the plant murder investigation. I caught up to her. "Hey, Jolene, do you have a minute? I wanted to talk to you."

"Sure. I was just on my way to the office to do some paperwork for TJ. What's up?"

"A secretary's work is never done. I won't keep you long. Have you heard about the break-ins at the greenhouse?"

"No, I haven't heard anything about any break-ins. I'm sorry. What are they doing?"

"They are destroying some special plants that I'm crossbreeding." I watched her closely for any changes. There was a slight frown, but that was all. Still, it could be enough to prove she wasn't happy that I was trying to create life.

"I'm sorry to ask, but I heard that you were involved with a group that protested laboratories that were experimenting with cloning. If I was genetically alternating plants, would that offend you?"

"I'll be honest, I don't think anyone should be trying to create new species or create a life by cloning. But I would never risk our food sources because of my belief. Our world has changed, and we have to do what we must do to survive, within the law, of course," Jolene explained.

I'd keep her on my list for now, but I'd keep looking. "Thanks, Jolene. Do you have any ideas who may be doing this?"

"Well, if we're looking for someone who may be offended by what you're doing, I would look at Bonnie Claydesta."

That surprised me. I held up my hand to stop Jolene, "Wait, why would a seventeen-year-old want to destroy my plants? That doesn't make sense. What do you know?"

"If anyone would have a reason, it would be Bonnie. Her strong religious beliefs should be obvious. Maybe she sees what you are doing as going against God."

"I guess I could see that; I will speak to her. Thanks, Jolene."

Back in my greenhouse, working with my plants, I reviewed everything I'd learned about who could be destroying them.

Our suspects included Ann Claydesta, who just denied it; Joanne Primm, whom Ann believed was guilty out of jealousy towards those smarter than her; Jolene Clean, once part of an anti-animal cloning protest group; and finally, Bonnie Claydesta. I don't know why someone would destroy a food source. Hopefully, we'd figure this out soon.

When I returned to the house that night, the plan was to go to bed as usual and then follow Ruffus and Adalinda when they left.

Gail, Shelly, Raven, and I met on the porch, ready to solve the mystery of the missing food. Again, we looked like rejects from a mystery movie, dressed all in black. Gail had painted her face with black stripes and was ready to paint mine.

"No way are you painting my face again. I still have black shadows of the makeup I can't get off."

Gail took my hand, "Okay, Nancy Drew, let's do this."

I closed my eyes and felt the tingle of magic bubble up, "*Sequi candentis vestigia,*" I repeated the spell, making my intentions known. "Show us where Ruffus is going, show us his paw prints, illuminate them. "*Sequi candentis vestigia, Illiumare.*"

"Yes!" I whispered, pumping my fist in the air, Ruffus's paw prints were glowing.

Raven fist-bumped me, "It worked. You're awesome, sister."

We quietly followed the glowing prints northeast through the woods, down the side of the hill to a cave entrance. It wasn't too far from the main house.

We had to duck down to enter the cave. Then, it grew into an endless expanse that seemed to go on forever, the ceiling so high we couldn't touch it. The walls of the cave had strange paintings, like pictographs, with numerous intersecting lines that all crossed in one place.

I was shocked to see Katie Adler, Melissa Primm, Noah Toume, Ruffus, and Princess Adalinda sitting around a little ball of fur, playing with her and cooing. Blankets and pillows filled the area, and food and bottles of water sat around the cave walls.

Katie looked up, "Um, I can explain, Mom. Don't be mad."

Gail was ticked off. She seemed to fill the cave with her anger. "What in the name of all that is holy is going on, Katie Alder? Melissa, Noah, Ruffus, and Adalinda, you all should know better. Why didn't you come to us for help? There was no need to steal! Where did you get the cloaking magic that you used to hide from us last night?"

Katie stood and faced her mom, "You saw us last night?"

Adalinda spoke up with a heavy sigh and shot smoke rings out of her nose. "I cloaked us. I wanted to protect the baby. I'm sorry." She hung her head, flew to Ruffus, and sat on his back.

"None of this is Melissa or Noah's fault. It was my idea. I found her lost in the woods, scared and crying. I couldn't leave her. I asked Melissa and Noah to help me take care of her. When Ruffus found out, he wouldn't leave, and then Adalinda joined us. We were going to tell you, I promise. We named her Lucy Bigglefoot."

"How did she get here?" I asked. I didn't think they would know, but I needed to distract Gail. Parts of her body were shifting. Her left arm had changed into a monkey's arm, and her left ear was a huge elephant's ear. Her right leg was a giraffe's leg, and she was standing lopsided. She was so mad she hadn't even noticed. She looked hilarious; we were trying not to laugh, but we couldn't hold it in any longer, Shelly, Raven, and I burst into a fit of giggles. Gail glanced around in confusion then noticed she was on the verge of tipping over. The only thing that saved her from falling was the counterbalance of the weight of the elephant's ear. She shared a little grin with us and then turned to glare at Katie again.

Katie looked relieved at the change of subject, "From what we've been able to piece together, she was with her mom when a bad man killed her mom. Then there was a bright light, and she went through, and that's how she ended up here, lost and alone in the woods."

"How do you know that?" I asked confused.

Melissa picked up Lucy, "Hi baby, can you tell them how you got here."

"Monster, Mama fell, red, mama pushed, in light." Then she patted her chest, "Me, Lucy." My heart broke for the little fur ball. I walked over to Melissa. "May I?" I asked as I held out my hands. Lucy jumped into my arms, almost knocking me over. She made soft cooing sounds as she snuggled her head into the crook of my neck. She smelled familiar. Vanilla and Bergamot, just like my body wash, and sandalwood and amber, which were the same as my shampoo and conditioner. *Oh, that's where that all disappeared too. Oh, well she smells lovely.*

"Where did you bathe her?" I asked

"At the river. We also brought fresh, warm water to rinse her. She loves bathtime," Melissa explained.

Lucy was one and a half feet tall and about twenty-five pounds, with soft, red fur covering her body except her face, hands, and feet. The kids had made a wreath of flowers that she wore around her head, and they'd styled her hair into ringlets. Her bright blue eyes sparkled with mischief, and her long lashes swept her cheeks when she blinked. Lucy had a cute little upturned nose and a sweet smile showing off her four little front teeth.

Lucy was dressed in little shorts and a t-shirt that said *Kiss me, I'm Adorable.*

"Where did her clothes come from?" Shelly asked.

Noah pointed to a neatly folded pile of clothes, "We found the baby clothes in the extra supplies in storage."

"I can sew clothes for Lucy like I did for Adalinda," Raven clapped her hands excitedly.

Gail had transformed back to her original self except for the huge elephant ear hanging from the side of her head. I grabbed her big elephant ear; I just had to see what it felt like. It was as rough as tree bark, and I bet it was heavy. Gail was holding her head at a slight angle, and I'm guessing it was getting difficult to hold her head upright.

Gail studied the little blue-eyed beauty with the intelligence of a veterinarian. She loved all animals; sometimes, I think she liked them better than people.

"In my professional opinion, Lucy's a baby bigfoot. She has all the characteristics that I've read about. The cute little feet that aren't that little are a big clue.

Raven scratched Lucy on her curly head, "I agree with Gail. In my studies, I came across some information about Bigfoot, although I didn't realize they were real. Bigfoot got its name from its enormous footprints. Adult prints are said to be twenty-four inches long. Also, a grown Bigfoot's estimated height is nine to fifteen feet tall."

"Cool, your fun facts come in handy quite often."

"I'm not leaving a baby out here. We'll figure something out back at the house" Gail said while rubbing Lucy's head.

I looked at the kids, "Clean the cave up. Wash the blankets, pillows, and dirty clothes. Then, bring the food, water, and clean clothes to the house. Please." I said as I turned to take baby Lucy Bigglefoot home with me.

When we returned to the house, Carlos and Joe were sitting on the porch having a beer. They both looked at the newest member of our family in awe.

Joe walked to me and peered at my little sleeping bundle, "Hmm, a baby bigfoot. She's a rare beauty. How did she come to join our family?"

"Let's have a seat, and I'll fill you in on what I know."

As I rocked baby Lucy, I shared what we had learned from the kids.

"This is quite a turn of events. I assume Lucy's mom was on her way to fight by your side. When she was attacked, all she could do to protect her baby was send her to you."

"You have no problem with any of this, I see. Why don't you tell us why you think that? Please tell us about the light Lucy went through. The cave drawings—the petroglyphs—were very interesting. What do you know about those?" I asked.

"I'll explain what I can. Let's get little Lucy taken care of first."

I grudgingly agreed.

"Okay, the kids, Ruffus and Adalinda, will need to apologize to Chef C, and as punishment for lying and stealing, they will be on KP duty for as long as Chef C sees fit. He will have them washing dishes, peeling potatoes, and any other kitchen duties he wants them to do. What do you all think?" I asked.

"That's a good punishment, I agree. I know the kid's hearts were in the right place, but they still should have come to an adult," Gail said, nodding.

The house started groaning, squeaking, and making other noises, like rocks grinding together.

"What now?" I asked, as I shook my head.

We all went into the house. I couldn't see anything different until I went into my bedroom. Oh, no. Deep-fried pickles! To the side of the sitting area was an opening to a cave-like room, the perfect size for Lucy, with a place for her clothes and a fluffy big bed.

"Like I told you before Mel, there are going to be more who want to come and fight beside you. I'm sure that was the case with Lucy's mom. The light may be a bit difficult for you to believe, but I promise that what I'm about to tell you is the truth." Joe took my hand. "When the attack happened a month ago, it opened doors, or you could call them portals to other worlds, allowing supernaturals to enter this world. Both good and evil creatures."

I couldn't hold my tongue any longer, "Is this like the Fairy Ring you told us about? That it's a portal to their world?"

"Yes, I told you before, there is a war coming, Mel. You will lead the fight for justice. The four of you will be at the center of it all, but you won't be alone."

"How do you know this, Joe?" Shelly asked.

"There is a prophecy that was written long ago. You four were prophesied to fight a war for the survival of all the worlds."

My mouth dropped open, making me look like a fish out of water. This was unbelievable.

Chapter 24

TJ

My dad, Joel, let us through the fence surrounding his house, or compound, as he called it. As soon as I was through the gate, I jumped out of the vehicle and pulled him into a hug, then introduced our team.

"Sorry about Dylan. We will retrieve his body as soon as possible," he declared.

"Thanks. We all need a place to catch a quick nap. We still have our snipers on the hills monitoring the area. If you have someone good with a rifle, it might be good to relieve them," I muttered, the weariness evident in my voice.

"Let's head inside and get your team into the bunkroom. Ellis, your sister's friend, is a former Army infantry soldier. He should be able to shoot straight." Dad said.

I keyed my radio, "Snipers. I might have one replacement. I will let you know in a few minutes."

They both sent a click back. They were probably too tired to try talking, as we'd only had about four hours of sleep in the last three days.

We walked into the house, where my mother, Moonbeam, was in the kitchen working to make breakfast for us all. I walked over and hugged her. She was wearing her typical sixties hippy jeans. They had holes in them, patches of peace symbols, love, war and embroidery of flowers along the lower portions of the pants. The flare at the bottom could easily hide a cat or be used to sweep the floor if unable to find your broom. To finish the look she had a tie-died shirt that might have been bought in the sixties. Her long gray hair was pulled up into a bun on the back of her head.

"I'll have breakfast done in a few minutes. Biscuits and gravy and some sausage," she gestured at the food.

"Team, grab a plate and eat before we catch a little bit of rest," I said, yawning and sitting down with my plate.

After breakfast I started to head to the kitchen with my plate.

"I'll take care of cleaning the table," Mom declared. "You all go get some sleep."

I looked at my dad. "Where are Damian and Zoe?" Damian my younger brother, could be smart when he wanted, and Zoe, my younger sister, liked bringing home friends like stray dogs and cats. I wondered how many were here now.

"Your brother is watching the security cameras, and your sister, well, who knows," Dad said with a look of unease.

I could tell that these were probably questions for another day. I shrugged my shoulders and headed for the bunkroom. "Team, follow me, and I'll show you the bunkroom. There are plenty of bunks for us, so grab some shuteye."

As we walked through the house, I saw my brother at the security desk, monitoring the cameras and sensors. I sidetracked a little bit. "Hey, brother. Our snipers are still out there. Let them know if you see anything. They are tired and might lose focus while keeping us safe."

"Hey, big bro," Damian said as he turned to look at me. "No problem. I can see them on our cameras."

I found a bed, took off my vest and boots, and laid down. As soon as my head hit the pillow, it only took seconds for me to fall asleep.

It felt like I had just fallen asleep when my mother woke me up.

"It's ten a.m. I wasn't not sure how long you wanted to sleep, but you've been out for five hours," she whispered so as not to wake up the others.

"Thanks. I will get up and help with packing up the ranch."

I went into the bathroom to take care of business and brush my teeth, then I headed out to my dad's receiving area, as he called it. When he'd built his ranch, he'd put in a receiving area like a factory or warehouse would have. That way, he could back up a large semi-truck trailer and load or unload it using a forklift. When they listed the term "Prepper" in the dictionary, they also included his picture.

I saw him running his forklift and loading a trailer. He stopped and left it running with his foot on the brake as I approached. "How did you sleep?" he asked.

"Not bad. I could always use more, in any case. Where is everyone else?" I replied.

"Damion is probably still on the security desk. Your sister is probably in the lower bunker with her friends," he scowled.

"Oh," I frowned, as I turned on my heel and headed for the bunker.

I entered the lower bunker, and my sister and her four friends were lying on the beds. "Why are you all down here and not helping Dad and Mom pack everything to head out?" I yelled. "You know the plan is to leave this place, right?"

If looks could kill, the look on my sister's and her friend's faces when I entered and yelled was priceless.

"We don't want to leave," she mumbled.

"Dad is packing everything. You will have nothing here. You and your friends need to get upstairs and help pack this place up." I glared at them.

My sister, Zoe, was five feet five, 110 pounds soaking wet, red hair. Today, she was wearing a shirt with a marijuana leaf on it that said, "Home Grown is best." Her blue shorts had seen better days.

Her friend Jace stood up and came face to face with me. He was six feet ten and weighed 250 pounds. His white T-shirt had the sleeves cut off, a pocket that held a pack of cigarettes, and gray 5.11 type pants. He had clearly not shaved in a few weeks, and was trying to grow a beard, though it was spotty. Maybe he was using his facial growth to hide his cigarette-stained and rotting teeth.

"What if we don't want to leave? We can stay here if we want to," he said..

"When we leave, no one is staying here," I said. "Get out of my face. Your breath stinks, dude!"

"You wouldn't be so tough if you didn't always have that pistol on your hip," he sneered.

I stepped over, pulled my pistol from its holster and placed it on the table near the door, then stepped back over towards him. "Feeling froggy, dude. Jump," I jeered.

I could see the wheels slowly spinning in his drug-cooked brain when he pulled his right fist back. I let him start his swing, stepped out of the way, and jammed my right fist into his belly with enough force to push him back, and as he was doubling over, I raised my knee into his nose and heard a resounding crunch as it smashed against my knee. He spun around and fell to the floor with blood running from his broken nose.

Zoe jumped up. "Stop, just stop it, TJ," she screamed. "Why do you have to be such a bully to my friends?"

I moved over to the table, grabbed my pistol, and holstered it. "Get your loser friends upstairs and help pack the house, NOW, Zoe. You keep bringing these losers here who take advantage of Mom and Dad," I snapped.

"They're not losers. Just because they like a little marijuana occasionally does not make them losers," she blurted.

"Do any of you have jobs? Where are you, or are they getting your money for your dope?" I hissed.

"None of your business. We work," Zoe said with stubbornness in her voice.

I figured this conversation wasn't going anywhere other than to raise my blood pressure and give me a headache. "Get upstairs and help pack so we can get on the road," I snarled. I'm not sure I really wanted this group at Freedom Ranch. They were probably going to cause trouble for everyone. Mel was not on Zoe's Christmas card list, as she usually told Zoe what she thought of her lifestyle. I would have to find time to talk to Mom, Dad, and the team about them.

As I turned to leave, I saw Jace sitting up. I made a quick move to him, and he raised his hands and jerked away. I laughed. "You all heard me. Get upstairs, or the rest of you might look like Jace," I said.

I went back to Dad's receiving area and approached him as he moved about on his forklift. "Zoe and her friends should be up here soon," I advised.

"What did you do, TJ?" he inquired.

"Nothing that shouldn't have been done a while ago," I laughed. "What is left to pack and load?" I queried.

"The armory is packed and loaded. The storage room needs things put into boxes and pallets so we can load them. Zoe and her friends can pack that up and wrap it with the cellophane wrap so I can load it with the forklift," Dad declared.

"Is everything going to fit in these two trailers?" I wondered aloud.

"I'm not sure. It will be tight. We have some stuff in the kitchen and then our clothing and bedding that your mother insists we pack," Dad said and shrugged his shoulders, as if saying, 'It's your mother, being your mother'.

"We brought a military heavy haul truck. I saw a couple of sets of tandem trailers out along the road. We can grab them with our truck for extra space if you think we will need it?"

"It might be good to grab them. They might have something useful in them, too."

"I will get a team to head out there."

I headed inside the house and found our team, minus Gavin, Nick, and Claire, in the kitchen, eating.

"Hey team. I hope you feel better after some rest. I have a little task for a couple of you. Remember the tandem trailers along the highway we saw. We are going to need a set of those to finish packing up the house here. Gunner. Pick a team to head out and grab one of those sets of trailers. I know we saw some not far from where we turned off the pavement," I explained.

"Not a problem. We'll get it done," Gunner replied.

He grabbed Liam, Skyler, and Isabella and headed outside. He returned a minute later. "Hey, did you forget we left the heavy haul truck over with the Humvees?"

"Crap, I was so tired, I forgot to have someone go get them." I saw John, Bonnie, and Madison sitting there.

"We got it," John acknowledged, as he got up from the table.

I knew that unhooking the dead semi-trucks that were attached to the trailers would take some work, though, but they would figure it out. "Hey John, also grab a couple of people and the MRAP and head over and bring back the Humvees."

I saw Zoe and her friends appear and head for the kitchen. They were probably headed for some food before I put them to work in the storage area. I planned to work them hard, as we still had over a hundred buckets to pack. I also knew Dad had a couple of large freezers that were usually full, and we would take those with us.

After a little while of not seeing my sister and her friends, I headed into the kitchen.

Zoe was yelling at my mother. "Mom, just make us some food. We are hungry."

"Come on, Mrs. B. I know you have some good food here that you can fix for us," Ellis commented as he waved his hands around the kitchen.

Ellis was all of five three and probably 200 pounds. Today, he was wearing a red T-shirt that matched Zoe's with the marijuana leaf on it. The shirt was old enough that I couldn't read the writing on it, though I suspected it had something to do with his favorite drug. His camo 5.11 shorts struggled to stay up around his fat waist.

"Hey, Mom. Head out and help Dad with the food from the storage area. I got this," I snapped. I saw the look of shock on all their faces as they realized I had entered the kitchen. "My mother is not your chef or servant. If you want something to eat, you fix it yourself. What have you been doing since you arrived in the kitchen? Giving my mother a hard time while she's trying to pack?" I asked, my voice low with anger.

"Ah, ah, trying to find something to eat," Zoe stuttered while looking down at her hands as she clenched them.

I opened the refrigerator and found some cold hot dogs and sliced meat along with the typical condiments. I placed them on the kitchen island. "I am sure there is some bread up there in that cupboard," I pointed behind Zoe.

Standing beside Zoe was her friend Constance. She was wearing a black t-shirt draped loosely over her bony shoulders, like she was trying to make grunge fashionable again. Her faded black shorts, frayed at the hems, clung to her hips as if out of sheer loyalty rather than fit.

Constance looked over at me and said, "I don't eat meat. What am I going to eat?"

"Are your arms broken? Open a cupboard or two or even the refrigerator to see what is there. I'm not doing it for you. Figure it out soon, we have work to do," I told her.

As I headed out of the kitchen, I gave a quick head nod towards Jace, and he flinched away. I laughed as I left.

"Jerk," I heard a couple of them say.

As I walked into the center of Dad's compound parking area, I heard Gunner and the team returning. I could see them towing a tandem set of trailers with no markings on them. *What could we have in these*, I wondered. The placard on the side showed explosives.

Gunner positioned the trailers so we could back them to the loading dock as soon as Dad finished loading his trailers. "I have a feeling these will have some cool stuff inside," Gunner said with enthusiasm. "I recognized the placard on the side showing explosives, and the military likes to use unmarked trailers to ship ammo and other cool explosives."

"Let's get these bad boys opened up," I said.

Liam met us at the rear of the trailers with bolt cutters. We had the locks removed in no time, and holding our breath, we opened the doors on trailer number one.

"Holy molly," I gasped as the light hit the inside of the trailer. Pallets with boxes labeled Rocket Propelled Grenades, were piled high. Each crate listed a count of twenty RPGs per crate. Gunner and I jumped into the trailer to count the crates and see what other goodies we had.

"These are a game changer," Gunner exclaimed.

"You could say that?" I said, a shocked look on my face.

"Anyone that attacks us with anything bigger than a standard vehicle, we can use these to change the dynamic of the fight," he proclaimed.

"I get it. I don't plan on us going on the offensive anyplace unless we absolutely have to."

"I get it too; trust me, I do." Gunner grinned. "I also see crates of new Sig Sauer MCX rifles and ammo. I would bet that those are full auto."

"Nice. We will have to restack some of this stuff to get stuff in here from dad's place," I advised Gunner as I headed out of the trailer.

As we moved to the back of the trailer to jump out, we could hear more whooping and hollering from the other trailer. I guess that trailer held more of the same things that we had found in the first trailer.

"What did you find, Liam?" I asked, looking at trailer number two.

"I didn't look at everything, though I did see a couple of cases of BMG 50-cal rifles and ammo, Sig Sauer MCX rifles and ammo, and some grenade launchers. Not sure if the grenade launchers are the handheld style or vehicle mounted ones," he revealed, a gleam in his eye.

"Wow, what a haul. Let me check on my dad and the rest of the house. Hopefully my sister and her friends are working to pack up the storage area that has a bunch of food in buckets. We can pack that stuff on top of this stuff if we need to."

I received head nods from everyone as I headed back inside to check on Zoe and her friends.

I passed the kitchen and did not see Zoe and her friends. I was hoping that they were in the storage area. Sure enough, they were, though, moving the buckets of food at a not-very-fast pace. At least they were working on packing the buckets on the pallets that Dad had positioned here. I saw four pallets completed with about ten buckets per pallet. "I will go get Dad with the forklift to move these to the loading dock," I announced.

"Fine," Charmaine announced. "What are you working on?"

Charmaine stood close to six feet tall, solid and strong like someone who might've benched her problems in her past life. She wore a pink t-shirt that read, 'I was left unsupervised once—just once,' and a pair or gray 5.11 tactical pants marked with what looked like paint ... or possibly lunch. Her red hair was short for the ponytail she attempted, strands jutting out like they had minds of their own.

I was thinking of something meaningful for my retort but then thought better of it. "Organizing the teams for the trip back to Freedom Ranch, we just inspected two trailers we acquired from the road. We needed a couple more trailers to ensure we got everything that we need or can from here," I told her.

I turned on my heel and headed out to find Dad and the forklift. He was in the loading area, and one of the trailers was full.

"Hey, Dad. How's it going? I'll get the guys to move that full trailer, and we can back in one of the ones that we acquired. We are going to have to reposition the contents in both. You'll be shocked when you see what's in them when we open them up," I said, a wry smile on my face.

"Sounds good. Are Zoe and her friends ready for me to move anything yet?" he queried.

"Yes. They've finished four pallets. We will probably have to unload the buckets and stack them on top of what is in the acquired trailers," I informed him.

He raised his eyebrows at me and smirked as I walked away. I was sure he was curious to know what we had found in the trailers.

I found Gunner and Liam chatting near the new trailers. "Hey, guys. Can you move the right-hand trailer and back in one of these?" I asked. "My dad knows he will have to move stuff around in them before we can load anything. He'll work on that as soon as one of them is positioned at the loading dock."

"Sounds good," they said in unison.

I keyed my radio. "Bonnie, Isabella. If you want to meet me at our vehicles, we will top them off with fuel while other things are getting moved around and prepped for our departure," I announced. At the same time, I was also thinking about our snipers. "Snipers. How are you guys doing? Do you need anything?"

"We are good. We have been taking turns napping and watching. Other than you all moving around, we have not seen anything," Gavin said.

"That sounds good, and I appreciate you guys on overwatch," I said, thanking them.

I saw my dad waving me over to him. "What you need, Dad?"

"The second trailer is about done. I probably have two pallets left for it, and then it can also be pulled away and staged for departure. I saw some of what your team acquired in the trailer. Wow."

"Sounds good. I will let the team know. I am going to top off our vehicles with fuel from your storage tanks while we get the last of this stuff packed."

"Good idea."

I detoured to Gunner and Liam as they were getting ready to reconnect the truck to the second trailer. "My dad is almost done with the second trailer, so it can be moved. He was shocked at what we'd acquired. I'm going to top off our vehicles, and we should be close to departure."

They gave me a thumbs up as I headed over to start fueling our vehicles. Bonnie and Isabella were already there. "I'll run the pump at my dad's fuel storage tank. It is temperamental. You two can cycle vehicles to me if you don't mind?" I said as we arrived at the fuel pump.

"Sounds good," they both blurted out.

I should have had someone check on Zoe while I was fueling the vehicles. Oh well. By the time we finished packing here, it would be dark. Did we want to travel in the dark? If we stayed here another night, could we use just the cameras to monitor the area, or should we pull all that stuff down at the last minute?

I keyed my radio. "Hey, Damion. Do you want to take all the cameras and sensors with us?" I queried.

"No, it would take too much time to get them from the hills. We have a bunch packed as spares that we are taking," he advised.

Well, that might make spending the night here easier. I could pull our snipers off the hill and use the security cameras to monitor the area. I love it when a plan comes together.

"Earth to TJ, earth to TJ," Bonnie blurted at me while also poking me in my ribs.

"Oh, hey. Sorry, I got lost in thought on the plan for the trip back to our ranch. What's up?"

"This is the last of our vehicles, and while we were waiting for you to manage the pump, we checked your dad's trucks. They are all full," Bonnie informed me.

"Great, and thanks for doing that. I was thinking about whether we could leave tonight or first thing in the morning," I told them.

Isabella spoke up, "I think we leave in the morning. That way we can see trouble coming, and we all can get some rest before the long drive back," she stammered.

"You are correct. We are all tired and could use some rest before the long drive back. Good call, ladies."

"Snipers, work your way down to the compound. Brother, please stay focused on the cameras and sensors. Once everyone is here and everything is packed, we will have a team meeting," I announced.

"Copy," they all responded.

I headed inside to find my mother and ensure that she had not packed all the food from the kitchen. We would need stuff for dinner and breakfast. In the worst case, we could eat Mountain House food pouches.

On my way to the kitchen, I saw Zoe and her friends working in the storage area. A quick detour revealed that they only had about a pallet's worth of buckets to load. Well, there might be hope for them yet. John was there helping and trying to motivate them to work faster. He was clearly outworking all of them.

"Hey, Mom. I hope you haven't packed everything from the refrigerator yet. I think we'll spend the night here and leave at first light. My team is tired, along with everyone else here," I advised her as I wiped my sleepy eyes and yawned.

"No, I have stuff left. I was hoping someone would make a sound decision on when we would be leaving. I like that decision and can support it," she consented while also yawning.

I headed back out to the dock area to see Dad backing the forklift out of one of our acquired trailers.

"Last load," he announced. He shut down the forklift and hopped off it.

I could see the bags under his eyes and knew that he was tired. I turned around and saw John standing there with a smile on his face. "What are you smiling about?"

"I had fun running herd on your sister and her friends. About the time they thought they could sit down and wait for your dad and the forklift, I took them out to the trailers to stack buckets since we had to do that anyway to make room for everything," he said while smirking.

When I looked at Zoe and her friends, they were all sweaty and dirty from handling the buckets and pallets and sending daggers with their eyes. I grinned and turned back to the group. "I made the command decision that we will leave in the morning. That is the best alternative for a couple of reasons. First, we can get some rest before we depart and have a long drive back to Freedom Ranch. Two, we don't know what we will find along the way back to the ranch. Let's try to go through Eureka with these trailers. The route over the mountain that we took on the way here has some sharp turns, and I don't want to get one of these trailers dumped over the side of the hill," I stated. "Mom has food left in the kitchen. It is every man and woman for themselves in there." The last part was so Mom could rest and not work over the stove to feed us, and Zoe and her friends knew they had to fend for themselves. If I was honest, I'd rather not eat my mom's cooking, it always left something to be desired.

Everyone agreed, though I heard some disgruntled tones from Zoe and her friends.

We ate, took hot showers and were about ready to climb into our bunks when I called out to John and Gunner.

"We need to set a watch rotation for security at the cameras. Damion can show everyone how to use them. I would say to include Zoe and her friends; however, I would not trust them to remain awake and alert us to any danger. Include me on the rotation."

"Good call, we'll get it done," John announced.

It felt good to get a hot shower, clean clothes and climb into a bed after the long couple of days that we had had. I sure wished it was my bed at home with Mel, though. My eyes closed as soon as my head hit my pillow.

Chapter 25

TJ

John woke me up around zero four hundred to let me know it was my watch rotation. I felt like my head had only just hit the pillow.

"I have some coffee in the kitchen for you. See you in a few minutes, buddy."

"Thanks for waking me. I will be there in a couple of minutes."

I sat up, rubbed the sleepiness out of my eyes, and headed to the restroom to take care of my morning business.

I entered the kitchen, smelled coffee, and saw hot water on the stove. "Coffee smells good. Breakfast pouches?" I asked.

"Figured the pouches would be the quickest, and your dad has buckets of them," he advised. I nodded in agreement.

"He is a diehard prepper. Go get a couple more hours of sleep. I will wake everyone around zero six fifteen and try to be on the road by 0700. I think Zoe and her friends will be our roadblock to a quick departure," I advised.

John just raised his eyebrows at me and turned and left the kitchen for me to eat in silence.

I was headed for the loading dock area when I saw Isabella sitting at the security station. "Have you been here a while, or are you just coming on?" I inquired.

"I got here about thirty minutes ago," she said between yawns.

"I'm going to take a quick walk outside, and then I will join you to keep you company."

"Thanks, I could use the company to keep me awake," she mumbled.

I headed outside to check on our vehicles and get some fresh air. After a quick lap around the edges of the compound, I saw nothing out of the ordinary, so I headed back inside.

I sat down next to the watch station and Isabella. "How are you doing? This has been a rough trip," I said, looking over at her.

"I'm doing all right. Gavin and Nick have been talking to me. We talk about what we have had to do to survive since the EMP. They also talked about what they had to do to survive in Iraq and Afghanistan. None of it is pretty, and it messes with your head a little bit." She sighed as she quickly glanced at the cameras and sensors.

"So that you know, I'd never had to kill anyone until the EMP. The first was while John and I were on our way back from the Rubicon. A guy was on a bridge, stopping traffic, and wanted to take our Jeeps. John shot him, and one of the guys there was Billy. Billy took us to the location where this gang was hanging out and had his family locked up. John and I eliminated six gang members. I have lost count since then. Sometimes, I have a hard time sleeping. I guess if it didn't bother me, then something would be wrong with me. If we like the killing aspect of what our world has become, then there is something wrong with us. You can talk to any of us. Gavin, Nick, and Carlos had counseling when they returned from their overseas deployments and understand the physiological aspects better than most of us," I explained. "I am going to start waking people up so we can take care of our morning business, eat, and pack the last few things so we can hit the road."

"Sounds good," Isabella sighed as she turned back to the monitors.

I headed into the bunkroom to start waking people up. I was going to wake John up last, he hadn't been down for long. I headed over to Zoe's room to wake her and her friends up. I was not looking forward to this group. I knocked on her door and then tried the doorknob. It was locked, so I knocked even harder.

"Wwhat," I heard from behind the door.

"Time to get up and get ready to leave this popsicle stand," I proclaimed.

I didn't wait for a reply and headed upstairs to the kitchen. "Good morning, Mom. Everyone will be here soon. John got us all breakfast pouches. Fast easy, and no dishes when we are done," I said, as I waved my hand over the coffee pot and pan of water.

"Appreciate him taking charge and making life easy for this momma. I was not looking forward to making breakfast," she sighed.

"John can be a forward thinker like that. Glad he is my friend," I announced.

"Is that all I am, your friend?" John asked as he walked into the kitchen.

"Ah, ah. You are more than a friend."

"Just messing with you, buddy. Have to keep it loose around here so we don't get too uptight and uppity," he grinned as he came in for a hug.

I turned around and saw a grumpy Zoe behind me. "What are you fixing for breakfast, Mom?"

Before my mother could reply, I grabbed a breakfast pouch and put it in front of my sister. "Bon appetite," I said, as I smirked and pointed to the hot water.

"Really, this is all we have? I don't like them. I think they taste like cardboard," she complained, as she pushed the packet away.

"I think you have these confused with MRE's sis. Those can taste like cardboard. When they do, add more hot sauce. These don't need as much hot sauce." I laughed.

Constance pushed her way to the counter. "Do these have meat in them? You know I don't eat meat," she explained.

"Let me see. Nope, no meat, though it does have red dye number 9," I laughed. "Eat up, buttercup. We are burning daylight."

Zoe and Constance ate in silence, barely touching their breakfast pouches as their eyes stayed fixed on me—sharp, unblinking, and anything but friendly.

Once we'd finished eating, we headed outside. "Everyone remember your vehicle assignments?"

"Yes," everyone chorused.

We got onto Highway Fifty and headed west. I asked Bonnie to drive so I could get out quickly if we had trouble. Our convoy had Bonnie and me leading in the Humvee. My dad was in one of his trucks, then the Stryker, Damion driving another semi-truck, John in the other Humvee, Liam in our heavy haul truck with the tandem trailers, and Gunner in the MRAP bringing up the rear.

The plan was for Liam and me, with the Stryker and Humvee, to separate ourselves from the convoy and approach Eureka to see if we would be allowed to pass through the town. The others would hang back out of sight until we gave them the all clear, and then they would approach.

Every plan is great until you have first contact. That happened when Liam and I arrived at the barricade at the city limits sign for Eureka. Six vehicles blocked the road, and it appeared that five people were on guard duty.

I keyed my radio as we rolled up to their blockade. "Leave me room to back up if this goes sideways," I announced to Liam in the Stryker.

"Copy."

I wished I had Gavin or Nick with me in the Humvee. I knew my sister could shoot, as I had seen her handle a pistol and rifle at times on the range. However, it had been a long time since I had seen her shoot. "Hey, sis. When was the last time you went to the range?"

"Oh, probably about four years ago when I went with you, Mom, and Dad on one of our visits," she informed me.

I grabbed my rifle from the storage location and press-checked the action to ensure I had a round in the chamber. "If bullets start flying, just start backing up. This thing is armored, so we are good," I reminded Bonnie and the others.

As we rolled to a stop, a tall, obese guy with black cargo pants and a black shirt that held a badge in the right pocket, stepped out with his left hand raised. He was wearing armor, though I think it was struggling to cover any part of his wide girth. His baseball cap said police on it, so I was hoping things would go well, especially since we were in military vehicles. He had an AR-15 on a single-point sling, and he had his right hand on the rifle. He looked a little tense, probably because he could see that someone in the Stryker was manning the machine gun. That thing just looked menacing sitting there.

I opened my door and stepped out, positioning my AR-15 in the low-ready position. "Hello, officer. Can we pass through your fine town? We are escorting some equipment through to the armory in Reno," I elaborated. I did lie a little bit, well maybe a lot. I wanted our convoy to sound official.

"We will have to inspect it first to ensure you are not hauling any contraband," he said with a laugh.

I wiped my hand across my face, knowing this was not going to go well. "This is government property, and you don't have the authority to inspect this cargo," I said with a sneer.

"Well, Sonny, if you haven't noticed, there is no government since the world went to shit," he snickered.

I took a deep breath. "Why don't you go and get your mayor and Chief of Police, and we can discuss this simple matter," I insisted with a little louder voice. Thankfully, we all had battle dress uniforms that we had all bought prior to the end of the world. None of us had rank insignia, and if he questioned me on that, I would tell him we were a secret unit that hauled special cargo around the country.

"I am the Chief of Police and the Mayor, so you have to deal with me," he replied, his voice a high-pitched whine.

"Well, Chief. Just let us pass through. We need this equipment in Reno to help defend the country from foreign invaders." I was trying to play to his duty to uphold the Constitution and patriotism.

He tilted his head back and laughed. "You all must have some important equipment. Now I think I really want to inspect it and maybe charge you a toll to pass through my town."

I could see his guards behind the cars getting fidgety and moving their rifles closer to their shoulders. "Chief. Two thoughts for you here. One, if you think you can hold us out of your town, you are a sorry officer of the law. If you look closely, you can see that we have some serious equipment here that can cause a lot of damage. Two, if your guys back there continue to be restless and pull their rifles up, my guys here in this Stryker will open up with that 50-cal. Those cars won't do them any good as cover." I scowled at him.

About that time, I heard Gavin in my ear. "TJ, Nick, and I are in a good position to see most of the town. He has snipers on the rooftops along the main street. I see probably ten of them. We also have a small team getting into position with a couple of RPGs."

I clicked my radio mic once in acknowledgment. "Well, Chief. I think we have a little standoff. My team is ready to pass peacefully, and as I said earlier, I will and can leave dead bodies in your town. I would prefer not to, though, if you continue to play games ..."

I took a couple of steps back, got closer to the rear of the Humvee, and keyed my radio. "Send an RPG on a car to show that we have some heavy firepower." I laughed at the chief. "You might want to move yourself and your people. You're about to get a quick demonstration of our capabilities."

"I think you're bluffing," he hissed.

"Fire One," I said into the radio. An RPG came out of the tree line from behind me and hit a car a hundred and fifty yards from him and his team. The heat from the blast was enough to knock us back a step or two. "Do I have your attention now? Put down your weapons, pull your people back, and let us pass."

The look of shock on his face was priceless. His security guys were putting their weapons down on the vehicles. "Nick, what are his snipers doing?" I asked.

"They are still in position. Want us to take one or two out as a message?" he answered.

"Negative. I would rather not leave any dead bodies behind unless we have to," I whispered. I could see the wheels moving in the fat boy's head. "What's it going to be, chief? He gulped a few times. "Still not letting you through."

I figured I would try another approach, so I yelled at his guys behind the cars. "What do you guys think? Should the Chief let us pass, or should we use him for target practice with our 50-cal?"

One of the guys I could not see yelled back. "He shot our regular chief of police. He is just a fat bastard on a power trip who thinks he can run this town with a fat iron fist."

"Shut up," he yelled at whoever was talking. "I will come back there and kill you myself if you don't shut the fuck up."

I'd had enough now after hearing that conversation. I pulled my rifle up, put my red dot on his fat head, and pulled the trigger. The round from my AR made a neat hole in his forehead and removed most of the back of his cranial and brain material in a red and gray mist that covered one of the cars behind him. He was dead before his body hit the ground for a dirt temperature check.

I keyed my radio. "Watch the snipers on the roofs. If they shoot at us, take them out," I hissed. I yelled at the guys behind the cars. "Come on out with your hands up. If you have a way to communicate with the guys on the roof, let them know they are in the sights of our snipers and the Stryker. They are to put their weapons down and back away from them."

The guy who had spoken earlier, called out. "I have a radio. I can tell them your instructions."

"Come out here so I can see you. Do not reach for a weapon. Are we clear?" I hollered.

"Crystal," he shouted.

He came out from around the car with his hands up. He was a tall, skinny guy with short blond hair, wearing a black 5.11 shirt and pants. I could see the radio hanging on his belt. "Slowly bring your hands down and get your radio. If I see you reaching for a gun, you are a dead man. Got it?" I snarled while looking over the top of my rifle.

"Y-yes," he stammered.

I watched him slowly bring his hands down and grab his radio. "Hey, guys. Put your rifles down and then back away. They have snipers watching you, so don't do anything stupid, please," he drawled into the radio.

"Bonnie, Liam. Let's search these guys once we get confirmation that the guys on the roofs have backed away from their weapons. Claire, man the fifty and shoot anything that needs to be shot," I muttered into my radio microphone.

"Copy," they all replied.

"TJ, rooftop snipers have laid down their weapons and are backing away from them," Nick informed me.

"Copy." I watched the group behind the cars. Bonnie and Liam were soon at my side, and we moved in to search the guards for weapons. Other than a couple of knives, no other weapons were found. I walked back to the guy who had been talking to us, and I asked him, "What's your name?"

"Cliff, Cliff Roberts, sir," he stuttered while trying to look around for our other team members.

"Morning Cliff. Here is how I would like to play this. Does the fat guy have any close friends that will be pissed that I killed him?"

"He has kin in the area, me included, though we are cousins a couple of times removed. I don't think anyone will be too upset that he has been removed. He always wanted to be the Chief of Police. He tried going to the academy but could not pass the physical due to his weight," Cliff laughed at his last comment.

"He is a ... or was a big boy. He knew where the chuckwagon was, that's for sure," I said, with a shake of my head.

Cliff just laughed again.

"Is there any leadership left in town?" I inquired.

"I am sure there is, though they scattered to the wind when Dean there took out the chief of police and the mayor three days ago," he described. "You are probably going to ask how Dean removed the Chief and Mayor. He was friends with them, as his family had money, and he asked to have a meeting with them in the Mayor's office. He ambushed them and killed them both. Then, he appointed himself as Chief of Police and Mayor. He has two close friends who are probably at the police station now. Donnie and Billie are his cling-ons, and they follow him around and do what he tells them. In return, they get drugs and booze, and now probably women. We have a couple of single ladies missing," Cliff sighed with his last statement. "He won't let anyone into the police station, so I am sure the women are there. Can you help us?"

"I need to ask my team," I replied. Stepping away so I could call the team together. "Pull the rest of the convoy up here," I announced over the radio.

The rest of the team and vehicles arrived shortly after at our location. "Snipers, remain in position. We have a couple of possible bad guys in the police station. If you can get eyes on it, please do and let me know what you see," I urged them.

"Copy," they both replied.

When everyone else arrived, they got out of the vehicles. Cliff was shocked at the number of vehicles we had with us.

"Gather up. Here is the deal. The dead fat guy appointed himself chief of police and mayor. The previous ones are dead due to that fat garbage pile. He has two friends in the police station that we need to remove, and they might be holding women hostage to use as slaves. Cliff, move a couple of these cars and the dead Chief, and we will take a Humvee and the Stryker down there to remove them from the police station," I said. "Do you think they will listen to you if you ask them to come out?"

"They might listen to me," Cliff hedged, while rolling his eyes.

"If they don't come out, John, Bonnie, Isabella, and I will be stacked up on the door. We will enter and give them their eviction notice," I explained. "Keep everything else here and stay alert." I saw Cliff looking at Bonnie and Isabella. "Cliff. Don't underestimate these two young ladies. They have been training with us and have seen enough action to know what will happen when we enter. I would let them have my back anytime we are headed into a tough situation. They have been well trained." I winked at both ladies as I headed to the Humvee.

When I got back into the Humvee, I remembered Zoe and Constance in the back seats. "Zoe, Constance. Get out and stay with the team here. We need to finish saving this town," I told them as I waved my hand in a get-out motion. "You know what, never mind," I said as I changed my mind, "stay there." I keyed my radio. "John, Isabella, get in the Stryker. My back seats are full."

"Copy," they both replied.

Cliff had the remaining guys at the blockade move the vehicles and Dean so we could pass with the Humvee and Stryker. He followed us on an old Yamaha 250 cc motorcycle that smoked badly and sounded like the piston was going to come through the top of the cylinder any minute as he revved it while going down the street.

We stopped a couple of buildings away from the police station, and the breaching team exited the vehicles. I pulled the team over to discuss our strategy. "Cliff, you knock on the door and then get out of the way. If they crack the door open, we will bum-rush it. If they don't open it, let's hope it's unlocked, and we can enter. John and Isabella, you go first and right when you enter. Bonnie and I will go left. You see a gun on them, shoot to kill. Questions?" I asked.

"None." John gestured. "Let's roll."

Cliff knocked on the door. "Donnie, Billie, open the door. Chief wants you at the roadblock ASAP," he yelled.

"What is going on? We heard an explosion a little bit ago," one of them replied.

"Someone threw a pipe bomb at us and attacked. The chief shot a couple of them. We need help, though; Joey is hurt," Cliff responded.

"Ok, we will be out. We need to lock up the girls first," one of them said.

The door unlocked a moment later and I grabbed Cliff and moved him out of the way as John hit the door, Isabella stacked up right behind him. Bonnie and I were moving and went to the left. We were a well-oiled machine performing this breaching. Once inside, I saw the guy who must have been unlocking the door on the floor. John had his rifle pointed at him and was yelling, "Don't move, dirtbag. This is not a game."

As soon as Bonnie and I entered to the left, I saw the second guy standing there with his mouth hanging open near the door to the cell area. He reached for his pistol and Bonnie and I both fired two shots at him, center mass. The four bullets entered almost the same spot and exited out his back in a red gore. He looked at us like he could not believe that we had shot him. He collapsed to the floor, leaking the rest of his body fluids on the tile.

Cliff entered the police station and saw the mess as the gun smoke curled in the air. He pointed at the one who was still alive and under John and Isabella's guard. "That's Donnie," he drawled.

"The dead one must be Billie?" I asked. They were both dressed about the same with dirty wife beater t-shirts that had not seen a washing machine since the lights went out and frayed blue jeans. Billy had on cowboy boots with the soles ready to fall off. Donnie had some old work boots on that had no tread left. I could smell their unkempt bodies through the gun smoke still hanging in the room.

"Yup. Neither are very smart. Dumber than a box of rocks," Cliff mumbled.

"We are not. Just been down on our luck, is all." Donnie grunted out with John's boot on his back.

"Bonnie, let's clear the back-room area." I headed to the door leading to the rear of the police station. I grabbed the doorknob and twisted, opening the door.

Bonnie was stacked up behind me as we entered the booking room and cell area. I was hoping we would not see the atrocious things we did in Austin on our way to Ely. It was dark as we entered the cell area, and I turned on my tactical light on my rifle hand guard. I saw the young ladies in the cells standing there. A few of them had welts on their faces and torn clothing, and they looked scared as Bonnie and I cleared the area. I finally spoke up. "We will get you out of here in a minute. We are not here to hurt you or take you away from here."

Cliff found the keys to the cells and entered to unlock the cell doors. "Hey, ladies. Dean is dead, along with Billie out front. These nice folks helped us retake our town. I hope these idiots didn't hurt you too much?"

One of the ladies was tall and had red hair. She was well put together and wore blue jeans with holes in them and a black T-shirt that said, 'In my previous life, I was a Navy badass. ' Right after Cliff unlocked her cell, she stepped out and slapped Cliff across the face. I thought she was going to turn his head all the way around like an owl.

"What the hell, Julia?" he whined as he brought his face back around to look at her.

"That is for not protecting us and letting that fat bastard lock us up. He and his two minions raped a couple of the girls. They knew I was too mean, and they left me alone. How come you didn't do anything to take the town back?" Julia asked, while jabbing her finger in Cliff's chest.

"He took all our ammo for our guns. All we could do was throw them at him if we wanted to do anything," he rambled while looking at the floor. "Sorry, cousin, for not being able to help you all."

"Tracy and Claire. We need you to go down to the police station to check out the women we rescued. Team, drive all our vehicles down this way so our medics don't need to walk," I called over the radio. "After our medics get here, they will check out the ladies, and once they are treated, we will need to get out of here. Can you all handle the town now? Find a few more people like Julia here to help run the town. Use your military leadership skills and manage this like a big team," I said. "I would love to sit and talk Navy with you, Julia but we are trying to get home today. We have a ranch near Minden and have been gone for a while."

"We can handle the town now that the trash has been taken out," Cliff declared. I could see the wheels moving in his head, as that was not what I had said to Dean at the roadblock.

As I walked out of the police station, I keyed my radio. "Everyone meet here in the middle of town. We will move on down the road after Tracy and Claire check out the ladies in the jail. Then we will stop for lunch outside of town."

While I was waiting for the rest of our team to arrive, I spoke to Cliff. "Do you have anyone in town with a ham radio? If you do, I will leave you the frequencies that we monitor, and we can check in once a week."

"We do have an older gentleman that has some old ham radios. His name is Del, I'll get the information to him so we can remain in contact with you all," Cliff said.

"Great," I replied as I headed to the Humvee to get a piece of paper and pen to write the frequencies down for Cliff. It took me a few minutes to find the paper and pen. Once I was done and climbed out of the Humvee, our convoy was rolling up. I also saw Nick and Gavin walking out of different alley's and headed our way. "Great job, guys. Let's get loaded up and blow this pop stand when our medics are done inside," I urged.

I shook Cliff's hand and looked at Julia. "Nice to meet you. Keep this town cleaned up."

She must have noticed the Senior Chief anchor on my Navy uniform. "Be good out there, Senior Chief. I would tell you what I used to do, but then ..." She laughed.

"Be good and take care of this town. Before we go, what do you have for weapons around here?" I inquired.

"Mostly hunting rifles. A few people have AR-15s, though not many," she replied.

"I might have a gift for you," I replied with a smirk.

I walked over to my dad. "What trailer has the Sig rifles and ammo?"

"There is some in both. We spread it out. Why?" he inquired.

"We are going to leave a couple of the rifles here along with some ammo," I told him.

I walked to the back of the first trailer and opened the rear door. I could see the boxes with the rifles and ammo. I climbed inside and opened a crate with the new rifles. I figured they had more 5.56 mm ammo than some of the other calibers that Sig Sauer made. I pulled out four of the rifles and a couple of cases of ammo.

I yelled at Julia. "Hey, Julia. Come on back here and bring someone with you. We have a gift for you and the team here."

When she walked around the back of the trailer and saw what I was pulling out, she gasped. "Where did you all get these? Oh, never mind, I don't want to know. Thank you. That will make defending this town so much easier." She pulled a rifle up, pulled the bolt carrier back, verified that the rifle was empty, checked the red dot optic after she turned it on, and sighted at a far object, handling it like a pro. She looked like Santa Claus had just come early this year.

"Enjoy the new toys. We need to head home to our families," I said with a grin as she continued to handle the new rifle like it was a baby.

I circled my hand over my head, indicating for everyone to load up and head out.

Chapter 26

Ruffus

"Come on, Ada, we need to go check on Lucy. She is probably hungry this morning, and we need to hide one or two of our little hoomans on the trip to the cave. It's not like we can feed her," I said while holding my paw up for Ada to look at. My little dragon friend did not like mornings.

"Can't you just go without me?"

"No. You have that witchy, voodoo stuff that can hide us in plain sight. Now, let's go. The little hoomans will be waiting for us behind the bunkhouse. Plus, I am hungry and need to stop and see the kitchen wizard for a snack." My stomach growled at the mention of food. I was waiting at the door for her as she fluttered her wings and headed over to me.

"Oh, yeah. Maybe he will have my favorite. Pancakes. Those things are so delicious, and so light and fluffy, just like a cloud. He is a snack master, that is for sure."

We headed down the stairs out of the house, with a detour to the kitchen wizard. I was so glad he was here, I didn't have to eat that kibble they put in my bowl. Yuck. That stuff looked like little rabbit turds. I had never eaten rabbit turds before, though TJ had pointed them out to me, and I had smelled them. They didn't smell good either, and that was about what the kibble in my bowl smelled like. Life was so much better with the kitchen wizard here. Entering the bunkhouse, the aromas coming from the kitchen wizard's work area were almost mesmerizing, and I knew I would be in a food coma soon. I could smell the bacon and hear it sizzling on the griddle. All I cared about was the bacon, though he would throw an egg or two on some potatoes, and breakfast would be served. Adalinda was not a fan of the bacon, though so I would take hers if she turned her head away long enough. I had let the kitchen wizard know that she

255

loved his pancakes, and he always seemed to have one ready for her. I don't know how he did it, though I didn't care about the how, just about what I got. We devoured our food and headed outside to find our little hoomans. Rounding the corner from the front doors of the bunkhouse and near the greenhouse, I saw Katie, Melissa, and Noah all standing there and fidgeting as they waited for Adalinda and me. Katie was the most nervous and was shuffling her feet back and forth. I ran up and sat in front of them to get some head scratches, and they didn't disappoint. I could see that the little hoomans had some food and other stuff for our new little bigfoot friend.

"You ready, Ada? Do your witchy stuff." I said, then asked her, "how do you know it's working and the others aren't able to see us?"

"When I cloak us, I can see waves in front of us, that is how I know it's working. Let's move along to the cave and our little Lucy."

"This is so cool. Wish I could do stuff like this," Katie whispered. "If we talk, can they hear us?"

"I'm sure the adults could if we were close enough," Adalinda responded and shushed everyone.

We made our way across the grassy field and knoll and then down the side of the hill above the river to the cave. As we entered, I could hear baby Lucy crying, so I jumped ahead of my hoomans to check on her. She was lying in the little bed that Katie and the others had made for her and crying. I could see the tears running down her little cheeks. When she saw us, she put her little arms out to be held by one of the hoomans. Katie ran up to little Lucy, who jumped up to be held, almost knocking Katie over in the process. It was funny, and I snorted. Katie gave Lucy the milk they had brought, and they all watched as she quickly finished the milk from the bottle and let out a little burb. Well, maybe a big burp.

Ada started flying around the cave while Lucy chased her. It was funny watching Lucy try to jump and catch Ada, though they made me tired just watching them. My hoomans were laughing and giggling, watching the antics of the two in the cave.

"We need to head back so we are not missed," Ada said. "Who is staying here to watch Lucy? We will come back around lunchtime with more food."

"I will stay," Katie replied.

"I'll stay with her too," Noah announced while looking at Katie.

I looked at them both, and I am sure they had googly eyes for each other. I nosed Ada. "We need to keep an eye on those two."

"I will find a way to cover for you two while I am back at the house. Take care of our little Lucy while we are gone," Melissa said.

Ada, Melissa, and I left the cave and hiked up the trail to the top of the hill. Ada sat on my back and held onto my collar while we walked back to the bunkhouse. On our way to the bunkhouse, I saw my momma Mel walk into her greenhouse. We went around the back of the bunkhouse, so we could avoid the greenhouse. Ada uncloaked us once we were there.

"I'm headed to see the kitchen wizard again. All this walking has made me hungry," I complained, as my stomach grumbled.

"Me too," Adalinda quipped.

"Me three," Melissa concurred.

Adalinda and I went inside the bunkhouse to see the kitchen wizard and check the menu for the afternoon. Have I mentioned how much I adore that man? "Hey, kitchen wizard. Ada and I are back, and we are hungry. What you got for us?" I queried.

"I always have your favorite, bacon, and for Adalinda, I have some pancakes. I know you two love those two food groups," Chef C exclaimed.

"Oh man, you are the best," I commented as I snatched the multiple pieces of bacon from his hand. He placed a pancake on a plate for Adalinda, and she quickly devoured it. I wandered around the bunkhouse and then the house looking for TJ, and then I remembered that he was away with a rescue team. I found a spot on the porch in the sun to take a nap and lie down. Ada joined me, and we curled up to rest. I don't know how long we had been napping when the screen door slammed shut, and I jumped up, ready to attack whatever it was. As the sleep cleared out of my eyes, I saw Shelly standing on the steps. Sorry you two. I didn't mean to interrupt your nap. She reached down and scratched the top of my head. I relaxed my attack posture and wagged my tail in appreciation of the head scratches.

"Come on, Ada. Let's find a quiet place to finish our nap," I said as I left the porch and headed back to the bunkhouse. Walking into the bunkhouse, I saw Joe sitting next to Mamma Mel, and they were chatting about something and laughing. It was good to see her laugh, especially with TJ away on a rescue mission. I headed over to them to see what they had on the table to eat. Something sure smelled yummy in the kitchen area. I walked up, placed my head on Mel's lap, and looked up at her with my sorry eyes. It worked most of the time when she had food and usually resulted in me getting a treat off her plate. Today was no different, and I think it was beef pot roast. After I quickly devoured Mel's bite, I placed my head on Joe's lap and worked the same magic on him.

Oh, yum, that was so good. These hoomans are so predictable, I thought as I licked their hands clean. Now it is time to visit one of my favorite hoomans here, the kitchen wizard.

"Hey, kitchen wizard? Do you have any of that delicious meat left?" I could almost take this stuff over bacon any day. No, bacon was the best. I soon had my fill of the wonderful beef pot roast that the kitchen wizard had prepared. I was so full that I thought my belly was going to pop. I might as well take a stroll past the little hoomans for a couple of head scratches and snatch some more food.

"Adalinda, where are you? I need another nap to let this food settle, and then we can find the little hoomans to go feed Lucy when it is dark," I told her.

"Sounds like a plan, Stan," she replied and then giggled.

We headed to the main house to nap on the porch again, though I sure hoped no one slammed the door again. I needed my beauty sleep. I was going to give them something in their shoes while they slept to remind them to leave a sleeping dog alone.

I heard Mama Mel and her ladies walking and chatting as they came our way. I sat up, rubbed the sleep out of my eyes, and nudged Adalinda to look alert as our hoomans arrived. Mel stopped to rub the top of my head.

"Good boy, Ruffus. Thanks for keeping the boogers out of the house," she said.

"No problem, Mama Mel. That is why I'm the attack dog here." I headed upstairs with Mel and Adalinda getting ready for bed. I hopped on the bed and curled up at the foot of the bed, and Adalinda curled up with me.

"You two stay down there, will you? I don't like it when you lie on top of me," Mel complained.

I picked up my head to look at Mel and shook it back and forth, then put my head back down on my paws and closed my eyes. I knew Ada, and I had to meet the little hoomans a little after dark to take care of Lucy. I heard Mel snoring away and nudged Adalinda, saying, "It's time to go meet the little hoomans."

"Can you go? I'm so comfortable here and warm."

"Again, you have to do that witchy voodoo stuff to hide us as we walk to the cave," I reminded her. "Move your scaley little butt, and let's go."

I crawled off the bed, hoping not to wake Momma Mel. We made a beeline for the back of the bunkhouse to meet Melissa. She had food and other things for Lucy, and we were soon headed to the cave with Adalinda cloaking us. When we entered the cave, I could hear Lucy giggling. She was playing with Katie and Noah, running around the cave as they chased each other. I ran inside to check on what was causing all the giggling and laughter. "Looks like you'll are having fun. We brought more food," I said.

"We are having fun," Lucy said. "They were keeping me busy, so I don't miss my mother as much."

We all gathered around her to comfort her, and Katie wiped her tears away. Lucy climbed into Katie's lap and hugged her, and it seemed like the world was right. We were sitting there feeding Lucy and playing with her when I thought I heard a rock or something out on the trail. I started to move to the entrance to check on the noise when I saw Momma Mel, Gail, Raven, and Shelly entering the cave, hunched over. Oh, this will not be good. I sat down and pulled my ears close to my head, ready for the yelling to start. Katie turned her head and gasped when she saw her mother just inside the cave. "I can explain, Mom. Don't be mad."

"What in the name of all that is holy is going on, Katie Jane Alder? Melissa, Noah, Ruffus, and Adalinda, you all should know better. Why didn't you come to us for help? Where are you all taking food from the house for this little creature? If you were, there was no need to steal. Where did you get the cloaking magic that you used to hide from us last night?" Gail yelled.

I listened to them, loudly talking, as they discussed Lucy, the food, and other items that we had brought here to help baby Lucy. Things eventually calmed down, and Momma Mel grabbed baby Lucy and headed out of the cave with the other adults. That had gone better than expected as I lay down to rest while the little hoomans picked up the stuff in the cave. They soon had everything ready, and we headed back to the house. When we were near the house, I could see Mel and Joe talking, and then they headed inside. Joe was out late tonight. It was like he knew something was up and had stayed around the ranch.

Adalinda was on my back when I went inside, and we headed upstairs. When we walked into our bedroom, I noticed a new addition to the house. A cave-like feature had been added, and baby Lucy was curled up in the little bed. Joe and Mel were talking, and I could feel the tension coming from Momma Mel. I walked up and sat next to her and leaned into her leg to get her attention. She rubbed the top of my head and ears, and my tail started racing on its own across the carpet on the floor. Joe left after they chatted for a few more minutes, and Mel headed to change for bed. Why did hoomans have to change for bed?

I climbed up on the bed and stretched out, placing my head on Mel's pillow, while Adalinda curled up on TJ's pillow.

Mel entered the room and saw us relaxing. "Hey, you two. One of you will have to move off a pillow. I need a pillow to sleep."

I gave a fake snore as she climbed into the bed and moved Adalinda, then she put her head down, letting out a sigh as she relaxed.

Night all.

Chapter 27

TJ

We had made such good time running along Highway Fifty, that it wasn't long before we rolled up to the top of the pass outside Austin. I keyed my radio.

"Same plan we had in Eureka. Liam in the Stryker, and Bonnie and I in the Humvee, will head down the hill to see what's waiting for us. I hope since we cleaned up this town the first time through, nothing bad is waiting."

Headed down from the top of the pass into Austin and clearing the last sharp curve, I could see a roadblock of dead vehicles across the road. I could see four people behind the vehicles, and I also caught a reflection from a scope on top of one of the buildings.

"Snipers on the rooftops," I informed the team.

Rolling up to the roadblock, Bonnie stopped the Humvee about forty feet from the vehicles. I recognized Doug from the earlier trip through town, he was still wearing his Desert Shield baseball cap. He waved as he came between the vehicles to approach us. I climbed out of the Humvee to approach him.

"Hello, Doug. How have things been in town since our last visit?" I queried.

"Been great. Everyone is working together to secure the town, work in the fields, and help the town survive. We have a policy of, if you don't help, no food for you," he grinned. "We did have one family that wanted to test that rule. They quickly found themselves outside the borders of the town, on their own."

"It sounds like things are going well, then. We are returning from Ely with my parents and headed home. Can we pass through?"

"No problem. We can move these two vehicles, and you can pass. I will relay this to the team on the other end of the town so they can let you through."

I keyed my radio, "No issues here. Come down the hill. We will be ready to roll when you get here," I communicated to my team on the top of the hill.

"Good job having snipers on the rooftops. I spotted them when I caught a reflection from one of their scopes. We have a couple of new rifles that we will leave with you that will eliminate that tattle tale.".

"What do you have for us?" Doug asked, as he leaned forward slightly, interested to hear what it was.

When the trucks arrived, I opened the trailer holding the rifles and the box containing the new Sig Sauer MCX Spear rifles. His eyes went wide like saucers when he saw the new rifles and the optics on them. I pulled out six rifles and then handed down around three thousand rounds of ammo. "Give these to your snipers. There is enough ammo here for them to train with them a little bit. Their optics gave them away. These new optics have all the cool Gucci stuff on them for no reflections," I said as I handed down the rifles.

"Man, thank you so much," he said with enthusiasm, as he checked out the new Sig MCX rifle. "What a gift. Thank you again."

"Use them wisely, and keep your town under control," I advised Doug.

"We will, and we have a good group that is leading the town. Our primary concern is keeping everyone safe and working together," he said, as he looked at the town around him.

"We need to get moving. We still have a lot of miles to go before we get home, and it will probably be dark by the time we get there. Take care," I said.

We shook hands, and I headed for the Humvee. He had the vehicles moved out of the way so we could pass through, and I waved to the folks manning their western barricade. Then we continued down the loneliest highway in America. At Sand Mountain, we turned off Highway Fifty to follow the Pony Express Trail around Fallon. We were kicking up a ton of dust that could be seen for miles. "Everyone, keep your head on a swivel and call out anything suspicious. We can be seen for miles with the dust cloud we are generating," I warned as I watched the area around us. Thankfully, no shots came our way from the hills along the trail. We soon passed Highway 95 and Alternate 95. That meant that we were getting close to Freedom Ranch. When we turned off the Power Line Trail, I keyed up the radio in the Humvee to see if I could contact the Ranch. "TJ calling Freedom Ranch, you copy?" I announced over the radio.

I was getting ready to try again when Katie replied. "Freedom Ranch, calling TJ. We hear you loud and clear," she replied.

"Good to hear your voice. We are about 20 miles from the ranch. It will be good to be home," I said.

"It will be good to have you all back. I will let Chef C know so he can have dinner ready for you all," she told me.

Food from Chef C would taste even better after this trip, as we had been eating nothing but packaged food. I could hear the excitement in her voice. I wondered what kind of trouble Mel and her team had gotten into while we were away. I pondered over that though the remaining miles to the ranch.

As we pulled up with our convoy, I saw everyone from the ranch at the front of the bunkhouse welcoming us back. Mel was right up front, a sight for these sore eyes.

I keyed my radio. "Welcome home, team—job well done. Park the vehicles near the bunkhouse, and we will worry about unloading them tomorrow," I advised the team. I would, however, ask my dad if the generator that was running to keep the freezer cold with Dylan's body, would last through the night.

Before the Humvee had come to a complete stop, I jumped out and ran to Mel. She ran at me too and jumped into my arms for a hug. We hugged and kissed, and she whispered in my ear. "You stink, mister. I will help you shower before you eat," she commented, a gleam in her eye and slight smirk on her face.

Ruffus was running around me, sniffing me, and sneezing. "I know. I probably stink and have lots of dust on me," I said, while I tried to rub the top of his head.

"I will take you up on that offer, though I have a question for my dad. Follow me while I find my dad, Love," I said to her as I headed to find my dad. I held Mel's hand as I searched and finally found my dad.

"Hey, Dad. Will the generators stay running to keep everything cold and frozen," I asked.

"Not sure, though I will add some fuel after dinner," he declared.

"One last thing, sweetheart, before we head to the house," I pleaded with Mel, as I stepped up on a fender of the Stryker.

"Everyone gather around, please." When I had everyone looking my way. "Great job by the team we took to Ely. Sadly, we lost Dylan in a firefight over there. We brought his body back, and we will have a funeral tomorrow for him. I think we will bury him overlooking the river, as I know he loved fishing in the river. Please lower your head in a silent prayer for his peaceful entrance to God's hands." With that, everyone bowed their heads in prayer.

After a moment's prayer, I looked back up. "Thank you, see you all soon for dinner." As I climbed down from the Stryker, I had tears in my eyes, and Mel hugged me tight. I then remembered my bullet wound that she did not know about. Well, she would soon see it and probably have a fit. As we were walking to the house for a shower, I figured I should tell her before she saw the bandages.

"I was shot also while in the firefight at Dad's," I whispered to her.

She stopped and looked at me with worry in her eyes and slapped my arm. "Where and why did you not radio that back to me?" she yelled. "You should tell me these things, you know. You could have died, like Dylan, and I would never see you again. You are never leaving the ranch again."

"It is but a flesh wound," I said quoting Monty Python to Mel. Ruffus followed us to the house as we walked, rubbing up on me and sniffing me. Once in our room, I stripped out of my gear and clothes while Mel started the shower for us. When I stepped in, I swear there was mud running down the drain. The hot water felt good on my body. Once we were out of the shower, Mel checked out my wound and wrapped it with fresh bandages. Afterwards, we dressed and headed back to the bunkhouse. My mouth was watering for some great food from Chef C. While walking up to the bunkhouse. I could smell the BBQ cooking something, and Matthew and Albert handling the grill duties. I detoured to check out the grills with Ruffus at my side with his nose in the air. "Something smells good there, boy," I said, as I scratched Ruffus's ears.

He gave me a little bark, as if to say, "You bet, Dad."

"What we got on the grills here, guys?" I queried as I sniffed the air.

"Steak, and vegetables from the garden," they said in unison. "James probably has a special treat also."

"Yum," was all I could say as I walked into the bunkhouse. The food aroma in the kitchen made my mouth start watering. I looked over at the steam rising from the pies that James and Cassie had prepared. *I'm going to be in a food coma soon*, I thought to myself.

I looked at Mel with a gleam in my eye. "I am going to go grab a couple of bottles of wine from our cellar. I think with those great steaks out there, we need to pair them with a nice wine," I said, as I smiled at her.

"That sounds good. Any idea what you are going to bring up, though with this crowd, you might need more than one or two bottles." She laughed, as she released my hand so I could return to the house for the wine.

I headed into the house and downstairs to our wine cellar. Quickly searching the multitude of wine racks, I found what I was looking for: Niner Winery, 2015 Fog Catcher, a great red blend. One of our favorite wines from our days in California. I grabbed four bottles and quickly returned to the bunkhouse so I could decant them.

Chef C saw what I had brought out and commented. "Excellent choice to pair with the steaks, and the little bit of spice that I added to the root vegetables will go nicely with that wine."

As we sat down to eat, Isabella asked, "Can I say a prayer prior to our meal?"

"Of course. It is always welcome," I said, gesturing at her to go ahead.

"Dear God. Thank you for this fine meal prepared by the team here. We are preparing to use this food to nourish our bodies and minds. Pray to remind us of Dylan's passing and that he did not die in vain as we successfully rescued TJ's parents and family friends. In God's name, we pray. Amen."

"Amen," we all replied.

"Great prayer, Isabella," Matthew commended his daughter.

We dug into the food on our plates, enjoying another fine meal with family and friends. I had poured wine for everyone to enjoy during our meal, and as we started our meal, I paused. "If I could have everyone's attention. I wanted to toast having everyone here—also, a moment of silence for Dylan and the loss of him to our family. Raise your glasses—to Dylan."

After dinner we headed outside to enjoy the evening air. As I looked at the group of people we had here, I knew we would have to do something with the bunkhouse so everyone could sit down and eat or relax.

The kids had asked if they could have a bonfire and s'mores. I looked at some of their parents and got nods of assent. The kids soon had a fire going, taking a little chill off the air.

I was deep in thought when Joe sat next to me on the log beside our fire pit.

"What are you deep in thought about, TJ," he inquired.

"Two things, really. The first thing is what we are going to do for beds for all these people. Currently, the Army tent and cots work. Before winter, we have to find a better solution. The second thing is that we are running out of space inside the seating area in the bunkhouse," I said, revealing my thoughts to Joe.

"We could find a mobile sawmill," he suggested, "and build something off the front of the bunkhouse." He pulled out a twenty-year-old bottle of scotch and held it up. "Here, take a snort of this, it will help you think better," he laughed. "I am glad you all made it home safe, though I am sorry about Dylan's loss. I liked the kid, and he had a great head on his shoulders."

"Thanks, Joe." I tipped up the bottle to take a shot straight from it. "Wow. That is smooth. It's a shame I'm drinking it straight from the bottle," I exclaimed.

"Figured tonight was as good as any to share this with my friends and family. You all, are my family, TJ."

We sat there for a while, contemplating life, staring into the fire, lost in our thoughts.

Mel interrupted my thoughts, "Ready for bed, sailor man?" she gestured as she pointed to the house.

"Yes, my love," I proclaimed as I pulled my tired body off the log to head to the house.

I squeezed Joe's shoulder as I departed. "See you in the morning, Gunny."

"Goodnight, Senior Chief," Joe replied.

Chapter 28

TJ

I woke up with Mel snuggled up to me, Ruffus on the other side of me, Adalinda lying across Ruffus, and the sun coming through the window. How long had I slept I wondered. I knew it would be a sad day as we buried Dylan, though I wondered about the rest of the day. I worked my way off the bed, though Ruffus gave me his usual early morning look, which told me he had to do his business, too. He was not too excited to get up and leave Mel. I watched Ruffus stretch as he worked his way off the bed and headed to the door. I headed to the bathroom to take care of business. As I walked out, I heard a growl from downstairs. I grabbed my pistol and headed downstairs, taking steps two at a time to see what had caused Ruffus to growl. As I reached the last step, I could see Ruffus with his ears back, lips pulled up, and the hair standing up on his back. I could see Jace lying there in front of the door that Ruffus wanted to go through, and Jace was stopping him. Ruffus heard me and turned his head, and I could see the anger in his eyes. He never relaxed his ears, and as I got closer, I could hear the low rumble in his chest, which was a warning to Jace.

Jace looked at me. "What is up with your dog?" he grumbled from being woken up.

"He wants out, and you are blocking his door. Why are you lying in front of the door to begin with? You might want to get out of his way, or he might move you," I muttered through my early morning fog. "He is highly trained, and being a killer is one of his better traits."

"I—" Jace was about to say something when Ruffus snarled, showed his teeth, and moved closer. "None of your business," he said like a teenager.

Jace tried to push Ruffus away, but Ruffus grabbed his arm between his teeth and started pulling him like a large chew toy.

Ruffus had only just pulled on his Jace's arm, dragging him, when I yelled, "Stop."

A sharp cry escaped Jaces lips, "Owww."

They both looked at me, and Ruffus kept Jace's arm in his mouth.

"Get up, Jace, and let him out. Ruffus, *'oust.'*" Ruffus released Jace's arm, and as soon as he was clear of the door, Ruffus pushed his way through the doggy door and headed outside to do his business.

Jace was rubbing his arm, and I could see he had a little line of blood running from a puncture wound from Ruffus. "Next time, you might not be so lucky. He is a trained dog and has killed someone before. He could have broken your arm with a shake of his head. Oh, one last thing. Just because you heard me use the command to release you, he is trained to only listen to a couple of people, and you are not on that list, I said, shaking my head. "You will need to see the medical personnel this morning for the puncture wounds on your arm. Again, why were you sleeping in front of his doggy door?"

Jace looked at me and was probably thinking of something to say when Ruffus came bounding back through the doggie door. He stopped long enough to give a little nip to Jace, who jumped back. I laughed at Ruffus's antics. Ruffus looked at me, and I was sure I could understand this thought about Jace.

"Not funny," Jace hissed.

I just laughed and headed to the kitchen to make some coffee. As the coffee was brewing, I heard footsteps coming down the stairs, along with the padding of Ruffus's claws. I headed to the front door, and heard Joe arriving on his ATV, so that gave me a pretty good idea of the time. I wonder what his shirt says today. As the coffee finished brewing, Mel was there with cups for us, and I heard John and Shelly coming out of their room.

"Hey, everyone. I hope you all slept well," I inquired.

"Better than I have been lately, as the bed is softer than the ground we have been using," John said, as he sighed.

I looked in the living room and saw Zoe and her friends still crashed out. Jace had found a place out of the way. Ruffus was sitting with us, getting head scratches and treats from his treat canister.

"Zoe's friend Jace found out that Ruffus does not play when he is on a mission. Ruffus just about took his arm off when Jace thought he could block the door. Ruffus snarled at him, and when Jace went to push him out of the way, Ruffus took hold of his arm and was about ready to shake his head, but I stopped him. Jace has some puncture wounds in his arm, so he needs to see Gail in the clinic this morning," I explained.

When I looked at Ruffus, he looked at me like I had tattletale on him to Mom. I reached down and scratched his head. "Good boy, Ruffus. You put Jace in his place."

Ruffus gave me a little bark that I was sure was a way of saying thanks.

"Now that this pot of coffee is finished, let's head to the bunkhouse and see what kind of wonderful food Chef C has for us this morning," I urged. Without waiting for a reply from the others, I turned and headed out the door to the bunkhouse. The moment we were outside, Ruffus and Adalinda took off like rocket's for the bunkhouse. "That dog has a one-track mind," I blurted out.

"Just like most men," Mel and Shelly exclaimed at the same time.

John and I looked at each other and shrugged our shoulders.

As we got close, I could smell the sausage cooking in the pan. "I sure have missed Chef C's cooking," I said, as we walked in the door. My mouth was watering.

"Me too," John stammered out, probably around the drool coming from his lips.

"Sausage, eggs, hashbrowns. James has made some fantastic cinnamon rolls for a sweet end to breakfast," he said, with a smile. Breakfast will be on the buffet here in a minute."

I could see a couple of the children helping him finish cooking breakfast and moving serving dishes to the buffet. "Thank you, Blake, Katie, and Melissa, for helping Chef C with breakfast," I commented to the children.

"We love helping Chef C. We learn how to cook, and we get first dibs on food when it is done," Katie gushed at the accolades being handed out.

I finished my breakfast and stood to get everyone's attention. "Morning, everyone. I don't want to ruin anyone's breakfast, though I would like to have a funeral for Dylan between 1100 and 1200. It depends on how long it takes us to dig a grave out on the hill overlooking the river."

"I know what Dylan liked to eat the best," Chef C said, "so I will make a meal in his honor. I will also work with James and Cassie to make his favorite dessert."

"To make the digging easier, we can use your backhoe," Joe said before hanging his head in a silent prayer.

"Thank you, Joe, for handling that sad chore," I said, hanging my head in sadness.

"There is enough lumber back there to make a nice casket," Albert informed us.

I knew he was a fantastic furniture maker and knew he would make a great casket for Dylan. "Finish your breakfast, and when you are ready, Joe, I will bring the backhoe over, and we will find a wonderful location for Dylan's grave."

As everyone finished, I headed outside and sat at one of our picnic tables. I don't know how long I had been sitting there when I felt Mel tap me on the shoulder. "Earth to TJ, earth to TJ, come in, Major TJ."

"Oh, what, sweetheart? Sorry, I was thinking about Dylan, and it is hard. I knew we could lose people; I did not think it would be like this," I commented as a tear ran down my cheek.

Mel wrapped her arms around me and held on tight, her voice soft against my shoulder. "TJ, I know how much it hurts losing Dylan. I remember how broken I felt the first time we thought he was gone. And now ..." she trailed off, her breath catching. "Now it's final. I feel it too. We all do."

She pulled back just enough to look me in the eye. "Matthew and the rest of the deputies headed out with the backhoe. They've got the grave handled. They *wanted* to do it—said it was their way of honoring him. Their way of saying goodbye." She gave a sad smile, brushing her fingers lightly down my arm. "You don't have to carry everything, not today."

I nodded, swallowing hard, my throat raw.

"And hey," she added gently, resting her forehead against mine, "like you always tell me—don't sweat the small stuff. Right now, we just need to be here for each other."

"You're right ... again," I whispered, the tears finally slipping free. "Let's sit a while—before the funeral starts."

I soon heard the backhoe returning, and Mel and I sat there in our thoughts with our arms around each other. Around eleven hundred, Albert came out and got the attention of Matthew and Russell. They all headed into the shop. When they came out, they headed my way.

"TJ, we are ready for the procession out to the grave. Albert made a fantastic casket that would make a king proud. We have everyone in the shop, and we have the casket with Dylan in it on John's trailer. John is going to drive it out there slowly, with all of us following," Matthew disclosed.

"Sounds good. We will join the procession as you pass," I said, my voice sounding tired.

We joined the procession as it passed, and we all followed the Jeep and trailer to the grave site. Matthew and his fellow deputies acted as pallbearers and carried the casket to its final resting place.

Before lowering the casket, Matthew placed Dylan's badge over his heart. Matthew and the rest of the deputies then placed their badges on the casket. They picked up the ropes and lowered the casket into the grave. Matthew spoke about Dylan's career with the sheriff's department and how he was always willing to help around the ranch to keep everyone safe. He was a great friend to everyone and will be missed by everyone. A few people stepped up and talked about Dylan. I knew I had to say something, as he was on our team to Ely. I stepped up to the head of the grave.

"This is hard. It was my responsibility to bring everyone back alive, I failed in that single mission. We all knew the risks, though, and Dylan probably knew that better than most of us. He was always willing to do anything for the team, and did, never with a complaint. Rest in peace, Dylan. You will be missed." With that, I stepped away from the grave.

When no one else had anything else to say, Matthew stepped up and spoke again. "We will take care of filling in the grave. Thank you all for coming. I know Chef C has something special for lunch planned. See you all there."

We all started making our way back to the ranch, and Mel and I walked with our arms around each other, knowing that life can be short sometimes. As I looked around at the group that attended the funeral, I noticed that Zoe and her friends were absent—something to talk to them about later on. *Way to make an impression sis*, I thought on our walk to the house.

When we arrived at the bunkhouse, Chef C was the first to enter. "Lunch will be ready in a little bit. I have a few final preparations to finish. I should be done about the time Matthew and the team arrive. We will eat when they arrive."

I knew Dylan liked tequila and figured I would get a special bottle out in his honor. I had some Cierto, Private Collection, Extra

Anejo Tequila that I would pull from my collection to share with everyone tonight.

I saw Matthew and the team arrive back from Dylan's grave and walk into the bunkhouse. Chef C came out and announced, "Lunch is ready. In honor of Dylan, his favorite meal was Chile with extra meat, cornbread, and, for dessert, pineapple upside down cake."

When I walked inside, Matthew and the deputies were in line to get their food first, as they should be. Dylan was a close friend and partner with these guys prior to the world collapsing. I was sure they were taking his death hard.

Matthew saw me and motioned for me to head outside. "Hey, TJ. Dylan knew the risks when he left with you guys. His loss will have an impact on all of us here, everyone liked him so well. As a deputy, he knew the risks, and he was part of the SWAT team, so he was well aware of the risks. Don't let it get you down or into a bad place. Remember the great things he did here for our team. We will all go at some time, and this was his time. I am sure he is looking down on us and wishing that we all remember the good times we had and not dwell on his death. Now, let's eat and enjoy his favorite food group. We might want to remain outside for a while after we eat," Matthew grinned as we headed back inside.

"Thanks Matthew, I needed that pep talk," I said as I clapped him on the shoulder.

When I got back inside, I could smell the chili and cornbread. Ruffus was circling everyone like a hawk over a field full of mice. "I hope no one has given Ruffus chili. If you did, he'll be sleeping with you tonight."

A few of the children hung their heads. Oh man, it was going to be a smelly night with Ruffus.

After lunch, we all helped clean up the kitchen and headed outside. We sat around listening to Matthew and the other deputies tell some of the pranks Dylan had pulled on fellow deputies and the pranks that were pulled on him.

When the sun set Chef C announced that he had freshened up the chili for dinner and had bowls ready for everyone. Sitting back out around the fire pit with a fire roaring, and finishing up our chili, I pulled out the tequila that Dylan enjoyed. I passed the bottle to Russell, "Start the process on this bottle in Dylan's honor, please," I announced. I'd had a few sips in Dylan's honor when Mel grabbed my hand and dragged me off to the house.

"Let those guys finish that bottle in his honor. Give them some space, and let's go to bed."

"Night all," I announced as Mel and I departed the fire pit arm in arm.

Chapter 29

TJ

I woke up with the usual suspects snuggled in close, and I could not roll over to get comfortable. "I might as well get up," I mumbled, "these bed hogs aren't going to give me any space to continue sleeping."

Ruffus picked up his head from the pillow and turned to look at me. I swear, I could hear what he was thinking. *Get up, pet. I need more room and my beauty sleep.* He pulled his paws up and rubbed his face as I wormed my way from between the three of them. Once clear of them, I left the bed and headed to the bathroom for my morning rituals and got dressed. As I was opening the door, I whispered to Ruffus, "Want to go downstairs for treats?" I figured he would also need to go outside. He jumped off the bed and jostled Mel and Adalinda at the same time. I heard them both mumble something unintelligible, but then they were snoring before Ruffus was at the door. I thought of waking Mel up, though she would argue that she needed her beauty sleep. She was gorgeous, and if she never got any more sleep, she would be beautiful well past old age. Down the stairs we went, with Ruffus leading the way. Passing through the living room, I saw Zoe and her friends sleeping on the couch and floor. Ruffus paid them no mind as he headed for the door, and I detoured to the kitchen. I could smell the coffee and knew that John was probably up and around also. Our women loved their sleep.

"Morning, John. How late did you stay up last night with the guys?"

"We left right after you two. I am too old to try and hang with them young bucks," he declared.

"On a different note, tomorrow is the Fourth of July. We need to plan something. The new picnic area along the river could be a good way to break it in," I declared, with a grin.

"I like it. We can fix up burgers and dogs, and we have a BBQ down there, that way we can give Chef C a break."

As we poured our coffee, I heard Ruffus growl at something. We headed for the door, and I grabbed the AR-15 I'd left in the corner. Pushing the door open and press-checking the action to ensure the rifle was loaded, I reached the porch. It was still dark outside. I clicked the tactical light on and saw a bunch of eyes glowing back at me. I told Ruffus to back up as I moved away from the door, I knew John would be coming out the door any minute. I heard John's footsteps as he came through the door and made his way to the porch and next to me.

He clicked his weapon light on and whispered, "What the hell are those things?" He gulped from his shock at seeing these strange creatures.

"I don't know, buddy. I wish Mel and the girls were out here. I think those things might be from another world or something paranormal."

The eyes twitched and blinked in chaotic rhythms—flickering on and off like faulty bulbs in a nightmare. My chest tightened. Each set of eyes locked onto me, and a cold dread spread through my veins. My skin prickled, heart hammering like it was trying to escape my ribs. I couldn't stop staring, couldn't breathe, as sweat beaded along my brow, hot against the icy grip crawling up my spine.

Ruffus was at my side, and his growling got louder as the eyes moved closer. I had my rifle up and ready. When I looked at Ruffus again, his body had changed. He now had the head and talons of an eagle, and the back half of his body looked like a lion.

"If they get to around twenty-five yards away, let's start shooting," I urged with a shaky tone to my voice.

"Yeah, sounds good," John gulped as he replied.

I heard the porch door open and heard Mel, Shelly, and Adalinda on the porch. Adalinda flew up to us and sat on Ruffus. She made a strange, guttural low-pitched noise that I felt rumble through my body, then spat a fireball at the eyes. I figured it was as good a time as any to start shooting at the eyes. John and I were firing our rifles, and Adalinda was shooting fireballs from her mouth. Our rifles appeared not to affect the creatures when Shelly yelled, "John and TJ, get down."

We dropped to the deck and Shelly used her magical powers, flinging rocks at the eyes. Mel was chanting something that I could not understand, and what looked like tree roots were circling and attacking the creatures. Ruffus took off with Adalinda and started attacking, using his talons and beak to rip the creatures apart. As the creatures died, the light slowly faded away as it left their eyes, and they disappeared. Ruffus and Adalinda finished off the last creature as a team. When I could no longer see its eyes, I got up and headed over to Ruffus. Mel and Shelly followed along. My weapon light was still on, and as I approached, I could see these dog-like creatures, though their heads appeared more cat-like, while the rest of their bodies appeared like a mix between a dog and a wolf. Their fur was a gray color, and their tails were long and bushy. When we were about five yards away, they all just melted into the ground, leaving a slime behind.

"That was weird," I muttered to Mel, who was next to me. Ruffus returned to his normal appearance. I looked at her, "Would you mind telling me what the hell just happened?"

"I am not sure, really. They should not have been able to enter the ranch, as we've placed wards around the property. The wards are supposed to protect us and let us know if something paranormal has crossed the boundary lines."

I looked at her like she was speaking Greek or some other foreign language. "What is a ward or whatever you called it?"

"They are special crystals that we placed at the four corners of the property, designed to keep out paranormal creatures," Mel explained while waving her arms around.

"I guess they didn't work," I harrumphed.

"Don't get uppity with me, mister. Your guns didn't work either," she grumbled, her eyebrows pulling down into a frown.

"Our guns work on living creatures," I hazarded a guess, "so they were most likely non-living creatures." I reloaded my rifle and slung it over my shoulder. "My coffee is probably cold now. We can talk about this more inside." I turned and headed back into the house, with everyone following me inside.

"You head back to bed, sweetheart," I said, looking at Mel.

"I don't think I can sleep after that excitement."

We entered the kitchen, and I grabbed Mel and Shelly a cup of coffee. "Oh, another thing. What did Ruffus turn into out there? He was terrifying with the head and talons of an eagle and the body of a lion." I sat on a chair at the large kitchen table and sipped my cold coffee.

Mel leaned forward, her eyes locked on TJ's. "This is the first time he's changed in front of us," she said, her voice low but intense. "I always knew he had some kind of edge—something beyond normal—but never guessed the full extent. His paranormal form is a Gryphon." She let that sink in, then gave a small, almost reverent shake of her head. "When he transforms, it's not just showy—it *amplifies* everything. Strength, speed ... instincts. He's a force." She finally took a slow sip of her coffee, like the weight of what she'd said needed a moment to settle.

Shaking my head, I raised my hands in defeat. "I'm changing the subject because I have no clue about the paranormal stuff, though you'll have to fill me in. I was talking to John about our Fourth of July celebration down at the river tomorrow. I figured we could have burgers and hotdogs, and some of us guys could man the grill and give Chef C a break. We can break out all the games and, in the evening, have a big bonfire down there," I suggested.

"I like it."

Matthew and Russell entered the house wearing their vests, helmets with NVGs and rifles ready to go to battle. "What were you guys shooting at a minute ago?" he asked.

"You probably would not believe me even if I told you the truth," I sighed.

"Try me," he said, between heavy breaths.

"We had these strange creatures out there that Ruffus detected. They had cat-like heads, and their bodies were a cross between a dog and a wolf. Our rifles had no effect on them, and it took Mel and Shelly's magical powers to defeat them." I shrugged.

"You been drinking all ready? I don't believe you, there is nothing dead out there."

"That is the other strange thing: after they were killed, they sunk back into the earth and left this slime-like substance behind for a few minutes. Then the slime disappeared also." From the look on their faces, I knew they did not believe me.

Russell looked at John, skepticism on his face. "Is he telling the truth, or has he been hitting the bottle all night and just thought he would touch off a few rounds this morning?"

John grinned, "God's honest truth."

Mel and Shelly put down their coffee cups with a grin on their faces. "Some of us have figured out that we have magical abilities. We haven't told anyone else, we're still trying to understand our abilities." Mel sighed. "We will have to share what we know with the team here, so if someone does see us do something, it doesn't scare them."

"Who else has these powers that you mention," Matthew asked.

"Obviously, Shelly and me. Raven, Gail, Joe, Carlos, and Ruffus," Mel said, while wringing her hands as she detailed them. "Oh, we think Chef C also has powers due to his ability to create some fantastic meals when we have few, if any, of the ingredients that he's used."

"He is pretty magical in that kitchen, I must say," Russell commented while rubbing his belly.

"We might want to start physical training more often," I said. "Speaking of Chef C, I am sure he is working on breakfast as we speak. Let's finish our coffee and head on over."

Approaching the bunkhouse, a tantalizing aroma of sweet and savory smells wafted from the kitchen, promising something absolutely delicious.

"What smells so delicious in here that it has my mouth watering so much that I could fill a gallon jug in a matter of minutes?" I asked, walking over to Chef C.

"I have prepared a spinach and ham souffle on top of hashbrowns. James has created a special sweet treat of brioche, a buttery, slightly sweet bread that's perfect with jam or honey," Chef C announced with an air of greatness and a wave of his arms.

"How soon before it is ready for us to devour, or should I start on my arm first as an appetizer?" I simulated chewing on my arm to show my desire to eat soon.

"Stop it, TJ. It will be ready when it is ready. You can't rush perfection." Mel smiled as she slapped my arm away from my face.

I headed to the coffee pot to increase my caffeine intake for the day. As any sailor worth his salt of the seven seas will tell you, 'Coffee is a sailor's mainstay to productivity.'

I had taken a couple of sips of the high-octane java when Chef C announced, "Breakfast is ready. The kitchen staff is placing it on the buffet for everyone now." He waved his hand over the buffet like he was waving his magic wand over the food.

I heard Joe on his ATV, arriving right on time for breakfast. Like everyone else, I wondered what Joe's shirt would say today.

"Morning Joe," I commented as I tried to read his shirt. It was navy blue today, and it said, "*Help lift someone else before you lift yourself.*" It showed one soldier helping another one up.

"Good morning, everyone," he called out as the kids came running to him for their morning hugs.

After we had filled up on the scrumptious food that Chef C had prepared, I stood up to address the group.

"If I could get everyone's attention. Tomorrow is the Fourth of July. I figured we would relax down at our beach and have hamburgers and hot dogs, play games, and relax. That way, the new folks here can get to know everyone as we celebrate Independence Day."

The rest of the team gave me thumbs up and said, "Sounds great."

"What is the plan for the rest of the day?" I queried.

"Why don't we work on cleaning out the trailers," Dad said, "and get as much put away as possible?"

"Sounds good," I nodded at him. I rolled my eyes a little bit, because I knew it was going to be tough work. We did not have a loading dock or a forklift, but we could make the bucket on the backhoe work. "Everyone, meet out in the shop in an hour."

Damion got one of the trailers positioned so we could start working on it. "Hey, Dad. Why don't you run the backhoe? We can strap the heavy stuff to get out of the trailer and set it close to where we are going to unload it."

"That sounds good, my back won't take much lifting anymore," he commented as he grabbed his back to remind us of his back problems. "Just point me where you want the heavy stuff."

"Put the weapons and ammo near the armory and the food and other items near the storage shelves," I explained, pointing out each area of the shop. "Mel will have a team near the storage area, and I will have a team at the armory."

We soon had things moved around the shop to their designated location. Some items would be placed in the tunnel between the house and the shop for long-term storage. I wanted to leave some of the new rifles out for the team to practice with. We developed a routine, and before long, it was lunchtime. One of the children stuck their head into the shop and yelled that it was time for lunch. Most of us needed the break. I looked into the trailer on the way to the bunkhouse and noticed that we were only about halfway done. We had another trailer after this one. We would not get to that one today. Arriving in the bunkhouse for lunch, I noticed that Chef C had prepared a minestrone soup and set out bread and different meats and items for sandwiches. Looking around, I noticed that Zoe and her friends were not present. I excused myself as I headed to the house. Upon entering the house, I saw Zoe and her friends camped out on the couch and chairs in the living room. "What are you all doing here? There is work to do around the ranch," I exclaimed, probably just a little too loud.

"We don't know what needs to be done," Zoe whined, her shoulders hunched in defense.

"If you come to the bunkhouse at a normal time, you would know what needs to be done around here," I snapped. "When did you have breakfast? Lunch is ready now."

"We went down a little while ago, and the cook made us something for breakfast, so we're not hungry now," Zoe hissed, her face flushed from me yelling at her.

Jace chose that moment to speak up. "Chill, dude. We will help after we take a nap."

I lost my patience at that point. "One. You will not call me dude. From here on out, it is Mr. Bush. Two. Chef C is not just a cook. He is also not your personnel chef, and if you don't eat when the rest of the group eats, you will wait until the normal meal times. Three. Mel or I should not have to give you a personal invite to help around here. Four. If you don't help out around here, you don't eat." I had spit coming from my mouth as I yelled at them. All their mouths were hanging open in shock. "One last thing. You have about twenty minutes to get ready and head to the bunkhouse and then to the shop to help put stuff away from Dad's." Not giving them time to respond, I spun on my heel and headed back to the bunkhouse and my lunch.

Walking back into the bunkhouse, Mel could see the strain on my face. "You okay?"

"No, I just finished yelling at Zoe and her friends, who have been hanging out in the house while the rest of us busted our asses working in the shop. I need to have a quick chat with Chef C. They came down here a little while ago, and it sounds like they requested him to prepare food for their lazy butts," I hissed through my stress of dealing with Zoe.

I saw Chef C in the kitchen and walked over to him. I took a couple of deep breaths to calm myself. "Hey Chef C. I heard Zoe and her friends came down here between breakfast and lunch. From now on, if they are not here for our normal mealtimes, you are not to prepare them anything. I am trying to make the point with them that you are not their personal chef. You have other things to worry about than feeding their lazy asses whenever they want to eat."

"No problem, TJ."

My mother overheard the conversation and determined it was time for her two cents. "They should be able to eat whenever they want. I let them do that in Ely," she retorted at me, as she looked to Chef C for confirmation.

I slowly turned my head so I could look her in the eyes. "Chef C is not their short-order cook or anyone else's around here. He is a fantastic chef who volunteered his talents to ensure our nutritional needs were met. That is his primary mission here—not to make specific meals for those who want something special for their special person. That is his kitchen, and the rest of us stay out unless invited in. He is also teaching the children how to cook and manage a kitchen and is doing a fantastic job of it. They adore him and his talents. Unless you want to cook for Zoe and her friends, specifically at my house, then you are free to do that. Again, you are not to take food from this kitchen. Are we clear," I spit out. I was getting stressed about this situation again.

"You don't talk to your mother that way for one. Second. I don't cook," Mom growled at me.

"You could burn water," I said a little too loud, and Chef C laughed.

She went to slap my face, and I caught her hand as Dad walked in. "Moonbeam, what are you doing in the kitchen? You know you can't cook. Leave Chef C alone, will you," Dad declared as he stared at her with his hands on his hips.

"While I never—," she stammered as she turned to leave the kitchen.

I headed to the dining area, grabbed a sandwich and soup, and sat down next to Mel.

"You all right?" Mel asked.

"I am now," I declared.

Lunch went quickly and we were soon back in the shop, moving supplies around as we pulled them off the trailer.

Chapter 30

Mel

I woke up snuggled up to TJ, and I felt so safe with him next to me. Well, Ruffus and Adalinda were also here, and they would keep me safe if trouble came to our door. I felt TJ start to stir. Ruffus gave us a little "Woof," as if he was telling us to stop moving. That dog loved his sleep as much as I did.

TJ rolled over to look at me. I saw his gorgeous blue eyes, and it felt like they were boring into me and seeing my most intense thoughts of him. "I need to get up. You know me, I don't like just lying in bed when there are things to get done around the ranch. Unless you want to, you know?"

"Ya-ya, I know, and not now. Take that darn dog with you so he will stop lying on my legs. Don't know how he can sleep like that." When I mentioned Ruffus, he lifted his head to look at me with his big brown eyes. He felt TJ getting out of bed, so he jumped up and bound off the bed. Adalinda crawled up closer to my head and snuggled up to me.

"Hey, Loverboy, my big strong warrior man. Before you leave and get wrapped up in stuff, we need to talk about getting the women who are held captive at CVI soon. I don't know if those women would want to come here or return to their hometown, though we can figure that out once they are free."

"I don't like those women being held captive and abused either. We will have to do some reconnaissance to figure out the best way to help them. That might take a day, at least. We need a plan when we head in there. At least we have some heavy weapons now to assist us." He chuckled as he headed to the bathroom.

I figured I might as well get up, but I was still daydreaming of him when he came out of our bathroom area dressed for the day, wearing his 5.11 tan pants and a tan moisture-wicking shirt. He sat down on the bench at the foot of our bed and put on his Merrell hiking boots, which he loved. He was heading out the door, with me admiring his backside, when I climbed out of bed. Ruffus followed him, and I soon heard the doggie door flap as Ruffus exited the house.

As I came down the stairs, I could smell the coffee. This must be some of the stuff that we acquired from the Starbucks roasting plant a while back. This stuff was good, and we had enough for at least a couple of years. Entering the kitchen, I saw John and Shelly there with TJ, sipping coffee. TJ poured me a cup.

"Yum, this stuff is great, though I do miss my visits to Starbucks for my favorite coffee," I smirked as the caffeine from the coffee woke me up. "Hey John, Shelly. How did you sleep?" I asked, while holding the coffee cup close to my nose and inhaling its aroma.

"Great, as we usually do," they snickered as they both sipped more coffee.

"It's a good thing your room is downstairs and on the other side of the house," I smirked at Shelly. "Before you men get busy around the ranch, we need to make a plan to rescue the women at CVI," I asked my two favorite guys, well, besides Chef C and Joe.

"We can get with the rest of our security team and make a plan," TJ said, as he put his coffee cup in the sink and turned towards the door.

He headed to the bunkhouse for breakfast. He and that dog had a one-track mind for food. Speaking of that darn dog, he must have headed for the bunkhouse after he finished doing his business and was getting treats from Chef C.

I heard Joe on his ATV heading across the field. He knew when food was ready at the ranch. If I didn't know better, I would think that Chef C called him five minutes before the food was ready. He arrived and jumped off his ATV, ready to head inside, but not before he hugged me. I checked out his shirt, and it said, *"I'm not your buttercup."*

Arriving at the bunkhouse, I could smell breakfast cooking as I crested the threshold of the door. It smelled like bacon, hashbrowns, and eggs, and I am sure James and Cassie also had a wonderful breakfast dessert for us.

"Chef C, our wonderful kitchen wizard, what masterpiece do you have for us this morning?" I drew in a hungry breath, my mouth watering from the fantastic smells emanating from the kitchen.

"This morning, we have hickory smoked country bacon, freshly grated potatoes, and fresh eggs from our own chickens. James and Cassie have also prepared a wonderful éclair for everyone," Chef C revealed as he waved his arm over the food on the buffet.

"You are a wizard at this kitchen stuff, and we are so grateful to have you here," I declared as I wiped the drool from my mouth.

"It is my pleasure to be here and take care of my extended family. Now eat and enjoy," Chef C declared with a wave of his hand and a smile on his face.

As we finished breakfast, TJ stood up to address the group. "If I could have everyone's attention. As many of you have heard, the gang in town has some captured women. Mel and the team think that we need to rescue the women. The security team will develop a plan to rescue them as soon as we can. Any questions?"

I saw Ann raise her hand, and then TJ's mom raised her hand, too. Ann stood to speak, as sometimes she had no manners and wanted her opinion heard.

"What are we going to do with them? If you bring them here, we have no room left in the bunkhouse?" she blurted out. "What will they do once they are here?"

I shook my head as I rose to address Ann. "One, they will be given the option of if they want to come here or not, and we will find room for them. We do have room in the Army tent, though we are working on other solutions prior to winter getting here," I sighed as I answered Ann.

"Yes, Mother. You had your hand up also," I said, my brows drawn tight in a scowl, lips pressed into a thin, impatient line.

"Do we have enough food for everyone. What kind of shape do you think the women will be in once rescued? I don't want us to go hungry because some of you do-gooders think you need to rescue everyone out there like they are a stray dog," she huffed out as she finished.

"We do have enough food in storage, and with what we grow and preserve from our garden and greenhouse, we can last a long time. A decision was made prior to your arrival that we would not reject anyone from the ranch. If you want details on that decision, come see me and TJ, and we will explain it," I said, as I rolled my eyes in her direction. If she wanted the details of that decision, I sure hoped that TJ would come to my defense.

"Well, you know I was coerced into an agreement on that decision," Ann piped up.

"Ahh—"

TJ spoke up in my defense. "Ann. You may have voted 'no' when we asked for a vote on letting people into the ranch who may not have had the skills that we needed. However, everyone else voted in agreement. I would not have held it against you for voting 'No' if you wanted to. Mother, that was a group decision prior to your arrival, and other than Zoe and her friends, everyone so far has brought skills to the ranch that we need here. Zoe and her friends are more than capable of performing work. On days that we preserve fruit and vegetables, Chef C can use some help, though that is his domain, and he picks the kitchen crew," TJ admonished Ann and his mother as he stared at them both.

Moonbeam let out a tired sigh and said, "Working in the garden, greenhouse, and barn—Zoe and her friends think that's beneath them. They won't lift a finger out there," she said, her voice cracking a bit as she pointed toward TJ. "I did my part for years, helping your father prepare for all this. But I'm worn out, honey. I know things are hard now, and the world isn't what it used to be—but I've spent so long taking care of Zoe and those friends of hers, doing everything for them. I just want them to be looked after the way I tried to look after you."

"They're free to walk off this ranch right now if they can't pull their weight," TJ snapped, voice sharp and unwavering. "You let them coast, and now we're paying for it. That kind of dead weight drags everyone down—and I won't let it slide." He took a step closer to Moonbeam, eyes blazing. "This isn't a retreat. It's survival. If they can't handle that, then go with them. Because around here, we *earn* our place."

"Security team. Meet in the shop in fifteen minutes for some planning," TJ snapped into the radio.

Moonbeam was about to open her mouth in response when TJ's dad grabbed her arm and pointed to a chair. She pulled her arm away and stormed out of the bunkhouse. "I will not be treated this way by my own son," she snapped, as she walked out the door.

Ruffus and Adalinda took off outside after her. I heard Moonbeam scream. I walked to the door to see Moonbeam on the ground and Ruffus making a beeline for the house. Moonbeam was on the path he normally took, and he'd knocked her down. *Good boy,* I thought as he jumped up onto the porch of the house and sat down with his tongue hanging out. I was sure he was smiling at me.

When I looked at TJ, he shrugged his shoulders and sat down to finish his coffee. I sat down next to him and asked, "Are you okay?"

"Yup. I am better than okay after seeing what Ruffus did on his way to the house. He seems to know when to finish knocking someone down. Let me finish this coffee, and we can head to the shop to discuss our rescue plan for the women at CVI."

TJ and I entered the shop, and the whole security team were present. As I started counting heads, I counted twenty-eight people, including me, on the security team. Wow, where had I been when all these people showed up? The newest were the ten from the National Guard depot.

"Okay, team," TJ spoke up to get the team's attention. "As you know, we plan to rescue the women held captive at CVI. We don't know how many women they have or how many gang members are present. We need a plan to get in and get them and possibly take out as many of the gang as possible to help the town."

I spoke up. "I want to remind everyone that some of the gang members, including who I think is their leader, possess magical powers, and our human weapons will not be effective against them, as we saw in a couple of other fights at the library and Starbucks roasting factory. We have the five of us with magical powers to help defeat those in the gang who do," I advised the group. Everyone on the team pretty much knew the five of us who possessed magical powers.

Nick walked over to our dry-erase board and started drawing the CVI building. "Most of us have a general idea of the layout of the building. It has a raised entrance facing the east. There is also the lower entrance on the north side and then the employee entrance on the west side. There are too many rooms to clear each one with our group. Two snipers can take a position on TJ's Corral and cover the two main entrances. The Stryker and MRAP can each cover the two main entrances, and a small group can cover the employee entrance. With the Humvees, we can carry those who will enter the hotel as part of the rescue team, though we need to leave people here to defend the ranch. We go in late at night and use our NVGs. TJ, do you have any IR illuminators in your bag of tricks?" Nick inquired as he finished drawing on the board.

"I do, though probably not enough for everyone. We have not gone through all the cases of new gear that we found in the trucks prior to leaving Ely," TJ informed the team.

TJ was looking at me with a quizzical look on his face. "What magic tricks do you have up your sleeve, love? Can you make people invisible?" he questioned.

"Not that I have figured out yet ..."

"Melly has not figured that one out yet. Chef C and I can help some of you become invisible," Joe commented as he and Chef C seemed to appear out of thin air.

All our jaws about hit the floor.

"What the holy hell," John shouted.

Joe stepped into the center of the room, commanding attention with a calm certainty. "Let me clear a few things up," he began, his voice steady. "You've all heard the legends—Arthur, the Round Table, Merlin the great wizard. Well, those stories? They're not just bedtime tales. Merlin was real. *Is* real. And Chef C here?" He gestured toward him with a hint of reverence. "He's a potion wizard—been brewing magic as long as I've been walking this earth. Between the two of us, we can cloak a small group to get inside unseen. Chef C will build the potion, and I will use it to take a small group inside. We can then start rounding up the women and get them ready to leave when you start shooting," Joe said as he pulled what appeared to be a wand out of his sleeve.

I stared at Joe, my mouth slightly open, heart pounding. Merlin? As in *the* Merlin? My brain scrambled to catch up, trying to piece together the quiet, steady man I knew with the legendary figure from every magical tale I'd ever heard.

"I knew you were special," I whispered, almost to myself, taking a hesitant step closer. "But I didn't know you were *this* special."

A mix of awe and worry flooded through me. I reached out and wrapped my arms around him, holding tight. "Thank you for joining us on this mission," I said, my voice thick. "But I don't want anything to happen to you—not now. You have so much to teach us. The world *needs* you."

He hugged me back, warm and calm as always, but now I couldn't help feeling like I was clinging to a living legend.

"I will be all right. Don't you worry, little one. He gestured with his wand.

TJ coughed to get our attention. "We have a mission to plan. John and I talked about this prior to our meeting, so he is aligned with this. Here are the teams as we outlined.

"Nick and Gavin are our snipers and will take a Jeep to get to their perch on TJ's Corral. MRAP will have Gunner and Skyler on the turret, and passengers will include Russell, Heather, and Walt. You will have the north entrance.

"Stryker will have Liam driving, Tracy on the turret gun, and passengers will be Cole, Madison, and Matthew. You will take the raised entrance. Snipers can take out any threats at the doors as you both arrive.

"Humvees will be driven by me and John, with Bonnie and Ryan on gun turrets. The passengers will be Mel, Shelly, Gail, Ravin, Carlos, and Joe. It will be cramped, but we're not going very far."

"Don't forget Ruffus and Adalinda," I said, reminding TJ of the two.

Ruffus picked up his head at the mention of his name and gave a little chuff.

"We will make them fit," he commented as he nodded his head.

"Joe, can you cloak a Humvee?" TJ asked.

"Hum, never tried. Is it necessary with all the firepower we will have out front?" Joe queried.

"I guess it would work better for you to cloak a team that comes in through the employee entrance and find the women first. If you can also take them outside, that would be great. Once you grab a few of them, you will have to question the women and find out how many slaves and if any are in other locations," TJ pressed.

"Are we taking prisoners?" Nick asked.

"Negative," John was quick to reply.

"We will all have radios and suppressed weapons so that we will have the element of surprise on our side," TJ said. "For those going inside, I want to run some drills this afternoon on the range, so we don't have a 'blue-on-blue' incident."

"What is a 'blue-on-blue' incident," Gail asked with a quizzical look on her face.

"That is where someone on our team shoots a teammate," I replied.

"Oh, okay," Gail responded. "Yeah, that would be bad for the home team," she said her lips turned down slightly, a frown beginning to mar her face.

"When you find a group of women, bring them out the nearest door and get them into a vehicle. It could be cramped, and if we must, some of us can flee CVI on foot and wait for a vehicle to return for us. Before you come out a door, call it out so those outside know you are about to exit the building," TJ advised the team. "Review the drawing and get some rest. After lunch, we will run some drills on the range for close quarters building clearing drills. Any questions?"

Shortly after the security meeting, we dispersed to have lunch and were quickly on the range soon after, running drills and shooting at targets. TJ and John even made some low targets, like they might be on a bed with non-threat targets, to represent the women. The training was tough, though it taught us to ensure our shot placement was accurate. No spray-and-pray while trying to rescue the women. Our goal was to avoid injuries to the women or ourselves.

TJ and John huddled us all together. "Great job on the range. We gear up at zero one hundred and roll out at zero one thirty. I want our snipers in place by zero two hundred, and the rest of the team to execute at zero two thirty. That is the witching hour when people on watch are most tired, and those who are partying are usually done and in bed. Questions?" TJ asked.

Hearing none, we headed for the kitchen and food and rest, as zero one hundred would come early enough.

Chapter 31

TJ

I woke up before my alarm clock went off, which is what I usually do, even with a planned early-morning mission. I woke up Mel, and we completed our morning rituals, dressed, and headed downstairs. Ruffus and Adalinda followed us down the stairs, and they headed outside to complete their business. About halfway down the stairs, I could smell the coffee and figured that John and Shelly might be up. To my surprise, the whole away team was in the house, coffee cups sitting in front of them. Joe was there also. It was strange, that I didn't hear him on his ATV arrival.

"Morning, everyone. I hope you all slept well." I commented as I grabbed two coffee cups and poured some for Mel and myself.

I heard multiple "Slept okay" from the team.

We were all a little bit tired since we had not gotten our usual amount of sleep. "Let's head over to see what Chef C has for us to eat before getting ready to head out. We need our energy," I urged the team. I received head nods all around as I turned to head out the door for the bunkhouse and kitchen.

As I approached the bunkhouse, I could smell the sausage cooking and hear the potatoes sizzling in the sausage grease, and eggs being made to order. Ruffus bound through the door as I opened it and just about knocked me down. I yelled at him, "Slow down, Ruffus." That darn dog always got food before the rest of us.

"Breakfast is on the buffet, and eggs to order up here," Chef C said as he pointed first to the buffet and then the bench top where the eggs were being served.

I saw Ruffus over near Chef C getting his usual treats of sausage and potatoes. We finished our breakfast and headed over to the shop and armory to get kitted up for our rescue mission. Our two snipers took off in a Jeep to get to TJ's Corral and positioned. The MRAP and Stryker looked menacing, sitting in the shop with their large tires and machine guns on the top turrets. Our Humvees even had an evil look, with the machine guns sticking out the tops of the vehicles. We were soon loaded up and moved out of the shop towards town. We completed our radio checks as we progressed slowly down the road and to our staging points in town. The MRAP and Stryker would be positioned to the east of CVI, and John and I would stage to the west with our team in the Humvees.

"Snipers in position. The East door has one guard. North entrance I'm not able to see anything since it is under the portico cover," Nick announced.

I announced over the radio, "Teams one and two are rolling in now. Three and four, standby for my call."

I heard Gunner and Liam reply, "Copy."

John and I stopped our Humvees near the rear employee entrance, and we all exited our vehicles. "Just like we drilled at home. Here we go," I called over the radio so the other teams would know we were entering the building. Thankfully, the door was unlocked, and we entered the long hallway. As we entered, I got a chill, and the hair on the back of my neck stood up. There were a couple of doors leading off the hallway. I pointed and a couple of team members went to clear those rooms.

We were about halfway down the hallway when Bonnie spoke up, "TJ. John. What are these? They say, 'Front toward enemy.'"

I now knew why the hair was standing up on the back of my neck.

"Abort. Run and get out of the building," I screamed over the radio. "Abort, get out of the building now." We spun on our heels and took off running for the door that we had entered. As we did, the claymore mines attached to the walls behind us started detonating, chasing us down the hall.

This is not the way I wanted to die, I thought as we sprinted for the exit, the hallway behind us erupting with a deafening roar, the power from the exploded mines making my head feel thick. . . I could feel ball bearings starting to hit me as I ran. Suddenly, a claymore three feet in front of me detonated. The world tilted. My team—people I, loved, knew, and trusted—were torn apart in a red mist. One second, they were there, the next gone. I stumbled forward, my vision blurred. I could feel something warm trickling down my cheek. I touched it and looked at my hand. It was blood. I didn't know if it was mine or from my team.

I looked down and saw a claymore next to me, and in that brief second, I wondered, *'Did this one malfunction? Am I going to survive?'* Then there was a white-hot blinding flash, I felt myself pushed backwards from the blast wave, an invisible hand coming from nowhere and slapping the shit out of me, then I felt nothing. The next thing I knew, I was looking down the hallway, and all of my family and friends were dead. I got them all killed by trying to be a hero!

Chapter 32

Mel

"TJ. Wake up. You're having a bad dream."

"Sorry ... what?"

"You were thrashing around, it was so bad the critters left. You even kicked me a couple of times."

"What time is it?"

"Zero fifteen. Time to get up and head down for coffee and breakfast."

"Can I sleep for another five minutes?"

"No, TJ, unless you want to send the rest of the team without you."

"I can't have that."

Adalinda also chuffed at us as she sat on the dresser to start preparing for our upcoming mission.

"Hey, Ruffus, Adalinda. You both ready to take out some bad folks?" I asked them.

They both chuffed at us as we started to get ready for the upcoming battle. We grabbed our 5.11 black pants and shirts, stuffed our feet into our Merrell boots, and stopped to brush our teeth. We headed downstairs when we heard voices in the kitchen. I heard my girls chatting in the kitchen and could smell the coffee before I hit the landing. "Morning, ladies and John. Good to see you all this fine morning."

Raven poured TJ and me a cup of coffee. "Enjoy this fine nectar of the coffee gods," she said, and then she slid the cups to us like a bartender sliding a mug of beer down the polished bar top.

"Thank you, Raven. Ah ... this smells heavenly," I said. I inhaled the aroma as I brought the coffee cup to my mouth to take a sip.

"You're welcome."

"Let's finish our coffee and head to the bunkhouse for breakfast. We will be moving soon," TJ announced as he put his coffee cup in the sink and headed for the door.

"Is TJ okay?" Gail asked as he walked out the door.

"He had a bad dream, well, more of a nightmare," I told the team.

"Whatever the nightmare was, let's hope it doesn't come true," Shelly quietly said, her hands pulled close to her chest, holding her coffee cup.

We placed our coffee cups in the sink and headed out the door to the bunkhouse.

The air was crisp and felt good. I knew winter would soon be upon us. I was deep in thought about how winter would affect us when we entered the bunkhouse, and I could smell the sausage that Chef C had on the grill, along with potatoes and eggs. "Ah, a nice hearty breakfast before we go to battle. Thank you, Chef C. You didn't have to get up so early. We could have fended for ourselves this morning."

"It's no big deal, Mel. I like to make sure my family is well-fed before we send out teams to save others," Chef C elaborated.

"We are lucky to have you."

"My family and I are lucky to be here. We are grateful for your generosity," Chef C said as he handed Ruffus bits of sausage.

Those two had a thing, and I was sure Ruffus would protect him before TJ or me.

We all had our fill of Chef C's delicious breakfast and headed to the shop and armory, where we grabbed our armor and kit. Buddy checks and radio checks were done, and we loaded up into our assigned vehicles. Nick and Gavin headed out a few minutes early in the Jeep since they had the furthest to go for their sniper position. The rest of us rolled out a few minutes later and positioned ourselves at our assigned staging areas. I was riding with TJ in a Humvee and staged to the west of CVI. We had been waiting for about twenty minutes when Nick called on the radio. "Team 6, in position. One guard at the east entrance. The north entrance appears deserted."

TJ keyed his radio and announced, "One."

I heard the other teams reporting in. When everyone reported in, TJ called out, "One and two are moving. Stand by for my call." I heard a little apprehension in TJ's voice as we started moving. I looked at him and grabbed his hand as we started moving. We rolled up to the rear entrance, and all quickly exited the Humvees, except for our gunners, who would remain on watch.

Joe suddenly yelled. "Stop. Don't enter yet. I feel some very strong wards protecting the building. Let me disarm them prior to entering." Joe stepped up to the door and waved his magic wand along the edges. The runes on his wand were glowing, and as he traced the door frame, his wand left a glowing trail of dust particles behind.

"Do your thing, TJ."

TJ announced, "One and two breaching."

We entered the rear door, which was thankfully unlocked, and entered an employee lounge area. "Clear," TJ called after him, and John entered and swept the room with their rifles.

I didn't feel any other magic in the area other than the wards that Joe had disarmed, so I wondered where the paranormal people were living if they were not there. Our plan called for our team to enter, try to get the women from wherever they were, and get out without being detected. We entered a hallway that went to the conference rooms, where we suspected that the women might be held.

TJ and I entered a conference room and saw two thugs sleeping near women who had been tied up to an anchoring point in the wall. I pulled my suppressed pistol up and shot the thug in the head. I really liked Athena, my Sig P365XL Rose edition pistol, but she wasn't able to have a suppressor installed like the Tacops. I heard TJ's suppressed pistol 'pfft' as he ended the other thug's life. The female heard my shot and her eyes snapped open. The sound also woke the woman, and the thug by TJ. Before the thug could move TJ shot him in the head, then put his hand over the females mouth to keep her from screaming. I had my hand over the girl's mouth as well, so she wouldn't scream.

"I am here to help you. Please don't scream. Nod your head if you understand." She nodded that she did, and I removed my hand. "I am going to cut these restraints and get you out of here." I pulled the cutters from my pack and made quick work of the restraints holding her to the wall. I could hear TJ having the same conversation with the female on the other bed. We were moving to the door when I heard gunshots from one of the other conference rooms.

I heard John on the radio. "A thug woke up and got a shot off. We are ballistic now."

That was the code for Nick and Gavin to take out the thug at the front door. About that time, I heard a loud report from one of their BMG 50-cal rifles. I pulled the girl we had just rescued towards the door and stopped when I got to Joe.

"Quick question." I asked the female I was rescuing, "How many other women are being held captive here?"

"There were seventeen when we first arrived. They killed a couple. The last I heard was around thirteen," she stammered.

I announced to the team, "There should be thirteen women here. TJ and I have two, we will take them outside."

Shelly called over the radio, "We have three women and headed to Joe."

The Stryker and MRAP teams announced their arrival at their respective doors. "Entering," Gunner and Liam announced as their respective teams entered CVI. With our NVGs and infrared illuminators, we could see our teams.

From the earlier gunshots, the thugs were now awake and shooting back. I hoped that no one on our team got injured.

"Walt is hit," Gunner declared over the radio.

"Team four has three women and is exiting," Liam declared.

"Conference room eagle is clear. Three women mobile and moving," Gunner informed us.

We were moving down a hallway, leapfrogging to each conference room entrance. Two thugs appeared in front of us. TJ hit them center mass with his Sig Sauer MCX rifle. He pulled the trigger so fast it sounded like he was on full auto. We opened the doors to the conference room when someone inside opened up with a rifle and shotgun, shredding the doors. John and TJ lined up at the doors, and when they thought they had a lull in the shooting, they entered. TJ went left, and John went right. I heard their rifles spitting death at someone inside.

"Clear," TJ called. "Mel, find Gail. We need a medic in here. One of the women is in bad shape."

"Copy," I replied. "Gail, where you at?"

"Main door with Ruffus and Adalinda."

"Tell Ruffus to find his momma, and follow him. He will find me."

I soon heard Gail, Ruffus, and Adalinda coming through the hall. I took them into the room that TJ and John had just finished clearing.

"NVGs up. We need a light in here," TJ declared.

When the light on TJ's rifle came on, I was shocked by what I saw lying on the bed. The lady had been badly beaten by the thugs. Her face was badly beaten, her jaw hanging to the side, and her nose was smashed flat on her face. Her breathing was coming through ragged, shallow breaths. There were blood stains on her shirt from what looked like knife cuts or stab wounds along her ribs.

Gail jumped up next to her and started talking to her.

"We got you, now. No one will hurt you anymore. Let's get you patched up and out of here," Gail said quietly to the woman.

Gail pulled her medical bag out and opened it, pulling out gauze and other items to treat her. I could see sadness in Gail's eyes as she examined the lady, coming to the realization that she might not be able to save her.

The lady mumbled, "I'm not going to make it.," as she wheezed, struggling for breath, bloody red bubbles appearing on her lips. "Don't waste your meds on me. Give me something to help me go quickly. Please."

Gail looked at us with tears in her eyes. We all nodded in confirmation. Gail pulled a different syringe from her bag and a bottle of something to administer and help her go pain-free. A few seconds later, we heard her take her last breath.

Joe came into the room. "TJ, John. I'll head outside to guard the women; you two go and help find the other women, " he said with a growl.

I could hear more gunfire from around the hotel and casino, and since it was not suppressed, I knew it was thugs shooting. Our team would soon have them under control, or at least I hoped they would. I could hear Liam and Gunner calling clear on different rooms as they moved through the building. From my count, we had one girl unaccounted for.

TJ called over the radio. "We have twelve of the women accounted for so far. One must be in a room. Not sure we have time to search every room in this place." I could hear the sorrow in TJ's voice over the radio.

Suddenly, Bonnie was shouting over the radio. "We need help out here. There is some strange magical shit happening."

I wanted to ask what, but then I thought better of it and took off for the exit. Ruffus and Adalinda raced past us in a blur. Adalinda spat a ball of flame at the door, which knocked it off its hinges. When we arrived outside, there was a tornado-like thing spinning around our Humvees being caused by a tazzy devil. Bonnie and Ryan were still manning the machine guns on the roof, though they were keeping their heads down. They had the women all crowded into the Humvees to protect them; I could see the fear in their eyes through the glass. Then, *I felt her.*

Not with my eyes. Not with my ears. It was deeper than that—like shadows crawling over my skin, like the air had suddenly grown heavy with smoke and secrets. My gut twisted, my blood turned cold and hot all at once. My breath caught. I knew that presence. Lillith.

How did I know her name? I just *did*. Like it had been carved into my bones.

Joe put his hand on my shoulder, steadying my racing heart. "You got this, Mel."

Lillith stepped out of the cloud of swirling dust and debris, holding balls of fire.

I took a deep breath. "I know. You've been training us for this day." I stepped towards Lilith, drew my sword, and yelled at her. "Just go away before I am forced to kill you, Lilith." I took a deep breath. "I know. You've been training us for this day." I stepped towards Lilith, drew my sword, and yelled at her. "Just go away before I am forced to kill you, Lilith." Suddenly, the tornado stopped, and I saw what was causing it. A creature emerged, low to the ground and spinning with such speed it blurred—its limbs a twisted whirlwind of claws and smoke. As it slowed, I could make out glowing eyes and a mouth full of jagged teeth, still twitching with the energy of its violent rotation. It snarled and settled beside Lilith, and standing next to it was BG—no, Azazel-the fallen angel himself.

I heard Joe mutter to Carlos, "So, Azazel, the fallen angel, decided to come."

"Well, this just keeps getting more and more interesting," Carlos replied in a low voice.

Joe waved his wand around us and shouted, "*Protego, Protego, Protego.*"

My ladies stepped up next to me. "Spread out so we can defeat her and hit her with everything you've got," I instructed my team.

Lilith sent a ball of fire our way. We raised our clasped hands, tightening our grip to magnify the surge of energy between us.

"*Spirits Ducentia Protego Me,*" we whispered, producing a glowing sphere over us that stopped the fireball.

"*Fulgur Temptatio!*" I screamed—once, twice, three times—my voice tearing through the air like a war cry.

The sky answered. Clouds churned above, thick and black, roiling like they were alive and furious. The wind snapped around us, electric and sharp. Then a bolt of lightning lanced down, striking Lillith dead-on. Another followed. Then a third. Each hit split the air with a deafening crack, lighting the battlefield in strobes of flashes.

Beside me, Shelly thrust her hands toward the ground, her crystal pendant glowing like a miniature sun. The earth trembled. With a guttural roar, massive slabs of rock erupted from the soil, tearing free like they'd been yanked from unseen hands. With a sharp flick of her fingers, Shelly sent boulders hurtling through the air—aimed straight at Lillith.

Ruffus let out a roar that split the air as he completed his transformation into a fully changed Gryphon and bounded forward like a living missile towards Lilith. Adalinda was on to his back, hanging on for dear life, her four tiny dragon paws buried in the thick feathers on his shoulder. Her eyes blazed as she spat fireballs after fireball over Ruffus's head as they charged toward Lillith. As Lilith deflected them, two struck the berserker, hitting him in the chest, knocking him down. Lilith and Azazel moved out of the way as Ruffus approached, leaving Bobby, the berserker, on his own. Ruffus grabbed him and started shaking him until his limbs flew. An audible snap indicated his neck was broken. Ruffus dropped him, the body falling awkwardly, and moved away. Adalinda hit him with a final fireball that destroyed what was left of his body to ashes.

I heard a loud crash and looked over to my left. I saw Carlos and BG, or Azazel, fighting each other. They were throwing everything they had at each other. This was a classic good versus evil type of fight. When I looked back towards where Lilith had been standing, she was gone. I sure hoped that she had left the fight. Carlos and BG were throwing each other around, hitting each other with their fists. When they threw one or the other around, it had the effect of knocking down walls and trees. Carlos got a good hit and launched Azazel away from him. Landing in a heap, Azazel looked around and realized that Lilith had left him. He abruptly took off into the night before Carlos could get to him.

"Stay alert, team. Even though I can feel them getting further away, they might only be going away to lick their wounds and then come back in a few," I declared. I looked down to ensure I was not naked, like the last time I fought Lilith. Though, in hindsight, she had hit me with a fireball. I looked around at my team and could tell they were spent from all the energy we had used. TJ and the rest of the team arrived outside. I turned to them and asked, "Did we get all the women from inside?"

TJ looked disappointed as he said, "From what we heard from the two we rescued, we are missing one. We don't have enough people to clear every room in the hotel," he sighed. "Although, I do have an idea. Let's see if Ruffus can find her. While a couple of us follow Ruffus, can you see where the women want to go?" Turning to look at Ruffus, he encouraged him, "Come on, Ruffus. Let's see if you can find the lone lady in the hotel."

I watched John and Joe join TJ and Ruffus and reenter the hotel and silently wished them good hunting. After what felt like an eternity, I heard muffled gunshots from inside and then heard TJ on the radio.

"We got her. She will need a medic when we get outside."

Gail came over with her bag to meet them at the door as they exited. Joe was helping her along, and TJ and John were backing out the door behind them. TJ shouted, "Get her loaded. We need to move now." Gail grabbed her other arm and put it over her shoulder, and they loaded her into the back of a Humvee.

"Joe, Carlos," TJ yelled over his shoulder, "you both drive, and when everyone is loaded, start backing out of here."

"Copy," They both replied.

"Ruffus. Heel," TJ commanded. Ruffus headed to the left side of TJ and stood guard, still in the form of the gryphon. As we were backing away from the employee entrance, three thugs attempted to exit what was left of the door. They looked like the three stooges as they fought each other to get out. TJ and John opened up on them with their rifles and put good hits on them. Bonnie opened up with the 50-cal Ma-Deuce on the Humvee to ensure they were dead as we moved away from the scene.

John and TJ walked near the front of the Humvee in case more thugs came out, and Bonnie and Ryan provided backup with their machine guns. I heard TJ on the radio. "Teams One and Two exfiling to rally point three. Teams Three and Four, see if there are any keys in the vehicles, and if so, bring them with you and clear out. Snipers, same for you, clear out."

All teams replied with, "Copy."

Once the Humvees had backed up far enough to turn around, TJ approached Joe's window. "You guys have full vehicles. Get to the rally point. John and I will meet you there," he said, as he slapped the top of the Humvee.

Joe dropped the Humvee into drive and started to speed away. My pleading eyes met TJ's as we drove off. "Joe, how are they going to get to the rally point? It's over a mile away," I said. Our rally point was over in Ranchos.

"They will walk or run while ensuring our tail is clear of threats. When we get there, we can have Gail and Tracy check the women out for medical issues and quiz the women to see what they want to do. We should have some vehicles that they can use if they don't want to come to the ranch," Joe said as he grabbed my arm. "Good job out there, Mel and team."

We arrived at the park, and Joe stopped us in the parking lot. We piled out and helped the women who had been captives just a short time ago. Gail started checking their injuries. She could help with their physical injuries. However, she wouldn't be able to help them with their psychological wounds. Those of us who were not helping Gail assess the ladies, set up a perimeter around us. We soon heard the growl of the diesel engines of the MRAP and Stryker approaching. They pulled up and parked facing out so the gunners would have a clear sight line on anyone who showed up. They had commandeered three vehicles from the thugs. We helped the rest of the women out of the vehicles so we could treat them. All of them had been raped repeatedly, and a few had been hit multiple times, probably for trying to fight the thugs off.

Gail pulled Shelly, Joe, and me away from the group. "I questioned them while I checked them out and what they would like to do now that they were free. Three would like to come to the ranch, they have skills we can use. The others want to head up to Carson City and try and find their families. The three who want to come to the ranch are single; two are nurses and have combat experience from the Army, and the other one is an engineer from the Reno water plant. She was also in the Army as a combat engineer."

"We need to find more beds so we can get everyone more comfortable than sleeping on cots in the Army tent. It would be good to separate the men from the women. I will talk to TJ about the plan tomorrow," I said as I watched the women realize that they were finally free, some began to sob with relief.

I heard TJ on the radio. "We are five minutes out. The back trail is clear."

While we were contemplating sleeping arrangements, TJ and John walked into our circle of vehicles. "How are the women doing?" TJ queried.

"All things considered, well. The one grazed by a bullet is patched up," Gail briefed John and TJ.

I pulled John, Shelly, Gail, and TJ further away from the group to discuss what I had learned from Gail. TJ and John nodded their heads, confirming our discussion.

"Gail, are they all good to travel? I want to get us back to the ranch as soon as possible. We will give the nine that want to head to Carson City two of the three vehicles. We want to give them something that will make the trip and not leave them stranded. Give them some of the ready to eat meals from the Stryker and MRAP, so they have some food while they travel. Ask the team that drove the three vehicles here which ones they think are the best and give them the keys. Then let's load up and beat feet," TJ said as he watched the team and scanned the perimeter.

The team scrambled to get the meals moved from the Stryker and MRAP and then assigned two vehicles to the women for their travel. I pulled the nine women off to the side and discussed the plan.

"We are giving you two vehicles. One is a four-door late-model Ford truck, and the other is an older GMC truck. Our team is sure they will get you to Carson City, and they have enough fuel to get you there. Who can shoot a gun? We have some weapons that we took from the thugs so you can protect yourselves." Five of the nine raised their hands. "You four might want to learn how to handle a gun to protect yourself," I advised them.

Two of the four said weapons scared them, and were not sure they could use one on another human being. I just let it go as I was too tired to counter their comments. "We are loading up in a couple of minutes to return to our place. The keys are in the vehicles. You are free to go. Please don't try to follow us if you change your mind." I watched them load up and head north, away from us. I wished them luck in their journey and said a silent prayer for their safe travels.

"Team, let's load up and head back to the ranch. I am hungry," TJ barked.

Ruffus also barked, probably indicating that he was hungry as well.

"Freedom Ranch, TJ. The team is headed home with three extra souls. All accounted for. See you soon."

"Ranch copies. Chef C will have food ready upon your arrival."

Hearing that, my stomach growled at me. I think Ruffus heard it as he put his head on my shoulder from the back seat. We were soon in front of the bunkhouse and pulling our tired bodies out from the vehicles. I pulled the three women off to the side.

"Let's get you fed, and then we will find you a place to sleep. See the Army tent over there. We have extra cots in there. We will put up more dividers to give you privacy. The Army National Guard group that joined us is also sleeping in there. I will take you into our house so you can shower. We have a stash of clothing and other essential items that we will get from our storage for you while you clean up. I need your sizes, and I will give it to our supply team. You want to eat first or shower first?" I asked.

"Shower," they all replied.

Shelly, Gail, and I took them to our house, as we had enough showers for them all to get cleaned up at the same time. "While you get your showers, I will have our team track down clothing for you. We can burn the stuff you are wearing now." I showed each of them the bathroom and showers."

"I will go find Jolene and Joanne and give them these sizes. I will be back in a few with clothing for you all. Enjoy your hot shower, and then we will get you over to the bunkhouse for something to eat," Shelly said.

"You have running water, and it is hot?" Lynn exclaimed.

I could see the excitement in their eyes. "Yes, we have solar panels on the house and shop, and they power a well and water heater." They were probably looking forward to the shower, though not expecting it to be hot water, as most of those necessities were no longer working after the EMP strike.

While I waited for the ladies to finish their showers and Shelly to return with new clothing, I started a pot of coffee to help energize me. *Ah, this tastes good*, I thought to myself as Shelly walked in with Jolene and Joanne, each with an armload of clothing for our new ladies.

"We each have clothing for one of the ladies. Point us in the direction of who is in what bathroom, and we will give them the clothing," Shelly informed me.

I called off who was in what bathroom, and they all headed in that direction and soon returned.

Lynn was the first one to return to the kitchen. "That shower felt so good. I really did not want to get out," she exclaimed. "Oh, that coffee smells heavenly. Can I have a cup, please?"

I grabbed a cup from the cupboard and poured her a cup of joe. I grabbed two more cups for the other ladies, as I figured they might want some when they made their way back to the kitchen.

"Glad you enjoyed the shower. The bunkhouse also has showers, though I felt you might feel more comfortable in the bathrooms here. Each bunkroom has a shower, along with our clinic, though you would have been in someone's assigned room for a little bit while you cleaned up."

I heard someone coming down the stairs. "You have a gorgeous house, and your bedroom is exquisite. The shower felt incredible. I think I forgot what it was like to feel clean," Val said . "Oh, is my nose deceiving me, or is that coffee that I smell?"

Without even answering her, I poured her a cup of coffee and set it in front of her.

"I think I have died and gone to heaven. It has been so long since I have had coffee," she squealed.

I heard Betsy come down the stairs to join us, and as she turned the corner into the kitchen, I put a cup of coffee in front of her. "I hope that you feel better after that hot shower," I asked. "Is there anything that we can do for you all. I can only imagine the horrors that you all had to endure while in the hotel with the gang?"

"It was rough" she acknowledged, looking over my shoulder as if she could see it happening.. "The gang did what they wanted with us, and we had no say. Thank you for rescuing us," she said. "The shower was fantastic, though I thought you might have lied to us about the hot water until it almost burned my skin off. Oh, this coffee is heavenly, I'm not sure the last time I had coffee. Do you have to ration it?" she asked, as she took a sip of her coffee.

"I'm glad you enjoyed your hot showers. And no, we don't ration the coffee. We raided the Starbucks roasting plant and can raid it again, if necessary," I revealed. "Finish your coffee, and we will head over to the bunkhouse for breakfast. I'm not sure what our fabulous chef has conjured up this morning, though he is a wizard in the kitchen." I thought I heard their stomachs grumble at the mention of food, so we deposited our cups in the sink and headed to the bunkhouse. On the way there, I informed them of the rules.

"Ladies, as I mentioned earlier, the rules here are pretty simple. We all work together to survive. We share our skills with others and learn from others. It is crowded out here now, and we are working on getting better accommodations for those in the Army tent. The house is off-limits unless invited in. We all eat together to conserve food. Any questions?" Not hearing anything from them, I opened the door to the bunkhouse so that all of us could enter and enjoy Chef C's savory food. As usual, the aromas from the kitchen were fantastic, and my mouth was watering already. The new arrivals just about pushed me out of the way to get to the buffet line to eat. Our small core of ranch leadership always ate last. With how much they put on their plates, I could tell they had not had a good meal in weeks. Chef C had prepared pancakes, bacon, and eggs, while James and Cassie prepared cinnamon rolls for dessert.

Val asked, "Aren't you going to eat Mel?"

"I will once everyone else has gotten theirs. We have a small leadership team, and we always eat last," I explained.

I soon felt TJ's arm around me. "How are the ladies doing?" he asked, pulling me in tightly to his side.

"So far, so good. They've had showers and are in clean clothes. It is more than they had a couple of hours ago," I told him.

I turned around to face everyone. "If I could have everyone's attention, thank you. As you may have noticed, we have three new people out here today. These three wanted to come to the ranch, and the other nine are heading home to Carson City. They are Lynn, Val, and Betsy. Betsy and Lynn are nurses, and Val is an engineer from the Carson City water plant. They were all in the Army for a few years. Matthew and Nick, please get them checked out and issued weapons."

"Copy."

TJ and I grabbed our plates and food from the serving line and found seats next to our new family. I saw Ruffus over near Chef C, who had a handful of bacon. Darn dog, he loved Chef C. When I called for Ruffus, he gave me a quick sideways glance, and then he returned to stare down Chef C for more bacon.

TJ stood up to make an announcement. "Hello. It was great to return home today with everyone, after our rescue mission. It was a success, as you can see. We have three new guests who are now part of our family here. Please show them around the ranch, and in a couple of days, we will get them into the chore rotation. Lynn, Val, and Betsy, feel free to take a couple of days to get comfortable here. If you need anything, please let us know, and we will track it down. For our team, we need to make a run into town and the RV dealers to see if we can find some RVs that we can use out here. Again, welcome ladies. Please relax and unwind for a few days."

"Great speech, honey," I whispered in TJ's ear after he sat back down.

"Thanks. Let's go take a nap for a little bit," he whispered back.

After a delicious breakfast, we headed over to our house and quickly undressed, falling into our bed with Ruffus and Adalinda snuggled up with us. TJ was snoring before his head even hit his pillow.

Chapter 33

TJ

After the rescue, we returned to the ranch. We had a quick breakfast, but since I'd had been up since zero one hundred, I needed a nap. I knew most of the team also needed a nap, and now that all the adrenaline was wearing off from the fight, it was time to rejuvenate ourselves.

"Hey, Mel, take me to bed or lose me forever, my darling," I said, the tiredness showing through my attempt at humor..

"Yes, my darling," she said, as she came and wrapped an arm around my waist to walk back to the house together.

We made our way into the house and quickly made our way to our bedroom. Passing the living room, I could see Zoe and her friends still sleeping. *Hum, should I stop and wake them up so they can get breakfast and help with chores, or should we head to our bedroom?* Mel pointed up the stairs, so I guess that was the path to take this morning, and Zoe and her three friends would get a pass. I pointed in their direction, and Ruffus took off that way and licked each one of them.

"Ruffus, you big oof, why did you do that," Zoe exclaimed. Then she saw Mel and me heading up the stairs. "That was not nice, TJ, telling your dog to wake us up like that."

I just laughed as we headed upstairs with Ruffus, who gave us that big doggy grin that he had. We had a quick shower before we got into bed.

Mel tried to talk to me. "Hey, TJ. How well did we ..."

That was all I heard before I was snoring.

I woke up around twelve hundred hours and felt refreshed after my four-hour nap. I slowly worked my way out of bed without waking up Mel. Ruffus picked up his head to look at me, and then, just as fast as he could, he squirmed his way up to take my pillow.

"Hey, what if I wanted to come back to bed? You big fur ball." I know he heard me because he thumped his tail. Adalinda was curled up at the foot of the bed, her tiny wings tucked tight against her sides, tail wrapped around her like a scaled blanket. Each breath came with a soft, whistling snore that fluttered her nostrils and occasionally sent a little puff of smoke drifting into the air—pure dragonette charm in nap form. I headed into the bathroom to take care of business, brushed my teeth, and got dressed. I was headed downstairs when I heard voices coming from our kitchen and wondered who it was. I walked into the kitchen and saw Zoe and her friends sitting at the counter, drinking coffee and tea.

"Morning, Zoe. When did you all get up, have you been out helping with chores?"

"Um, yeah. We have been out doing chores," she quipped. "We needed a break and came in here to relax for a few."

They did not look like they had been outside working yet, and her friends would not look at me. That told me that Zoe was lying to me.

"You know, sis, I will go check. Just because you are my sister does not give you a pass on helping around here." I told her. I didn't want to argue with her, so I turned and headed for the door and the bunkhouse before she could reply. Just as I reached the door, I heard Ruffus and Adalinda coming down the stairs. As Ruffus passed the kitchen, he turned his head and gave a little menacing woof, causing Jace to jump. I held the door open, and as he passed me to go out and do his business, I'm sure he winked at me. Adalinda was holding tight to his collar as he kicked it up a notch, clearing the porch and heading for his favorite tree. Adalinda spread her wings and took off to find her favorite spot for her business. That got me wondering: *did* dragonettes do their business? I made a beeline for the bunkhouse to see what Chef C was preparing for lunch.

As I walked into the bunkhouse, I could hear voices raised, and it sounded like Ann and my mother. They were yelling, or rather, talking loudly to our three new guests.

"We have enough people out here. We don't need more mouths to feed, and we don't need your kind out here," Ann snapped at them. Moonbeam was nodding her head up and down like a bobblehead as Ann tried to dress down our three new family members.

I looked around the room as the door slammed shut behind me, and all heads turned my way.

"Ann. You will not talk to our new members that way. We offered them a place to stay, and they have skills we can use out here. And who appointed you in charge of who can and can't come to the ranch?" I snarled at her.

"I appointed myself as the de facto leader when you were away from the ranch. No one else was willing to step up and lead. We don't need more mouths to feed around here, and we also don't have enough beds for everyone as it is, so they need to leave the ranch."

She was red in the face from having to defend herself to me.

"No one appointed you as a leader around here. You have zero leadership abilities. You are nothing but a pain in my ass." Shit, did I say that out loud. "We have enough food to survive for a couple of years. If you aren't careful, you will be banished from the ranch."

"What, you will banish me from the ranch like people got banished from the island in that survival show," she sneered.

Before I could speak again, Val stood up. "If you don't want us here, and if we will be a burden to the ranch, we can leave," she sighed.

"I don't—"

I cut Ann off before she could finish her tirade. "Shut up, Ann. You have done enough damage today. And, yes, the leadership team will ban you from this island if you are not careful." I took a deep breath before speaking to Val.

"You three are more than welcome to remain here. This ranch belongs to Mel and me. Ann has no say on who is allowed here or not allowed here. You three bring more talent to the table than Ann does."

"How dare you talk about my friend that way, and in that tone," Mom said, waving her finger at me.

"Since you want in on this discussion, Moonbeam. You suck at being a mother. You let Zoe and her friends walk all over you and do as they please. It shows now that they don't want to do anything around here. I just caught Zoe lying to me about helping today with chores. So, if you are not careful, you will be off the ranch right along with Ann." I hardly ever called my mother by her first name, and when I did, she could tell I was pissed. Chef C was trying to pull Ann out of the bunkhouse, but she kept trying to push his hands away.

"Well, I never thought my own son would throw me out on the street," my mother snarled, and turned away to head out of the far door of the bunkhouse. I heard the door behind me and turned to see Mel, John, and Shelly coming into the bunkhouse.

"What is all the yelling about in here?" Mel asked, as she looked around the bunkhouse. Mom was standing at the other end of the bunkhouse with her hands on her hips and her lip curled in visible disgust. Chef C had Ann over in a corner of the kitchen.

I took a deep breath to relax. "My mother and Ann were telling our new guests that they were not wanted here. I walked into the middle of it and then proceeded to tell Ann and my mother that it was not their role to determine who we allowed into our family. I unceremoniously told them both that they could be out on the street if they were not careful."

Chef C came walking over. "TJ, Mel. I'm sorry for the way that Ann behaved. I talked to her and let her know that we need to remain here for our safety and the safety of our children. It won't happen again," he said.

"Chef C. You should not have to apologize for your wife's behavior. You are all welcome here and do a lot for the ranch. I know if we kick someone off the ranch, it will probably be a death sentence for them. Let's all relax, but please tell your wife that it's not up to her to make decisions that affect people out here. We won't put up with bullying, either. If you will excuse me, I need to go talk to my mother now." I sighed as I walked away.

Mel caught me in the hallway to the back door of the bunkhouse. "You sure you want to fight that cat now? Maybe let her cool off for a bit before you go all Navy on her again," she suggested.

She knew me all too well. "I need to deal with her now while this fire is hot. I need to find my dad as well and explain the situation to them. I don't want to banish her, though I want peace out here."

"It will be all right. We are all learning this new normal. We should expect that some people won't be happy because they want the old world to return," she said as she held me close.

"I guess I know that. Ann has been a pain in the ass for a while, and now Mom is siding with her. We can't have that type of division in our lives here. I know you understand my reasoning on that."

"I do. Let's get the core leadership team together later today and talk about this. Maybe use a multifaceted approach to get them to acknowledge that the ranch must have tranquility to survive. If we go after each other, we will fail and will probably end up killing each other."

"You are so smart. Can you gather the leadership team? We can meet in the house later to discuss this."

"Sure thing," Mel responded as she let go of me and headed out to find the rest of our leadership team. I went to find my mother to talk about her standing with someone abusive to our guests. She had slipped out the back door while Mel and I were chatting, and when I looked outside, I couldn't see her. Oh well, I'd find her later. I headed to the house to wait for the other members of the leadership team. On the porch, Ruffus and Adalinda were lounging in the sun.

"Hey Ruffus, Adalinda. What are you two doing out here?" Like they could really answer me.

As I crossed the porch threshold, Ruffus gave me a couple of woofs, and Adalinda gave me a squeak. When I opened the door, they both got up and headed into the house. In the living room, I saw Zoe and her four friends spread out, my nice highball glasses and a bottle of my good scotch sitting on the coffee table.

"What in sam hell are you doing with my good scotch?" I yelled. I could feel the blood rushing to my head from the anger I was feeling. "I see no one has gotten out to finish chores. Get the fuck out of the house now." The shock of being yelled at had them frozen in place. "Get—Out—Now!"

Jace hooked the bottle on his way, scrambling to get out of the house. My hand clamped around his arm, stopping him in his tracks, "Leave the scotch. It is not yours to take," I said, as I pulled the bottle out of his hand. I let go of him and he nearly fell over in his haste to get out of the house. I saw him rubbing his arm where I'd been holding him.

As they passed the door where Ruffus and Adalinda were sitting, Ruffus gave them all a quick bark causing Jace to take a step to the side and hit his shoulder on the door jam on the way out.

I took a few deep breaths as I watched them leave, trying to bring my anger down a notch. Looking past them, I could see Mel with our leadership team walking towards the house. Our leadership team consisted of Mel, Shelly, John, Russell, Matthew, Joe, Chef C, and me. They watched Zoe and her friends rush past, before climbing the porch to enter the house.

As they were making themselves comfortable, John commented, "Breaking out the good stuff for us to sip on while we have a discussion?"

"Don't get up on my last nerve. Zoe and her friends thought they would help themselves. I wouldn't drink from those glasses. Let me get some clean ones, and we can all have a taste while we have a discussion," I advised the group. I pulled down fresh glasses for the group and gave everyone two fingers' worth of the fine scotch. The bottle was empty after we had all gotten a taste of it, Zoe and her friends had helped themselves to a good portion of it.

"Let this fine twenty-year-old scotch breathe for a minute, and then we will get down to business here," I told them.

"I asked for you all to meet here so we can discuss some issues," I said, starting the discussion. "Chef C, if you don't want to be here to discuss your wife, I fully understand and respect your decision."

"I will stay, and what is said in here, I understand and respect," he said, his face downcast.

"First of all, I am not up for banishing anyone just yet, though it is getting close. About an hour ago, Ann was chastising our new guests and telling them that they were not needed or wanted here and that they should leave. Only this group gets to decide who will be banished from the ranch. While Ann was ranting, my mother stepped up to side with her, and I went nuclear at that point on both of them. I have not seen my mother since, though I will track her down. No. I do not plan on apologizing for the way I talked to her. Her parenting skills suck, and that is why Zoe is the way that she is. I need to talk to the Army National Guard guys to see if they have another tent and cots. I want to put Zoe and her friends in one. That way, they can't hide in the house. Any comments?"

"What do you think your mother would do if we decided to banish her?" John asked.

"She probably would drag my dad back to their ranch, and I am sure Zoe and her friends would go with them. If they did want to go there, we would have to help them and give them back the supplies that they brought here. I do think it would be a death sentence for them, as they don't have many people who could fight off a gang. Zoe and her friends are useless with a weapon," I elaborated to the group. "Please pass this on to those who are managing areas where we have chores, and if they don't see Zoe and her friends out helping, track them down. If they get any grief from them, let me know, and I will put a boot on their ass. I might even let Ruffus have a go at them." Hearing his name, Ruffus thumped his tail on the floor. "The other thing I want to discuss is that we need to find more beds before winter gets here. We have talked about getting a bunch of RVs from the dealership in town and bringing them back here. If they have a bunkhouse-style one or two, it will work better. A couple of weeks prior to the EMP, I thought I saw three of the bunkhouse-style RVs on their lot. We can get them wired for power and water and dig a sewer line. We have most of the stuff that we would need, though if not, we can hit the Lowes in town. Let's plan on a scavenging trip tomorrow for the RVs. Any questions? None? Ok, let's relax, finish this scotch, and determine who is going on the scavenging run."

We all sat there relaxing, drinking our scotch until it was time for dinner. After dinner, the children asked if they could build a fire for s'mores. I pulled another bottle of scotch for the group to enjoy and some red solo cups to drink from. I had not seen Ann or Mom since this afternoon.

"Hey, sailor. I'm headed to the house to get ready for bed. Don't stay up too long with the boys," Mel urged as she started walking in the direction of the house. Ruffus and Adalinda followed her to the house, while I stayed near the fire, soaking in the heat from the flames and relaxing.

I saw a light come on in the greenhouse, so I pulled myself up and headed over there to see if I could figure out where the light had come from. My night vision was gone from sitting near the fire, and I was slowly moving through the greenhouse so I wouldn't knock anything. I heard a sound behind me, then suddenly I felt a hit to the base of my skull, causing an excruciating pain, and then my lights went out.

I came to, wondering how long I had been lying there. Something didn't feel right, though, and as I looked around me, I realized that I was standing, floating five feet off the ground. I looked down and I could see myself lying on the ground in the greenhouse. *Am I dead? Is this what death feels like? Am I headed to heaven or hell?*

Characters

TJ (Theodore James) Bush-Retired Navy, professional shooter and trainer

Melanie (Mel) Bush-Prepper, blogger/creative hobbyist, horticulturist, amateur archeologist

Ruffus the Dog-TJ's trained service dog

Gail Adler-Veterinarian

- **Katie Adler** (14)

John Packard- Retired Army special forces soldier, Tactical training instructor

Shelly Packard-Prepper blogger

Joe Brown-Retired Marine Gunnery Sergeant and neighbor

Clarence (Chef C) Claydesta-Chef

Annette (Ann)Claydesta

- **Brian Claydesta** (15)
- **Bonnie Claydesta** (17) -Security

Sean Steel-an Army Ranger stranded on the Rubicon Trail (KIA)

Raven Steel-Teacher and seamstress

Billy Primm-Security and Maintenance

Joanne Primm-Teacher

- **Charlie Primm**-(14)
- **Melissa Primm**-(15)

Albert Tinkerton-Furniture Craftsman

Anita Tinkerton- Pharmacist

- **Denise Tinkerton** (16)
- **Donny Tinkerton** (18)

Tracy Cole-Trauma nurse
Claire Westland-Trauma nurse
Matthew (Matt) Clean- Deputy Sheriff
Jolene Clean- Secretary

- **Isabella Clean** (17)-Security
- **Blake Clean** (12)

Russell Toume- Deputy Sheriff
Scarlett Toume-Dental Hygienist

- **Henry Toume** (16)
- **Noah Toume (14)**

Dylan Hart- Deputy Sheriff
Cole Whitlock- Deputy Sheriff
Madison Quill- Deputy Sheriff
Quinn Pherson- Deputy Sheriff
Nick White-Marine from the VFW
Gavin Smith-Marine from the VFW
Carlos Tejas-Marine from the VFW
Kyle Johnson-Retired Navy Chief Petty Officer, prepper, gunsmith, and ham radio operator in
Mississippi
Adalinda Goldenflame – Princess dragonette
Lucy Bigglefoot – Baby Bigfoot
Barney Donald – Parents of James Donald
Betty Donald – James Mother
James Donald - Baker
Cassie Donald – Baker

Branson Fox – NANG team member
David Doresy – NANG team member
Erica Carmichael – NANG team member
Gunner Brooks – NANG team member
Heather Yarbrough – NANG team member
Liam Parker – NANG team member
Ryan Jensen – NANG team member
Sara Thatcher – NANG team member
Skyler St. James – NANG team member
Walt Reed – NANG team member
Joel Bush – TJ's father
Moonbeam Bush – TJ's mother
Damian Bush – TJ's brother
Zoe Bush – TJ's sister
Constance Merriweather – Zoe's friend from Ely
Ellis Murphy – Zoe's friend from Ely
Jace Whitlock – Zoe's friend from Ely
Charmaine Lockwood – Zoe's friend from Ely
Lynn Shaker – Nurse, rescued from CVI
Val Johns – Nurse, rescued from CVI
Stelly Shaw – Ghost Librarian
Fred Wilfred – Ghost (Killed by Fiona)
Wilma Wilfred – Ghost (Killed by Fiona)
Fiona Malefic (Wicked) – Lilith
BG Belial (Azazel Fallen Angel)
Bobby Savage (Beserker)